DEAD RUN

DEAD RUN

John Steiner

DEAD RUN

DOUBLE DRAGON

Prologue: Till Death do Us Part

Exhaustion had befallen Corneliu Galca long ago, yet he kept running through the gloomy woods. Though tattered, his clothes reflected a man of fair wealth in the year of Our Lord sixteen hundred eighty-eight. But it wasn't the fiery razing of Brasov by Austrian soldiers that had spurred Corneliu to flee his estate and homeland without possessions. It was what stalked amid the chaos, unnoticed by conquerors until too late.

"Papa, don't leave us!" Corneliu heard his son and daughter cry out, far behind him.

Their voices invoked terror in him that overrode feeling fatigued, and Corneliu shifted to a staggering sprint. Each misty huff of breathe came with a whimper and the smell of the dinner he'd eaten nine hours ago. Despite a frigid winter's night, his chest, shoulders and legs burned. Many backward glances he cast in fear of what may come from behind.

Neither the soft pounding of dogs' paws nor the hard thump of horse hooves did Corneliu hear. What swished were deft feet lighter and faster than his heavy booted steps. They knew Corneliu had one avenue of escape. He couldn't count on help from fellow Romanians, who dreaded the advancing Austrian banners, nor the aid of the invaders. He had to leave his country behind, if he could.

"Papa, we love you! Help us!" His children's desperate pleas sounded from either side.

"No!" Corneliu's lips trembled as he begged under his heaving breath.

Even with gaps in the forest canopy, Corneliu couldn't be sure in which way he headed. Clouds consumed the starlight, leaving him only to hope he had maintained a roughly north-west heading. Anywhere else meant being boxed in by the Carpathian Mountains.

Nearly falling several times more during his panic-fueled run something caught his next rasp in his throat. He frightfully clutched at a tree. It was sobbing. A woman sounding like her face was covered by her hands and her heart buried by grief. Corneliu knew that wail too well.

Cautious as to avoid making any sound, Corneliu advanced with slow steps, feeling out where to plant each foot. Though his eyes adjusted to dark as best they could, he strained to see the ground under the abyssal night time forest. He couldn't risk being found by his children. That would only draw the others who had wrought the disaster in the night.

Yes, he was sure now, it was Alina who wept. Corneliu's beloved wife, whom he thought lost.

"They're dead," she wailed, allowing Corneliu to home in on her. "All dead!"

At last came the relief of light, for Corneliu found Alina kneeling next to a weakly burning torch she'd brought with her. The torch had been stabbed solidly upright into the frozen ground. Alina too had fled, but she couldn't bring herself to run any further, when her grief burst through. She rocked on her knees, her bare feet uncovered by her simple nightgown. Hugging herself against the cruel night's chill, Alina cried alone.

"I can't believe they're dead!" She screamed so loud at the heavens that it gave Corneliu a jolt.

Feeling his own tears well up, Corneliu approached with assuring hushes.

"Dead, dead, dead," Alina sobbed, beating the cold earth.

Corneliu gently gripped her shoulders, which brought no start from his devoted wife.

"Yes, my love, our children are dead. I know," he whispered, giving her a soft shake to bid her stand.

In a furious spin at waist level, Alina flashed her bloodless face and a morbid gaunt grin at him. But it was her eyes that foretold Corneliu's end: opaque grey irises and pupils encroached by inky black at the fringes. In the failing torchlight he saw that Alina too had become a walking plague.

"No," her corpse hissed with in sadistic glee at the ruse. "Me! I'm dead!"

Before he could think to get away, she grabbed Corneliu's head and drew him in.

He felt many stabbing pinches, as a mouthful of sharp teeth sank into his neck. In a backward rip of her head, Alina tore away a sheet of skin, a strip of muscle and much of his windpipe, slashing open his artery in the process. Warm blood splashed them both, as his dead wife plunged her face into his gaping flesh.

Unable to help himself, Corneliu tried to scream and thrashed wildly. The only ones to hear didn't come to his aid. No, Corneliu's own children

7

rushed in to have their fill, before Alina drained away all of his living red essence. As with his wife, all seven of his progeny had been slain by vampires. Yet two children had refused to remain in the earth. They had come straight home once risen, and must've bled their mother dry.

So too was Corneliu's fate as his strength evaporated and his body stilled. The horrified expression on his face and filling his eyes remained long after he breathed his last in the dead of night.

Chapter 1: Lupercalia Day Massacre

Maybe it was fitting, Hayden Cornell thought, as he texted into his phone. The sandy-blonde chemical engineer, his hair speckled with gray and more grayed at the temples, had set up an online messaging account a minute ago. Fitting that the outbreak started on the fourteenth of this month of all months.

He heard a distant metallic clink and turned his head. He had crouched down in the hall. Hayden shifted from one heel to the other. His white dress shirt sliding against his skin and the crack of one knee were the only sounds he made.

To each end of the hall, most of the overhead lights were off, but not those at the corners. It revealed to him that the office building he'd broken into was on emergency lighting, and that meant most of the building's power was off. The city's power grid remained up for the time being, but a number of documentaries he'd seen and books he'd read warned how short-lived that might be. Hayden wasn't sure if the backup power here would've lasted as long as that of the chemical engineering lab where he formerly worked. Regret over his choice of hideouts welled up. He needed to find the main breakers for the building.

However, the ground floor of the office building appeared, upon first entering, to have few entrances. He lucked out on finding keys that proved to belong to a security guard, because they worked on all the building's doors. The basement floor, into which he retreated further, had but one stairwell now locked off, and two elevators that he had since shut down.

Reassured just a little more now than a moment ago, Hayden still found himself nervously rolling the knot of his black, silver and gray tie between fingers. After rereading his text, he posted it, and began drafting another.

Today, people think of Valentine's Day as being about love, Hayden keyed in with his right thumb. Well, hearts are involved. That's the number one organ to stab or rip out.

Another sound, one Hayden couldn't identify, came from the floor above somewhere. He glanced to the metal door next to him, and wondered what people would think if they saw what he brought with him. Terms like sick, insane and death- wish would enter loud conversation.

It's not just people that come back, Hayden began his third post. Animals too, or at least mammals. And there's no rhyme or reason for why some species are susceptible and others not.

Here's a clue, he entered a fourth posting. Don't waste your time on apocalyptic pathogens, mutant DNA, ancient curses or space aliens. This is more world changing than any of that shit.

After sending that to his account, Hayden stopped and shut the phone off. He had to consider how much more survivors could handle at this point. For that matter, Hayden wondered if it would be good for him to spread so much so quickly. A lot of people looked suspiciously on those well informed.

With joint-creaking sloth, Hayden stood up in the hall. He listened with intensity to the sound as his gray slacks shifted. Putting the phone in his pocket, he gripped the door handle and braced his other hand between it and the doorframe. Half-expecting someone to burst around the corner, he eased the door open and went back inside.

Hayden entered the mailroom again, and gazed down its length to the freight elevator he'd used to move everything he brought. That included two gurneys with partial human outlines under several heavy white sheets. Lacking the lab's best equipment and facilities, Hayden asked himself, yet again, why he had brought these two bodies. As widespread and crazy as things got throughout the city, the chemical engineer doubted he could produce useful answers in time to help anyone, maybe not even himself.

And to think yesterday morning it all seemed like a normal day—.

* * *

After parking in the staff-reserved lot, Hayden shut off his car and grabbed his briefcase before heading into work. On the way through the front door, he unbuttoned his crimson and white sport jacket Inside, Hayden spotted James, the security guard behind the desk as usual for the morning shift.

"Season's over, you know," James called out, having noted the large, white stylized 'A' on the left side of Hayden's coat. "And 'Bama took a beating last year. Don't look too good next year, either."

"Yeah, yeah," Hayden dully accepted, holding out his ID badge with emphasis on his answering middle finger.

James scanned his badge with a chuckle and buzzed him in. Hayden left behind the reminder of just how the Crimson Tide got rolled, and headed first for his office.

Several folders, many more individual sheets of paper, and scores of Post-Its covered his desk in a haphazard arrangement around the computer, obscuring the keyboard. He peeled off the one sticky-back memo that looked new and read it. Afterward, he pulled out a felt tip marker to scribble the entire piece black and then drop it into a shredder. A full sheet printout caught his eye, which Hayden picked up to read as well.

A knock at his open door drew Hayden's attention to one of the lab aides who stopped at his office. "The shipment's in."

"Alright, I'll be down to sign off in a minute," Hayden said, and sat at his desk. He noticed that his computer monitor showed black rather than being off, indicating the power saver mode had kicked in after he'd left it on again last night.

"Son of a bitch," Hayden cursed, while reaching under the mess of paperwork for the mouse.

Waving the mouse back and forth on the desk brought the monitor up, and a moment after that, the computer. There appeared the progress report file that he had left open. Over it was an automatic

12

timeout notification for his log-on. Given the subject of his report, Hayden wanted to bang his palm against his forehead.

Instead, he logged on to access his profile history between then and now.

Satisfied nothing undue had taken place in his absence, Hayden logged off. Then his cell rang with Vincent Price's laughter.

"Yeah, hello," Hayden said after pressing talk, standing up and placing his other hand on his hip.

"We need results," the cryptic voice ordered.

"We just got these things a month ago," Hayden explained. "Half the equipment I requisitioned hasn't even shown up yet. You're just going to have to give me time, like I said from the start."

"We're out of time," the man's low tone countered. "It's already becoming a problem in Eastern Europe, and heading your way at one thousand, seventy miles an hour."

"Whoa," Hayden said in mild alarm with his hand out, as if the caller could see. "Wait a sec. I thought the outbreaks were few, isolated and sporadic."

"That was last week," the unknown caller informed him. "The situation's changed."

"Look," Hayden pressed his case, absently turning around. "We're barely starting here."

"Do you think the lab is safe?" the mystery voice asked.

"What's not safe? Electronic locks, mandatory ID checks, armed security..." Hayden listed.

"Safe from them." The other man emphasized just enough for Hayden to get his point.

"Oh," Hayden caught on, and paused for grave consideration. "No, I imagine not."

"Grab what you can and get out," he warned, sounding hard but not cross. "You got nine hours."

The connection died on that, and Hayden lowered the phone slowly. At first, he eyed the confines of his office, and then stared at the floor gnawing at a thumbnail in thought. Then he walked out at a brisk pace. He headed for the makeshift quarantine lab, formerly a walk-in freezer. Inside, lay two gurneys and some of his lab equipment, around which his lab aides and a Fed Ex driver were standing.

Hayden accepted the electronic clipboard and scribbled a rushed signature. "Cornell," the driver asked, after reading the LCD copy. "Like the university?"

"Yes, the spelling's the same," Hayden said.

"Did you go there?" came the driver's inquiring attempt for small talk.

"Does it look like I went there?" Hayden said, showing his jacket letter.

He waited for the driver to leave before grabbing a roll cart and starting to pile on the new boxes.

"Where do you want that to go?" one of the assistants asked him.

"Take this down to that armored truck in the garage," Hayden said, and pointed around. "This other stuff too. Everything we were setting up here's going with us. I'll handle these two."

"Going where?" the other aid asked.

"Apparently," Hayden prefaced. "They think the effect's going to escalate and hit us tonight."

"Serious?" the second aide questioned.

"Yeah," Hayden nodded, starting to feel his breathing rate increase. "We can't do this here."

Hayden loaded up a second cart and sent the aids on their way. Then he walked to the front security desk to see James still alone, but flipping through security cameras on his terminal.

"Who all else is with you?" Hayden asked.

"Just Sarah," James answered, turning in his seat. "Why?"

"Shit's gonna hit the fan, and I need you guys riding shotgun."

Familiar with the possibility of an epidemic but not the nature, James asked, "When do we leave?"

"Soon as I get things loaded up," Hayden informed him. "We're taking the armored truck, so grab a set of keys for it and meet us down there. Bring whatever weapons you got."

James shot up from his chair and left the front desk, while Hayden returned to the lab for the first gurney. He passed the aides with empty carts, one at a time, heading toward the elevator, and told both to reload them with everything else that was portable. Down in the warehouse floor, Hayden rolled the gurney up to the security truck. James, who stood six-four, easy, waited next to a woman in matching security uniform, with high cut, dark curly hair, who stood nine inches shorter.

"What's that?" Sarah asked, pointing to the bulge under the many sheets.

"Never you mind," Hayden admonished, more curtly than he intended. "Just stay up front."

Hayden pushed the gurney into the open back, which caused the first set of wheels to fold up underneath. Halfway in, he came around and folded up the second set before rolling the gurney all the way to the back. Lifting the sheets just enough to see whether the straps were tight, Hayden dropped them without looking at what they held down. Looking around a moment, he found some bungee cords he then used to secure the gurney in place. Then he went back for the second.

"Comet UFO cults, evangelical raptures, Mayan doomsday, crazy polygamists," Hayden muttered on the way to the elevator while rubbing the knot of his tie. "Guess this one's for real."

* * *

Staring at the closer gurney, Hayden noticed subtle movements coinciding with the sound of skin against fabric. He was sure both were active, and took relief at the fact they had been rendered immobile. He went back to the freight elevator to pick up the shotgun, and studied the bloodstain on the pump action handle. He needed to know who or what was upstairs.

He strapped the bloody police-design utility belt around his waist. Next, he put on Sarah' light bullet-resistant vest and covered it with his sport coat. Where a tonfa- fashion police club would hang, Hayden inserted the pry bar. One side ended with a hooking wedge, but it was the conical tip that

Hayden had used as a weapon to protect himself. Despite that the steel bar remained rather clean after a cursory wipe-down.

As prepped as he thought possible, Hayden went to the stairway and quietly produced the set of keys he'd found. After he unlocked the door with care, he entered the stairwell, shotgun barrel first. With a glacial pace he ascended, listening with muscles tense between every step. The sound of an errant foot bumped against something hollow and plastic. A small trash can, Hayden imagined.

Someone up there made a shushing sound, which made Hayden's grip on the shotgun turn his knuckles white and his Kegel muscles clench as if he were on a roof ledge. The intrusive but light steps grew distant, and so Hayden advanced the rest of the way. He came to the ground floor door and unlocked the door. The building had twenty floors, and Hayden had spent the remains of the day ensuring the stairwell accesses were all locked down. He wasn't up to being surprised again like that.

On the other side of the stairway access, Hayden slung the shotgun over one shoulder to lock the door once more. He hated every weak metallic clink of the key ring, and he made a mental note to do something about that later. Right now, however, Hayden needed to figure out the random noises he'd heard.

Not Daring to stray too far from the stairwell, Hayden checked every corner more than once before moving on. What put his nerves most on edge was coming to the main lobby, where a wide bank of full height windows permitted easy views both of half of the ground floor and one long hallway. Yet Hayden saw no movement inside the lobby or on the other side of the tempered glass.

So far so good. With only a handful of overhead lights working, Hayden willed himself to approach the large, accommodating reception desk to the left of the front doors. There, Hayden took a moment to gaze out into the foreboding night. The fluctuating glows of a couple of distant fires alluded to the magnitude of madness out there, though the siren songs of midnight had stopped. He thought a distant scream penetrated the windows, but a quick glance revealed nothing in his line of sight.

Yet a shift of shadow down another short hall caught his wide anxious eyes. It came from a break room, which Hayden closed in on with more dread than he had in daylight hours. A couple of whispers reached his ears, but he couldn't make out what was said. One of the shadows shortened, leading him to think someone or something had ducked low, maybe to feed.

Hayden edged right up to the door, shotgun leveled across his chest. He'd never been a gun owner, though he had once considered buying one or more, and so wasn't sure what was the best way to do this. Steeling himself, Hayden jumped out into the doorway with the weapon's butt stock up against his shoulder. Four people whirled around startled, and with it he got one woman's short scream and one man's longer cursing plea.

But their complexions were normal and all four pairs of eyes retained healthy colors within

18

white sclera. They were alive, and they quickly recognized that Hayden too counted among the living. They had gathered around one of the vending machines, redefining what Hayden thought to involve feeding. At least they were smart enough not to break the glass with a ruckus.

One man, a Black man in his late twenties, wore outdoor working clothes, a tool belt, and was holding a machete that, as yet hadn't been marked with use. Another, barely out of his teens, on one knee, wore a tee-shirt, jeans and a hoodie with some blood splatter. He was gripping a long metal pole. The older Hispanic woman who'd screamed had a pistol sticking halfway out her pocket. It contrasted with her school teacher attire, made complete with glasses. The woman who hadn't given the vocal start stood out to Hayden the most among the group.

The other three wore backpacks with the sales tags still on them, and full of whatever else they came across. While all four also carried bags or purses, the younger woman with long, straight red hair carried a military style duffle bag, which clashed with her long earthy brown dress, burgundy top, long coat, boots covered in felt, two or three necklaces and a considerable number of rings.

"Jesus-fucking-Christ," the construction worker's chest heaved in relief. "'Scared the shit out of us!"

"'Feeling's mutual," Hayden offered back, beads of sweat showing on his red face.

"Are you, like, a security guard?" the redhead asked.

19

"No." He shook off his denial. "I was just hiding out here. My name's Hayden Cornell."

"Evelyn Gwinnett," the redhead said. "Or just Lyn."

"Salma Lopez," the other woman introduced herself as well.

"Isaac Morgan," the construction worker added.

"Kael," the younger man uttered in brief.

The red head glared at Kael for a moment, but Hayden let it pass. If the young man thought his last name was his own business Hayden was fine with that. He realized he was still pointing the shotgun at them and lowered it while searching for the safety.

"Anyway, sorry about the gun," Hayden apologized. He finally figured out the safety, before slinging the weapon. "I didn't expect anyone else would come here."

"The stores and restaurants and places like that were cleaned out," Isaac informed him.

"Did you see what's happening out there?" Salma asked Hayden.

"Oh yeah," Hayden breathed heavily, arching his brows. "I started out with four others."

"Why is this happening?" Salma's question sounded more like a prayer.

"News was sayin' some disease went around making people crazy and eat each other," Isaac recounted, and gave the machete an assuring shake. "Good thing for those zombie survival books."

"How can dead people get up and do things like–" Salma choked on something unspoken.

Evelyn and Kael shared a look that caught Hayden's attention. He figured they knew each other, from the wordless admonishment Evelyn gave the man, but Hayden felt there was something else.

* * *

The airport lounge was half filled with people, Evelyn noticed while sitting on one of the benches. So many people walked back and forth she had to move side to side to be sure of seeing every face for the one she would recognize. He got good at slipping by, but never that good. It was just that no one needed to know his whereabouts or habits as much as they did now.

Watching the news on the overhead flat-screens reminded Evelyn of that. Two separate cable news channels showed the same video feed of a Norwegian fishing boat from the viewpoint of a Coast Guard helicopter. The ship was reported to have been missing for a week, according to what Evelyn could hear above the din of commuter chatter and foot traffic. In the video, yellow sunlight shown on the vessel's deck at an angle. One of the channels switched back to a news anchor with a banner underneath indicating an update.

Then Evelyn caught sight of the person she waited for. Wearing a hoodie, with the hood pulled up and his head tilted down, Kael would've escaped Evelyn's notice but for one brief glance in her general direction. He didn't alter his pace, indicating he didn't notice or recognize Evelyn.

After Kael picked up his luggage and headed for the terminal exit, Evelyn slung her purse and

21

followed him at a brisk heel-clacking pace. She noticed that Kael went to a bus stop and sat on a bench. From there Evelyn went back to the airport parking lot and got into her car. She drove out and across the street from the bus stop into a restaurant parking lot, but didn't get out. Instead, she waited for Kael to board a bus, and then followed it.

However, Kael didn't get off until well into the night, even though the bus had circled its rounds twice over. Eventually the bus pulled into a stop for a couple of minutes before Kael stepped off. He immediately walked down the street with his head low, as before. Evelyn gave him a minute before she pulled close to the sidewalk and slowly drifted up next to him. Kael made a deliberate effort not to notice her, even after she had the window roll down and leaned over to for him to see her face.

"I'm not going away, Kael," she called out. "So you might as well get in."

"How long can you keep this up?" Kael tossed back, without turning his head.

"Unless you're prepared to sleep under freeway overpasses and eat from soup kitchens, longer than you can," Evelyn challenged. "My finances are better than yours."

"Are you going to tell me how worried everyone is?" Kael threw back at her. "Since you already know, we're covered," Evelyn quipped without hesitation.

"I can handle it," Kael declared, before a scream captured both their attentions.

At first, Evelyn took it to be a woman's scream, but hearing it again and for longer, she

22

realized it was a man's. Kael dashed off toward it, right as she was about to demand he get in the car. Thinking he'd only get shot for his curiosity, Evelyn accelerated to catch up with Kael. That is, until he broke off across a park. Gauging where the screaming came from, Evelyn kept going along the road.

Arriving at the corner before reaching sight of the event, Evelyn stopped and got out. By now she could hear several people exclaiming their horror; the original victim kept screaming for help that none witnessing answered. Then she heard Kael come onto the scene.

Taking a peek around a building corner, Evelyn saw a man pinned down by someone whose features she couldn't make out. Kael was grabbing at the assailant's shoulders, trying to pull them off. Except the best he got was lifting both people off the ground. That Kael was strong enough didn't surprise Evelyn, as she knew what kind of jobs he worked and the martial arts training he had. Yet, the attacker didn't budge from having its face buried between the man's shoulder and neck. Kael then took to landing heel kicks onto the attacker's head, but nothing came of it.

"C'mon," Kael yelled at witnesses to the scene. "Someone give me a hand!"

Finally, two other men jumped in, the second being a construction worker who only just come upon the scene. The three of them struggled to pry loose the fingers of what Evelyn now recognized was a child who was ravenously biting at the grown man's neck. And still the violent child didn't yield.

"Break his wrists," the construction worker yelled, and pulled out a hammer from his tool belt.

A wet crack sounded, as Evelyn started to approach. More sounded when the first produced nothing. She saw Kael take something off the Black man's tool belt and used it to beat down on the kid's other wrist, while the third man kept ineffectually pulling at the attacking child's ankles.

Joining the rest of the crowd, she heard them gasp or speak out in disbelief at what they saw. Evelyn noticed that the child hadn't cried out from pain despite the assault from the two grown men. Kael at last flipped around what Evelyn saw to be a screwdriver to use the flathead to stab into the wrist bones. She noticed, under the light of street lamps and store fronts, no blood came from the injury.

Working the screwdriver around, Kael twisted the child's hand to a grotesque angle before the screwdriver snapped. Then, he was able to pry the smaller hand off the man, who now lay in a large pool of his own blood and hardly moved. The construction worker saw Kael's results and used the claw side of his hammer to similar effect.

The two of them lifted the child off, but each stepped back when the kid attempted to bite at their holds. The other man who had been helping backed away with horror written all over his face. Apparently many others got a clear view of the child, and decided in a hurry that they'd seen enough. The bystanders didn't run away all at once, but flee they did when each registered on their own that the kid was dead and still moving.

24

Much to the construction worker's surprise, Kael took charge by flinging the kid against a brick wall. When the child got up unphased and rushed at him, Kael hopped onto his left foot and drove a snapping heel-kick with his right. It landed squarely into the dead kid's chest, and he slammed the wall again. When his head struck there came a sound Evelyn could only think of as coming from a hardboiled egg breaking. All that, and the child-sized horror still stood.

Lacking coordination from brain damage, it attempted to charge Kael and the construction worker. However, Kael threw a palm heel into the kid's forehead to knock it onto its back. Then he grabbed the child's legs and swung it around to crash into the wall a few times. More bones broke, and the kid could no longer walk, though it started an ineffectual crawl toward them.

"Come on, Kael," Evelyn yelled. "Obviously, you're not killing it! Let's go!"

Kael and the Black man both followed Evelyn to her car, which she didn't argue on understanding what lay behind them. She opened her door to let the man get in back, while Kael got into the passenger side. Then she heard screaming from several different directions at once. Elsewhere, came the growling of an angry cat, and slobbery grating snappish barks from a dog in a different direction.

Amid the growing chaos Evelyn distinctly heard a person laughing with sadistic glee, and that it drew closer with frightening speed. The source appeared as a man ran diagonally across an intersection. Her mouth agape, Evelyn hopped into her car quick, slammed the door, started the car and pushed the gas pedal all the way down.

Her car built up speed, as Evelyn checked her rear-view mirror. The man, or dead man she supposed, maintained a world class sprint until he leapt off the road. A prolonged moment passed before the human-shaped monster landed heavily onto the roof of her car.

Evelyn yanked her steering wheel to the right, only to catch sight of fingers appearing on her passenger side window. She threw the car that way, amid shouting from Kael and the other man. Yet, the dead man reached for the opposite side in time to avoid being thrown off.

Then a fist pounded down on her windshield, causing it to crack in one blow. Another hammer blow widened the fractures, to where Evelyn couldn't see through it well. A third hit landed far to the left, where the roof was supported by the frame. The entire corner bowed in, and another pounding fist caused the corner to snap. One more hit broke the ruined windshield from the frame, allowing the man's fingers to wrap around the edge heedless of cuts to his hand.

"Slam on the brakes!" Kael shouted.

By then, the man ripped upwards, with his other palm slamming onto the hood in opposition. The whole corner of Evelyn's car roof peeled up with the superhuman effort, invoking a scream out of her. She hit the brake pedal, and the dead man rolled off into a sideways spinning arc clear of the car, and a couple dozen feet beyond. He hit the road in a firm thump, and rumbled further out, making Evelyn wonder just how fast she'd been going before stopping.

The man rose up onto his hands and knees, before shots rang out and bullets struck him. It slowed his effort to stand, but when he did his head swung around to seek out the source of gunfire. He dashed off toward the right, causing Kael to swing open his door and run out as well.

"Kael!" Evelyn screamed at the top of her lungs. "Kael, don't do it! He'll kill you!"

Undaunted, Kael ran – not straight at the dead man, but to a pile of debris left out on someone's front yard. Evelyn heard a long metallic slide, as Kael freed something he'd spied from inside the car. Then he raced after the ravenous dead man.

Whoever carried the gun fired off more shots, and bullet impacts ripped both cloth and the flesh of his knees. He buckled and tripped, given Kael the vital seconds needed to catch up with the Olympian sprinter. Several more shots hit the dead man in the face, causing his head to recoil just a little. By then Kael was able to reach the man, and swept the pole across the other's legs.

That's when Evelyn realized the shooter was a woman, as she advanced to improve her aim. Evelyn also noticed that as the dead man dropped to his knees, he now appeared to be blind. He swung for Kael, but always missed thanks to good footwork. Kael counter-attacked with expert strikes from his improvised staff, mustering every muscle in his considerable body.

The dead man's head jolted one way and the next with each stroke Kael administered. Yet the corpse refused to lose its motivation for afterlife carnage. The woman fired more shots into his head at point blank range, when Kael was safely away. Knocked onto its back, the body still moved, and arms flailed with a spastic twitch.

Finally, Kael thrust the end of the pole into the chest. Everything just seemed to stop at that moment.

"Kael!" Evelyn screamed again, but with less fear than before. "Get over here!"

He did, and the woman with the pistol also approached, setting Evelyn on edge.

"Holy shit," Kael cursed in trembling exhilaration. "What the hell's going on?"

"Are you people alright?" the woman asked, herself sounding scared out of her wits.

"Yes," Evelyn heaved her relief, hand to her chest. "It's a good thing you were here, but... he could've killed you. Thank you so much."

"I can't believe this," the woman said, as Kael made room for her to get in. Surprisingly the passenger door still opened without too much creaking. Once Kael got back in, having left the pole, Evelyn drove off. She and the others all cast fretful glances every which way, as she cruised down the street at legal speed.

"I thought zombies were supposed to go down when you shoot 'em in the head," the Black man said from the back seat. "Oh, I'm Isaac Morgan."

"Salma Lopez," the woman introduced herself in turn. "I only just lost a couple other people like that who were after me. Had to shoot their knees."

"I'm Kael. You were pretty cool and smooth back there," he praised. "What do you do?"

"I'm an undercover cop," Salma revealed, "Part of the gang unit."

Evelyn introduced herself last, and then asked, "Now what?"

"Gotta hit up a hardware store," Isaac said.

"I don't think now's the time to go five-finger shopping," Salma condemned.

Evelyn thought that Isaac would take offense by Salma's assumption, but he didn't. "If those're really dead people goin' round, then we better get prepared."

"I think Isaac's got a point," Evelyn reinforced, while checking both for store fronts and anything dangerous coming for them. "I gotta grab some things, myself."

However, they were far from the first with that idea. Evelyn passed by a few businesses with people pouring into and out of shattered windows and broken doors.

One such looting was broken up by still more attacks. Evelyn noticed a brown cat with its entrails hanging out clinging to a woman's back. It savaged her neck as she reached back to pull it off. However, as she fell to her knees, another woman ran up to her and grabbed the profusely bleeding woman's wrist.

Evelyn only assumed biting came next, as she sped off rather than test their fate.

A couple of intersections later, and Evelyn noticed what she took to be rats racing out into the street at her approach rather than flee her coming car. She served wide to avoid them. From the corner of her eye she noticed several leapt impossibly high. Isaac was quick to snatch one that would've made it into the huge gaping opening in her roof, and threw it back before it had a chance to bite him.

"Is it some kind of rabies?" Salma asked, a shiver running through her face and shoulders.

"No rabies I ever heard of lets you shake off gunshots," Isaac observed.

Evelyn took note of her fuel gage, and said to the others, "We better find somewhere to hide and quick. I can't drive around like this all night."

"There," Isaac pointed by her left shoulder. "It doesn't look like anyone else has been there yet."

"That's what worries me," Salma warned. "I gotta reload, and then we can go in, but stay close."

"No problem," Isaac accepted with a tremor in his tone.

Evelyn parked around back, and as everyone got out she went to her trunk.

Opening the huge dull green army bag Evelyn had packed for her trip, she fished out a couple flashlights and spare batteries. Meanwhile, she could hear Salma trading an empty clip for a full one. Then Kael led them toward the mega-retail outlet's receiving bay. Using Isaac's claw hammer to pry the code lock from the door proved a little too easy.

"You've done that before, haven't you," Evelyn accused, with a mildly stern brow.

"Yeah, but never with a roofing hammer," Kael admitted, and handed it back. "Thanks."

They stopped at the sporting goods section, with Salma leading the way, pistol first. Everyone strained to hear what else might be inside with them, but nothing jumped out of the dark. And to no further surprise, the shelves were bare of guns and most ammo.

"Huh," Kael scoffed at what Evelyn's flashlight revealed. "Everyone bought up bullets for the Bushmaster assault rifles and left the nine mils."

"That's actually been a going trend for a few years," Salma explained, while panning the other flashlight around. "Most of the three-fifty-seven rounds are gone too."

"Big bad go'ment is gonna take ma guns," Kael mocked.

"Right," Salma tisked, as she scooped up boxes of bullets and a couple extra empty clips. "If only. Let their kids go to school through gang-contested neighborhoods."

Further scouting of the store let them pick out backpacks and other bags. Isaac selected something he figured would be more effective for the next ravenous charging corpse. Kael found various sizes of knives, the largest of which Evelyn guessed he liked because of action movies, and he located a six foot pry bar. Heavy as it sounded when he set the tip onto tiled floor, Evelyn wondered if it were too heavy to use, or if Kael were planning far ahead for something else.

The place didn't have much in the way of food, except for end-caps of chips and whatever hung from pegs by checkout counters. Those they quickly packed away, while Salma kept watch toward the storefront's windows. The four of them slipped back out of the retail outlet through the same rear door, and checked around before returning to Evelyn's car.

Finding an office building in a particularly quiet part of town hadn't taken long.

Kael was about to work his felonious magic on the door, but Salma stopped him to test the handle first. Whoever left last must've been in a rush, Evelyn figured. Her assessment changed minutes later.

Not practiced in criminal entry, Evelyn had bumped a small trashcan, while checking behind the front courtesy desk. Kael quietly verbalized admonishment to her, for a change, and looked around to see if anyone else inside had noticed. He spied a short side hall and waved the rest toward it. His attempt to empty a vending machine was when they met Hayden Cornell.

Chapter 2: By Dawn's Illuminating Light

Evelyn and the others collectively explained how they ended up here, after which Hayden checked his watch. They had about an hour before dawn, giving Hayden a sense of some comfort. However, the horrors of the night weren't done just yet.

Everyone froze on hearing the lobby doors swing open fast. Hayden came out of it first, and brought forth the shotgun again. Isaac stood to his right with machete ready. Kael waved off Evelyn and Salma before joining them.

Up ahead, Hayden saw five more people spilling through and then pulling the doors closed. A thump startled the new cluster of humanity. Hayden heard rapid vicious barking, as something scratched at the glass. He and the other four rushed out to see a German shepherd standing on its hind legs pawing at the doors. Two of the night's refugees noticed Hayden and the rest.

"Help us," the Asian woman cried.

"Gonna have to shoot it," said the man wearing a hat that reminded Hayden of Indiana Jones.

"We need the doors to stay intact, so no," Hayden refused.

The dog exhibited traits Hayden recognized: darkly bordered opaque eyes, grayed nose, and mouth full of nightmarishly deformed teeth. Otherwise it appeared rather muscular and absolutely immaculate, as if groomed for a show. It bit onto the door handle, but because the doors had closed all the way its tugs were ineffectual. Its paws scraped as it leaned back, though its strength was limited by body weight, and so nothing happened for a moment. Once the dead animal's paws braced against the metal frame of the door, though, the handle popped off with a metallic ping.

"'Fucking kidding me," the hat-wearing man cursed his disbelief.

"Ah." Hayden took a moment to recall the name of the man in the hoodie. "Kael. You think you could use that on a dog without getting hurt?"

"Why don't we just shoot it?" Isaac asked.

"You mean like Salma's headshots you guys told me about?" Hayden reminded them. "I think we've all established that guns are overrated against them."

"Yeah, I think so." Kael nodded, and then raised the pry pole up for a two-handed spearing.

"Okay, you with the hat and Isaac get on opposite sides of that door," Hayden instructed, and pointed to the Asian woman. "I need you to open the door just a crack, and then you haul ass."

"You didn't see what one of these things did to her car," Isaac protested.

"That was a man," Hayden said. "Just do it, and be ready with that machete."

The man with the hat and black leather jacket also packed a leather roll with two double-barreled shotguns, both lacking butt stocks, projecting out of

34

it. Hayden pictured a number of other weapons holstered or otherwise crammed inside. An image reinforced when the man produced a good sized bowie knife.

Seeming to have forgotten his own advice about guns, Hayden kept the shotgun ready. He nodded to Kael and then to those around the door. The rest backed away or ran to hide in side rooms or behind the courtesy desk. The small woman opened the door, but not enough to give the monstrous dog purchase with his newly sharpened claws.

"A little more, please," Hayden said.

"It get in and kill us," she pleaded.

"We want it to get in," Hayden advised her. "Otherwise it'll keep making noise and more will come."

Pensive about Hayden's plan, the woman pushed a bit more and let the door close several times. At last, the dog's one and a half inch long claws made it into the crack amid its maddened pawing. Lacking any human sense of doors, the dog kept scratching until it could press its nose through.

"Okay you two," Hayden ordered them. "Be ready to hack at its face and legs."

"This some crazy goddamn shit," Isaac grumbled, but kept a firm hand on his weapon of choice.

The animal wedged its way through, though the two men chopped at it before the dog got even halfway. Kael rushed on with the pole to stab at the beast's head. The tip binged off with only a line of skin scratched into the animal's head.

"No, Kael," Hayden yelled. "The chest! Stab it behind a foreleg where its armpit is!"

Kael readjusted his grip, making Hayden flash to some decades old Kung Fu flick. He thrust the pole in with deft accuracy. There came a crunch, as the steel pole passed between ribs. Yet, the dog just snapped wildly at it. The dog's paws scrambled and slipped over the tiled floor. It attempted to crawl out from under the tip Kael kept pressing home.

The dead animal made a half-circle, until Isaac managed a good whack with the machete at its hind quarters. The man in the hat and black jacket came around to help Kael push the pry bar further in. Together, they managed to penetrate deeper, as Isaac continued to hobble the ravenous canine, until it just went lifeless all of a sudden.

The guy with the hat sighed while giving Kael a look. He then pulled up a sleeve to check a scab-covered injury, which Hayden figured the man had gotten some time before coming into the lobby, and was aggravated by the struggle. The rest had come back out to see the results of the struggle, and then they noticed that the guy was bleeding a little. Salma and the others seemed to realize that it was a bite, and the undercover cop produced her pistol to aim at the man.

"Whoa, what are you doing?" Isaac protested. "He's one of us."

"He's bitten," Salma declared to everyone. "We can't risk that he'll turn into one of them."

"Oh shit," Hayden scoffed, rolling his eyes and turning his head away. "Give me a break."

36

"We don't know how it spreads," Salma warned him. "He has to go."

"*You* don't know how it spreads," Hayden admonished, and waved the injured man over.

"Don't move!" Salma yelled, even though he didn't budge.

Hayden put the shotgun barrel right up between Salma's shoulders. "Lower the gun—now."

"What in god's name are you doing, Hayden?" Salma's voice cracked as she attempted to scold.

"He's not going to turn," Hayden said with dead-level calm. "Lower the gun and lay off him. Victims have to die and be completely drained before this thing takes over."

"What?" the woman with the boy questioned. "Are you some kind of expert on the undead?"

"No," Hayden rightly denied. "I'm a chemical engineer, which is even better."

"How do you know he won't change?" Salma asked, still unwilling to relinquish her aim.

"Was that from the dog?" Kael asked, as he looked it over.

"Nah," the leather-clad walking arsenal said. "Got jumped by some amped-up whacko when I got home late, or, ya'know. 'Figured she was a tweaker who broke into my apartment looking for drugs. She came out of my bathroom and slammed me into a wall like a linebacker."

Salma cast uncertain eyes to the side, to size up Hayden's determination, before she lowered the pistol and set its safety. "How did you get away?"

"Threw the bitch through the goddamn window, of course," the hat-wearing man explained, now clamping a hold onto the bite. "I tried to box her crazy ass, but she brushed it off like it was nothin'. So, while she was biting my forearm, I scooped her up by the knees and ran for my living room window. A five floor drop to the pavement, and she got up to chase after someone else."

Kael had disappeared somewhere, but came back after having found a first aid kit. He and Evelyn worked together to wrap up the man's wound, while a new round of introductions came; Nick Farnsworth in the hat, the Korean woman was Hyun Jae Seoh, then there was Wanda and her son Brad as well as Valerie, a girl not yet in her teens.

"Now, if we're all back to being one big happy hunk of humanity," Hayden said. "I can explain what's going on; or at least what I found out to date."

Kael was going to remove the pry bar, until Hayden stopped him. Instead, he had Kael and the hatted man named Nick Farnsworth carry the limp and bloodless corpse. After locking the front doors, Hayden led them to the stairs. He ushered them through before locking them off again and following the rest down.

Most lingered in the hall that Hayden had been sitting in before their arrival. A few poked their heads into other rooms. One of those offices had a computer still on and set to watch online news casts. However, Hayden stepped around to stand before the door to the mailroom.

"Okay, before I let you in here I don't want to hear any screaming, shouting or comments about why I got all this inside," Hayden advised them. "Alright?"

A few nodded, even the two kids, and some said so aloud. Then he opened the door and walked in first. He trotted over to the freight elevator to roll over an empty cart that had been in there before he arrived.

"Just sit the dog here, but keep that bar in where it is," Hayden instructed.

Kael and Nick did so, both mindful of the nasty array of slashing teeth and claws atypical for a living canine. Hayden waved everybody over to one of the tables, where he had earlier seen movement under the sheets. Once they gathered around, he then reached an arm high over the front. In sharp tugs he pulled the sheets back to reveal a woman's face with grayed skin and death clearly in her eyes. There was a hard rubber handle in her mouth. It was locked in place with stainless steel chains running through the handle and wrapped around the back of the head. Hayden pulled that off, and quickly withdrew his hands before the woman could get her teeth into them.

Isaac was about to voice his protest and disgust, when Hayden stayed him. "Just listen."

"Her skin is like porcelain," Hyun Jae Seoh observed.

The dead woman's tussled shoulder-length hair was black, but a glossy hue of lifeless gray shined in the light. Drawn a little taut over bone, the skin revealed no signs of blood vessels, though

39

Hayden knew they remained. The corpse didn't heave for breath, and blinked its eyes on very rare occasion.

"Her arms and legs are gone," Evelyn stated, while searching Hayden's features.

"Ah...." Hayden nodded in admission. "Yeah, whoever sent this one and the other to us had the good sense to reduce the hazards. Anytime we fed this corpse in tests we made sure to cut off any newly restored parts of the limbs."

"So," Isaac spoke up, waving his fingers back and forth. "You're sayin' these ain't zombies."

"Wish they were," Hayden confessed, looking over the ineffectually writhing corpse.

Evelyn stepped closer without fear to search the dead woman's neck. "No bite marks."

"Before you get to speculating too much," Hayden prefaced. "Let's throw out all the nonsense from movies or books. They don't keep the scars from before they turned."

"Do you know who she was?" Evelyn aptly questioned, seeming to understand the real personage of this body was gone forever.

"Say hi, Alina," Hayden lightly prompted the quadruple amputee vampire.

"Say hi, Alina," the dead woman taunted right back, with an anticipatory toothy grin.

"See," Hayden began, as he pointed a finger more than a foot away from the mouth. "There's a small number of changes that take place. For one, all the original teeth crumble away to get replaced by that mouthful of razors. Pretty much the same number of teeth they had before, but strictly for slashing and nothing else. You'll see the same's true for the dog over there, only that people don't get the elongated fangs."

"Why?" Kael asked, while appearing the least reluctant to look at the formerly human vampire.

"It's an issue of biomechanics," Hayden explained. "Though how this, er, phenomenon knows to do that beats me. We were only just starting our work after the World Health Organization biohazard docs had their turn. The dog also gets sharper claws, just not razor sharp."

"I thought real vampires would be a lot faster'n us," Nick commented.

"Again," Hayden interjected. "Modern cinematic mythology."

"But the heart thing worked," Nick reminded.

"Yes," Hayden agreed. "And it worked hundreds of years ago in the Carpathian region, when people staked the dead into their graves. In fact, let me use your knife and I'll show you something."

Hayden waved summoning fingers toward Nick, who then passed over the bowie knife. Once he pulled the sheets back more, Hayden noticed someone covered the younger kid's eyes. The corpse named Alina wore the tattered remains of a hospital top, but the breasts were clearly visible. A spot was labeled with an X by a marker on the inward side of the left breast.

Switching his grip, Hayden came to realize the weapon was never built for a downward stab. Yet he readied himself to do that anyway, using both hands. He hammered the blade down at with a

41

grunt. As the weapon sunk to its hilt, the vampire let loose a shriek. The scream was cut short before it could fill anyone's ears. Like the dog, no blood seeped out from the point of attack.

"Dead as a doornail, right?" Hayden presented to them.

He put the meat of his own hand in its mouth and looked at the others. "And it doesn't have to be wood, I take it," Evelyn noted.

"Wood, silver, plastic if you wanted to try that," Hayden concurred, while taking his hand away.

"That one who attacked her car." Salma reflected, indicating Evelyn. "I shot it through the heart once or twice. And before that there was the first one I ran into. Why didn't that work?"

"That brings us to the second half of what's going on," Hayden announced, and restored the gag before ripping the knife back from the limbless corpse's chest. "This'll take a bit."

Twitching in the body was the first sign that the vampire hadn't truly been laid to rest. Its shoulders thumped, as the once-female thing attempted to rise up. The head moved slowly at first, but built up to wild swings both ways until the eyes opened to stare straight at Evelyn.

"Like a switch," Hayden pointed out, as he traded focus with each adult in turn. "Only we can't be turned back on like they can. It's got to completely cross through the heart and stay there. Not sure why yet. Though they renew lost or damaged tissue, it's not cellular regeneration that you'd see in a living animal. Their cells get reassembled someway. We were just getting to that when everything went to pot. No cellular respiration, no heartbeat, no need to breathe. The WHO guys found that they use their lungs to create a vacuum, so that in fact they do suck fluids out of the bites."

"If they don't breathe," Kael began in preparation for his question. "Why do they need blood?"

"Turns out it's not blood specifically," Hayden corrected, waving to a set of external hard drives he had brought there, and that now stood on a nearby shelf. "It's any nutrient-carrying body fluid. Blood's just the easiest and most abundantly flowing from a fresh injury. Give them time, and they'd try to completely desiccate their victims. The World Health people think it's because vampires need the water and adenosine triphosphate that their own bodies no longer reproduce. I could list all the other crap they need, but really, you get the point."

"And, from what you said upstairs," Evelyn speculated. "If they des– well, drain someone completely, is that when they turn?"

"So long as they're not left out in the sun, yeah, that's the going theory," Hayden said.

"But," Wanda, one of those from the second group, started to suggest, "Sunlight was just from that old silent movie, I thought. It's the one with the rat-looking vampire. Wouldn't Romanians have been pulling vampires out into the sun if that really worked?"

"I doubt they knew back then," Hayden suggested, while covering the Alina vampire back

43

up with sheets, and then checked his watch. "Yeah, we can do this now."

"Do what?" Nick asked.

"Somebody get behind that cart with the dog and follow me," Hayden said, and grabbed a sizeable battery-powered light and a couple of other things. "This'll weird you out."

Feeling perfectly secure, Hayden rolled the gurney toward the freight elevator.

He turned it on with another of the building keys, and pushed the vampire specimen in. Kael pushed the cart in after him, keeping one hand on the pry bar, and the rest followed.

The elevator raised one floor. Hayden noticed that Wanda's preschool-aged son kept to the furthest corner he could and was hugging his mother's leg. Hayden pondered the original composition of their family before they'd gotten there. Hayden's mind soon turned to thoughts of his own lost younger boy and deceased ex-wife. His older son, now a grown man, still refused to talk to him.

"It's okay," Hayden assured the small boy, and got a child's faithful nod in answer.

His mother ran her hand back and forth through his hair, as everyone else studied the exchange. The pre-teen girl Valerie, to her credit, seemed to have shed most of her fears last night, and looked like a promising brunette Buffy-in-waiting.

"I hesitate to ask, but how did you guys fare before coming here?" Hayden inquired of them.

44

The doors opened, and Hayden rolled the gurney into one of the offices. During his scouting venture through the office building last night he'd closed all the curtains and blinds he could, to ensure no vampire could see in. The room he chose was on the eastern side, and would serve well for his impromptu demonstration.

"'Far as I know," Isaac started his brief backstory. "My girl's still doing fine over in Florida with her grandparents. As for her mother, who cares? Serves her right, for gettin' it on with some dude she brought to my house, while I'm out bustin' my ass payin' bills."

"I here on student visa," Hyun said. "I hope my family is safe."

"We..." Evelyn hesitated a moment, throwing a glance at Kael before she continued. "...haven't had a chance to check up on everyone else back home. I should probably do that."

"Give me a minute with this, before you do," Hayden implored.

The mother-son pair, Wanda and Brad, had been a trio the day before. However, from her tearful recounting, the father hadn't been terribly fatherly before being taken down by vampires. He unwittingly gave her and the boy a chance that he probably should have been willing to sacrifice for. Salma wasn't married or seeing anyone, had no children of her own and grew up in a different state, where her parents presumably remained. Valerie turned out to be a foster child who had no idea who her parents were, and didn't think much of those the state had allowed to adopt her. She had stormed out of the house, and was a few blocks away when the nocturnal horror show began. Nick didn't say anything, just shrugged, so no one pressed him for more.

"So," Hayden announced, as if addressing a class gathered for a field trip, and hoisted up the battery powered light. "Here we have an ultraviolet lamp."

"Yeah," Isaac acknowledged, eyeing Hayden over. "Okay."

"Right," Hayden called out, as he pulled the sheets off the vampire again. "So, bodies can't turn if exposed to sunlight, and if you were to look outside you'd see no vampires scurrying about. Daylight hours are perfectly safe out there. Everybody with me so far?"

"I can't wait to see this thing fry," Kael let slip with morbid fascination.

Isaac stared at him with discomfort, but returned his attention to Hayden.

"And, presto change'o," Hayden chanted, as he flipped on the light and turned it to shine down.

The vampire's muffled laugher was aimed at Hayden, as he panned the light up and down her fully exposed face and torso. Just to be sure the image sunk in, Hayden repeated the sweep barely an inch over the limbless and strapped down animated corpse. Then he moved the light up to blast UV rays directly into the vampire's clouded eyes, and lingered there. She tried to bite her way through the gag, but Hayden kept his hand away just to be sure.

"If not UV, does any light work?" Kael asked.

"A big fat goose egg," Hayden answered. "We tried X-rays, pretty much every part of the ultraviolet spectrum and what's below the visible range."

"Is there anything above X-rays?" Isaac asked.

"Yeah, there is, but gamma rays produced in the sun don't reach the surface, and I can't think even vampires could see them," Hayden said, as he walked around and picked up a mirror panel, and then pointed to the curtains. "Pull those back just a tad from the side there."

Isaac obliged him, and the splash of daylight on the wall opposite of the window gave the vampire cause for alarm. It tried to use its shoulders and buttocks to worm away, but the straps held it in place.

"She's terrified," Nick observed.

"It," Hayden iterated. "It's simulating terror, probably to play on our sympathies.

Now watch as I direct a little sunshine onto it."

Placing the mirror into the light, he moved around to aim the reflected power of the sun onto the creature of the night. Alina's corpse appeared more panicked and even tried to beg and plea in the dead woman's original language. Hayden played the redirected light all over the frantically recoiling body. And yet nothing happened to support the dramatic Hollywood fiery vanquishing of undead.

"What was she saying?" Evelyn inquired.

"Romanian, I imagine. That's where I'm told this one was found," Hayden explained, and then thumbed to the curtain that Isaac let go of. "So no solar spectra will do it, as you can see. But if I pull those open this thing'll cook. We don't know what it is."

"But it's afraid—" Evelyn caught herself and tried again. "It reacts as if sunlight will destroy it."

"Yeah," Hayden acknowledged while sizing up the gurney-confined specimen. "That probably is a secondary stimulus it uses to avoid what the sun's actually doing. And whatever that is, it apparently can't get through stuff like these curtains or even fabrics if they're woven tight enough. Glass lets the effect through, but they burn a lot slower. Go figure."

"What would it take to find out and recreate it?" Evelyn asked, giving him an odd expression.

He leaned on the gurney to survey the corpse again trying to bite him, and pondered a moment before saying, "Give me a consistently functioning particle lab and twenty million dollar annual budget? Sure, I could've banged out a solution in ten to fifteen years. But that was yesterday."

"Only direct sunlight and impaling the heart are weaknesses," Kael recounted, staring at the vampire. Then he turned to Hayden. "So what are their strengths?"

"Decapitation works, but it'll be hard as hell," Hayden added to the group's possible defenses, while he covered the vampire up again.

"I guess that machete was a good call," Salma directed to Isaac.

Hayden ran down what he'd gotten from the prior WHO quarantine study. "Strength is the operative word there. It varies between species, but because nature turned us into such underpowered weaklings, human bodies tend to see the largest multiplier. The estimates are somewhere between eight to ten times. As you can imagine, it's hard to get one of these things help us know exactly."

"Damn." Isaac voiced the discouragement Hayden guessed the others were feeling.

"Fortunately, however, they're not light-speed fast," Hayden went on. "While being strong helps someone run faster, it seems there's a peak depending on body type. They'll match just about any sprinter on Earth, other than that Bolt guy from Jamaica, I suppose. Even fat ones, if there are any, will run us down. But they get to full speed in two or three steps. Plus, they never tire. They can jump high and climb anything their fingers can pinch or hook onto. To go along with that, as Nick can attest, their bones are a shitload tougher. Soft tissues don't tear so easy, and a fresh feeding fixes what's damaged."

"But their reflexes are the same," Evelyn tested out loud.

"True, but there's going to be a lot of animal vampires out there," Hayden warned. "And a lot of them are quite a bit sharper on that. What's more, they'll be several times stronger than they were when alive. Vision aside, they'll also retain their sensory abilities, and that has me worried."

"What about vision?" Nick chinned toward Hayden.

"Visual acuity doesn't change," Hayden began. "But from the documents and files I read,

49

every specimen develops receptivity to infrared. The wavelength they best see pretty closely matches human body temperature. Despite that milky stuff in their eyes, they can pick up ambient light better, which makes sense considering the night-time restriction. We might find human vampires wearing glasses, but they'll still get around in the dark pretty well."

"Anything else?" Kael asked.

"Yes," Hayden answered, and then gave them all a dead-level stare. "Their sense of smell changes in only one aspect. All vampires, every one of them, are better at detecting blood at slightly longer distances. The WHO studies showed that can be thwarted with enough rusty iron mixed into water, but the messed up part is this: Regardless of what species the body is, they all prefer human blood. They can get by sucking down other mammals, but they're selectively geared for people. Birds are warm-blooded, but they don't get attacked, and as with a lot else, no one knows why."

"What species?" Evelyn questioned.

"Dogs, but not wolves," Hayden started, focusing on what he could recall off the top of his head. "Nor any other wild canines they tried. The bodies of some domesticated breeds appear more likely to become vampires. Gorillas are susceptible to rising, but not chimps. I don't even know what to make of that. I think there were a few monkeys on the list. One of the videos had this big gray baboon that just about ripped its cage apart.

"Domestic cats and male lions will turn. Apparently, some naturalist found an entire pride of female lions and female cubs bled dry. The teeth marks matched the male when changes in dentation were accounted for. But none of the females got up and no male cubs were found, making them think they turned after being fed on. Black rats, but not the brown ones, even though they both originate from China. Also, those big rats found on New Guinea."

"Great," Salma bemoaned. "It'll be just our luck to have elephant vampires escaping the zoo."

"I don't recall that idea being tested," Hayden added, after some thought. "But what freaked them out were reports of bottlenose dolphins torpedoing out of the water to snag crewmen off fishing, shrimping and whaling boats. There could be a bloodsucking Moby Dick for all anyone knows."

Kael snickered at Hayden's choice of phrasing, which forced him to realize what joke he'd inadvertently set up. Evelyn just shook her head with a sigh toward Kael.

"Bats?" Nick dared pose the obvious question, with his palms out.

"Yes, now that you mention it." Hayden remembered just then. "Though, oddly enough, not vampire bats as I would've expected. The quarantine tests came up negative on all three kinds. A lot of the insect-eating species also don't turn, but the fruit bats and nectar feeders come back."

"With so many ways this, I don't know, this effect can spread?" Wanda, who was largely incurious about the details, asked. "Why didn't it spread so fast until now?"

"Who knows?" Hayden replied. "Maybe it's because people think you can have a romantic relationship with them."

The sarcastic tone and mocking expression he gave drew a small degree of ire from Wanda and Valerie, though Hayden noticed Evelyn presented a bemused face.

"Maybe something was holding it in check until now," Evelyn offered.

"Could be," Hayden accepted, and arched his brow looking away before shrugging.

"Hey, wait a minute." Kael sounded as if he'd found brighter prospects. "Isn't there a book about slayers? Yeah, these guys would go out with spears and flamethrowers and some other stuff. No superpowers or anything, just normal guys out of the army, or… something like that."

"Right, go ahead and have at it," Isaac tossed to an exuberant Kael. "Let us know how that turns out for ya. We'll be all right here waitin'. How that be?"

"You never know," Kael defended, and waved to Hayden. "He says the World Health–something was looking into this. Government does all this other stuff about swine flu and terrorists. Why not?"

"I think that's what they were starting to do," Hayden said, to help Kael out. "The R and D firm I work for was awarded one of the contracts to figure this crap out, once they discovered it wasn't a disease and that a subject's DNA wasn't involved."

Hayden went over to the, as yet, still impaled and motionless vampire dog. He rolled that cart out of the room toward the lobby entrance. The others followed, unsure if he had still more to show them. Hayden had given them everything he could think of.

"Is there a cure?" Valerie, the pre-teen girl asked.

"They're dead," Hayden reminded her, while he unlocked the doors. "And that's that. Connections in the brain deteriorate. Only fragments of the mind are left. Yeah, there's a cure alright. This is it."

He gave the cart his best shove, and leaned against the doorframe to watch it roll unsteadily out into the advancing light of morning. The other eight gathered behind him and Valerie to witness Hayden's therapy of disinfecting sunlight.

It didn't burst into flames, which he guessed disappointed more than one of the survivors. However, a rapid sizzling swept down the stilled dog carcass as if exposed to a seamless row of blowtorches. The cart stopped half way into the sun, letting everyone see that nothing less than direct exposure did the deed. The soft tissue broiled and then burned down layer by layer, and the previous flesh fell away. From the start of the burn down to the bone, it took sixty six seconds, Hayden noted, studying his watch. The pry bar slid out about halfway, but the devilish dog didn't stir in time.

The bones lasted around four to five minutes, with a bubbling of brain matter that started up the moment the skull degraded enough for the light to get through. Where the upper half of the animal lay, it quickly dried under the sun's sanitizing power. Hayden walked out to run his hand into the pile of crumbling remains, and then showed the rest still inside the lobby.

"Leaves quite a mess, but nothing that a push broom and shovel won't fix," Hayden remarked.

He grabbed the intact rear half by the ankles and tossed it out into the light, before picking up the steel pole and brought the cart back. The others said not a word, as he rolled the cart to the freight elevator. Next, he included the gurney with them in tow, and returned to the basement floor.

Chapter 3: A Price Too High

Research assistance is what Hayden said he needed, though he was selective about who to ask. However, that same morning Evelyn overheard him approach Hyun, and heard her beg him to be one before he got a word out. Then Hayden came to Evelyn next, and she also accepted. She wasn't sure Wanda or Valerie would be interested, or if the chemical engineer would offer. Salma and the guys were needed to keep watch, despite the daylight hours.

So Evelyn entered the mailroom to find Hayden already at work. He was bent over one of the animal specimens that he had rendered into the normal kind of unmoving dead. The rat's body was dissected and the skin pinned back. The heart was still impaled with one scalpel, which he cut open with a second.

"Find anything interesting yet?" Evelyn asked him.

"Same as the others," Hayden answered, as if everyone were up to speed on his work.

"Which is...?" Evelyn drew out, while Hyun entered in behind her.

"Oh, right," Hayden stood up to face her. "I don't want to get too technical, but there's a new bunch of chemical changes. Namely, that everything in the bloodstream gets meshed together through covalent bonds. It's like one giant molecule, and it happens in the muscles and other

55

places as well. It appears to take the place of circulation, but the amount of energy is low. Impaling the heart works because that's where the central driving force of this mega-molecule is."

"So what's confusing you?" Evelyn asked after gauging his expression.

"Some of the chemistry here isn't possible, or," Hayden backtracked. "Shouldn't be."

"Do you know what make them burn in sunlight?" Hyun asked with sudden enraptured interest.

"No, but it's probably linked to the discrepancies with known chemistry," Hayden guessed.

"Huh," Evelyn remarked, as she leaned over to see all four chambers of the rat's heart exposed.

Off to the side, Evelyn noticed Hyun pull back the sheets for the second human subject. Up until yesterday, Evelyn had watched Hayden give both of them limited quantities of animal blood mixed with interstitial fluids, so that they wouldn't shut down completely.

"So sad she ended up this way." Hyun's voice carried a hint of sorrow. "And so pretty, too. She will be like that forever. What is her name?"

"That one was," Hayden ensured to emphasize, "named Janelle Harrington. The information I was given stated that she was killed up in West Virginia a couple months ago. The corpse of Alina Galca back there died some time back in the late sixteen hundreds, or so they think."

"Did they cut off their arms and legs before capturing them?" Evelyn asked in a clinical tone.

"Uh, after," Hayden recollected aloud. "And we kept up on that when we fed them. Especially the older one. If that thing gets off the table we'll be in real trouble. Whoever hired us apparently had the bright idea of sending only female specimens. As if women are less dangerous or something."

Hayden's laugh at that brought a smile to Evelyn's face. "Sounds like you were married."

"Was," Hayden confessed. "Things soured after losing our younger son to leukemia."

"Oh... sorry," Evelyn apologized with deliberate pause.

"It's not like it was your fault," Hayden chided with a pained smile. "But thank you."

"So," Evelyn changed the subject. "What do you need first?"

"Away from populated areas," Hayden said, diverting discussion further. "That would be nice."

"I don't think we can all do that," Evelyn suggested. "At least not together.

Someone's got to get a hold of Valerie's foster parents, which'll piss her off. Isaac wants to try checking on his kid and grandparents. I'm not sure what Wanda wants to do."

"What about you and your brother?" Hayden asked.

"We're from out of town," Evelyn skirted the issue without answering.

"Hmm," Hayden voiced, clearly appearing to have let her evasion go. "Okay, start with Valerie. If your car still runs I think you should drive her home just long enough to check on her folks. You got

57

plenty of daylight left, but be careful about going indoors. Always stay in the sun."

"And you?" Evelyn asked, while fishing out her keys.

"I'm going to poke around at this crap, until I figure it out," Hayden answered, but not the question she meant, at least not at first. "Not much else to look forward to."

Evelyn approached Valerie in one of the offices, where the girl was fixated on social media posts about the outbreak, and braced herself before asking, "Do you need a ride home?"

"What for?" Valerie spat, without turning her head.

"I'm not saying you have to stay, but," Evelyn paused to phrase references to foster parents carefully. "It's so you can see if they're alright. Then I'll take you where you want, if it's not too far."

"It's that chemical guy's idea," Valerie deduced with scorn. "Right?"

"After everything else, you don't have to worry about being busted for running away," Evelyn pointed out with chosen bluntness. "Up to you."

"I suppose," Valerie conceded at last and put away her phone.

Hayden had left the stairwell doors of the basement unlocked for the moment, along with the doors on the first floor. Evelyn and Valerie walked to the lobby doors where Kael and Isaac both sat on chairs from other offices. They were staring out into the midwinter morning for signs of any other survivors.

"Where you guys going?" Kael asked.

"We're going to check on Valerie's foster parents. We should be back in a couple of hours."

"Hey," Isaac called out, as he rose from his chair. The machete was sheathed to his side, and he was holding one of Nick's double-barreled shotguns. "You want me to come with you, just in case?"

"Yeah, that would be nice," Evelyn agreed.

She exited when Isaac held the door for her.

Seeing her car in the day for the first time since it had been mangled let Evelyn remember just how dangerous vampires were. But the engine still worked, and she needed this opportunity to see if any gas station pumps remained functional. With the three of them in, Evelyn pulled out, and chuckled to herself at the image of casually cruising in a car that had been peeled like an orange.

"So Isaac," Evelyn called to him in the front passenger seat. "Did you get a hold of your kid?"

"Nah man," he answered, and then braced the bridge of his nose for a moment, before continuing. "I don't know if service is out over there, or if her grandparents are just bein' assholes."

"I take it it's her mother's side?" Evelyn queried without stepping into marital status.

"Yeah," Isaac answered, becoming more open about it. "I caught her once goin' around my back, and I thought we had things patched up. She's tellin' me how sorry she was and it won't happen again. Two years later, she went out and got another guy. So I filed divorce papers on her ass."

"Maybe it's good everyone's family is messed up," Evelyn sought out the bright side. "That way we're already set up and ready to go for when the world goes nuts."

The made Isaac laugh, as she intended, and then he said, "'Cept Wanda and Brad seem normal."

"Which way, Val?" Evelyn asked, testing a truncation of the girl's name in hopes of cooperation.

Following the tween's directions brought them to a suburban stretch of road.

Once Valerie pointed out the house with a high foundation, and well windows, Evelyn pulled over, and everyone exited the car.

"Hayden says we need to be careful going inside," Evelyn warned in preparation.

"In the daytime?" Valerie doubted.

"Don't need to tell me twice," Isaac eagerly said. "They don't get blasted but by direct sunlight."

"Oh," Valerie recalled, as they set off for the front door.

The girl opened the door, but Evelyn was relieved that Valerie didn't just walk in. She instead called for the foster parents – by their first names, Evelyn noted – and got no response.

"What do you want to bet they saw me with a gun an' freaked out?" Isaac joked.

"In that case, they'd probably want to burn me at the stake," Evelyn suggested.

"They're not like that," Valerie countered, and took one cautious step inside.

"Hello?"

"Where've you been?" a woman called out, sounding cross.

"They're okay," Valerie said, and attempted to go further.

"Wait," Evelyn whispered, and then turned to Isaac. "We all go together."

"Yeah, I got'cha," Isaac assured her. He checked the gun before he popped the strap off the sheathed machete that kept it from sliding out by accident.

They crept across the living room just far enough to peek down a hall and the neighboring dining room. Evelyn made a point of seeing that all the blinds were up, and took that as a good sign. A door slammed, making all three of them jump.

A woman started down the hall, but stopped once she saw all of them. "Valerie, who are they?"

Evelyn, her nerves on edge, studied the woman for anything unusual. Her eyes and skin appeared normal, and she thought nothing of stepping into indirect sunlight spilling from the other rooms.

"They helped me out last night," Valerie said, pointing back to them. "This is Lyn and Isaac."

"We don't mean to scare you, ma'am," Isaac apologized. "Just with all this craziness goin' on, we thought you might need help or something."

"Valerie," the woman said, as if she hadn't heard Isaac. "Go downstairs and talk to your father."

"Okay, alright," Valerie acceded with her hands up. "Just wait here a minute."

"No, it's alright if your friends want to go with you," the foster mother permitted.

That brought one brow down on Isaac's forehead, though Valerie seemed unconcerned, so Evelyn went along with it. Going down the stairs, however, Evelyn noticed less light than she thought would be normal for a bottom floor halfway above ground level with window wells. Yet the foster mother followed them down without hesitation, so Evelyn again pressed on behind Valerie.

"He's in his office room, Valerie," the woman goaded.

"Mark?" the girl called out in query.

Evelyn noticed she used his name rather than address him as her dad.

Following Valerie, all of them entered a wood-paneled room with shelves, computer desk, liquor cabinet and office chair. And in the middle of the floor lay a man so white Evelyn knew he'd been bled dry sometime in the night.

That's when Evelyn felt Isaac bump into her from behind, and the door slam behind them all. A lock sounded, informing her that Isaac had been shoved into her by the woman. Now, all three of them were locked in with a corpse.

"He went out looking for you, you little tramp!" the woman screamed. "And that's what happened to him! You're going to give him what he needs, so help me!"

"Tara!" Valerie screamed as she ran to the door and pounded on it. "Let us out!"

Evelyn and Isaac both locked eyes on Mark's body, both fearful it could jump up at any second.

"You bitch! Let us out," Valerie screamed again, still hammering at the door.

"When your father gets up he's going to teach you a lesson," she screamed back in fury from further away. "He's the one who wanted to bring you into our home! And look what you did!"

"He's not moving," Evelyn observed at just over a whisper.

"Maybe they didn't work him over enough to turn," Isaac speculated, and handed her the shotgun, to then pull out the machete. "Kneecap his ass if he moves. I got this."

Isaac edged closer, while Valerie kept up her verbal and fist barrage.

"Is that another bite on his wrist?" Evelyn asked as she stayed at Isaac's side.

"Yeah, I think he got tagged by a bunch of 'em," Isaac suggested.

"I don't think he's getting up." Evelyn sounded hopeful more than observant.

Risking putting the machete away, Isaac returned to the door. "Ma'am, your husband's dead!"

Evelyn heard the woman scream something back, and wasn't sure if it included a racial slur.

"Did I hear that right?" Evelyn checked with the others.

"Gawd," Valerie condemned, and offered a sympathetic face to Isaac.

"Yeah, tha's what I thought," Isaac nodded, and reached back toward Evelyn. "Let me see that."

"Sure, here 'ya go." Evelyn passed him the shotgun.

63

"Ma'am! You don't let us out I'll use my key," Isaac called out in warning.

Another vitriolic verbal backfire made Isaac's head droop in disappointment, and then he waved Valerie back before leveling the shotgun barrel. "Last chance...!"

"Shit, just do it," Valerie insisted with a dismissive wave at the door, while she turned away.

"Breaking and exiting," Isaac muttered, and then stepped back wincing. "That's a new one."

It sounded more like a bomb than a gun blast, and with his background in construction, Isaac blew away the wood next to the knob instead of the handle itself. And he only used one barrel, in case the bang was loud enough to wake the dead. Evelyn checked, while Isaac kicked the door the rest of the way open, but the man's body never twitched.

They still rushed for the stairs and charged up with Isaac keeping the gun ready. At the top of the stairway, they saw the woman was more fearful. She ran into another room, locking it behind her. But the trio simply went for the front door, though Isaac paused and turned.

"Next time don't make people shoot up your damn house," he shouted, and ushered them outside.

By the time they got back to Evelyn's car, she stopped to ask before getting in, "Don't you think we should help get that body out, just in case it does turn?"

"Fuck her," Valerie seethed, her voice dripping loathing.

"Now I'll second that," Isaac concurred. "Crazy bitch wants to sleep with a dead man, tha's her business. She'll probably accuse us of kidnapping his ass. Let's just go."

* * *

"A disturbing development," the field reporter on the computer monitor stated, as he stood among national guardsmen. "It's a little after two a.m. We're on the roof of a thirty story building, and these, ah, people are scaling the outer walls straight up for us. Haley, get a shot of this."

"Right, fuckin' stand there and look," Nick declared with his feet up on the desk and fingers laced behind his head, as he, Salma and Hayden all sat around the desk watching online news video.

Hayden checked his watch again, both for sundown and for the results of what he had left going on in the mailroom. Then new developments on the flat screen drew his attention up. The camera operator aimed down to show vampires climbing up the sides of the tall building, as flashlights and larger lights cast down on them. A shot rang out, causing one dead hand to slip, but the vampire reacquired purchase with a faint dark hole through its hand where the bullet hit.

"Sir," one of the guardsmen advised in formal tone. "I need you to step inside now, Sir."

"Okay, yeah," the reporter answered, and waved his camerawoman on, but paused to keep doing his thing. "We've been told to go inside where it's secure. But, just to update you, the infected people are definitely becoming violent. We're getting sporadic reports that pets and other animals are also contracting this epidemic and spreading it around. People are advised to stay in

65

their homes, or wherever they currently are, and not to admit anyone in even if they're familiar. Authorities are–"

From above someone landed on the reporter, invoking a scream from him as the biting started.

"Contact, contact," Guardsmen shouted. "Everyone else fall back inside!" Assault rifles blazed away, racking both living and dead bodies with multiple hits.

Yet the vampire kept sucking away at the prize in hand, as more leapt the last few stories up to the roof. Without warning the camera fell forward with two distinct cracking sounds; one being glass. Hayden felt the other was the camerawoman's skull.

"Shit," Nick cursed, and pulled his feet off to sit up and grab the mouse. "I've seen enough."

"Where was that?" Salma asked.

Nick stopped what he was doing to back up to the previous page hosting the video. "Somewhere over in Atlanta, it says here. The user's posted six of these, all from different cities."

"You said they have to be drained completely," Salma said to Hayden, as he was about to stand.

"I got videos in the mailroom of laboratory recreations with test animals." Hayden thumbed.

"How long does it take?" Salma asked.

"The rat-to-rat contact was clocked at two minutes, seventeen seconds," Hayden explained. "The live subject turned about fifteen minutes after its vitals flatlined."

"But that's a rat," Salma reminded.

"You'd have to upscale it, that's true," Hayden admitted. "I don't know what ratios, though. Mouth-to-body mass probably has to be factored in. They use the lungs as a pump and to store a lot of the fluid sucked out when the stomach and intestinal tract are too full. Just guessing here, but it probably takes maybe a couple hours or better for people to turn."

Hayden stood to check up on his experiment, but Salma stayed him again. "The night before last we didn't see anything like this in precinct reports."

"Look," Hayden began while laying it out between his hands. "It's a logarithmic progression. So say it's two hours. That's ignoring transmission through small animals. This time of year, that means you're getting thirteen hours of night-time, so that's at least six doublings in their numbers."

"I don't understand," Salma said, furrowing her brows at his description of the math.

"That means two times two times two, and so on," Hayden rephrased. "Meaning they end with sixty-four times as many vampires as there were at dusk. Now I'm ignoring a lot of other factors, like those who get caught in daylight or any that get destroyed by survivors. But, like you saw, taking them down isn't something the world's set up to do."

"Tonight's gonna suck," Nick pointed out, having followed the conclusion Hayden left out.

"There's a capping off point isn't there?" Salma suggested. "They'd run out of – food."

"I'm just a chem freak who's got a minor in particle physics," Hayden stated, as though that exposed all his limitations. "I don't know the ecology implications of this. All I can tell you is natural selection doesn't just act on living things. It also works on complex reactions. There're molecules that reproduce copies of themselves without having to be alive, but undergo random changes if the process is allowed to cycle long enough. My job was – is – figuring out how this crap works and maybe coming up with something that interferes with it."

Salma appeared to have been given enough, allowing Hayden to go back to the mailroom and take a look at the small rat he'd previously dissected. He'd put it back into the thick-barred cage with a petri dish of pig's blood, before removing the scalpel lanced through its tiny heart.

However, after verifying that the blood was completely consumed, Hayden noticed Hyun sitting next to the body of Janelle Harrington. The short Korean woman was sending texts through her phone. She occasionally talked to the futilely writhing corpse about her telecommunications exchanges.

"Are you practicing bedside manner to be a nurse?" Hayden asked.

"Oh no," Hyun suddenly answered with awkward cheer. "I tell her it okay, and that she soon can join her lost loved ones. She like that, I think."

"I keep telling you, she doesn't have feelings anymore," Hayden disparaged. "You're seeing an incomplete neurological imitation used to lull us into lowering our guard."

"But she talk to me," Hyun insisted with enthusiasm-laced Korean syntax.

"Because it can't get up and do anything else to you," Hayden reiterated, going back to his work.

With care Hayden opened the cage a crack and thrust a set of prongs in.

Brutally, he squeezed a hold around the rat's middle, causing it to flail and writhe in attempts to gnaw through the glossy stainless steel. That is, until he stabbed the scalpel through its heart. All the previous cuts he made in dissection vanished as a result of feeding, and that's what Hayden wanted to study.

He listened to Hyun talk to the vampire again, as he jotted down the weight numbers for the scalpel and petri dish. Then Hayden put the stilled rat carcass onto a scale, and did a double-take of the reading. Checking over his older data, Hayden then recalibrated the scale and tried again.

"No, that can't be right," Hayden gave voice to his doubts.

"What can't be right?" Hyun asked, giving all her attention to him again.

"Weight's wrong," came Hayden's nondescript answer. "I administered a two hundred gram sample of blood, but the rat's weight went up by about two hundred, five."

"Maybe scale is broken?" Hyun offered.

"Yeah, checked that," he said absently, while turning the dead rat over in the tongs.

"Do you think they, ah, the vampires stop being ugly when they turn?"

69

It was an odd question from her that Hayden, turning around and lowering the rat, had to be sure the young woman wasn't joking with him. Hyun Jae Seoh presented him the same chipper expression she had before, when justifying her talking to the corpse.

"They stop being nice when they turn," Hayden sneered with irritation. "They stop being your friend. They're no longer your relative, your acquaintance, your lover, nosey neighbor bitching about your lawn, or that person who says hi to you at work. All that's left is a walking, talking supercharged health hazard. And be glad there's nothing left of the person. Who'd want to be like that anyway? Skulking in the dark forever and sucking down any warm body you run across."

"But look how cute she is," Hyun praised of the corpse casting its evil smile Hayden's way.

"Until someone cuts her head off or she gets barbecued," Hayden honed his words into the most stinging barb he could conjure at the moment, while running a calibration of a different scale. "She'll be an adorable pile of incinerated shit."

The vampire threw a hurt expression to Hyun, who pointed it out. "You hurt her feelings."

"Why all the sympathy for it, anyway?" Hayden asked, trying to walk back the attitude.

"I don't want to be ugly," Hyun uttered, taking him by surprise.

Examining the measurement, and affirming there was an extra five grams, Hayden studied Hyun Jae again but without saying anything. She couldn't be any older than mid-twenties, though Hayden might've estimated low because of her girlish size. At his age, the young woman held little attraction for him, but he deemed her pretty enough any man her age, be they Asian or not.

"My mother tell me I'm ugly," Hyun groaned. "She say I won't find husband."

"No offense," Hayden began, while carefully putting the rat back in its cage with the scalpel in place to keep it dead. "But your mother sounds like a real bitch. You can tell her I said so, if you want."

A sob escaped from Hyun. Hayden didn't have time to issue an apology if the comment about her mother was what upset her.

"It's gettin' late," Nick said, leaning through the doorway. "And they're not back yet."

"Dammit," Hayden hissed, as he headed out to follow Nick to the stairs. Then Hayden stopped in the hall on realizing something.

"What?" Nick asked turning around, uncertain.

"I just realized I hadn't heard Brad running around all day today," Hayden recalled.

"I figured Wanda and him left to go find the dad," Nick shrugged.

Hayden stopped by a room he saw Salma in. "You didn't see Wanda or Brad today, did you?"

"Wanda was upstairs, last I saw," the Latina cop answered. "Said she was going to get through to emergency services, and see if we could get help."

"By the way, anything from your station?" Hayden inquired further.

"No one's answering," she said, and waved to the computer. "Whole system's in trouble."

"Alright, thanks," Hayden concluded, and resumed moving toward the stairwell.

Up on the main floor, Hayden saw Wanda seated at the front desk and focused on the computer.

"I guess everything's alright," Nick said prematurely.

"Wanda, where's Brad?" Hayden asked, rising on his toes for her to see him.

Forgetting everything, she swung her head around to discover the little boy wasn't around.

"Kael?" Hayden asked.

The scrappy young man turned in his chair with a head shake.

"There's a fire exit, right," Nick suggested. "Maybe he slipped out through one of those."

"Brad!" Wanda's voice rose sharply in alarm, as she shot up into a run. "Brad!"

Then, through the glass doors, Hayden saw a big security truck with a bank logo on it. Coming outside with Nick and Kael, he realized Isaac was behind the wheel, and both Evelyn and Valerie riding with him. They parked front-on to the curb and got out.

"What's wrong?" Evelyn asked, seeing Hayden throwing concerned glances around.

"That little boy's missing," Kael said.

"We ditched Evelyn's car for this," Isaac explained, bouncing a fist off the front wheel well.

"We got some more supplies and stuff," Valerie added.

"Good," Hayden praised without emotion, and looking distant. "Park it around back later. Right now we need help finding Brad."

Other than Wanda, no one shouted out the boy's name, lest they give away the general area of their shelter. Hayden wished she wouldn't call out, but didn't admonish her for it. However, he only had Nick follow Wanda around, while others broke off in pairs to search elsewhere.

Then, as Hayden realized the sun had dipped below the buildings, Brad called out, "Mommy!"

"Brad," she shouted back. "Hurry over here, we have to get inside!"

"I found daddy," the little boy declared.

"Shit," Kael cursed, as he and Hayden raced toward Brad's voice.

Isaac and Evelyn arrived at a gap between a brick wall and some houses around the same time Wanda and Nick had. Hayden and Kael showed up not long after, and the six of them saw Brad bouncing on his toes behind one of the houses and pointing back somewhere.

"I found daddy," the kid triumphantly declared. "I found him, I found him! I'm a big boy now!"

Brad raced off, pulling at the fears of all six adults who broke into a run after him.

"Brad, don't," Wanda screamed. "Come back!"

They reached a home with a long deteriorated door and paint flaking off. Wanda hesitantly stepped toward the doorway and then back, shaking her fists with pained trepidation against maternal

73

impulse. Evelyn and Isaac passed around small flashlights, before the six all entered single file.

"Of course, the lights are off and the windows are small," Nick griped under his breath.

"Daddy's here," Brad's voice rang from further in the house.

Wanda ran off without waiting for anyone to follow, and got a few yards before the others could catch up. However, by then her screaming rang out in conjunction with Brad's angry sounding grunts. The others came to a bare bedroom on the west side of the interior. Wanda was crumpled in a corner, and Brad locked into a hug on her with both of his arms and legs despite her attempts to pull him off.

Everyone grabbed onto Brad where they could, and Isaac drew out the machete. There wasn't much coordination between the five adults, but all the tugging ripped Brad loose and tumbling back. The boy rose first, but Kael was next and threw a waist-level front-ball kick right into Brad's chest.

Isaac held the machete up, but hesitated to use it. Brad rushed Kael, who was the closest, but the young martial arts trained man blasted the ravenous tyke back with another fast foot. Then Kael turned and took the machete away from Isaac, and whirled it about the wrist in anticipation.

This time the boy sprang above head level straight at Kael, who swept the heavy blade across as the child projectile drew near. Wanda shrieked a horrified refusal against the outcome. In a flinch, Kael deflected the severed head, but took the limp body impact full on. The long blade clattered to the floor, as Kael frantically pushed at the headless attacker.

Hayden and Evelyn rushed over to find blood soaking Wanda's entire left shoulder and breast along with more coming out of her mouth through screaming sobs.

"Put pressure here," Evelyn instructed Hayden, while placing his hand on the large neck wound.

Skin had been torn away, when the group separated son from mother. Hayden's bare contact on her exposed flesh drew an ear-piercing scream with the lost child's name in it.

"Hold on, Wanda," Evelyn called out over her cries, and pulled something from her purse.

Hayden expected the gauze, but the black glass bottle with its aging paper label and pockmarked cork smacked a dumbfounded look onto his face. Evelyn popped the top off before dumping a healthy pile of brown powder onto a portion of gauze. She pulled off Hayden's hand and slapped the strange remedy onto Wanda's injury with a subtle rub. He also glimpsed a battery in Evelyn's left hand.

"Alright, let's get her up," Evelyn ordered, after she wrapped and tied the gauze into place.

Nick and Isaac each took a side, while Evelyn repositioned around them to support a loudly distraught Wanda's head and keep her hand on the bandage. Kael just sat there staring at the twice-dead boy. Hayden knelt down to roll the head over and pointed the flashlight at the lips. He wasn't wrong about decapitation, but that was only to incapacitate the body. Brad's lips kept biting beneath a snarling nose and fierce-browed eyes. Not one baby tooth remained. Only tiny razors meant to kill.

"Kael, it's night-time," Hayden prompted, shining his light on the young man. "We gotta go."

Once alone, Hayden picked the head up by its hair and the body by an ankle. He lingered behind the others, so as to find an ideal spot to leave Brad's remains for the morning sun to eradicate. Then he ran as close to a sprint as he could, with adrenalin superseding concerns for his joints.

The interior of the abandoned house remained seared into Hayden's mind all the way back to the office building. He didn't recall seeing anyone else inside, and was pretty sure the father's whereabouts remained unknown. Brad must've wandered into another dark hollow and been turned there.

Isaac had moved the armored truck into where Hayden had parked his earlier. Hayden locked the front doors, and sent everyone down stairs. He locked all the other doors along the way, and turned off the freight elevator again. While the others attended to Wanda in an office, he went straight to the mailroom. Hyun still sat next to the second vampire corpse, but stopped talking to it when she saw all the blood covering Hayden's tie and shirt.

That look of Hyun's, one of a kid caught doing something bad, mustered up a father's anger in Hayden. First, he ripped his tie off and wadded it up to throw at a shelf behind him. Then he gave the Korean college student his best scolding parental glare.

"Cold fucking dead!" Hayden roared, to Hyun's recoiling fear of his rage. "Get it now?"

She ran out, staying closer to the vampire than to Hayden, he only just noticed.

Once the coast was clear Hayden fished out the short pry bar from the security guard utility belt, and came back to Alina's corpse. He ripped the sheets off entirely, letting them fall to the floor. Then he pulled the gag loose before repeatedly plunging the tip of his metal stake into and back out of the chest.

Amid his screams of frustration and mourning-fueled wrath, Hayden heard the body's mocking loop growing more sinister. "Corneliu will save me. Corneliu will save me. Corneliu will save me."

The final stab he left, on seeing it shut the dead thing up at last. Then Hayden kicked at shelves, threw around whatever his hand rested on, knocked over anything offending him with its presence, before finally sliding down along the back wall. There he bawled into his blood-streaked hands.

No one dared enter to investigate all the noise he made.

Chapter 4: All Fronts

"Okay," Isaac said to the rest gathered around a table piled with new weapons. "We got bows, crossbows, a spear gun–" the third item he raised up. "Not sure that's as helpful, but I figured might as well grab it. There's some more knives here, swords from a hobby shop, and machetes too. We picked up a few axes from hardware stores, and I found these bags of lawn pegs. They're plastic but pretty sharp, so stick'em in and that's one less dead guy walkin' around."

"Not bad," Hayden praised, sizing up the haul.

Isaac, Salma and Kael had left several hours ago but didn't get back until a little after sundown.

"There were only two thermal sights, but this way we'll be able to know who's dead and who isn't from way out. Also brought a few guns," Isaac included in afterthought.

"Why?" Kael asked.

Hayden noticed Isaac traded glances with Evelyn and Valerie before explaining, "In case some asshole decides they wanna feed us to a vampire pet they's keepin'."

"Seems reasonable," Nick remarked, while he picked out a few for his ample collection.

"How's Wanda doing?" Hayden asked Evelyn, as he laid a hand on an expensive black crossbow.

"She, ah, cried herself to sleep," the bejeweled red head answered. "We don't have anything for the

78

pain, so I just let her drink up some Jack Daniels we found in someone's desk."

"Everybody else hit up the pharmacies before we got to them," Isaac added while testing a bow string. "All the pain killers, antibiotics and bandage stuff was gone."

Hayden was going to ask about moving her into one of the trucks in the morning, when something echoed through a nearby vent. At first it sounded like a flexing of sheet metal, as if from a sudden rush of air, but scratching and rubbing came through the ceiling.

"Damn, didn't think of that," Hayden realized aloud.

"They're coming through the ducts," Nick observed.

"Something is," Hayden said. "I'm not sure people could get through those."

As if to confirm his point, a bat squeezed halfway out of a vent in the drop ceiling. Once its head aimed their way it popped through and flutter straight at them. Everyone except Salma and Hyun grabbed something sharp, as it darted for Isaac. He batted it away with a machete, and it whirled right back around as if it were a yoyo. Isaac swung back and forth while leaning back, lest the blade pass too close to his face.

Several more bats burst forth from vents and a few rats dropped out. All of them wasted no time in going for the living. Isaac halved the first one to come out, and Kael grabbed another by the wing before it could reach him. Kael swung the thing around rapidly, before flipping it onto a table and quickly taking its head off as though he were cutting vegetables.

At first, Salma tried getting a bead on one with her sidearm, but realized it pointless and reached for a sword. Hyun just ducked down under a table, but then saw the rats making their way for her. Evelyn also noticed, and cracked her boot heel on the skull of the first, before reaching down to pin and behead it. Hayden skewered the second with a knife, and then rocked the tip of the blade against the floor to be sure he had cleaved the heart.

Just after that, one bat landed on his back and started up for his neck. He cursed, "Shit!" as he reached behind himself in vain for the animal.

Next, he felt his shirt being pulled back as the weight of the small turned corpse disappeared. He heard rips before the flying terror lost its hold. He saw Nick toss the bat into the air before delivering a clean stroke that separated one of the wings from it.

When it hit the floor, Hayden was able to chop its head off with a new knife that he grabbed off the table.

After a moment of unpracticed swipes and tee ball swings, the bats were incapacitated and their heads cut off. Evelyn's footwear did a fine number on the scurrying terrestrial bound vampires, but there was more still to come. Hayden heard as much from one of the vents. Everyone recognized angry growls of a cat, but seeing its pawing catch onto, and then bend a vent made more than one jaw drop.

Running up under the vent, Kael waited with what Hayden took to be a samurai sword. Kael thrust the tip in repeatedly, getting the undying

80

feline's ire. Hayden wondered why the beast bothered hissing when it didn't have to breathe and obviously wasn't scared. However, the thing stuck its head in too far, giving the group a good look at its grayed inky eyes, before Kael managed an overhead swing that decapitated it.

"Like I was saying," Hayden huffed looking at the damaged vent with traces of dull gray ooze smeared on it. "It's the animal vampires I'm worried about finding us in here."

Realizing that the severed heads still moved, Evelyn found a mail sack and Hayden's tongs to gather them up. However, more sounded through the vents, and worse was heard from the floor above. Someone up there fired a gun, and glass shattering preceded the sounds of paws against tile.

"Normal people?" Isaac asked, as everyone eyed the ceiling.

"Doubtful," Hayden said. "Not leaving an opening like that without being in a rush."

The four-legged vampires, dogs most likely, Hayden imagined, trotted all around the ground floor. However a single set of clomping steps slowly paced around, as if listening between each foot fall. The lone human sounds went from room to room in a loop, before it stopped at the stairwell. Hayden distinctly recognized the sound of the door being pulled on. After a single footstep, the next tug on the door ripped it open and off its hinges.

"Shit," Nick cursed at a whisper. "Alright, guess it's game on."

The set of heavy shoes or boots started up the stairs, instead, bringing more than one silent sigh of relief. Once the ascent became too faint to hear, everyone went for ranged weapons.

"Kael, you should probably stick to a sword or something like that," Evelyn suggested.

"What for?" Kael asked, stopping in the midst of drawing back a crossbow.

"In case he gets that close," Evelyn explained. "No one's better at that stuff than you."

Kael let out an exasperated breath, but complied and passed the crossbow to Nick.

"No, I'm good," Nick refused, picking up his own rolled bundle of weapons and both shotguns.

"Those won't work," Kael reminded.

"I'll slow them down for you," Nick assured.

"Good idea," Hayden agreed with a chin to Nick. "Or take out its arms so it can't shoot."

Isaac, Salma, Valerie and even Hyun all armed themselves with crossbows.

Hayden selected the spear gun and Evelyn picked up one of the bows. Kael strapped on a couple knives, sheathed the sword he'd used before, and slung it across his back. Then he grabbed a bag of lawn stakes and an ax. Everyone else made sure to stock up on arrows or bolts and one or two backup weapons for hand-to-hand. They returned to the hall to occupy doorways facing the direction of the stairs.

The clinking patter of animal feet came down the stairs first. A couple of people were jolted by pawing at the locked stairway doors. It grew to a violent scratching with growls of what everyone knew to be a dog. Hayden recalled the door was metal, and hoped that meant the blood-feasting beast couldn't claw its way through. Part of his brain said it wasn't possible, but he reminded himself that the dead shouldn't be up and wandering around at all.

He didn't hear where the second dog went. After half an hour of nerve-racking scratches and unholy gurgling barks, the human vampire's footfalls returned. It came to the bottom of the stairs and checked the door as above. Then the door thundered with a kick, but held. More kicks sounded with increasing frequency, but didn't appear to get any results. Hayden recalled that the doors opened out from the stairwell, which explained the greater difficulty the vampire had.

Another kick cracked with a metallic squeak that made Hayden think something bent. Two more hits from the battering ram of a foot blasted the door open with a rattle indicating how much damage it must've taken. That cleared the way for a scramble of four canine feet.

A golden lab with glossy fur, but devoid of its adorable charm, bolted into view with a nightmarish rack of scythes for a mouth, snarling its unnatural hunger. Nick got off the first shot, which mangled a foreleg of the dog, and Valerie fired her crossbow immediately after. The bolt struck in the chest dead-on, but missed the heart, as the thing kept coming. Evelyn let loose an arrow that shut the horrid creature down in a tumbling slide.

Next to come around the corner was a pale hand wielding a pistol loaded with an extra-long magazine. Squeezing off shots without looking, the vampire made everyone withdraw into the rooms as lights shattered overhead. When the weapon clicked empty it stepped out. Nick and Hayden dared take a peek. It proved to be the body of a soldier with an armband showing MP. Nick again took the initiative and blasted a kneecap, so that Hayden could choose his time and squeeze the spear gun trigger.

Not used to the unorthodox weapon, Hayden's shot arced more than he anticipated, leaving Isaac and Valerie to fire their crossbows, while others reloaded. Hayden didn't catch whose shot did it, but the vampire fell forward into a heap just like the dog.

"There's still something up there," Nick reminded in a hiss, as he exchanged shells in his gun.

"We definitely can't wait until morning, now," Hayden warned. "We're wide open."

"Yep," Nick agreed, while looking to Kael. "Wanna do the honors?"

It took him a brief moment, but Kael realized Nick's meaning and rose up to remove the two vampires' heads with the ax. He cleaved the soldier's with two strokes, but appeared to have difficulty on the dog because of hesitation.

"Come on, man," Nick said. "I like dogs too, but ya gotta do it."

Kael traded off for a knife and gently lifted the canine's head before sawing it off.

"Who wants to watch the stairs?" Hayden asked everyone.

"I'll do it," Valerie answered, quicker than Hayden thought the girl should have.

84

"Fuck that," Nick protested, and stood up before Valerie could argue.

"Yeah, be right there, Nick," Kael said, following him.

"Everyone else, we're going for the freight elevator, so let's get Wanda ready," Hayden ordered.

Evelyn and Salma went to get Wanda, while Hayden led the rest to the mailroom.

He gathered up his equipment and rolled it to the elevator, which prompted others to follow suit.

"What about these vamps?" Isaac asked. "You sure we should take them with us?"

"Yeah," Hayden answered with a single nod, as he got behind one gurney and pushed. "I still think I can use 'em. Whatever's going on, it's just physics and chemistry, and that I can do."

"My momma always told me white people was crazy," Isaac chided and rolled the other over.

Once everything was in the spacious elevator car, Hayden went to the stairs to recall the improvised rear guard. "We're set, you two. Let's go."

With everyone piled into the car, Hayden closed it up and brought out the keys. While turning on power, he noticed Hyun looking after the two corpses, and shook his head. The tone sounded to indicate they reached the first floor, and with Isaac's help Hayden raised the other door. He had backed his armored truck right up to the door, and Isaac had moved his into a diagonal position next to it.

Hayden searched Isaac's face, to which the construction worker replied, "I was thinking we'd need to be able to get the hell out of here fast if anything went down."

"Got that right," Nick offered up from across the elevator car.

Hayden opened the first truck, and everyone loaded things in as he went to the cab. Inserting the keys, he didn't start it yet, lest the engine draw more trouble. What didn't fit easily went into the second truck, along with Wanda. Having her in the same vehicle as two vampires didn't strike anyone as a good idea. They were ready to leave before midnight.

"Valerie," Hayden came back and said. "You up front with me, and then I'll need two people to stay in back in case we run into problems."

Hyun Jae volunteered, which annoyed Hayden, but he let it slide for now, and Nick offered. The other four piled into the second truck, with Isaac driving and Salma up front with a crossbow. In the previous day, those with cell phones had programmed everyone else's numbers, and so Hayden speed-dialed Isaac's phone and waited.

"Yeah?" Isaac answered.

"We'll start our engines at the same time, and gun it away from the building," Hayden said.

"Cool," Isaac agreed. "Where we goin'?"

"I haven't worked that out yet, unless you got any ideas," he answered.

"You think the National Guard might be around the city?" Isaac asked.

"Honestly, I couldn't tell ya," Hayden admitted. "But I doubt containment was ever an option."

"Why don't we just drive to Salma's police department?" Isaac suggested, and then paused. "Ah, never mind. She's tellin' me no one answered when she checked in. The nearest onramp to the freeway sounds good to me. Didn't you say get away from where there's a lot of people?"

"That sounds like a plan," Hayden accepted. "Okay, turn her over— now."

He hung up and started the engine, and Isaac's truck started up a second after. Then they pulled out with Isaac in the lead. When Hayden pulled out into the street he checked all his mirrors for signs of the second animal vampire from in the building.

Valerie readied her crossbow and looking around repeatedly. In back, Nick crouched down with one hand on a rail and another on his shotgun.

The trucks sped up gradually, but they got to a good speed, before Hayden noticed a large mixed breed dog vampire sprinting out from the building. The truck engine revved up over and over, as Hayden shifted gears. Even at fifty-five miles per hour, the dead canine managed to keep pace. However, Isaac must've also seen the animal and kept accelerating. At a little over sixty they began to pull away. The dog seemed to see something else and veered away at full speed to disappear into the unlit night.

"God, that was scary," Valerie heaved with a hand to her chest.

"You ain't kidding," Hayden agreed, and then blew out his anxiety.

Hayden's phone rang again, and he answered, figuring it was Isaac, "How're things up there?"

"Up where?" the rough voice from two days ago asked. "Where are you at present?"

"Getting the hell out of Dodge," Hayden answered. "Don't suppose you could help, could ya?"

"Whatever you think your problems are, it's worse here," the mystery man said. "Did you find anything new we can use?"

"It's all one molecular complex throughout the circulator system," Hayden answered, eyeing Valerie for an instant, unsure if she should be listening. "And it's centered inside the heart, so score one for Carpathian superstition. Staking it must change the covalent dynamics somehow. Also, I need to ask something. Has anyone established if these things metabolize air?"

"They don't breathe," the man said. "You know that. Why?"

"I fed one two hundred grams of fluids, but it added two hundred five in mass," he explained.

"Are you sure that's not an error?" the caller asked.

"I recalibrated my scales to double-check," Hayden assured him. "Yes, it's really there."

"What was the subject?" the unknown representative asked.

"A rat," Hayden answered. "I dissected it, opened up the heart to examine, then put it in the case and un-staked the damn thing. Drinking the

88

two hundred fixed all the damage, and then I weighed it again to compare with what I got before feeding."

The other man ended the call, and Hayden held out his phone to look at it. "You're welcome."

"Was that the people who hired you?" Valerie asked, as she set the crossbow in her lap aimed toward the door. "That world health thing you told us about?"

"World Health Organization didn't contract us," Hayden corrected. "We just got all the data they had. I'm not sure who this guy represents. I figured it was someone at the federal level."

"Shouldn't the government be doing that kind of research?" Valerie questioned.

"They contract out all kinds of things," Hayden offered, realizing that Valerie wasn't in high school yet, and so hadn't been educated on the reality of how governments worked. "In fact, I'm surprised they haven't privatized everything. Used to like that idea. Now I'm not so sure."

His phone rang again in his hand, and Hayden pressed talk before bringing it up. "Hello."

"Off ramp's comin' up next," Isaac advised. "There'll be a bunch of trees next to it, so look out."

"Will do," Hayden acknowledged and then pointed his phone at the passenger window. "Watch your side there, Valerie. We're about to go for the freeway."

Isaac hung up, and Hayden placed the cell in his shirt pocket under his coat.

Feeling around to put the phone away reminded him that his shirt still smelled of blood even after he had rinsed and wrung it out several times in a restroom sink. Wanda's blood, he remembered.

* * *

"Kael," Evelyn called over the drone of cruising the freeway. "Bring me a water for her."

"Sure," Kael obliged and pulled a bottle out of a pack.

He made sure to steady himself with his left hand on the truck wall's bottom shelf, while passing the bottle of water to Evelyn. However, Wanda noticed Kael getting close to where she lay and threw a kick his way. The act startled Evelyn, who threw a jolted face to her. However, Kael just backed away to the opposite corner from Wanda and tossed the bottle to Evelyn.

"Thanks," Evelyn said, to be sure Kael knew one person appreciated what he did.

Then she opened the bottle and pressed it to Wanda's mouth. "You need to get something in you."

Instead, Wanda shoved the bottle away with enough force to spill a little in a splash up from the mouth. Evelyn twisted the lid back on when she saw Wanda roll over away from them both, toward the wall. Her eyes moistening, Evelyn said nothing. Kael just huddled up staring at the floor, when she looked to him in sympathy.

"Heads up," Isaac tossed back to them. "Something's up with these horses."

Evelyn made her way up and opened the door in order to stand between the front seats to look out the windows. Isaac pointed out to their right, and

Evelyn saw dozens of horses all in a hard gallop along the road. Then, in the side mirror, Evelyn noticed two more running so fast they managed to overtake the two trucks. She wasn't sure how far away they were, but after a moment Evelyn realized from their body proportions that they were both foals.

As the two younger animals got closer, which Evelyn noted from the speedometer, meant doing more than sixty she realized they had to be vampires. Both animals yawned their mouths wide, revealing upper and lower rows of menacing teeth no equine should have. One was already stained red with blood running down its mouth.

"I'm changing to the inside lane," Isaac said into his phone after selecting a number. "You saw that too? Yeah, they're both fucked up. I'll tell her."

"What?" Evelyn asked.

"Pull that crossbow in and lean back," Isaac said to Salma.

Evelyn withdrew further into the door separating the cab from the compartment, but watched in fascination. The foals caught up with the adults in short order, and leapt impossibly high to tackle one each. Stallion or mare she didn't know, but it didn't matter. They both tumbled along with the younger animals that attacked them.

The rest bolted out onto the road behind the two trucks, and onto the other lanes heading back into the city. However, one horse at the rear of the herd was struck by a car making even better time away from the city on inbound lanes. The animal crumpled the car's front end as it flipped over with an equine scream. The car spun out of control and slid toward the ditch between lanes ahead of the trucks. Despite skidding down sideways into the ditch, the car didn't turnover. That allowed the driver to climb out and break into a run.

Another foal appeared under the indirect illumination of a freeway sign. It zeroed in on the maimed adult horse, until catching sight of the one person fleeing from the car. It bowled over the individual, just as Isaac passed the scene. It wheeled around to prance on the stranger before biting them. Only as the screams started, when the foal easily lifted the victim in head tosses, did Evelyn realize it was a woman.

"Vampire horses now," Isaac bemoaned, shaking his head. "Now that's just messed up."

"But none of the adults," Evelyn observed.

"Maybe the young ones were slower and easier to catch?" Salma suggested.

"No," Evelyn countered. "Foals can run about as fast as adults after around a day."

"Only male lions," Isaac recalled of Hayden's long description. "And now only baby horses."

"So it appears," Evelyn affirmed. "Stuff like that's got to drive Hayden nuts."

Salma pulled on a necklace to bring out a small cross which she kissed and put away again.

"Whoa," Isaac said, leaning forward to look ahead. "Something goin' on here."

Evelyn noted the flashing lights and headlamps. After a second, she saw that many cars and trucks lined the road with a few people walking through the beams.

92

Isaac's phone rang, and he answered. "Hayden, are you seeing this?"

"Yeah," Evelyn barely heard Hayden's voice on the other end. "Slow down when you're close."

"You think they might be vampires trying to catch people getting out?" Isaac asked.

"They don't work together like that, from what I read," Hayden explained.

"Selfish, huh," Isaac surmised, and applied the brakes. "We're comin' up on the roadblock."

Hanging up and putting away his phone, Isaac moved both hands on top of the steering wheel and slowed the truck to a complete stop. Salma put her hand over her eyes to see what details she could. Then several spotlights from the sides of the police cars aimed into the cab, making sight beyond the windshield near-impossible.

"Vampires all over the place and a Black man still can't get a break," Isaac remarked with a grin.

"You in the vehicle! Turn off the engine," an amplified voice ordered.

"Yeah, yeah, I know the drill," Isaac muttered, and switched the truck off.

More than ten people approached with caution, all pointing various weapons. Once within a few feet, Evelyn realized they were highway patrol, and despite their arsenal they were clearly scared. Isaac made a point to show his teeth to them without looking foreboding, and then they loosened up a bit.

"Yours too," someone on the right said.

Salma and Evelyn both tilted their heads up to bare their teeth in the beams of several flashlights.

Isaac and Salma each opened their windows, careful not to move too fast. Other officers went by to check out Hayden's truck, while one stepped up to Isaac's window.

"How many inside," the Black highway patrolman asked.

"Five of us," Isaac answered and thumbed back. "There's four more in the other truck, but we're all normal. There was a car back there that hit a horse, and one of them jacked up horses went after the driver. You guys might want to keep a look out that way just in case."

"Is anyone bitten?" the cop asked.

"Officer," Salma interjected at that point and produced her own department badge to show. "I'm an undercover for the gang unit. Just so you know, they don't turn because of bites."

"Is anyone bitten?" the patrolman asked slower for emphasis.

"Yeah, but," Isaac answered in preparation to explain. "Like she told 'ya, that don't do it."

By then the back door opened with three men holding shotguns or assault rifles. Turning around, Evelyn saw that Kael had put his hands up and was about to step out, until he was told to stay put.

"How long ago was this one bitten?" one of the rearward cops asked.

"Yesterday around sundown," Evelyn said. "The guy in the other truck will explain it to you, but it only takes a couple hours to turn people. She's not going to become one of them."

"Get a gurney and wheel her over to the paramedic," another of them said.

"I want you to pull behind the roadblock," the cop next to Isaac ordered while pointing.

"Yes sir," Isaac answered.

After they took Wanda out, and a gap opened, both Isaac and Hayden drove through the line of patrol cars and other emergency vehicles. They pulled to the side of the road, and everyone climbed out. Evelyn saw Wanda wheeled over to an ambulance, where the paramedics looked her over. Hayden and the others joined them by Isaac's truck, and they gazed with concern toward Wanda. The paramedics called some of the cops over and began keeping a close watch on Wanda for a couple of hours.

"I don't know which makes me more edgy," Nick said. "Bloodsucking horses or state police."

"Really?" Evelyn taunted Nick, turning to give him a bemused look-over. "Clean cut guy like you?"

"Ahh," Nick rebuffed, feigning anguish with a palm out, reluctant to talk about it.

"Excuse me," one of the white shirted guys attending Wanda called over. "Which of you was treating this patient up to now?"

"Gimme a minute," Evelyn said, and threw Kael a look. "Watch the road, just in case."

"Yeah," Kael acknowledged, and ran his tongue against his cheek without returning eye contact.

As Evelyn crossed over, one of the paramedics pulled back the gauze, asking, "What's this?"

"It's a disinfectant," Evelyn straightforwardly answered. "I had to improvise."

"Well," the other said. "Looks like you guys are right about this; she's not turning.

There're signs that healing is taking place in the normal manner. In fact, when did you say she was attacked?"

"I told them it was more than a day ago," Evelyn reiterated.

"But for clotting, this injury looks a week old," the medic explained. "You improvise well."

"I get that a lot," Evelyn divulged. "Can we get her to a hospital?"

"If she's going that good," the first man began. "Then she's better off with you."

"Why? What happened?" Evelyn questioned them both with an alarmed voice.

"Hospitals were among the first major services to collapse," he revealed. "Not all the patients were brought in living, and you can imagine what the coroners' offices are all like."

"Is it like this everywhere?" Evelyn queried.

"Some parts are just now getting cases, and others are much worse off than we," the second medic laid out. "We don't know about outside the state, but rumor is that some places have droves of these things sweeping through cities and towns killing everyone."

"You're saying no help's coming," Evelyn inferred.

"Not at the federal level, no," the second guy specified. "A lot of networks are down, and some

96

power plants. Of course the military's scattered all over hell too far away to help at home."

Evelyn wasn't used to hearing that kind of an opinion since coming to the state, but set that aside to kneel down next to Wanda and ask, "Do you want to stick with us?"

"It'd really help us out if she did," the second paramedic confessed.

"Wanda?" Evelyn tried again.

"Aw shit, here they come," one of the cops yelled. "Everybody get ready!"

That made Wanda jump out of the stretcher, though Evelyn had to catch her as she wavered. The two women ran back to the trucks, as everyone else climbed in.

Evelyn assumed Wanda would rather not be with two vampires, and so put her back onto Isaac's vehicle. The trucks began moving before Evelyn could close the door.

However, curiosity compelled Evelyn to again come up to the cab and look out the side mirrors. Among the pallid masses of human bodies that refused to rest, she picked out two of the foals from before. Something else that was not man, horse or dog bounded well ahead of the human vampires. Salma appeared to be right about zoo escapes, but with the wrong animal.

Guns blazed, as Isaac pressed his foot to the floor, and there came some shots from the undead mob. Yet the night stalking gorilla ignored the barrage, as though they weren't even flies to shoo away. It could've easily caught up with living horses, had the bulky ape encountered them.

Instead, it ran headlong into the blockade. With a high overhand swing of both arms, it flipped a squad car over lengthwise to land in place, collapsing the roof.

The gorilla bounded up the sloped undercarriage and jumped off toward one of the cops who fired full automatic into it. Bits of the ape's flesh blew off from the barrage. In a pounding land, it then sunk its unnatural teeth, including slightly longer and much sharper canines, into the officer's head. It tore away a major portion of skull, before Evelyn squeezed her eyes shut to the carnage.

In seconds, the gorilla's ferocious roar lessened compared to that of the trucks speeding away side-by-side. Looking again, Evelyn saw in the rapidly receding scene that the ape batted away other vampires daring to bite into its prize. Then it sucked away at the man's head, while a couple human vampires slipped in to go for a wrist and the inside of a femur. Every one of the apparitions stopped for the feeding frenzy, that is, except for one of the undersized horses.

"Oh shit." Isaac cursed on seeing the frighteningly fast foal gaining on them. "Kael, one's coming up on us," Evelyn shouted as she went back.

A loud double-knock sounded off one of the walls, lending her to think the animal was able to somehow rear up and attack with its hooves. There came a delay before the next impact that put a dent into the back door. The third hit came, before Kael could grab a bow and notch it.

"Evelyn," Kael said to her. "You'll have to open this up for me."

"I really don't think we should," she shouted back.

"It's going to keep at it until we're out of gas," Kael hollered back. "You know that."

Or until dawn, Evelyn considered, but doubted they would last that long. So it was she reached over to the door handle and turned to Kael. He threw her a nod, as he raised the weapon. She pulled the handle and pushed the door with ineffectual force. It flipped open for an instant and slapped closed, before either of them could sight the vampire steed.

"Gotta hold it," Kael stated what she already knew and dreaded.

Evelyn subtly put a battery in her left hand and tried again. Barely slapping past the hinges, she forced the door open again, and caught a glimpse of those adorably large but spiritless opaque eyes. Yet she forced herself to focus on its ribs. The equine horror flashed its atrocious razors and reared up in a forward leap. An arrow sank into its chest, throwing the limp horse into a violent tumble with slack limbs flailing against asphalt in loud clacks.

Kael ushered Evelyn back, so that he could stretch out and close the door. The two just stared at each other for a long moment, before both realized Wanda gazed at them as if she hadn't seen either one before. She couldn't call Wanda's expression fearful, but one of unpleasant surprise.

Chapter 5: The Finer Points

"Never been so glad to see the sun," Hayden remarked, looking into the side mirror.

"Yeah," Valerie agreed, leaning against the window, propping her head on her palm.

The truck's forward projecting shadow became more distinct, as the sun crested above the horizon behind them. Half an hour after that, they came to a roadside motel in a very small town and pulled in. Hayden parked in such a way as to keep the daylight out of the back compartment, even though both his specimens were completely covered.

Everyone climbed out and walked up to the front entrance, but they all hesitated at the same time. Hayden had made it pretty clear about how things worked. Although he neglected to tell them that vampires never slept, he figured it was self-evident and hoped nobody would act otherwise.

"Crossbow time?" Isaac asked, throwing a glance to Hayden.

"Yeah, crossbow time," he nodded in answer. "Nick, I guess you'll stick with your guns?"

"Fuck that," he tossed back, and started for one of the trucks. "Too goddamn close."

"Sleep during the day?" Evelyn asked Hayden, once the rest walked away.

"I'm damn tired," Hayden breathed, and checked the spear gun over. "Gotta sleep sometime. And eat. Also, a shower would be nice. Those things don't need to be invited indoors to creep around and kill us. We'll check it out first, and that way no one has to be on guard."

Once armed, Wanda being allowed to stay in the truck, the other eight survivors entered into the front office of the motel. Hayden noticed that, along with a bow, knives and lawn stakes, Nick had an unusually wide looking pistol in his belt. Nick picked up on what held Hayden's attention.

"Two-barreled Second Century AF Twenty Eleven? Forty-three hundred dollars," Nick started his pitch. "Thirty-six hundred eighty grains down range in three seconds? Seven dollars, fifty six cents. Blowing a vampire's heart out his chest? Priceless."

"Just what the hell possesses someone to design a gun like that?" Hayden said in disbelief.

"Well, obviously, zombie plagues are all the rage among gun manufacturers," Nick chided. "Shit, I don't know. Imagine what today will do for the crossbow industry."

Evelyn just shook her head, but Hayden has a good chuckle at the thought, as they sized up the interior. No one took much surprise at the sight of blood streaked across the counter, back wall or the huge slick smear all over a cell phone lying on the floor.

Bloody paw prints, likely belonging to many cats, and a set of small hooves told the tale. However, they never found any sign of the turned or whom they'd fed on.

Checking around back some yards out, he did see one pile of charcoal remains of vague feline shape, and guessed it didn't make it inside in time.

He pictured the others hiding out in houses and barns just waiting for the sun to set.

"Place is clean," Nick called out to Hayden from the back door.

Lowering the spear gun, Hayden walked back and took off the arrow quiver he'd filled with three other spears and an ax, but kept the lawn pegs in his back pocket.

Everyone broke off to their own rooms, washed up, ran through whatever other hygiene, and came back to the motel kitchen. Hayden had started making a breakfast with what he found in the large fridge.

"Serving up some pancakes," Hayden listed off, facing the stove wearing an apron, as people filed in. "Frank'n'beans. We got grits, of course. Corn flakes up in the cupboard. Milk seems okay. A few eggs here, hash browns, spaghetti sauce and meatballs, but no noodles. Toast and fresh fruit's over here. And an all-time American fave: lots and lots of bacon."

"Mm, frank'n'beans sound real good about now," Isaac relished, as he set out plates.

"Meatballs right here," Nick added, pointing to his plate, after seating himself.

"You're one of those dads who just loves cooking breakfast, aren't you?" Evelyn observed while pulling the milk out. "The ex must really miss that."

"Wanda? You want anything," Hayden asked, without turning around.

When he didn't hear anything out of her, he turned to find she still hadn't joined everyone else.

102

"Hey, ah, someone watch this for a minute," Hayden said, taking off an apron.

Evelyn and Kael volunteered, as Salma started up a pot of coffee. Hayden scooped up the spear gun and walked to Wanda's room. He fought the first impulse of readying the weapon to sneak in, and just knocked. She didn't answer, but Hayden heard the shower running, and figured it safe to enter.

Wanda had discarded her clothes in a trail to the bathroom, Hayden noted as he approached it. This time he didn't knock, but just listened. Amid the continual blast of water he made out Wanda's soft crying and begging half-coherent prayers.

"Give her strength, God," Hayden whispered and gave the door a gentle pat, before leaving.

Hayden entered the kitchen again and took over the stove. He doled out the first serving of pancakes, and then brought Isaac's order over, before checking on the spaghetti sauce.

"She coming?" Evelyn asked him, as she poured milk into a small bowl of cereal.

"No," Hayden offered a muted answer. "I think she needs time alone."

Once everyone had what they wanted, and a serving plate piled high with bacon sat in the middle of the table, Hayden sat down to join the rest. Nick reached for several bacon strips to mash up into his sauce and meatballs, and then Kael grabbed some.

Hayden caught of glimpse of something on the inside of Kael's left hand, and a second look told him it was a pentagram.

"Odd place for a tattoo, isn't it?" Hayden probed, and pointed a fork to it.

103

"Oh, sorry," Kael offered an immediate apology out of habit.

"It doesn't bother me, I was just curious," Hayden elaborated. "I take it you're Wiccan?"

"Ooh, let me see," Hyun chirped in fascination. "I have tattoo on my ankle."

"Lotta Jesus freaks get on our case about it," Evelyn interjected on Kael's behalf.

"I see," Hayden remarked, and resumed on his pancakes before speaking again, "On behalf of Jesus freaks across the country, you have my apologies."

"You don't seem like one," Evelyn observed. "As a compliment, I mean."

"I don't wear it on my sleeve, that's true," Hayden explained, as he pushed a triple layered chunk of pancake through syrup before forking it up. "Scientific facts are still facts, regardless of what I want to believe. And they will not be ignored. No more flat Earth, geo-centric universe or Adam's rib stuff. Have to broaden our definition of God is all."

"Or goddess," Evelyn tested.

"I'm not that broad, but I'm okay with others who are," Hayden replied, and cast his eyes toward Kael's tattoos. "Now is that one inverted? Someone told me it's a symbolic goat head."

"Not in my case," Kael revealed with a little more ease. "This is more to do with the sun."

"Even with that quarter crescent on the left side of it," Hayden quizzed.

"It's kind've like celebrating seasons," Evelyn explained in Kael's stead.

104

"So you all do spells out in the woods, then?" Isaac half-heartedly asked.

"Right, spells," Evelyn mocked. "With pointy hats and all."

"Don't matter to me," Isaac assured, glancing at Nick, who was chowing down quietly.

In fact, Kael also looked at Nick's ravenous appetite, and soon everyone was watching.

"What? Yeah, okay, I haven't eaten this good in a while," Nick defended, and took more bacon.

"What kind of work did you do again?" Salma asked from across the table, before taking a sip of coffee in both hands and studying him.

"You could call it..." he tactfully worded, between chomps of bacon. "Human resource management and job placement services. People need work done and people need work to do."

"And that requires two sawed-off double-barrel twelve gauges," a skeptical Isaac remarked.

"I believe the street term is coyote, and it's a federal offense," Salma pointed out.

"You wanna Mirandize me," Nick offered with his wrists out, inviting the ratcheting clink of her cuffs, and added, "Or should I just read them to myself?"

"Do you ship product with your clients?" Salma baited with emphasis.

"You mean drugs," Nick flat out elaborated with his return question. "No, and I don't take people that I know are smuggling any."

"Ah," Salma gave mocking praise. "A kinder gentler brand of human trafficker."

105

"Los Zetas doesn't like any competition," Nick added quickly, and swiped up sauce from his plate with a piece of toast, before going back to the bacon.

"Speaking of which," Hayden began. "Just how many guns did you bring when we all met?"

"Seven and some other shit. That's so someone doesn't jack my load," Nick explained, and then threw a look to Salma. "There's criminals and then there's ruthless mother fuckers. Everyone I smuggle pays up front, but they all show up alive. We go our separate ways, and that's that. Better than gassing indigenous Columbians with American-made defoliating agents and rocketing their villages. After that comes turning a blind eye from loggers who rape and murder any survivors."

"So," Evelyn spoke up, hoping to lighten the mood. "Hyun, you're an exchange student?"

"Yes. I been in America for two year," she answered.

"What do you study?" Hayden asked, and recalled the moment in the mailroom when she turned to him and froze up. "I'm sorry, Hyun, about blowing my temper back there."

"Oh, is okay," she accepted with her original chipper tone. "I study to be software engineer."

"From one engineer to another," Hayden congratulated with a smile and a fist out to her.

Confused, Hyun saw Isaac's nod and bumping of his own knuckles together, before she put her smaller bunched up fist against Hayden's.

"Okay, we have a cop, a border-jumping guy, a chemistry geek," Valerie counted off, and getting a chuckle from Hayden, as she went on, "and a programmer. Isaac, you're in construction?"

"Yeah, concrete and steel mostly," Isaac specified, lifting up a glass of milk. "Also I do framing and drywall. That building we was all in I worked on a couple years back."

"Evelyn," Valerie circled the question to the bejeweled red head.

"CNA," she answered, and added once seeing Valerie's confusion. "Certified Nursing Assistant."

"And Kael," Valerie addressed in finality.

"Odd jobs," he replied cryptically, and eyed Nick for an instant. "Mostly legal ones."

"You're pretty handy with a lot of those weapons," Hayden complimented.

"I've been doing martial arts since I was eight," Kael revealed what Hayden guessed before, and included something he hadn't known about the young man. "My parents had me on the high school archery team to keep me out of trouble."

"What were your career plans?" Evelyn asked Valerie.

"Either gymnastics, marketing or trying for the Air Force academy," the tween just rattled off.

Hayden blew out his disbelief at her lofty ambitions, but otherwise said nothing.

He'd forgotten what child aspirations were like. They finished up their beverages, though Hyun finally decided to initiate conversation with Hayden.

"Can I ask question, Mr. Cornell?" Hyun Jae's accent made a Q into a K sound.

"Sure," Hayden said and waved out to her.

"Why old vampire call your name?"

107

"Ahh—," Hayden drew out with uncertainty. "She doesn't."

"Oh, she does," Hyun insisted with a vigorous nod. "She say, 'Cornell will save me.'"

Everyone's gaze affixed onto Hayden at that moment, to which he surrendered.

"She's saying *Corneliu* will save her. It's a man's first name. Probably her husband from seventeenth century Romania. The corpse heard my name around the lab and morphed it into that."

"But why she talk in English," Hyun wondered, and faces around the table also seemed to ask.

"They think human vampires can parrot back what they hear," Hayden offered, honestly believing that explained the vampire's picking up a new language. "You know, so they can lure us in."

"Oh! That make sense," Hyun Jae acknowledged with a bright smile.

"I've got to get some sleep," Hayden said, while turning to his watch. "I've set my alarm for sundown, so that gives us maybe six hours before we need to be up."

"Good enough," Isaac said and rose up from the table.

The rest did likewise, and after piling dishes into the sink, left for their rooms. Hayden stopped by Wanda's just long enough to find that she'd gone straight to bed. However, she stirred in her sleep and mumbled about the trauma she had gone through. Hayden left it at that and went to his room to collapse into his own bed. Wanda wouldn't have the only fitful day's sleep.

* * *

Neither of the security guards in the lab receiving bay, Sarah or James understood Hayden's urgency. They were mystified about why one of the aides was nervous when saying he couldn't come, because he had to deal with family matters. The other aide went along with Hayden into the back, and kept talking about all the zombie shooter games he played.

If only it worked out in real life the same way. Their first location was the lab aide's idea, that being a clinic his mother ran. However, as Hayden watched, the aide spent half an hour trying to explain over his mother's shouting. As a doctor, she saw two patients needing attention, and it was a physical wrestling match to keep her from rolling a specimen out into the sun.

Hayden convinced her to take vitals inside the truck, and that didn't improve matters at all. The doctor nearly fell out of the truck, when she backed away in horror. Hayden explained as fast as he could how he'd gotten involved, and what he needed, but she would have none of it. Hayden actually hoped she might call police, but instead she simply refused to let them in and told her son to go.

That's when the security guards, James and Sarah learned what the lab had been contracted to study. James suggested an empty building that had been an indoor gun range, which seemed sound at the time. Over the course of the evening they were bringing a few things inside, but the human and animal vampires were still on the truck along with the supply of pig body fluids the lab had been sent to use. By nightfall they had the front entrance locked and removed the external handle from the fire exit using the pry bar.

"The place still has power," James said. "So you should be able to do your thing."

"For what it's worth, I'm sorry I couldn't tell you," Hayden apologized, knowing James was still having trouble with the idea. "I was told this wasn't getting out of control, and that I'd have time to work on this. We were part of a program to stop an outbreak before it started."

The rest of the day and most of the night went by uneventfully. Using a laptop, James kept track of news reports about a spike of assaults. No one yet realized what happened, until hospitals started encountering problems with their mortuaries, coupled with bizarre break-ins, often not at the ground floor. So many patients became hapless victims, and just as many physicians, nurses and orderlies died in attempts to rescue them. However, it still seemed surreal.

It was at the coming of dawn when Hayden met the outbreak in person. It seemed the lack of windows and few entrances were just as appealing to the dead as the living seeking shelter from them. The vampire had been an older homeless man who ripped the door open without difficulty. James stood up first and drew his weapon. Sarah, further away, contributed to the barrage with a shotgun. However, the hits only slowed the charging corpse.

It grabbed Hayden's aide and kept feeding on him regardless of what the two guards did. Sarah knelt down and put her pistol to the vampire's head in a direction that minimized ricochet risks, and squeezed the trigger a couple times. But so long as the dead man had a food source it both ignored the attack and slowly renewed from the damage.

On a hope, Hayden scooped up the pry bar and drove it through the vampire's back. However, he hadn't put enough force into it, and the tip only sank a couple inches.

James jumped onto the bloodthirsty body, and helped push the steel bar all the way through, causing the vampire to go limp. It penetrated into the aide, but he was already still and beyond hope.

Sarah went over to the door to improvise a way to secure it, when a dog rushed through and attacked her. Hayden pulled the bar out to use on the vampire canine.

Backed by adrenalin, Hayden was able to stab deep into the animal the first time, but he missed the heart. Trying a couple more times, he at last stilled the beast. By then, however, Sarah lay gulping with half the front of her throat ripped open and blood pumping in weak spurts from arteries.

Once she died, James took off her shirt to get at the bullet resistant vest, and removed the utility belt for Hayden's use. However, by that time the first vampire was getting up again. James rushed it in a yell, and grabbed something off a table before he collided with the reanimated corpse. The two fell over with James on top and yelling for Hayden to run.

Fear narrowed his vision and suppressed pride, as Hayden bolted for the fire exit. He jumped into the truck without bothering to close any doors, and drove off. After a couple blocks he finally stopped in an empty lot to lock the truck's doors and then drove off again under the cover of morning. That's when he found the office building, which remained empty into the day.

Through the night Hayden had seen or heard a handful of attacks. On his phone and the disaster alert radio, Hayden picked up reports of bats and rats forming the bulk of the first wave. Sporadic attacks by the city's pets or stray cats, dogs, and the destitute, the lattermost of whom were seen as vermin before they died, swelled the ranks of the restless dead after midnight.

Back in that mailroom, Hayden felt himself pulled close to the Alina vampire strapped to the gurney. Only now she had her limbs and the gag was missing. Curiosity regarding the sudden change brought him to lean right over her. Then she suddenly opened her eyes and grabbed him.

"Corneliu, my love," she hissed before her hands snatched his head and her teeth flashed.

* * *

A bloodcurdling scream ripped Evelyn out of sleep and sitting upright. One hand slapped onto a double-A battery on the nightstand, while her other reached for the bow at her bedside. Heart racing, it took Evelyn a minute to realize it was Hayden.

Forgetting her shoes and still in pajamas, Evelyn took up the bow and plastic rack of arrows before going to the door. First, she turned to see that daylight still lit up the room's curtains, before she ventured out with the bow notched and ready to draw back. The battery she curled in with her left

112

hand grip on the weapon. Isaac, Nick and Kael all came out armed around the same time, and the four of them closed in on Hayden's room.

"You alright in there?" Isaac called through the door.

The door opened so fast it startled them all, and Hayden appeared ashen but not pale as death.

"I'm okay," Hayden gasped, sweat having beaded up on his forehead. "Just a nightmare."

"You sure," Nick asked as he looked up and down the hall.

"You'd know if it wasn't," Hayden assured, and went back to grab his watch leaving the door open. "It's a bit early, but if everyone's phones are charged we might as well get ready to leave now."

"Leave to where?" Evelyn asked.

"First," Hayden began as he put on his watch and then his dress shirt over the undershirt. "We should check around for a gas pump and take as much of the fuel as we can. Also, we might want to swipe whatever canned and packaged foods we can. Then we'll want to get out to an open field far from towns or other buildings. That'll give us a better chance of seeing them coming."

"Alright," Isaac said turning to the others. "Get'chr stuff and let's go."

Evelyn went back to her room and quickly changed into fresh clothes from her large bag, this time with jeans. Just before she finished putting on all her jewelry, there was a knock on her door.

"Come in," Evelyn said, once she finished.

Kael entered and closed the door softly before speaking, "Wanda's out in the dining room just sittin' there. She just stares and doesn't move."

"She lost her son, Kael," Evelyn reminded him, and thought back to this morning. "Archery team?"

"Just as good as your CNA story," a defensive Kael accused her at a whisper.

"That's what I mean," Evelyn said, while gathering her stuff. "You're getting better at this."

"Our school didn't have an archery team, though," Kael pointed out.

"No one's going to have a reason to check," she returned. "It'll be fine."

Evelyn went to the dining room with Kael, and then Salma joined her. As per Kael's description, Wanda just sat at the end of the table with her hands laid flat on the surface, staring into the glossy sheen. Evelyn noticed the bandage loose and in need of change.

However, when she came around and reached to check on it, Wanda swatted her hand away in a burst of searing anger. "Keep your fucking hands off me!"

Palms up and now in her own bad mood, Evelyn backed off looking down and away.

"I'll take care of it," Salma promised to Evelyn, and then spoke softly to Wanda. "C'mon."

When she stepped outside with the others Evelyn gauged the sun's position and figured there was an hour and a half of daylight left. As everyone board she was about to step into the same truck as yesterday, until Wanda suddenly got off in a huff and stood with arms crossed.

"What now?" Hayden shot, seeing the display.

"I'm not riding with her or her brother," Wanda declared.

"Okay then," Hayden answered, uncertain why. "You can ride with me if you want."

"And I'm not getting near those two things," a vehement Wanda added.

"That's fine," Hayden accepted after looking around and shrugging. "Ah, Nick, would you and Hyun trade with Evelyn and Kael? Yeah, I don't know, just go with it."

Evelyn guessed they gave Hayden questioning looks, because she didn't hear any protest from them. Once the switch was made, Wanda at last climbed into Isaac's truck and all doors closed. Within an hour the group found a gas station and filled up, after Kael discovered a dead station worker with keys. They also scooped up as much of the food as they thought useful.

Salma advised that everyone grab more of the candy than they were willing to, for the short term energy boost. Everyone went for the coffee makers and filled thick double-layered insulating cups to the brim. Then they drove out of town with a full twenty minutes to spare. Evelyn pulled out her cell and earphones, to then select an app to catch the news.

"Issuing a statement from an undisclosed location," an anchor began on the news site video she played. "The President has ordered a unilateral recall of all U.S. forces from overseas. The massive recall, effective immediately, includes bases in some one hundred thirty countries. Officials from the U.N. and NATO have decried the withdraw which, some say, leaves America's allies unsupported in their own efforts to combat this phenomenon. And it has been confirmed that former victims of these attack are returning to a life-like state through this contamination. Authorities are advising people that these corpses are dangerous and should be avoided at all costs."

Above the news crawl, the tag bar showed the woman reporting from an aircraft carrier. Yet the room behind her looked like a normal production room, if a tad on the bland side. She went on to cover related stories, as the screen switched to a piece of video of soldiers approaching abandoned buildings in daylight hours.

"While most emergency services appear to be down," the anchor's voice continued. "Some military bases have organized their own counter-offensive against the contaminated individuals. We have to warn our viewers at this time that what they are about to see is disturbing."

To say the least, Evelyn thought, as the video reached the point of the night vision equipped camera entered an unlit room with a skinny naked boy standing in the corner.

"C'mon son, it's alright," one of the goggle-wearing soldiers said. "We're here to get you out."

Instead, he turned with a soul-racking scream that made the camera operator and every soldier jump out of their skin. His eyes had turned into the cloudy empty slates with which Evelyn had become familiar. His wide open mouth more resembled a pitch-black abyss. He ran straight for the first soldier, as they all opened fire on him. The recoil was the only reason the boy fell back, though with his contorted face rising up it was clear he wouldn't stay down.

At that point the camera view became too jumbled and shaky for Evelyn to see much. She suspected the operator was running away from the scene. From the shouting and many boot claps, she figured the soldiers were also escaping. That they ventured so far in meant simply that they ran headlong into more vampires. Those who were once people, dogs and cats all bore similar unnatural faces with the shrieks of human voices pushed to the limits being the most frightening.

The video cut off at that point, but came back on with some, but not all, of the group outside. The camera turned to the sound of glass shattered from several floors up. A soldier grappling another man in shredded civilian clothing both fell to the street below. The searing effect of the sun had already started, but the thing continued to writhe after impact with his flesh burning in a sizzle.

A hand on her shoulder, made Evelyn jumped with a start. She saw in the outdoor lamp's light that Kael was trying to get her attention and she pulled the earphones off. "What?"

"Hayden says he's found a good spot to park, but there's a farm house in view," Kael said.

"Why doesn't he just keep driving?" Evelyn asked, thinking being on the move was safer.

"He doesn't know where we should be heading, and wants to save the gas," Kael answered.

The truck engine shut off, and then Hayden and Valerie came into the compartment. Hayden closed and locked the door to the cab and sat on the low level extension from the side wall.

"We've parked the trucks back-to-back," Hayden revealed. "So that we shouldn't expect anything from the back door in case they find us. There's a house out there, but all the lights are off, so we're going to stay away until day break."

"What do we do in the meantime?" Evelyn wanted to test Hayden on this. "In fact, what's wrong with finding some bunker or tornado shelter and just staying put?"

"For right now," Hayden began knocking down questions one at a time. "We stay awake. Every now and then I'm going to sneak into the cab and use the thermal imaging scope to check around, and Isaac's doing the same for the other side. As to long term, I don't know. I was hoping the people who contracted us would maybe call me with a suggestion about that. On shelters or whatnot there's still the issue of supplies, and I'd like to have electrical power for phones and my equipment."

"You still think you can crack this with test tubes and Bunsen burners?" Evelyn shook her head toward him waving a hand out at the futility. "You said it yourself, there are things going on that shouldn't be possible. I just saw a video showing that even the army can't handle this."

"Physics and chemistry, physics and chemistry," Hayden repeated like the words were their own spell and pointed to her. "Everything's bound to natural laws. I just have to figure out what we've missed that was always there."

"What if it's forever intangible?" Evelyn inquired while straightening up with level calm.

"There're no unsolvable problems in the world, there's just a failure of human imagination and hard work," Hayden contended. "I'm sure other people are on this, but if I can help I will."

Evelyn noticed goose bumps on Kael's arm from what she had said. Adding emphasis and giving even her the creeps, the Alina vampire stirred under its sheet covering. That alone was enough to ensure Evelyn wouldn't drift off into sleep. She nervously thumbed at one of her rings.

Seeing that, Kael became conscious of his left palm and stole a glimpse at it, when he saw that Hayden and Valerie weren't looking. Then he and Evelyn traded glances but said nothing.

Every half hour or so, Hayden crept into the cab with the thermal imager.

Ducking below the dash at first, he would rise to sweep a half circle with the scope up before his face. In the back, both vampires wriggled in their restraints, causing a sharp intake of breath from Valerie. Hayden got more or less accustomed to it, however. She scooted closed to Evelyn for security, with a hold on Evelyn's upper arm.

Hayden glanced over to the source of the girl's concern, but then ignored it. He pulled out his own phone and thumbed over it in thought. After,

119

he selected something that shone brighter in his face and started texting.

Evelyn went back to her cell, thinking she knew what website he was on and did a search. Trying variations of Hayden's first and last name, she at last discovered Hay-Corn and figured that to be his account when reading his long list of posts over the last three days. From Hayden's own online confessions, he felt over his head, and rightly so, Evelyn thought.

At daybreak, Hayden drove down the road further, with Evelyn squatting in the doorway between the cab and the back. Kael stood behind her, and the two watched as Hayden turned off onto a dirt road. Expecting a creepy rundown wooden relic of a hundred years ago, long bereft of paint and wood aging badly, Evelyn was pleasantly disappointed. The sizeable building, with attached greenhouse, was in an excellent state. Its bright yellow paint reflected a new era of sun worship with solar panels on the roof. There also stood electricity-generating turbines in the backyard spinning happy praises to natural wind.

"Suppose there's someone home?" Valerie suggested.

"Living someone or dead?" Hayden asked, and then realized he might've hit close to home with that remark. "Ah, sorry. I didn't mean to upset you there."

"You're fine," Valerie offered back with ease. "And I think it's the living kind."

"I suppose we'll share what we got and maybe they'll share with us," Hayden then answered.

Hayden settled into a spot some twenty yards away, and Isaac's truck pulled around the side to match. Hayden was about to get out with others, but stopped himself to check the angle of the sun first. Then he threw a glance over his shoulder and waved Evelyn back to check on the vampires.

"Yeah, okay, we're good," Hayden declared in a grunt, as he pushed the gurneys against a wall.

"What about the rat vampire?" Kael asked, looking around.

"Are you kidding?" Hayden shot lightly. "That thing's in its cage inside two strong boxes."

"Just so I know," Kael said in contrition.

Hayden had everyone climb out the front doors, and passed weapons over to them. Then he closed up the back compartment and exited. They came around to find Isaac's company gathered at the back of their truck and prepping their weapons.

"Reminds me of the start of a western horror movie," Nick remarked, before lighting up a cigarette. He paused to look at everyone. "You guys alright with this?"

"Might as well," Isaac acceded with a long blink and raised eyebrows. "Maybe we get lucky and nicotine repels vampires better than garlic an' crosses."

With the smoke in his mouth, Nick hefted his leather roll of weaponry and cracked one of his shotguns to check the shells. "Want me to get the door on this one?"

At first Hayden appeared ready to let Nick have at it, but changed his mind. "Let me do this."

121

Hayden, Isaac, and Nick approached the door, while having the rest hold back. Nick swung two fingers to Isaac in a signal of covering the other side of the door. Then Nick slipped out his bowie knife and nodded to Hayden. Evelyn watched an ever more nervous Hayden flex his fingers toward the door, with his other hand holding up the spear gun that had become his staple.

"Sure you want to do point?" Nick asked the chemical engineer again.

"Yeah," Hayden answered with a quick nod. "Just need to get my nerve up."

They were covered by an ample overhang, though the sun shone directly onto the porch and door. Hayden clenched a fist before just going ahead and snatching the stylized handle. He pressed the thumb lever and threw open the door that banged against the interior wall.

"Way to go, Jack Crow," Nick praised, with his cigarette wagging in his mouth.

"That a guy from that movie?" Hayden asked with his weapon nervously pointed inside.

"Yeah," an eager Nick nodded, and stepped in before Hayden.

The three of them surveyed the front room before letting the others in. Evelyn's eyes went everywhere from floor to ceiling in admiration of the décor. Salma and Nick paired off to sweep the rest of the floor, while Hayden waved Isaac to accompany him upstairs. The other five stayed put, though Evelyn paced around to examine the armoire of glass and wood and tables with vases.

While admiring a framed photo hung on the side of the staircase, Evelyn heard a door creak behind her. A thump of a heavy shoe or boot caused her to whirl around with a scream.

Chapter 6: Old Testament

"I didn't mean to scare the dickens out of you like that," the lean elderly man named David Judd said to Evelyn, as he sat in a recliner with everyone else in chairs or on his couch.

Hayden had rushed back when he heard Evelyn unleash that short, but urgent cry out, though Nick beat him to it. She and David nearly let loose crossbows on each other, with Nick bringing his shotgun to bear from the floor above. David and his Vietnamese wife, Anh, had emerged from a door that looked like it was a closet.

"It was rude of us to just barge in," Evelyn traded apology in kind. "But we didn't think anyone would still be here. The lights were off all night."

As a demonstration of contrition, Nick put out his cigarette into his palm with a wince.

"You were out there in the dark?" David asked with alarmed incredulity.

"Believe me, sir," Hayden added from a side seat on the couch. "I'm amazed you and your wife survived in this house day after day. How do you do it?"

"That's a little shelter we got down there," David explained with an absent point toward the front of the house. "Built it myself shortly after we moved out here. Storms get bad round these parts. Even got steel doors and good locks in case of trouble. One into the house and the other goes out back, in case a tornado brings the whole house down."

"When we saw on the news all this stuff about rabid attacks," Anh added, as she brought in more beverages to pass around. Her voice had the barest hint of a Vietnamese accent. "We started going down there every night to seal up good and tight."

"I assume by now you know it's not rabies," Hayden suggested.

"Yep," David acknowledged with a nod that made Hayden think he should be chewing on a wheat stalk. "Cable news said that too. That's when I went into town to get crossbows instead of more bullets. Wasn't sure if they'd work or not, but I could tell from the TV shootin' 'em wasn't doing any good. Lotta people in town were gone, of course."

"It's pretty much all of them now," Hayden revealed. "Or from what we saw."

"Figured you were from the city, such a wide group of people all mixed together," David observed without implication. "I'm guessin' it's worse there than out here."

"Pretty bad," Kael affirmed. "Shit got nuts quick! Or– sorry sir."

"That ain't the worst language I heard, son," David dismissed before taking a sip of his iced tea. "Hell, you should'a heard them boys out in Nam."

"You were in the service," Hayden asked.

"Hundred And First Airborne," David replied, which Hayden thought meant the army. "'Course I wasn't in country before nineteen-seventy."

125

"Is that where you and Anh met?" Evelyn surmised while waving to the old couple.

"We couldn't get enough of those men in their uniforms," Anh reveled when bringing back the last drinks. "David looked so handsome. He needed a little looking after, though."

That forced out a few smiles among the group not yet comfortable talking. "Have you had to take out any vampires here?" Nick asked.

"There's nights we heard something creep in here, but with one exception they seem wandered around only to clear out by morning," Anh explained.

"And that one?" Hayden pressed further.

"It realized that door in the front went to the shelter, and waited at the bottom all night," David revealed, at which cold shudders ran up a couple of spines. "Apparently those things don't need to sleep in the day, just hide out from the sun. Anh got behind the door to let it in, and I was right there ready to lay that nasty ole thing to rest."

David made a pistol shot gesture with his right hand, indicating his old soldier's edge hadn't faded completely. Hayden took a long swig on that thought, and looked around the room. The fireplace appeared to have only recently gone into disuse.

Sensible, as Hayden suspected it might give away signs of habitation. Above it on the mantle he noticed a number of photos. David and Anh Judd had raised two daughters and a son, that latter of who appeared to have made Eagle Scout.

"Have you checked on your children?" Hayden inquired, hoping at least someone received good news.

"We keep trying," Anh explained. "But it seems more and more phone service is out where they each live. What about all of your families?"

Right then Wanda lost it, and the tears began to flow. Anh dropped what she was doing to stand next to where Wanda sat and comfort her by rubbing her shoulders.

"It's not looking good," Hayden spoke first about that. "Though, I haven't tried with my son."

"Ours seems alright so far," Evelyn offered up, though gave no specifics.

"Not sure I wanna check with my folks," Isaac said, and suppressed something. "Sorry."

Valerie said nothing, lest she reveal her lack of grief over stepparents, Hayden suspected. Salma likewise didn't broach any details, though Hyun did. Nick passed the question on with a wave in front of his face, but didn't seem broken up about it.

"You're welcome to stay," David offered in his laid back country manner.

"I don't want to impose," Hayden said. "We just need the day to sleep, and we'll be out of your hair before sundown. Our food situation's good for now."

"You got some place you need to be?" David seemed to challenge him as he leaned forward.

"Not that I'm aware," Hayden prefaced, unsure how he could phrase what came next. "I, ah, there's things that I do in order to figure out how to deal with this problem."

"Like a doctor," David asked.

"Not in medicine, no sir," Hayden denied. "I'm actually a chemist. My PhD's in chemical engineering and I was studying samples before everything melted down."

The rest of the group stared at him, knowing fully what Hayden meant by "samples". But the elderly couple didn't, and that gnawed at Hayden.

"How's a chemist come up with a cure for vampires?" David asked.

"By getting a look inside the things once medical people have established it's not a biological disease." Hayden advanced another step in admitting the nature of his cargo.

"They don't strike me as cooperative folk," David remarked.

"Yeah, uh… it's like this, Mr. Judd," Hayden sputtered humbly, bracing David with his hands up from across the room. "I have three of them in that security truck out there."

Anh and David both tilted their faces down to cast their eyes at him, as if they weren't sure they heard right. Anh recovered first. "How could you manage?"

"To be honest, the hard work was done for me," Hayden admitted. "I work for a research lab, and we were sent these things to figure out what's going on inside them. Two human vampires, and there's a rat that turned in testing. We used to have a lot more animals, but I had to leave all that behind in a bit of a rush, you understand."

"Are they tame?" David leaned back more relaxed than Hayden thought he should be.

"No, actually. The people who sent the two human bodies removed their arms and legs first."

"Disgusting," Anh spat out, but didn't seem that horrified.

"They don't actually bleed, so it's largely a clean affair," Hayden confessed. "And, because they're not feeding both have become pretty inactive. I doubt they'll starve to death."

"Could be worse things you scientists tinker with." David took it better than Hayden had dared hope for. "What you come up with so far?"

"More questions than answers, really," Hayden revealed, truly at a loss on some aspects.

"We got electricity, if you need it," David offered to Hayden's astonishment.

Isaac and Evelyn both turned to Hayden, who caught himself nodding and speechless.

Nick and Kael got on moving the gurneys down into the shelter, while the others, minus Wanda, carried weapons and supplies in to stash below ground. Hayden saw no need to create a more inviting target for the Judds. After, they all took turns at the showers, each floor having a full bathroom. Some of the group also helped Anh Judd prepare meals. Despite being up all night, most of them didn't sleep, but, after freshening followed David in a morning tour around the house. Later in the even they helped with some chores.

With nightfall coming, Anh threw together dinner early and had help bringing it down into the shelter, before David locked everyone in for the night. The underground sanctuary had multiple rooms, which let Hayden keep the vampires out of

129

Wanda's sight. Even with eleven people it wasn't that cramped, though he figured it might feel more claustrophobic should the house be flooded with restless dead seeking out victims.

After adding a few sections to the Judds' main dining table and bringing out another, everyone gathered around to eat. Ready to dig in, they noticed that David and Anh had interlaced their fingers and bowed their heads for prayer. Out of respect, everyone held off eating, though Hayden, Salma and Isaac were the only ones to utter amen on David's thanks to God.

"I hope y'all like chicken," David drawled. "Damn things ran off all our sheep and killed the cow we kept out back. I guess there's some things that don't turn, bless their souls."

"What did you do with the lost stock?" Hayden wondered aloud.

"'Didn't dare eat'em, so I buried them in a grove out yonder far from the house," David explained. "'Makes me wonder if animals need a good Christian burial too."

"Is that why you let us stay?" Valerie asked, which drew more than one warning pair of eyes.

"The people of Israel were dead set on preserving hospitality," David praised. "Violating that was about the biggest sin you could commit back then."

"Those days are befalling us again," Anh assured, to show herself just as much the believer.

Hayden tossed knowing glances to Evelyn and Kael, but they each kept their proverbial heads down to focus on their dishes. Nick's attention to his plate came from an entirely different place, which drew snickers from Valerie and a shake of Isaac's head. Apparently, small time Coyotes rarely ate home-cooked meals.

"That vampire you took out," Kael started. "Did you bury it too?"

"Tried to," David said turning to the young martial artist. "Mrs. Judd and I hauled that thing up the stairs to go out back, but the durned thing started to broil once it was in the morning sun. So I shoveled it up into a wheel barrel and dumped it over by the cow. Kept the arrow, though."

"And none of the sheep turned?" Hayden asked, before taking a bite of chicken.

"No, but I'll tell y'all what I did see," David wound up for a tale. "A whole nest of dead rats all huddled up in a deep hollow where there used to be a big ole tree. Poured kerosene down there to burn 'em out. 'Cept they didn't squeal or nothing like that. Were it not daytime I think they woulda come outta there and rip me to shreds while still on fire. There's something else out there at night too. Roars like a lion, but I don't know if there's other big cats that sound like that."

"I'm sure you heard right," Hayden agreed. "Did you see it? Was it close?"

"No, no," David dismissed his questions to ease any fears. "It was way out. Must've come from the city zoo or somethin'. News said a lot of peculiar animals turn an' they ain't figured out why which ones can. I did see one of them dead fillies out there, though. Must've come from my neighbors a couple-three miles down the road. Thing wasn't

131

born but a month ago, and then one night it up and went after his whole herd. He said he never seen anything like it."

"Is he still out there?" Salma asked with peeked up attention and concern. "You neighbor?"

"He hasn't answered his phone in a couple days," David answered in a more subdued tone, Hayden guessed to be in mourning. "Whole family of eight, an' they was good people."

"Damn," Isaac muttered, and drew in a bit, possibly in thought of his own relatives.

"An' there's something else goin' on, too," David threw in as a finale. "We see it during the day. Some rather odd folks walkin' out in the woods half a mile out."

"Survivors?" Salma expressed renewed hope in her question.

"They'd have to be, but they're strange ducks," David drew out, inducing suspense amongst all gathered at the couple's table.

"They wear robes," Anh revealed, before sipping at a spoon.

"But they's hands were exposed, so I'm sure they're livin' folk," David added. "Don't know what they all're doin', but so long as they don't bring it here I'm alright with it."

After diner Hayden noticed that David and Anh spent a few hours reading out of the same Bible in a love seat with David's arm draped behind Anh on the back. Then they readied for sleep in a separate bedroom as though they were any other empty-nest golden-years couple.

132

"Kinda got a rule for you folks," David stated, before he was about to close the door to the underground bedroom. "This place is pretty sound proof, but you wanna keep it down just in case. Me and Anh got fair to middlin' ears, but it's those things you wanna worry about."

"Animal vampires you mean," Hayden observed, and nodded. "Yeah, we're careful on that."

Everyone else camped out in their own spots around the large central room, after David had closed the door. They lacked the privacy of the motel, but Hayden realized the doors David had put in stood with more reinforcement than he thought was needed for just any tornado. It didn't make drifting into sleep easier in the night, but at least then Hayden knew it was just fear.

* * *

The following morning brought heightened tension upon opening the door leading up into the house. Eight people readied themselves to turn whatever might lurk on the other side of the steel door into a pin cushion. Then Anh, Valerie and Hyun all gathered to open it. But nothing sprang out, and a check of the two above-ground floors led to no other surprises. The closets proved to be the most nerve-racking as the only dark places in the dawn light.

Breakfast let anxieties evaporate like dew under the sunrise. Then, with everyone else above, Evelyn went down into the shelter again to open her heavy bag. The Judds observed their spiritual practices, and she had hers. On pulling out a few natural herbs, she ground them up into a palm-sized cast iron pot. With subtlety she brought the mixture and a couple other things up with her. She then headed out the back door, where she saw Nick splitting logs with David's ax.

"Is that, uh," Nick paused, selecting another log, "Some Wiccan thing?"

"Yeah sort of, I'll be over in the grove," Evelyn answered, and then had a thought. "Don't tell the Judds. They're really sweet, but I'm not sure how they'd take this."

"I didn't see anything," Nick offered, easy enough.

Walking toward the tree line, Evelyn checked directly in front of where she was stepping to avoid holes or pits. The vampires with claws might've buried themselves to escape the day. Those once human could use tools to similar effect or to create traps, allowing them to catch and feed while shielded from the sun. She was just as concerned about snares set to hold a person until nightfall without killing or much blood loss. There was no telling what knowledge remained in a dead brain before the rising.

However, a clear and safe route Evelyn found, and she soon approached the first trees. They ranged from saplings to maybe a couple of decades old. Further in she could see others that were older, and felt a tug at her heart for such a place. Cautious under diminished daylight, Evelyn was warmed inside by the surrounding greenery that ran up trunks despite midwinter's bare branches. Ivy vines snaked up trees without much apparent harm to the woody hosts. In close inspection Evelyn noticed that in fact their fusion seemed perfect, and closed her eyes while placing a hand over her chest.

"So beautiful. So special. I feel it," Evelyn uttered to the gentle cold wind caressing her checks.

What Evelyn found to be less natural was first the pile of charred flesh David Judd had left. Behind rose a mound of fresher browner dirt, which must have been the cow's unmarked grave. Stepping around the blight to nature, she knelt down by the earthen pile and sunk her splayed hand into it. Working her fingers into the dirt, Evelyn embraced the connection with a blissful expression.

Opening her eyes once more, Evelyn noticed a patch of burnt ground, and recalled David's retelling of the vampire rats. She trotted over for a closer look. The liquid-powered fire had erased any evidence of how the hollow came to be, though Evelyn suspected the work of a badger. In the dark pit something stirred slickly, and a foul caustic odor wafted up in concert with the vague movement.

Daring to lean close, Evelyn cast her eyes to the left, to be sure the sun still shone through the gap between her face and whatever horror awaited discovery. She pulled out a small Maglite and turned it on to light up the hole. Scant few rat corpses clung to their power of movement, but she guessed that wouldn't last long without feeding. And yet starving into stillness didn't mean they were destroyed. The palm-sized monsters would linger forever, on the verge of reanimation unless cast into the light.

"I'll come back for you critters later," she assured the tiny, clouded eyes staring hungrily at her.

Rising up, she noticed yet one more sign of restless ravenous dead. Evelyn liked to think she knew the prints of cat paws rather well. However, placing her hand within the impression Evelyn asked herself just how large a typical lion would be.

Recalling her original purpose out here, Evelyn pinched out a small amount of the dry mixture she put together. Casting before the surrounding trees, she spoke a prayer to all of them and to the four elemental forces of nature governing their immotile lives. Evelyn then went back toward the house.

However, she stopped some twenty yards out to look around. Seeing that Nick was in the garage with David looking over an engine, and no one was peering outside through the back windows, Evelyn decided it was safe. She quickly knelt down with a Double-A battery she palmed into her left hand.

"Protect this house and all who dwell within," Evelyn chanted and pushed the battery into the earth just beyond the back porch, sprinkling some of the granule powder over it.

After, she pinched a little dirt over the offering and moved to another spot to repeat the ritual with another battery. "Protect this house and all who dwell within."

Leaving thirteen in all, Evelyn forged a subtle circle around the Judd home. In front of the eastern side, she had noticed Anh Judd working in a vegetable garden. Despite the season, the greenhouse was still a source of produce. Evelyn wondered if David had wired the interior to keep it warm.

Next, Evelyn went to the front door and set the undersized iron cauldron onto the walkway. Taking out a lighter, she flicked it, and then tilted the metal pot and set the rest of the offering to flame. As it burned she fanned the smoke to either side with backhand waves, and then cupped her palms to push larger billows toward the entrance. All the while Evelyn struggled against anxiety of being seen in order to maintain inner quiet and good spirits.

"This good home is of the sacred Earth," Evelyn expanded on the prayer. "It bears forth pure water we drink. It harnesses the air we breathe. It warms us with beautiful fire gifted by the sun. Let David Judd and Anh Judd be kept whole of body, pure in blood, full of breath and alive with spirit."

Assured that the unauthorized circle was sealed by the fact the fire in the bowl was burnt out, Evelyn picked it up and went inside to put her things away. Heading down into the shelter, she saw Hayden coming out of the room where the vampires were kept.

"Oh, hey," Hayden greeted her arrival. "I might need some help on something here."

Unsure whether he saw the pot in her hand, Evelyn dared not put it behind her leg, lest the movement draw the chemist's eyes.

"Sure," she accepted with a light tone. "Do you need me now?"

"In a bit," Hayden said, turning halfway back into the room.

Presented the window of opportunity, Evelyn bent over toward her bag to shove the cauldron and flashlight away. Then she joined Hayden by the doorway. He had re-established a miniature version of his impromptu lab back in the city, which itself was likely a chopped down version of what Hayden was used to back at his place of work. Both vampires remained strapped to their gurneys but were fully exposed. In a brief moment of paranoia, Evelyn wondered if the older man enjoyed gawking at their bare torsos and the fact the corpses seemed to never have a bad hair day.

"I thought Hyun Jae became your unofficial assistant," Evelyn commented.

"Yeah, she is," Hayden affirmed, while typing onto a calculator, and then thumbed upstairs in abstract. "I got her on the Judds' computer looking stuff up for me."

"They have a computer," Evelyn marveled.

"Just because they live out in the sticks doesn't mean they aren't hip to the century," Hayden playfully admonished. "Hell, they're even up on the green energy movement."

"I noticed Anh's got quite the little harvest going on in the greenhouse," Evelyn said.

"Okay, that's got it," Hayden stated without explaining what he'd gotten, and then realized that he'd zoned off the fact he called Evelyn over. "Oh, I want to open up the rat body again and extract some of the crap that's in its veins. I just need an extra hand to keep that thing staked while I do it."

Waving her over, Hayden opened the first, and then second lock box to pull the cage out with his tongs. He dared not get his fingers close to the thick bars and invite a lucky bite from the bloodthirsty rodent within. Then he grabbed what Evelyn thought was a broken antenna to aim, while the creature shoved a tiny paw through and grasped in vain for his face or hand.

In one thrust Hayden had it impaled through the chest and made still. Thereafter, he had Evelyn keep a hold on the metal rod, while he opened the cage and reached in with the tongs. First, the vampire rat came out, and then the other end of the rod followed, with Hayden and Evelyn frequently trading holds. Hayden then placed the rat flat to its back on a cutting board with small clamps.

"Looks like the product of redneck engineering," Evelyn chided.

"Yeah, it is," Hayden admitted, while he clamped the limp animal in place. "One of the lab aides put it together in a metal shop near his house."

Dissection was carried out quickly, making Evelyn wonder just how many times Hayden had performed this procedure before. Wads of elastic moist goo inside the blood vessel yielded with reluctance to Hayden's scalpel and tweezers, and appeared to bleed a little where cut. Evelyn noticed how more substance seemed to excrete through the arterial and veinal walls with the appearance of wet epoxy.

"Have you figured out where their strength comes from?" Evelyn was riveted by his work.

"I think it's this same stuff," Hayden speculated. "Somehow it spreads out from the circulatory system into every tissue. It contracts with electrical current kind've like how muscles do. I got to run some tests to see what molecular functional groups are involved here. Maybe there're portions that are enzymatic, though how it all starts by simply dehydrating the body blows my mind."

"Still using science to pry open ancient mythology, huh?" Evelyn asked.

"This would have Solomon himself pulling his hair out," Hayden boasted, "Granted, he never had access to nuclear magnetic resonance spectroscopy, so that gives me an unfair advantage."

Hayden placed a sample of the strange material that animated the dead into a test tube solution. After, he inserted the glass container in an opening atop a blue and beige hard plastic-encased machine, and started it. On a laptop, into which the machine was plugged via an Ethernet cable, a program started. Hayden spent much of the day studying its results.

* * *

"That bitch doesn't fucking touch me!" Wanda's voice screamed throughout the house.

Two days later and Hayden was in David Judd's hobby room on his computer when the shouting started. Rushing out and up the stairs to a sunroom Hayden saw Wanda sitting in a chair holding her left hand on her neck bandage defensively while Isaac, David, Evelyn and Salma stood around her.

"Wanda, I need to see how it's healing and change the bandage," Evelyn argued hotly.

"You two did enough," Wanda accused, and turned to David. "She did something to me!"

Kael ran up behind Hayden and looked at everyone. "What's all the yelling?"

"I'm still working on that," Hayden said before he thought about it.

"You," Wanda's voice stabbed at Kael. "And your bitch sister ruined my life!"

"What the fuck're you talking about?" Kael shot back, his mouth also faster than his brain.

"She's paranoid, Kael," Evelyn sniped. "Don't worry about it."

"Even those paramedics on the road knew you were up to something," Wanda shouted.

"Wanda," David spoke softly, hinting to Hayden that the senior was an old hand at dealing with squabbles under his roof. "Tell me what's wrong. Don't look at them, just talk to me."

"Look," Wanda said, pulling the bandage noisily from her neck, as if a little girl presenting a case to her own father against a sibling. "She did that. It's changing me into a monster."

"It seems fine to me," David observed, and Hayden agreed in thought. "What's the problem?"

"Mr. Judd," Evelyn tried to explain before being cut off.

"It's a bite," Wanda whined. "And she put something on it to make me into one of those things."

"She was attacked by vampire, Mr. Judd," Evelyn threw in as fast as she could. "It was her

141

son. Kael and the rest of us saved her life. Then I used an antiseptic on it before wrapping it up."

"He murdered my baby," Wanda screamed loud enough to hurt several pairs of ears.

"Kael," David asked of the young man. "What's she mean by that?"

"It's before we left the city," Kael managed before he too was interrupted.

"He killed Brad!" Wanda's sharp voice pierced the air.

"Wanda, this is my house, and I expect courtesy from every one of you while you're in it," David scolded without raising his voice. "Now Kael?"

"Some time during the day her kid wandered off outside the building we were all hiding in," Kael reported, also addressing David as a father. "So we went out looking for him. He was ducked behind some wall behind a bunch of houses and we couldn't see clearly. He lured Wanda into one of them and attacked her. It took four of us to pull her son off her. He tore a sheet of skin off her big as my hand. He was turned, Mr. Judd, I swear to god."

"How big again was this injury," David inquired to be sure, as he looked at the wound.

Kael approximated with both hands to frame out an area, "About like that, I think."

"Whatever Evelyn put there's doing more than keeping infection at bay," David Judd observed, and then turned to Evelyn and Kael. "I've seen my share of life threatening injuries. This must've been pretty bad, but it's comin' along good. So what happened after that, Kael?"

"'Kid kept comin' at us," Kael recounted, now flush red with the horror of the moment coming back. "So I knocked him back a couple times. He got up again and—."

"And what, son?" David demanded with just enough hard tone to invoke an answer.

"I used a machete on him," Kael slowly confessed. "He was dead, he was killing her, and he would've killed all of us. It, ah, the way I did...."

He couldn't finish with Wanda burning a glare straight through him. Kael instead stepped sideways, so that David was between Wanda and made a lopping gesture across his own neck.

"That must've been tough call, son," David soothed with a forgiving tone that reddened Kael's eyes with grief, and Hayden himself felt tears welling up.

"He murdered him!" Wanda shot up and screamed into David's ear, then and stormed off.

"What about what all else she said?" David asked Evelyn, as everyone else arrived to investigate.

"That part about the roadblock, Mr. Judd," Evelyn began.

"You all can call me David," he permitted. "It ain't discourteous to use my first name."

"By the time we found the police roadblock it was sometime the next day around midnight or after," Evelyn resumed her version, neither side of which Hayden had heard up to now. "I don't remember exactly. The injury was a little before sundown of the previous day. But the paramedics said that it looked like the wound was a week old

143

and still clean. They asked us to take care of her, because all the hospitals were down from the attacks."

"Them vampires, or whatever they are, heal quick too," David stated.

"It's not like that," Hayden, at last, interjected. "They go through a non-living renewal. The cells get rebuilt, but they don't divide like living cells do."

"Well, let's see this stuff she was carrying on about." David waved his fingers in summons.

"I don't have it with me," Evelyn said. "It's in my purse, in my bag down in the shelter.

"Alright, alright," David nodded, and then turned to Hayden. "She's gonna want to think we checked on this… whatever-you-call-it that Evelyn here used. I don't wanna be a liar, Hayden. So you have a look-see at this stuff she's keepin' usin' your exper'r'ments," David's last word carried the full weight of his southern small town inflection. "You see if they're not the same. Then tell everybody that Wanda's okay, and that it ain't makin' her into no monster. N'kay?"

"Yes, I can do that," Hayden answered with a conceding nod.

Hayden, Evelyn and David all went to the shelter. Evelyn broke away to retrieve the bottle Hayden recalled seeing only once. That left Hayden and David by themselves a moment.

"It's been a while since I read my Bible," Hayden confessed, and added an afterthought to his admission of guilt. "And there's most of it I haven't read."

144

"Hm-mm," David prompted.

"Is there anything remotely like vampires in there?"

"Revelations, if you really need 'ta stretch it," David informed him. "But the dead rising aren't supposed to be evil. They're the souls who accept Jesus as their Lord and Savior. Does got unicorns in there, though. Dragons too, if'n I recollect right. Some say there's satyrs, which're them goat devils, but that's really just about goats."

"Dragons are something I chalk up to somebody finding a dinosaur fossil," Hayden dismissed.

"I reckon that's possible," David conceded. "Don't matter to me none. I don't choose to get myself stuck on things like that. But now we got them vampires comin' out in real life."

"Here it is." Evelyn popped up with the bottle raised for Hayden to see.

"Okay," Hayden said to her and David both. "I'll do a run-through and let her know it's okay."

"I'm not asking for a thank you," Evelyn rued. "But I wish she'd just stop being a pain in the ass."

"Tell 'ya what," David consoled Evelyn, again shifting into sagely father gear. "I'll look after her bandage from here on out. I done dressed a few wounds in my time, so it'll be fine."

"Thank you so much," Evelyn appreciated his offer deeply. "I feel bad for her, I really do. It's just—."

"I know," David smoothed over her worry with a pat on her shoulder. "Time's is tough on a lotta folks."

Once Evelyn left, Hayden did a quick check of his cell phone for any calls, and then went downstairs with David in tow. Hayden began taking samples from the aged bottle, as David studied the vampires.

"Anything new on your figurin' this out?" David inquired.

"Yeah, actually," Hayden brightened up while saying, "Seems this continuous chain of stuff through the rat's body is largely composed of Glycine and Alanine."

"What all does that mean?" David asked on, as if Hayden's answer were gobbledygook.

"Don't know yet," Hayden said, and leaned to support himself on a table with both hands, his eyes distant as if picking something out through a fog. "It's familiar, but I can't remember why."

"And they don't sparkle," David noted.

"Not unless you throw one into a building transformer," Hayden quipped, and let his thoughts drifted toward more serious quandaries. "Why is it just mammals?"

"They suckle," David pointed out. "Their young suckle for milk. That's what make 'em different from other animals. I reckon that's sort've like suckin' blood."

"You know, that never occurred to me," Hayden declared.

"Just you ain't raised on a farm is all. But you got schoolin' and whatnot. You're a smart man, Hayden" David complimented him, offering an encouraging pat on the shoulder, and tightened his

146

grip in a consoling manner. "I'm sure you'll come up with somethin' useful."

"Yeah," Hayden echoed, not quite sure he believed it, and then checked his watch. "It's late."

"Time to get all everyone in here for the night," David agreed from further away, and then added more to himself. "'Nother night of Exodus, and ain't got no lamb's blood for the doorway."

Chapter 7: The Ties That Tangle

"Out here, you say," Hayden turned to ask David, as both men walked with shovels.

"Yeah, whole nest of 'em," David assured, nodding up to the grove ahead.

Over three days no additional night-time trouble befell the house, and sunlight tensions between Wanda and Evelyn or Kael were kept in check with healthy distance. Posting more of his thoughts onto his account, Hayden noticed the number of views were in the thousands. People were surviving out there, he realized with a restrained sense of hope.

Or it could just be vampires still locked by habit to tinker with phones they obsessed over while alive. The closest known location of ravenous fiends still lingered in that hole where David had found and set fire to them. Hayden handled turned rats more easily.

They entered the grove, an hour after sunrise, and approached the scorched pit. However, some of the dirt had been disturbed and the upper side of the earthen hollow was torn away. Leaning over what was now a trench, Hayden saw a slimy layer along the floor and sides that carried the stink of burnt flesh and animal hair. Yet there were no whole bodies or material remains indicating they had been exposed to sunlight and destroyed by it.

"Right here," Hayden checked, pointing into the hole.

"Uh- huh," David remarked as he bent over just enough to get a look. "They was there."

Hayden searched around for signs that they might've crawled away. Instead, human footprints stood out, and one stretch of those led to the place David had disposed of his drained cow. Pacing around it, Hayden noticed a patch where it looked as though someone grabbed a handful of dirt.

"Well, that's peculiar," David stated the obvious. "I know I didn't put my hand in there."

Hayden studied the shoeprints, but doubted he could make out the pattern of tread, as the thick layer of detritus prevented an exact impression.

"Well, at least we don't need to worry about anything else getting turned trying to take shelter in that pit," Hayden observed, and they headed back to the house.

Once inside, Hayden noticed Anh approaching with a billfold. "I found this on the washing machine after Kael ran his clothes through."

"I'll get it to him," Hayden said, accepting it from her. "He must've taken it out and forgot. Not sure there's much of a point in having wallets anymore, much less ID's."

Going downstairs and back into the work room, Hayden tossed Kael's wallet on a table closest to the door as a reminder to grab it on leaving again. Except it landed open, and Hayden couldn't help but notice the full name on the out-of-state ID: Kael Weylyn Monaghan.

Though struck by different surname, Hayden set that aside in order to quickly wrap up his tests on

Evelyn's bizarre powder. Via the aid of a still functioning internet he discovered high traces of collagen, which, after to a surf to a medical website, revealed the value of being able to rapidly rebuild tissue with minimal scarring. However, there also came up high concentrations of Glycine and Alanine.

It was the same to amino acids in the ubiquitous material in vampiric corpses, and in similar long unbroken sequences of the amino acids.

"Oh, you better not," Hayden uttered as if warning Evelyn.

Having a flash of insight, Hayden went to the hard drives containing WHO articles and videos. He didn't have his own microscope, and so couldn't reproduce the experiment. Instead, Hayden brought up the corresponding videos outlining why the affected bodies didn't decay. The substance pervading the necrotic tissue proved aggressive in depleting the water and nutrients of bacteria and other microbes, be they originally mutualistic to the human body or the source of disease. It didn't matter, and didn't even spare animal parasites present during the time a victim turned.

Though it was daytime, hearing Wanda's scream had Hayden out the door swiping the spear gun and lawn stakes along the way. Pounding up the stairs, he found David, Anh, Hyun and Valerie in the bathroom with Wanda before he got there himself.

She had the bandage off completely, and Hayden noticed that almost no trace of the injury was left.

"It seems fine," Valerie said and shrugged.

"Where's everybody else?" Hayden asked, looking around.

"They're out on a scavenging run," David answered. "Eleven people take a lot more food."

"David," Hayden addressed him with a questioning tone, and then waved him to follow.

Once downstairs Hayden glanced up toward the ceiling before saying, "I hate to say it, but she might be onto something with that stuff. It's got a lot of properties in common with what I'm finding in my specimens. Obviously, it's not making Wanda into a vampire, but it's weird enough that we should be concerned. There's something Evelyn said when I first met her that I remember. At the time I didn't think anything of it. When I explained what I knew about vampires someone asked why the outbreak only happened now. I didn't know, but she suggested maybe something held it back."

"From what you done told me, I don't see why anyone would spread that around," David said with distaste at the suggestion. "Even those weirdoes I saw once wearing robes."

"I'll straighten this out with her when she gets back," Hayden assured. "Maybe it's nothing, but it's looking like a more coincidental nothing than I thought possible."

With that Hayden went back to his work with Hyun's help. By this point both human corpses had joined the rat in complete inactivity. However, Hayden refused to trust that. At any moment of carelessness he expected to discover that last reserve of energy used to latch their teeth onto a living reservoir. Yet by mid-evening they hadn't, when he heard a familiar squeal of security truck brakes.

Going upstairs to encounter the foraging group first, Hayden was bumped by Wanda rushing down into the shelter. Nick entered first with several large boxes, followed by Isaac next with a similar load, and Salma carrying necessities of a different sort. They headed straight to the kitchen, while Salma went downstairs. Kael and Evelyn were on their way to the front door.

"I had a look at your antiseptic," Hayden said with a flat tone, as he met them on the porch.

"Is Wanda talking shit again?" Evelyn hissed. "Getting tired of her shit."

"Did you know her injury's pretty much healed up?" Hayden asked.

"I figured it would be," Evelyn said dryly and tried to get around.

"I'm not an expert on medicine," Hayden said, putting a gentle hold on her upper arm. "But I would've figured that kind of recovery needed a skin graft. And there was no aggravation that tore it open. Even the scabs went away easy."

"Never underestimate a CNA." Evelyn's harsh tone edged up in pitch.

"We need to talk about this, and in front of everyone," Hayden warned, trying not to sound accusatorial or angry. "I'm not kidding, Lyn."

"Whatever," she shot back and went inside. "Fine!"

Kael gave him a cold eye and shook his head walking past. Hayden dropped his chin with a sigh,

152

and also went in. After Isaac and Salma listed off what they'd found in a different nearby town, including more weapons, they then described what they had witnessed where they'd made the pickup.

Apparently survivors who ventured out during the day got into fights over supplies, despite the bounty available. While the group avoided trouble, they'd witnessed shootouts and beatings over material goods. Those who managed to find or create nocturnal shelters were now stockpiling whatever they could get for the long haul.

"Ah," Hayden spoke up, once the supply adventure recounting wrapped up. "We need to discuss something about Wanda and the drama around that."

Wanda then stormed into the kitchen, as if Hayden had introduced her as the next act, and dumped several items onto the kitchen counter. Evelyn went white on seeing the iron pot and large, decorative, black-handled knife among the oddities Wanda brought up as her case exhibits.

"Yeah," Wanda shouted at the other woman. "Now your dirty little secrets are out."

David and Anh appeared to have the most stricken reaction.

"Do you go through everybody's shit?" Evelyn shot once she recovered.

"Just satanic witches," Wanda fired back just as hot. "'Seems I was off by one letter!"

Hayden then caught a glimpse of Kael's hand, where he saw the three quarters full pentagram tattoo, though what concerned Hayden was more practical. "Evelyn, are you married?"

"What?" she blurted, having been distracted by the odd question. "No. Why?"

"Gwinnett's your original name then," Hayden stated.

"Yes, so what of it?" Evelyn answered, seeming more annoyed by the lack of a point.

"Which means, unless Kael Weylyn Monaghan is married and took his wife's name," Hayden prefaced. "You two aren't in the same family. Cousins maybe, but not siblings."

"So the hell what?" Kael exclaimed with irate confusion.

"A big knife with a satanic star on it," Wanda proclaimed louder, eager to bring the argument back to Evelyn's things. "And some weird pot for, what, spells? Evelyn?"

"Okay, so I'm Wiccan," Evelyn admitted without shame. "That's part of my beliefs. You don't see me getting on your case for prayers, or your crosses," she directed to Salma, and then turned to the Judds. "And I'm even fine with that little churchy alcove you got in the bedroom up there."

"You run your own church in here?" Nick asked, blowing off everything else over that tidbit.

"Anh and I are getting' on in years," David started. "Kids is out of the house, and we didn't have anything else to do with their rooms. So I remodeled on with a single pew and a podium up front. Sometimes our pastor comes by to offer us services, but mostly we just go up there to worship and sing hymns. We don't do incantations and we've never needed a big ole knife for the sacrament."

"It's a Celtic pagan thing," Evelyn announced, as if that alone settled it. "You wouldn't get it."

"That doesn't explain the antiseptic stuff you used," Hayden reminded. "I'm not even up on my own faith, but I figure something like that would've long stood out to the medical community. And Kael's star tattoo is upside down. Odd place for that, isn't it? On the palm?

"Yes it is," Salma acknowledged. "They wear away quickly. That's why gang members don't tattoo there, nor does anyone else really."

"Yet yours looks fresh," Hayden pointed out. "In fact I thought it was only a quarter full."

Kael became defensive, and clenched his left hand to hide the pentagram.

"Best show us, son," David ordered.

Dropping his gaze and looking away, Kael delayed a moment before raising his right hand.

"Your other one," Evelyn called out, surprising Hayden with her veracity against him. "You don't have to be ashamed of it, and you shouldn't hide it."

"Now I mean it," David declared. "Just what is it you two are into?"

"Those vampire rats David tried to incinerate are gone," Hayden added. "Not burnt down, but gone, as if someone dug them out. It had to be at night. And the site where David disposed of his cow appears disturbed. Someone in this house went out there and came back. I saw those prints. I just don't know who. Evelyn, you said something kept

155

vampires from spreading before. I'm curious what makes you think that?"

"Because obviously they didn't," Evelyn shouted, her face turning red. "First morning after we got here I went out to the grove. Nature's part of our religion. I prayed out there, and I saw those rats. I was going to go back later to be sure they got hit with the sun. But little baby there-" she slapped Wanda with the label "-pitched a fucking fit over the fact she got better. She's so guilty over her son that I guess she wants to die instead, but that didn't happen. I don't know!"

"The rats," a cold Hayden reminded her, though he noted Wanda breaking down in silent weeping.

"I went out there next day, and they were gone," Evelyn answered. "You're probably right, that someone picked them up at night. I don't know who'd want to, but that's what must've happened."

"That's not good enough," Hayden stated, with a slow shake of his head.

"Hey," Nick ventured. "I saw her go out that first morning. She was worried about the Judds not approving of her, whatever she believes in, and so I kept it to myself."

"That was the first time," David stated with a prosecutor's logic. "By her own admission, she went out a second time, but no one seems to have noticed."

"What?" Nick turned to him jerking his head back, bewildered. "At night? Don'cha think we'd notice someone opening up that door of yours?"

156

"Unless she did something to all of us to make everyone sleep through it," Wanda accused.

"Oh God!" Hayden rolled his head toward her, and then remembered David and Anh. "Sorry about that. Just that–"

"I told y'all I heard worse," David recalled. "Just that I and the wife don't use that language."

"The idea of using sleeping potions or what-the-fuck-ever does sound farfetched," Nick said.

"Dead people running around killing is farther fetched," Salma put forth with emphasis.

"I don't believe this," Isaac pointedly declared to everyone else as he started walking through the middle of them, eyeing each one in turn. "We don't got enough shit goin' on that now we gotta have some kind of damned lynching party. What'cha all gonna do next? Burn them at the stake?"

"That's an interesting idea," Wanda teased with a malicious grin, as though dangling keys before a prisoner. "Or we could all take a little trip to the river. If she drowns we'll all know I was wrong."

"We sure as hell aren't going there!" Hayden suddenly shifted his advocacy, brows high with adamant resistance to the notion. "Isaac's right. I don't feel like reliving the Salem Witch Trials. Even those vampires out there aren't so bad that they screw each other over like that."

Hayden stabbing a finger out the window appeared to bring down the tone for the majority, though the case so far still didn't look good for Evelyn and Kael.

157

"Until we know for sure I can't have you in this house," David announced.

"Whoa," Isaac again stood in the middle of it with a hand out to David. "Now hold the fuck on. We can't just be leavin' people out in the night to get torn to shit."

"It's my house, son." David's blunt tone visibly jarred Isaac. "I took y'all in, 'cause that's the Christian thing to do. But if y'all gonna bring the devil in here I can't accept the risk."

"Wait, wait, wait," Nick stepped forward mirroring Isaac's gesture. "David, you don't want to do that. I'm sure if these two were pullin' shit they'd have fucked us a week ago."

"I don't want to throw anyone out in the middle of all this," David said. "But I can't have them in the shelter with us until I know what all they doin'."

"I'm sure they'll be fine," Wanda hissed with sarcastic sting. "Evelyn's got enough batteries."

"What?" Hayden shot, turning around.

"Oh yeah," Wanda continued to stoke the fire. "There's a huge stockpile down there."

"That doesn't mean shit!" Kael shouted back, after shaking off the brief surprise.

"I agree," Hayden added, again crossing the battle lines. "I've seen a few witch movies, myself, and I don't recall a battery curse in any of them."

"You could break them open," Wanda suggested. "Aren't batteries toxic?"

"Not since some bunch of tree-huggers demanded they be safer to dispose of," Hayden stated, revealing his own political slant. "Sure, the

158

alkali materials are bad for you, but it's not an ideal poison. Besides, have you ever tried to bust one of those open? It's not easy."

"You know, Wanda. If all you wanted was a recharge for your vibrator all you had to do was say so," Evelyn remarked off-the-cuff with a side-to-side bob of her head. "Since your chicken shit husband isn't here to satisfy your need to replace your kid."

"Fuck you," Wanda screamed so loud everyone but Evelyn recoiled, and then stormed out. "Fucking witch! Fuck you! I hope those goddamn things suck you dry!"

"Jesus Christ," a stunned Nick let slip, turning to her. "Talk about stickin' it in and breakin' it off."

"That was not helpful," Hayden explained, with brows arched high in warning.

"You can be in here during the day, so long as someone's watchin' you two," David announced his final judgment on the matter. "But not at night. You can get your things out of there if y'all want to, but it's gotta be done before nightfall."

"I'm sorry, Mr. Judd," Isaac said to the older man. "But if you's leavin' them out, then I go out with them. This shit's not right, and you know it."

"Me too," Nick stated as he stood to Isaac's side. "You guys don't need that many shooters in your little bunker. If you need us, wait until dawn before you knock on one of those trucks out there."

"Alright then," David nodded, looking to feel bad about it, but not showing regret. David and Anh went into the bedroom Evelyn mentioned. Hayden noticed that, true to Evelyn's description, the room

159

was repaneled and lit up with colors revealing that the late sun was shining through stained windows.

"Well," Evelyn said, as she descended to the main floor. "I guess it's off to witch's prison."

"Ah," Hayden addressed the matter directly. "Lyn, I'm sorry. I didn't want it to come to this."

"Right, I'm sure," Evelyn uttered, sounding irritated with a hint of hurt. "You just got them thinking I'm trying to mutate everyone into fucking vampires. Yeah, thanks a lot, Hayden."

* * *

"Lyn!" Valerie shouted, as she headed for the front door with Kael, Isaac and Nick.

"Get into the shelter, Val," Evelyn called back, eyeing the last sliver of the sun over the horizon.

"We did this before, we can handle it again," Isaac assured her, as he went for the other truck.

The rest climbed into the one Hayden brought, and Isaac pulled the other around to be parked sideways at the back of the first. Then Isaac came through the cab into the back, and locked the door. Inside, Evelyn turned on a camping light, and noticed Nick and Isaac studying Kael's mark.

"You guys said that was related to the sun," Nick recalled. "But I think it's a moon."

"It is," Evelyn admitted. "But what is moonlight but albedo from the sun."

"Why didn't you tell us that before," Isaac asked.

"Let's just say we haven't had a lot of good luck around Christians," Kael answered.

160

"Yea, but it's the twenty-first century, man," Isaac said.

"And here we sit," Nick pointed out. "This shit's always gonna be with us."

"Kael and I belong to a unique pagan tradition," Evelyn began. "It's not Wiccan. Everywhere else people see the sun as making things warm, growing the crops, heralding the bounty of spring and saving people from winter. But the sun can't be there all the time. So we tell ourselves that the sun made mankind a promise to protect us even at night."

Kael raised his left palm to emphasize the point.

"Yeah, but his tattoo, if that's what it is, didn't look like that before," Nick said.

"And what is with them batteries?" Isaac asked, "I don't recall seeing you pick that many up during this entire time. In fact, you had that bag before shit all went crazy."

"All that's a little tougher to explain," Evelyn gave her guarded answer, and then realized that being here with her and Kael, they deserved better. "I knew about these things long before the outbreak. Kael would have learned had he stayed with the group. I came out here to bring him home."

"Wait," Isaac stayed her at that point. "You knew about this shit before?"

"I didn't know all the scientific details Hayden and, apparently, the World Health Organization figured out," Evelyn admitted. "But yeah, I knew. I'm not just a member of our pagan

161

religion, but a high priestess of it. There are nine of us. Kael was raised to be a kind of bodyguard."

"People been putting swords'n shit in my hands since I could walk," Kael revealed. "Being enrolled in martial arts when I was eight wasn't a lie. They don't enlist us in the military because they won't take people with tattoos that are visible below the shoulder."

"And of course guns have their limitations," Evelyn added.

"Why, why would you need a bodyguard," Nick asked, and then specified. "I mean before now?"

"Other than since the third century A.D.?" Evelyn asked the question that was redundant to her and Kael. "It's also to protect us from vampires, though they weren't called that until recent times. It's the original form of chivalry; defending priestesses. That's the mark for their order."

"It seemed stupid in modern times, so I took off," Kael jumped in, and cast a scornful look to Evelyn before going on. "Apparently, there's a final rite where they explain that I gotta fight off dead fuckers. The mark is supposed to empower me to do that."

Evelyn noted that Kael wasn't yet comfortable explaining the rest, so she didn't.

"I guess the batteries are for lights, then," Nick assumed, which she let go for now.

"They're important, yes. Enough so that I use them as offerings during prayers."

"Anything else you wanna share?" Nick asked with an expectant expression.

"I don't know who those robed people are," Evelyn admitted her ignorance. "But I can only assume that's who picked up the vampire rats. Who knows what they'd want with them."

"There's some sick mothahs out there," Isaac nodded seriously. "That's for damn sure."

"And there's a lion," Evelyn included after remembering the prints.

"Yeah, David told us about hearing it," Nick said.

"It gets closer to the house than he thinks," Evelyn revealed. "It might just be staking territory, if it's a living lion, but honestly I wouldn't expect it to survive long."

"What if it's dead?" Kael asked, himself no more familiar with vampires than the others.

"Then it's doing what the rest do," Evelyn replied, "Though it still will do lion things."

"Hayden thinks your stuff was like what he pulled out of the vampires he has," Kael said. "Why would he think that?"

"I don't know," Evelyn forthrightly answered, shaking her head. "I mean the only thing they'd be weirded out by is the use of spider webs...."

"What?" Isaac asked.

Evelyn had stopped all of a sudden with a serious stare at the floor.

"I was just remembering him pulling material out of that rat corpse's veins," Evelyn recalled, her mind back at that moment and seeing everything at the time. "He thought it was the source of the vampires' strength. It was stretchy and hard to cut—like spider silk."

163

"Well, that's all fascinating," Nick grunted, as he shifted to lie down. "But, we should sleep and be sure not to snore. And hope vampires got better people to suck down than us."

Isaac and Kael followed his lead, and Evelyn at last leaned back while pulling the blanket close. Despite her concern about being outside at night, she drifted into sleep after a few minutes. However, it only felt like an hour before her eyes opened wide.

Something dragged against the wall of the truck, which if Evelyn had to guess, was a hand. She lightly tapped Kael, who was closest, with her foot. He stirred, but quietly, as instilled into him from childhood. He sized up the room, since the light remained on, and then slipped out two lawn pegs into knife-fighting holds. He rose up, while Evelyn awoke the others, one at a time, with her hand over each of their mouths to keep them silent.

Then she heard the passenger side door open. A subtle squeak ensued from a weight being applied to a seat, and then the sound of it relaxing. Something thumped lightly, as if by accident with a knee or foot. After that the handle on the door to the back clicked stiffly. Next came a grind Evelyn knew meant more force than mortal man could exert.

But the lock held.

Isaac drew back a crossbow string deliberately slowly while staring at the door. Nick slid out an arrow, careful not to make noise, and notched it in a bow with a faint stretching creak of the fiberglass. Evelyn palmed a battery before selecting a green plastic stake between her fingertips.

Then the noise stopped, and the intruder reversed the sequence of disturbing noises on the way out, minus closing the cab door. Evelyn heard only a couple steps leading toward the house. Throwing a look to the others, she then went for the door and strained to unlock it in silence. Opening it just a crack, she peeked through to be sure other vampires hadn't entered.

It was always told that they heard no better in death than before, and that no supernatural stealth followed crossing into the shadow side. Evelyn found nothing, and dared open the door wide enough to see out the truck windshield. Indeed a human form of immaculate physique in a tattered wedding dress strolled toward the house, dragging a sledge hammer as if it were a sadistic surprise.

"She might be able to take down the shelter door," Isaac breathed below a whisper right next to Evelyn's ear. "I think we need to do something."

Nick gestured to get past them both into the cab, and so they made way. He didn't strike Evelyn as having ever been a soldier, but Nick did carry himself as someone familiar with shootouts as well as stealthy evasion. Crawling into the cab below dashboard level, Nick rose up just enough to look out the side windows and check the mirrors. However, he couldn't look under the truck, and that concept became terrifying to Evelyn.

The dead bride entered the house after opening the unlocked door, giving the four of them an opening to exit. As Nick crept out the open door, Isaac went next and Kael after that. Before Evelyn climbed out she went back to her bag for the ceremonial knife called an Athame. Unlike classical Celtic tradition or modern Wicca, her sect granted the artifact one additional purpose.

Once Evelyn had both boots on browned winter grass, she stood behind Kael and pressed the knife handle into his clutched hand. He slipped one of the pegs away to take the blade from her. Then Evelyn put her own lawn peg into a back pocket and brought up her bow and an arrow. The three men scanned the immediate area for more unpleasant surprises.

They watched the white gowned creature survey the front room. She seemed to notice something on the floor which then led her to the white door concealing the shelter stairs. Opening that, the vampire descended with a nerve-racking slow pace, and the hammer banged loud onto each step. A moment after she was out of sight there thundered a huge bang of steel on steel. Evelyn jolted in place, and froze as if she herself were stunned by a blow. A second slamming of the shelter door followed, and then a third.

The four of them trotted toward the house, but avoided stepping onto hard cement until running out of lawn. Evelyn placed a soft hand on Kael's shoulder, causing him to straighten up momentarily and study their surroundings again with a new perspective that he lacked a moment ago. As a defender, one of the Marked, he was nearing his peak time, but that was days yet.

As with the first time they had come to the Judds' house, Nick and Isaac each leaned a shoulder just beyond the doorframe. Kael pressed Evelyn

166

against the wall to his rear, as he fell behind Isaac. Isaac pointed to the side Nick couldn't see and showed a thumbs-up, allowing Nick to enter. However, as the rest stepped in, Nick reached back for the open door and gave the barest rap of a knuckle.

The hammering stopped.

Wooden groans slowly ascended with the sledge again banging each time.

Evelyn wanted to press knuckles into her teeth, but needed to draw the bow back, as Nick was doing. When the dress and the corpse in it entered view, Evelyn saw the contrast from the virgin white of the back, when it had gone into the house. A blackened horror of dried blood covered most of her front from the jaw down. Nearest the center of the woman's delicate frame glistened signs of a fresh victim.

In the dark of starlight from the window Evelyn couldn't see eyes, just two shadowy pits. They were joined by a third abyss when the vampire saw them and screamed hoarsely. Raising the hammer, she ran at them, but Isaac squeezed his trigger, while Nick and Evelyn let go of their bow strings. Evelyn ensured all three shots made their mark, and the corpse turned limp in an instant, tumbling to the floor. The arrows pushed through her back, and the sledge hammer clattered loudly on the hardwood floor.

"I'm going to check around outside," Nick whispered. "You guys stay in here and watch out."

"I ain't lettin' you go alone," Isaac insisted.

"Thanks, man," Nick accepted with a light tap against Isaac's upper arm.

After the two of them left, Kael moved up next to the door and became even more edgy. He frequently looked outside and then surveyed the interior again, as though surrounded by danger.

That's when Evelyn heard the shelter door handle crack and the door open.

Kael moved around her, and squared off with the empty opening toward the stairs. Evelyn noticed Kael's grip on the motley combination of weapons tighten. She notched another arrow, and the impulse to do that left her conflicted. The feet coming up the stairs this time were more tentative, but Kael ushered Evelyn out the front door anyway.

Back outside and tucked against the wall next to the front door, she found it easier to see. A slight pickup in the breeze startled Evelyn. She knew it meant a moment of diminished capacity to hear what approached. A dark lump appeared on the opposite side of the house, from where Nick had departed. Once it emerged in full form from around the corner, the weak outline of Nick's bow brought assurance. Isaac's shadow came around next.

Inside, meanwhile, the steps neared the wide open front door. Evelyn couldn't imagine who would be coming out from safety like this. Wanda's distraught face popped into Evelyn's mind. Could she be so devastated about her husband and son as to throw her life away?

Nick seemed to register what Evelyn heard and gestured for Isaac to stop as he did. That the person stepped around the felled vampire bride in

168

the front room scared Evelyn as much as the idea the shelter was now open to whatever wished to crawl in there and bring havoc.

When a pallid hand gripped the doorway Evelyn's jaw dropped into an unheard scream contorting her entire face. The hand was small enough for her to know it wasn't Wanda. And then the rest of the female form emerged devoid of clothes. In a flash it turned its soulless gaze on Kael, and lunged for him that instant. He tumbled back into Evelyn and they both fell onto the porch under the force of the creature's charge. Evelyn only just thought to turn her bow and arrow away to avoid stabbing it into Kael's back, but otherwise was pinned from any action.

Angry grunts and rasps, of a mouth that didn't bother to draw in breath to vocalize, were drowned out by Kael's cursing and the hard bumps against the house as they wrestled. Evelyn heard a knife drawn, and then caught a glimpse of Nick behind the lithe female corpse. A sick wet puncturing sound brought quiet from the ravenous body. Kael threw it off in panic, and then rolled atop it to drive his own plastic stake into the thing's chest.

Maybe it was out of habit, or for following up by cutting the thing's head off, but Nick had drawn his own knife out. Isaac stayed by the door to cover the inside. Nick pushed Kael away to cut off the vampire's head with two sets of sawing actions and a stab he twisted into the spinal column.

Evelyn finally got up, and looked down at the headless, undersized but monstrous human form. It took her a minute to recognize Janelle Harrington,

Hayden's American born and American died specimen. Her pristine arms and legs had been restored completely, as if she always had them.

Chapter 8: Dark Desires.

"Hayden," he heard Isaac call to him through the door to the storage room, one of three around the main room of the shelter. "Hayden, who's all in there with you? You guys alright?"

After the banging on the main door to the house, and the screaming event, Hayden dared not believe that the four banished to the security trucks had made it. Checking his watch, his discovered it wasn't even midnight yet.

"We're not asking you to let us in," Evelyn spoke at the door loud enough to carry through. "Just let us know how many of you got in safe. Hayden, your second specimen came after us out on the front porch. Are you listening? Its arms and legs came back. It fed on someone, Hayden."

David and Anh in the next room had been there all night, and they too weren't answering. Looking behind himself to Valeria and Salma, Hayden put his finger to his lips. Then he slowly put his head to the doorknob and closed his eyes.

When it had started, he ushered everyone he saw into the storage room. The lights were off, so he just threw the door open and let every shadow of living humanity run through that he saw. Hayden didn't know who had gone in and who hadn't. Not hearing anyone else left, he figured them all inside and stepped in last. After he turned on the overhead light he realized who was missing.

By then Hayden had heard the stairs door open and gritted his teeth and pounded a fist in air several times, angry at himself and at the fact that door remained open to his memory of what he heard. The main room could be filled with vampires, and only two were talking. He couldn't know.

"We can't lock the door from outside, Hayden," Isaac said. "But we'll close it behind us."

It was maybe three or four sets of steps that left the main shelter room. Not hearing anything else, Hayden none the less kept quiet and waved both hands down to Salma and Valerie. They went to one corner of box-lined walls and huddled up together for the night. Unsure how he could sleep, Hayden did eventually drift off after a couple hours.

Hayden awoke again to the sound of his watch alarm. It was dawn, or maybe past that, since he'd neglected to keep up on growing day cycles. Valerie moaned before waking, and clutched at him, before she realized only living people occupied the room.

Unsure if he'd brought the spear gun, Hayden nonetheless saw it leaning against the wall by the door with a crossbow. He then guessed that Salma had the sense of mind to grab weapons. Hayden picked his up, while Salma drew back the crossbow and signaled for Valerie to get behind the door to open it. Valerie hesitated for a long minute, which Hayden understood, for he wasn't so sure about leaving either. However, he knew they'd have to sooner or later, and better that they try to in the day.

When the door opened slowly, Hayden saw nothing dead waiting to lunge in. Salma ventured out first, making Hayden feel a surge of shame, before he followed to watch her back. A sound of fabric moving made him jump, as he and Salma aimed at a sleeping bag piled up by the opposite wall. They made pensive steps toward it, hoping their footfalls didn't sound as noisy as Hayden seemed to hear.

Everything sounded louder, Hayden realized, when he was scared out of his wits.

He went over to flip on the lights, and re-joined the woman cop, with Valerie staying in the storage room. Salma kept more visibly calm, when she took her supporting hand off her weapon to reach for the topmost sleeping bag. She ripped it off and jumped back ready to shoot. Under it was another sleeping bag, but the scream that her action caused rang in Hayden's ears with familiarity.

"Wanda? Is that you," Hayden asked, and regretted saying anything that instant. Foolish, he thought, until Wanda threw back the rest of the bedding to see Hayden and Salma. With her hands up, Wanda shook with uncontrolled terror. However, Hayden and Salma both lowered their weapons in relief. Next, the door to the Judds' underground bedroom opened, giving all three a brief start. David, too, had his crossbow ready for whatever might've lurked at the other side.

"Is this everybody?" Hayden asked looking around.

"Just me and David in here," Anh answered from behind the door she opened for her husband.

"Where's Hyun Jae?" Valerie asked, coming out into the main room searching.

"Hyun!" Wanda shouted louder, making Hayden cringe.

He came over to her in a crouch and said, "Not so loud. They can still be the house above."

"Sorry," Wanda quickly apologized.

Recalling what he was told last night, Hayden went to the other room where his equipment and the vampires were kept. Except one gurney was bare save for a few smears of blood. To Hayden the traces appeared to have been licked at. The Alina Galca specimen still appeared motionless under the sheets. Lifting those carefully, he found that it in fact was perfectly still, and there was no sign of renewal to its four stumps. The gag remained in place also.

David had set himself up for the door to the stairs, and Anh dutifully readied to clear his line of fire. Hayden rushed to stand alongside him and Salma; however he didn't quite get in place before Anh did her thing. Nothing stood behind that door either.

Hayden approached the threshold before anyone else and aimed the spear gun up the stairs. Indirect rays of blessed morning shone down, giving him perfect clarity while checking for vampires hiding from the sun. He led the six survivors up the stairs, and found bloody drag marks in the front room leading straight to the front door.

Without fear from that direction, Hayden threw open the door to discover the blood trail ended at a heap of a freshly burnt corpse. He guessed from the ruined mass that it has been a woman wearing a dress. Off to the side a couple yards were a couple more charred masses of vampiric flesh, one small enough to be a severed head.

"We should check to see if they got into the trucks," Salma said to Hayden's back.

"I gotta find Hyun first," he answered, and went back into the house.

They split off to check all over the house. Hayden went up the stairs by himself feeling a need to bone up on his virility. Wanda was perfectly fine with standing outside clutching herself, until she knew the house was free of vampires.

"Hyun?" Hayden ensured his voice carried throughout the entire floor. "You up here?"

"So pretty," Hyun's voice, making Hayden stop in his tracks to listen.

It seemed like it came from the one-room chapel, which a tentative Hayden neared. One-handing his spear gun, Hayden reached his entire left side out to open the door. It was still relatively gloomy inside, given that the room was on the west side of the house. He saw no one inside, however, and ventured on into the chapel room hoping to catch Hyun's direction when next she spoke.

"Hayden," David hollered up the stairs, "We ain't found nothin' down here."

Turning around in the room, Hayden sized the place up in a whisper, "This is kind've nice."

"I so pretty now," Hayden heard Hyun Jae say. "So pretty I get husband."

"Shit," Hayden breathed to himself, closing his eyes and raising his head in angst.

175

The closet Hyun Jae had hidden in was to Hayden's back. And he heard it open slowly. Whirling about on his heel, Hayden was just fast enough to see the small woman in air right toward his face. Both of them fell to the floor hard enough that Hayden was winded and the deathly pale Hyun atop him.

"I get husband," Hyun Jae rasped with a gurgle, her opaque eyed glaring at Hayden from between a curtain of black locks, lips drawn to expose newly forged killing teeth, as she clutched at him. "Husband! Mother say only pretty girls get husband. I pretty now! You see!"

"Help!" Hayden screamed with a shrill, as he wrestled to get the spear gun free.

"Pretty! Blood so pretty," Hyun's corpse hungrily insisted, and she snapped at Hayden's neck.

It took Hayden everything he had to keep the tiny form back, and that included him getting a leg free to continually knee at her light body. Hyun kept pulling Hayden's arms down from their barring position, but before she could land those cutting teeth he managed to get his guard up. He felt that mouth full of razors latch into his forearm, and he let loose another scream.

Then Hyun's body just went limp after momentarily pressing down on him in a thump.

"Next time you don't accuse us of being in a goddamn satanic cult, asshole," Kael's voice shouted, as he pulled the fully dead Hyun off Hayden. "By the way, you're welcome!"

Hayden eyed his bleeding arm, while Nick and Isaac helped him up. On his feet again, Hayden gazed down at Hyun Jae's body along with everyone else, minus Wanda who wasn't present.

"Shit," Nick cursed, sounding more disappointed than upset. "Poor girl."

"When do you think it happened?" Salma asked, looking to the others.

"I don't know," Hayden huffed, shaking his head. "God help me, I should've watched her closer."

"What do you mean?" Nick asked, as he stared at Hayden from behind.

"She was obsessing over how beautiful she thought the two specimens I had were," Hayden explained. "She told me once her mother kept saying she was ugly and wouldn't get married. After Brad tried to kill Wanda, I kinda lost it with her and blew my stack."

Grief ambushed Hayden at that point, and his face pinched before tears flowed.

With a sharp vocal intake, Hayden reached up to cover his mouth and turned away. Had he not been so upset, Hayden would've been surprised to find Evelyn embracing him and providing a shoulder to cry on. She also teared up while squeezing him, and he heard Valerie start sobbing through her hands.

"If you guys want," Nick spoke softer than Hayden thought possible for the outlaw. "We can arrange a burial out in that wooded area. We won't let her burn up until then."

Evelyn guided Hayden down to the dining room and consoled him, while Anh brought him and Valerie some water and handkerchiefs. She set about to bandage his wound but stopped.

"Are you alright with me using this?" Evelyn checked.

"Yeah, I'm sure it's safe," Hayden dully answered.

"I think I know what it was you were worried about," Evelyn commented, as she applied the powder and began wrapping his arm. "Spider silk. That's part of my recipe."

That seemed important, but Hayden let the thought go, to focus on his memory of Hyun Jae as a living woman dreaming of being a software engineer. Isaac, Nick and David set out to dig a plot away from the other scenes of vampire carnage. After wiping down the gurney that had formerly held the vampire Janelle, they used it to bring Hyun's covered body out. David conducted the funerary service at around noon, offering readings from a large ornate bible.

Then the many sheets were pulled back, so that the sun could ensure Hyun found everlasting rest in the Earth, before Nick and Isaac began covering it up. Going back into the house, everyone noticed the hurry with which Wanda went down to the shelter and returned with all her things.

"Hold up," Isaac said, "Where you goin'?"

"The hell away from here," she shot hotly.

"You all don't wanna take more than that," Isaac offered. "I'll get you the keys to the truck if you want. We'll break out some food and a couple weapons too."

"I don't know how to drive those," Wanda stated without looking at anyone while she packed extra food and crossbow bolts into her bags.

"Wait there, girl," David stepped forth, fishing out his own keys. He took one off to offer her. "It ain't much to look at, but the gas mileage's alright, an' she kinda fast too."

Wanda first just looked at the ignition key David was giving her. She appeared unwilling to take it, but then allowed him to place it in her palm with appreciation. "Thank you for being so nice to me."

Isaac offered her a crossbow, which she did accept before heading out the front door. The group followed her out, minus David, who went somewhere else into the house. As Wanda opened the garage and put her things in the car gifted to her, David came back out with an automatic colt pistol and its holster together in both hands.

"What's this for?" Wanda asked, as David raised it out toward her in offering.

"It ain't just dead folks who're dangerous," David said, and then turned a glance toward Evelyn with some remorse. "Though, I ain't always right about who that might be."

"Thanks," Wanda said, and put the weapon on the passenger seat with the other, before hugging David tight. "I'm sorry we caused you so much trouble."

"No, no," David said, hugging her back.

"Wanda," Evelyn called out, as Hayden turned toward her. "I didn't mean what I said."

"I'm sorry too." Wanda traded apologies, though Hayden wondered how heartfelt hers was.

Closing the passenger door, Wanda then went around to the other side and got in. She started the engine and pulled back with an arm over the seat and head turned to see. Once reaching the road, she waved at them all again, and backed into a turn before driving off at normal speed.

Half the group jumped, Hayden himself, when his phone's Vincent Price laugh sounded off.

"Man," Isaac scolded animatedly. "Change that goddamn ring tone, will 'ya!"

"Yeah?" Hayden answered into his phone.

"You haven't updated your online observations in a while," an unfamiliar voice said. "Hay-Corn."

"If you're with whoever hired us, now is not a good time," Hayden said back.

"Of course it's not a good time," the voice remarked. "It never is. That's why we're calling. It hasn't been smooth sailing where we're at either. They only just solved the problems aboard here."

"Sailing? Aboard?" Hayden posed the two single-worded questions. "And what is 'here' anyway? Are you on a ship or something?"

"Don't worry about that," the voice admonished.

"Well, if it helps you, I think the stuff is a complicated version of spider-silk or something along those lines," Hayden reported, though wishing he could hang up. "I could post a few formulas for the functional groups, and a rough guess of the monomer connections. But I'm surprised anyone had that kind of time to spare going online to see what I think."

"Have you checked your following lately?" the voice asked.

"Sort of," Hayden said quieter, and paused. "Hey, ah, look. We just lost a couple people, okay? Can't this wait? It's not like I really care about getting a paycheck at this point."

"We need you to investigate something for us," the voice demanded, as cold as before.

"Really," Hayden started. "It's not a good time. There's some bunch of people who appear interested in collecting vampire rats and we might have a lion that's turned and roaming around."

"It's on that first thing that we want to check," the voice said. "There's some structure a few blocks from your lab that people are gathering toward a few hours before dusk."

"Uh," Hayden said, unconsciously turning from everyone else. "We're not in the city anymore. Don't you have people? A military squad or something? Living people are going after each other, and I'm not sure the cities are that safe while the sun's up. Plus, getting much information and getting back out before dark isn't going to be easy."

"Isn't there a shorter way for you to say no?" the voice chided.

"Cute," Hayden said to the new stranger he was starting to like more than the last, which is to say not at all. "Okay, just give us a while, please. Is there a number I can reach you at? My phone isn't showing yours. Give us an address and we'll try in a few days."

Instead of an address, the caller gave him references from the lab and a building description as though it were seen from above. It made Hayden think they were on a military vessel and using satellites to see what happened on the mainland. The person refused to provide a return number, and instead said that they would call back in two days.

"Those them people you was workin' for?" David asked.

"Yeah," Hayden admitted, putting his phone away. "There's something they're curious about."

"But not so curious they get off they's ass and look for themselves," Isaac doubted.

"I don't know, but I think they're on a ship," Hayden said, shaking his head. "He hinted that they just had a bunch of problems. I'm curious to see what those might've been."

* * *

Evelyn heard Hayden call out from David's hobby room, "Everyone, in here quick!"

Inside the greenhouse near the door, Evelyn had been helping Anh water plants and checking on what, if anything could be harvested around the end of the day. Being late February, that was mostly herbs, some of which Anh told Evelyn were from Vietnam.

Evelyn went back inside to see what had excited Hayden. Once everyone else other than Anh had gathered around the large monitor – which David said was necessary for his eyes, though

Evelyn had her doubts – Hayden selected play for a news video.

"What's this?" she asked, as she saw sleet wash over asphalt through an unsteady camera.

"It's the *John C. Stennis*," Hayden said. "An aircraft carrier, and I think it's around the Florida Keys. I'd read somewhere that it was being refitted for all-electronic power. The stated idea was to detect problems with *Gerald Ford* and *John F Kennedy* carriers before they went into service, but I've always suspected they were in fact making it the test bed for a fourteen kilowatt laser."

"Ur, okay..—." Evelyn drew out, unsure why that was interesting.

A reporter that Evelyn recalled from an earlier news announcement stepped into view, amid a number of men in camouflage with body armor and rifles. She first described incidences of dolphins hurling themselves out of the water to attack sailors on the deck. What stunned Evelyn was that this took place while other dolphins were purportedly using sound to attack the ship directly. They said there were some cases of metal fatigue on the outer hull and steam pipes to the turbines bursting.

"Dolphins can do that?" an incredulous Evelyn asked.

"It's in the WHO materials I got downstairs," Hayden said. "Seems even normal bottlenose dolphins can exceed the maximum capacity for sound. Of course the default form of waste energy is heat, and so pressure on pipes near the ship's propulsion screws grew until something gave."

"But, you said living dolphins," Isaac iterated. "These're vampire ones. They don't breathe."

"All other vampires use their lungs for sucking. I guess these keep their lungs from filling with water to keep their original buoyancy. Though they make sound with this stuff in their foreheads in some way, they don't have to let out air to do it. But here's the point of the video."

It was night, but many bright lights lit up the entire surface of the floating city, and helped keep visibility in the rather angry storm. A couple of minutes passed before Hayden's interest manifested itself. When the ship was stationary in the storm, the camera picked up the sight more than a hundred yards away of someone climbing to the flight deck. The reporter commented on the fact that the ship's hull curved out from the water line, and that no handhold was possible for multiple stories worth of smooth steel.

However, Evelyn noticed something stretched along the blacktop off the edge.

From the yelling over the weather by flightline crews, she gathered that a cable of some sort had come loose or broken and was being blown about. The sailors rushed toward it alongside the armed men that the reporter identified as marines. Shooting began, but the pallid bodies that might as well have come from a ghost ship, persisted in their advance on the living. Most of the clothes they wore were shredded as though each person had been attacked by chainsaws. Many appeared to have once worked at sea themselves.

Some of the human vampires ran for other sailors who tried to retreat to the ship's interior. Two of the hatches didn't close in time, and vampires forced them open to grab men and some women, whoever was closest. Other vampires entered the ship to get those still fleeing. This as a couple dolphins vampires lunged much further out of the water than anything Evelyn had imagined at an oceanarium performance. However, one suddenly caught fire without anything appearing to touch it.

"That's fourteen kilowatts," Hayden exclaimed with a victorious pointing finger.

The thing flipped and thrashed to get around on the deck with more strength than living dolphins would've had. Yet firefighter crews counterattacked with high pressure hoses, and blasted the partially cooked horror back into the water.

"It was still moving," Evelyn observed.

"Yeah," Hayden agreed. "But it's off the ship, and I guess that's all they're worried about."

"So what was the point of this?" Isaac asked.

"Those people who called me are probably on that ship or another one," Hayden said.

"So they're the government or military," Evelyn speculated.

"Maybe, or they're a contractor for one or both," Hayden offered.

"Great," Evelyn sneered. "Training live dolphins wasn't enough. Now they want to make vampires into weapons. Same old shit."

"Maybe a weapon against other vampires," Nick speculated. "At least that I can make sense of."

185

"At first," Kael said flatly.

"Alright everybody," David's fathering tone echoed throughout the house. "Gotta wrap it up."

Evelyn hesitated halfway to the shelter, but an expression of conciliation on the elderly man's face reinforced his prior admission that he'd misjudged her and Kael.

Isaac and David entered last, stopping to look over the door that the bride of death had attacked in the night. Its outside surface was scratched and dented as if were lumpy dough, but otherwise it still closed and locked. Isaac mentioned the need to possibly find replacements, but that would have to wait.

David and Anh took up their nightly ritual of reading their Bible together. Nick, Isaac, Salma and even Valerie engaged in a poker game, with Valerie still learning the ropes. However, Salma and Nick stole glances from each other to suggest something more endearing. Hayden disappeared into his makeshift lab, though Evelyn wondered if he should be alone after what had happened.

About to get up after leaving texts on her phone, Evelyn was stopped by Kael, who showed her the palm of his left hand. The mark had filled completely, meaning that one way or the other everyone would know the full scope of what it meant. And they had just patched things up with David and Hayden.

Yet, Evelyn still wanted to check on Hayden, and walked up to the closed door to the room. After a light knock she heard Hayden ask her in. He wasn't working on anything. Instead, he sat atop two crates, one on top of the other, and stared at the now bare gurney.

"You holding up okay?" Evelyn asked, leaning forward to peek at his face.

"Not really a choice, is it," Hayden intoned with resignation, and waved at the gurney while adding, "We either hold up or we become like them. Time's on their side, you know."

"It's not certain," Evelyn contested. "We have the sun. The days are getting longer."

"Until dusk? Until autumn?" Hayden asked. "That's what will always be waiting for us. Get sloppy, get depressed … or just unlucky and bam! They get us."

He slapped one hand against another so hard Evelyn jumped inwardly, but didn't show it when speaking, "It's always been like that, Hayden. That's what made us, all people. We always feared the night, dreaded the coming of winter and suffered through all of it. And that's before street lights and before cops. Way back to the first villages and cities, we walled ourselves away from nature."

"Weird," a confounded Hayden said, turning to her. "I would've expected pagans to tell me how wonderful nature is. Go out and talk to trees or visit with animal friends."

"There is that too," Evelyn explained. "But it doesn't mean pretending the thorns aren't there."

"And those," Hayden's bitter question seethed as he shock a finger at the remaining human vampire. "One more thorn we have to put up with?"

"Hayden, the group Kael and I belong to didn't put up with them," Evelyn revealed through a

187

tone elevating in rhythm and strength. "We dealt with them, or at least as best we could. We didn't have all the techno stuff of today. But we figured out how to get by with things that go bump in the night, and maybe knock one or two of them flat on their ass!"

Hayden was about to say something, until a distant clank sounded.

"What was that?" Nick was heard asking from the next room, as he rose up from his chair.

Evelyn rushed out into the main room with Hayden behind her. A groan from Kael brought from Evelyn a quick glance. He looked sore all over. Something outside the shelter door had become curious as to what lay inside. Metal cracks and clatters suggested something being applied to the door. With the noises issued the soft chuckle of a malicious prankster.

In the house above, Evelyn heard more footsteps enter, drawing everyone's attention upward. But the sound of an entire bank of windows shattering and a deep throaty rumbling told of something more formidable than the usual brand of terrors shaped as people.

Kael's pains got more people's attention, and Hayden silently dropped down on one knee to get a closer look at him. However, the yellow cast of his eyes caused Hayden to pull back quickly.

"Nick," Hayden yelled, forgetting the troubles outside.

Going for his bundle of weapons, Nick brought forth the twin-barreled monster pistol and his bowie knife for good measure. Evelyn jumped over to stand between him and Kael with her hand out to him, and then another out at Hayden, "Don't! Just let me explain!"

"Shit," Kael's rougher voice grated. "Gawd, every fuckin' time!"

"Nick, Isaac, grab him," Hayden called out to the others, and dared approach Kael to roughly seize his upper arms. "We'll just put him in the storage room until we know what the hell's going on!"

Then a ratcheting sound started, and David's seeming invincible barrier to the darkness gave way in a slow inward bowing. Kael flailed weakly at the three other men, but he was in no position to resist being carried off and locked away with a slam. That the door could unlock from the inside didn't matter. Kael was in the throes of his mark now.

"We'll talk about that shit later," Hayden hotly threw at Evelyn, before grabbing his spear gun.

Everyone else, Evelyn included, followed his lead at readying weapons to aim at the door. Even Anh Judd drew back a second of David's crossbows. She had the practiced hand of someone who had backed up her man by reloading for him many times before.

With a pop the door swung open to strike the wall with a reverberating clatter. Before them stood a robed figure dangling a carjack and extra rigging from one hand. Dropping the door breaching assembly, the figure reached up and threw back its oversized hood with theatrical flair. In the shelter light Evelyn knew right away the clouded irises and pupils, encroached by the oily black of death.

Bloodless pale skin was drawn taut with the grayish sheen of the grave. All topped with a silky gloss of long blonde hair.

David got off the first bolt, but its tip stuck into something with a chuck, as the man of long golden hair and semi-gothic dress rushed them. The vampire brushed that off, as two more projectiles struck nearly on target. Evelyn loosed her bow to it hit dead on, and realized that the vampire had the sense of mind to wear something underneath for protection.

Nick tightened his grip on his knife, as Isaac went for his machete and Hayden reached for an ax; they all presented a wall of flesh to protect those behind. But the vampire appeared ready for that as well. It clung to the bar it had used in conjunction with the hydraulic jack to pry open the door. Though crude for defense, the dead man used the bar to deflect slashes and chops. In both hands it used the steel bar to keep Hayden's ax from splitting its head. It pushed the weapon back with ease, and threw Hayden off balance.

Evelyn ran for her bag, while David, Anh and Valerie all stepped around for clean shots that didn't come. Grabbing one of the D-cell batteries and some lawn pegs, Evelyn rose up with the small modern source of power cupped in her left hand.

"Nick!" Evelyn shouted at him, as he jumped on the vampire's back and tried hacking at its neck.

The blonde night terror grabbed Nick and ripped him off with ease. He twisted Nick's head sideways to clear the way for a bite, when Isaac brought down an overhanded slash. The vampire rose its arm up in defense, and the blade stuck partway in. Isaac attempted to pull the weapon back, but a twist about the vampire's elbow tore the handle out of Isaac's grip, while the machete remaining embedded into the corpse's arm. However, at least Evelyn now had a clear shot.

As though throwing a small dart, Evelyn let loose the plastic stake with a flick of her fingertips. A loud pop accompanied the unusual projectile's path straight into the dead man's neck, where it protruded through to the spinal column. The vampire fell forward over Nick, who in turn jumped up onto his knees and went to work with his knife. Isaac grabbed onto the machete, yanked it out, and started chopping at the body's wrists that it couldn't again grab anything or anyone.

A growl and a thump came from the storage room to which Kael had been dragged. Then, a much louder roar from upstairs answered, shaking the walls and rattling windows. The claws of the new threat didn't tap lightly against linoleum, but seemed to crack with weight like sickle points. The turned lion didn't descend with effort paid to stealth, but at a trotting clip that let it pounce to the bottom of the stairwell.

Evelyn ran for the storage room, as others backed from the wide open door in dread.

After romping into view, the medium-sized vampire lion lunged atop Nick. He pressed a palm to its nose with one hand and threw knife stabs with his other. All the while he shrieked with horror that Evelyn had never heard from him before. Isaac and Hayden both attacked the vampiric animal with

191

their weapons, but it just ignored the chops and slashing cuts to its sides.

Despite the lion's far more ferocious strength, the unnatural beast withdrew its muzzle to get around Nick's undersized hand instead of just ripping it off. Evelyn realized why, as stray knife thrusts had gone into one of the lion's eyes, and now Nick was desperate to put out the other. Only feeding on Nick's blood would restore the monster, which it seemed to realize when going for Nick's throat. His only chance lay with Evelyn freeing Kael, she knew as she threw open the storage room door.

"Kael, c'mon! Get up!" Evelyn shouted to the heavily furred form beneath shredded clothes.

The mark fully emboldening him, Kael ran out on rear legs with a wolfen huff.

Evelyn went back out and to her bag once more, in order to complete the plan that was her last-ditch effort to save everyone. The therianthropic Kael leapt onto the lion, and thrust snapping bites into a mane thick and immaculate, as if freshly washed and groomed. It complicated Kael's animalistic attacks toward a much tougher spine than any man who had been turned.

"Kael!" Evelyn screamed, and then threw the Athame to him.

Rearing up atop the lion, as if riding it in a rodeo, Kael's gray, black and white lupine face sighted the edged weapon twirling toward him. He snatched it with a strong paw-like hand already armed with menacing claws. He flipped it around the back of his hand once, before gripping it in both hands and pulling outward. The handle extended to Kael's full arm span, stunning those who saw.

Careful of Nick's position below, the very therianthropic Kael swept what was now a spear around his right, then left shoulder to line up the attack. He thrust the knife-bladed end into a spot behind the vampiric big cat's left shoulder. With a twisting swing to one side the living supernatural animal brought peace to the restless dead beast.

Rising up on his crooked rear legs, Kael reached down to pull the felled monster off Nick. Kael issued a huffing growl as he struggled a little against the weight.

Speechless, bloodied, rattled and shaking, Nick just stared at the lycanthrope looming over him. He appeared to be unsure, propped up on one elbow, whether he should shield himself with his other arm as he scuffled back. Evelyn realized then that everyone else wasn't just transfixed on Kael's inhuman form, but were trading unbelieving glances between the two of them. However, Kael's unreadable expression aimed up as he pivoted around and ran for the stairs to the ground floor.

Above, Evelyn heard more snapping growls and gurgling gnashing of teeth as Kael set about clearing the house of any other vampires that ventured in for prey.

Heads were dropping like bowling balls before the sound of Kael's paws carried outside into the foreboding night.

Isaac recovered first, and ran to close the door while shouting, "We gotta barricade it!"

"What about Kael?" Valerie shouted, as if her very brother were about to die.

"We have to let him go," a grave Evelyn answered, shaking her head. "Besides, we could never catch up to him anyway. Let's just hold up until morning."

They piled what they could from out of the storage room and Hayden's lab, though Evelyn was sure it would be insufficient if another vampire wanted in. No one slept for the rest of the night, and just sat facing the door, expecting another denizen of the dark to burst in. Evelyn focused more on the human vampire now lying beheaded.

The thing's mouth still kept biting at air, but it was the body that interested Evelyn. The style of clothes, which she noted before, would appear gothic to the casual observer, but Evelyn's own familiarity with clothing design let her make out distinctions. Reflecting on Hyun Jae, Evelyn suspected this to have been someone who, with romantic notions in mind, had wanted to turn.

Chapter 9: The Art And The Craft

"God, this thing weighs a fucking ton," Hayden grunted, as he, Isaac, a heavily bandaged Nick, and David all pulled the massive headless lion corpse up the stairs in the growing light of dawn.

Each held the monstrosity by a finger-length black claw-bearing paw. The four men coordinated their lift to get the thing onto David's wheelbarrow. From there, Hayden and Isaac both grabbed a handle to walk the monstrous corpse out the front door. With morning sun shining through the window, the remains darkened as if they'd been placed in an oven. Once out the door, however, an all-out sizzle of burning flesh kicked in, minus the flames.

"Damn, that's hot!" Isaac exclaimed, as the two hastily dumped the body just off the porch.

David brought up the massive head, which in the light allowed Hayden to see the characteristic horror show of dentation that made even a lion's normal teeth seem downright cuddly. Nick backed away with visible alarm, as David tossed the slow-moving thing out. Next, after removing its bullet resistant vest, came the human corpse, and that took much less work. After that, they pulled out the others found in the house. Everyone but Kael, who was still missing, had gathered out on the porch to watch the dead incinerate under the sun's rays.

"Okay, group meeting," Hayden declared with finality. "In the living room everyone."

"Since my beautiful dining room is ruined," Anh sighed though there was less disappointment in her tone than the words implied.

Hayden swung a chair around to sit on backwards, as others selected their seats, and Anh brought something for Nick to drink, which he accepted with a hand that still possessed a tremble.

"Okay," Hayden said with a hard look to Evelyn. "Let's start with Kael's, uh, episode."

"That's what you meant by him being empowered by that mark, right?" Isaac said, causing Hayden to turn toward him. "When it fills up that's a full moon and the boy goes crazy. 'That it?"

"Yes," Evelyn nodded. "The pentagram marks him as Son of the Wolf."

"This shit isn't over some high school girl, is it?" Nick's humor re-emerged, before he took a swig.

"Please," Evelyn disparaged, rolling her eyes. "Don't make me sick."

"Is that why wolves don't turn?" Hayden asked.

"I doubt it," Evelyn answered and went on, "We've got stories, fables and oral traditions teaching us why some animals turn and others don't but, really no one knows."

"What about that pentagram whatchamacallit?" David inquired with a sideways look.

"The two top points are supposed to represent ears, and the bottom one is a snout. The last two are like fur that comes off a wolf's face," Evelyn described. "Kael was trained from childhood to be a protector, just like I told Isaac and Nick when we were out in the truck the other night."

Hayden sensed a hint of sting aimed his and David's way for that, but given what they'd witnessed he believed it fair to press the matter. "So it is a curse of some kind."

"No," Evelyn declared with a hard tone. "It's a rite of passage. The nine of us award it to those who were chosen at birth and succeed in their training. We call it the sun's promise to protect us, even at night. Every full moon, they're at their peak and can fight whatever lurks in the dark."

"That's not how I remember them wolfman stories going," David said in a slight accusatory tone.

"According to our tradition," Evelyn began. "There was once an attempt to train German Christians to do the same. They called themselves the Hounds of God. After a few full moons they had Shadow Siders on the run. On one full moon they had pursued those few left fleeing the morning sun into a cave. By then their strength was entering the wane and they turned back into men. But the Hounds of God fearlessly pressed into the dark, put down the Shadow Siders and came out alive."

"Y'all don't call 'em vampires," Isaac asked.

"Our tradition's older than that," Evelyn revealed. "It's older than the Celts, older than Christianity and even predates Judaism. We say of vampires that they're from the Shadow Side: the world that cannot survive in the sun. I think that's where that extra weight came from in your tests, Hayden. In deference to you guys into particle

197

physics, it's probably the reason there's dark matter, but they can't produce it in experiments. No one knows where the stuff comes from or how it managed to fall to Earth before the sun could destroy it."

"Particle Supersymmetry," Hayden uttered to himself, and then leaned the chair forward with intensifying interest as he asked, "What happened to these Hounds of God?"

"They were killed by other Christians at the behest of the pope," Evelyn stated with something of a glare at no one in the room. "No good deed goes unpunished, apparently."

"Just killed?" David asked. "As in nothing special needed to kill them with?"

"Nope," Evelyn's hurt sounding voice alluded. "Iron manacles when thrown into a river, steel swords for those who fought back, or burnt at the stake. Just like some of the priestesses who healed sicknesses. So, as you can imagine, we ducked out of sight and did our thing in secret."

"And now this problem's probably worse than ever before," Hayden remarked.

"We're told by the keepers of our stories that there were other waves of turnings," Evelyn told him, "There were a few small outbreaks during the plagues. Sometimes they'd grow in numbers during wars and invasions. But no, never before did it go worldwide like this. Everything reaches farther and goes faster with technology."

"Well okay then," Isaac called out, as he stood up. "We best get on finding something to fix that door before night. David, I think you should come with me while...."

"There's something else," Evelyn said, drawing Hayden's attention back to her. "The one that broke the door and attacked us. I can't help but feel he let himself be turned."

"Humph." Hayden looked distant, thinking about the building mentioned in the last phone call. "Maybe we should go check out that place sooner than later."

"Oh!" Anh's exclamation from another room abruptly stole Hayden's attention, along with everyone else's.

A few of them rushed to where she stood, and then found Kael, bare naked and looking exhausted, standing in the front doorway with the knife in hand, both back to their normal sizes. Evelyn rushed over without embarrassment and walked Kael down into the shelter. As per her description, Kael had regained his human form.

Unsure how he was going to follow through with this, Hayden asked that Nick accompany him, as he readied up some weapons for venturing back to the city.

However, Evelyn re-emerged dressed in an outfit similar to the one she'd worn when he first met her, but with jeans under an open front dress-vest combination. With that came some additions he suspected weren't for fashion sense.

The leather girdle looked like it was meant for battle, and not of the bulge, the latter of which Evelyn didn't have to fight. Knee-high boots were fitted with steel-plating on the front side. Leather shoulder pads, strapped on over the trench coat, likewise appeared to enwrap metal to offer better protection. Part of the shoulder armor included a high collar and a chainmail covered band around the neck. Over her arms she wore bracers of plate over chainmail, and leather which partly covered her palms with a wrap between middle and index fingers around over the back of her hands. Strangely, Evelyn still wore rings, but so many of them, Hayden figured they'd improvise well for brass knuckles. The belt around her waist carried double-A batteries the way a bandolier served for holding bullets, with an extra strap of D-cells down the left side for easy access. Even her black leather Newsboy cap displayed steel on the brim, supported by a metal band under the leather, from his guess.

The seemingly witchy priestess wished to disclose more of her practice, as Evelyn waved them to follow her. She led the two men out toward David's garage, as Hayden heard Isaac and David get into one of the trucks and drive off. Looking around in search of something, Evelyn dropped her bag and spied a large square composed of cross-grained two-by-fours. She moved it over in front of the cement wall within the garage away from the house. Her eyes next sighted a collection of ball bearings and picked one out.

"Regular metal ball," Evelyn said, as if ready to do stage magic.

With a flick of her fingers came the sound of a gunshot, and an impact from the boards that sent chips of wood flying. Then Evelyn selected another and repeated the act.

200

"How did you do that?" Hayden inquired, truly mesmerized by the scientific mystery before him.

Evelyn revealed the D-cell in her palm. "The power came from this."

"But…" Hayden wasn't sure how to broach this. "You– wait. That's nearly a quarter million joules of energy in one of those. And you can just pull it or drain it out that fast?"

"The nine of us each have something to help," Evelyn hinted. "I like to call it a familiar, but I suppose guardian angel works well enough. They're not actually beings or personalities, or cats, so we can use them for whatever we want. But I don't have any power of my own other than metabolic, and my familiar has none whatsoever. All we can do is draw off whatever does. Most of us now just go with using batteries. They're small, they hold a lot, and the whole process is pretty straightforward."

"That pop," Nick started to say, paused, and then continued. "That was like a gunshot."

"It's that fast, yes," Evelyn agreed, turning to him.

"How many can you do off one of those?" Nick inquired.

"Ah, Nick," Hayden raised his head to ask. "What's the impact energy from one of your forty-fives?"

"Sh, ahh…," Nick uttered, trying to think. "About five-hundred foot-pounds."

Hayden's eyes turned up as he approximated the math in his head, and his finger working in air to

201

carry numbers over, before saying, "So imagine sending off three-hundred rounds off one D-cell."

"Whoa," Nick gasped at Evelyn in awe, then turn to Hayden. "So why hasn't anyone invented a way to do that without her little pet?"

"You need to increase the amps, and there's a limit to how well that can be done," Hayden said, feeling himself returning to well-trod turf. "Of course the battery heats up. Maybe it explodes. But I guess she can pull out however much she wants."

"In the old days," Evelyn began, "we had to cook up something with complicated recipes and special ingredients that were a bitch to get. You know, all that boil, boil, toil and trouble stuff that we're known for. But, as I said, no pointy hats."

"And your little clubhouse let Christians push you around all that time?" Nick doubted.

"Whatever we put out, we get back thrice-fold," Evelyn recited like a mantra. "I'm sure someone like Hayden will figure out the exact amount of feedback, but that's our little rule of thumb. So there's no world domination plan going on. When we die the familiar moves onto the next girl born who will take our place, so the sisterhood isn't always at full strength. The past outbreaks were around those times, but this one's different. A few priestesses have gone bad, but they never get far on that."

"Do the rest of you go after them?" Hayden asked.

"No," Her definitive answer was itself passive. "We sit back and watch until they smarten up or lead themselves to ruin. Then we wait for a new girl to be born with the familiar and train her up."

"What about that shit with the spear?" Nick asked, ever more impressed. "That was bad-assed."

"It's meant for Sons of the Wolf who're assigned to protect a priestess," Evelyn explained. "It's the mark that lets them draw it out like that, and no one else can, not even us."

"But they can't change except for full moons," Nick asked.

"The Marked makes them stronger and faster toward the full moon, and more of the animal comes out," Evelyn detailed. "With a little nudge their senses can be heightened. Last I knew, Kael could normally bench press something around two-seventy. But at his peak it's a bit over four hundred thirty. He's not vampire strong or anything close, but he'll be quicker than most any of them we run into. True to a wolf's nature, the mark makes him tough as hell and improves his endurance."

Kael arrived dressed in clothes Hayden doubted came from anything he'd imagined in David's closet. He brought an armful of weapons and equipment, with Salma accompanying him. The canvas pants had double-wide legs Hayden imagined were to be worn in a dojo somewhere, but stayed snug around the waste and pelvis.

Two long slits appeared on the shirt instead of sleeves, and around that was a harness strapped into an X with the ceremonial knife sheathed on the back of Kael's right shoulder.

"Two things," Hayden said to them. "First, Salma, I think it better that you stay here in case we don't get back before dark. And Kael, are you sure you're up for this? You look beat, son."

"Not an option," Kael announced, and then took a deep breath. "She goes, then I go. Oh! I found this other bulletproof vest among your stuff in that room."

"Is this more of that macho shit?" Salma questioned with some irritation.

"No, because Evelyn here's coming along with us," Hayden answered matter-of-fact. "And from what she just showed us we'll need her. I'd have Kael stay behind to rest up."

"Hey Kael," Nick called out. "Do that thing with the stick, again."

Setting the other stuff down, the young man pulled the knife out to full length. He handed it over to Hayden and Nick to hold in turn, and then took it back.

"Weighs the same as before," Hayden observed to a nodding Kael, and then said to him. "You or Nick might as well wear those vests. I had it on when we all bumped into each other, but I realized how ridiculous that was with vampires going for arteries."

"So if he's coming," Salma demanded Hayden's attention again. "Why not me?"

Nick paced over to soothe her with his arms on her shoulders. "It's gonna be okay. We're just going to poke around at this place Hayden's talking about and hustle on back. 'Ya kinda need criminal sorts to do that, not cops. You got that whole To Protect and Serve thing goin' on."

"And you?" Salma returned with her smile at his smirk. "Your guns aren't more useful than mine."

"Hey, I softened up that lion, you know," Nick defended in good humor, and made a tongue click with a downward stabbing motion before pointing. "So that Kael could do his little thing."

"Yeah, sure," she teased back, and patted his chest affectionately.

Nick strapped on one protective vest; Kael, however, passed the other over to Salma to use.

"Okay, let's mount up and get rolling," Hayden announced.

Once the four of them were inside the remaining truck, Hayden pulled out to turn east. Evelyn rode in the passenger seat, while Nick and Kael rode in the back. The door between them was open.

"So tell me," Hayden said to Evelyn. "About that getup of yours, nice by the way."

"Thank you," Evelyn said while looking it over.

"If you're wearing protection why doesn't Kael?"

"Speed and staying power," Kael shouted from the back.

"That's basically it," Evelyn agreed. "In the final phase of his training he's expected to practice night-time raids by vampires, or if he has to go after them, that lasts until dawn. Armor would wear him down and slows his reaction time."

"And you're not really a CNA," Hayden deduced. "So what was your job before all this?"

205

"I worked for a fashion designer," Evelyn answered with a shrug. "Nothing big time, but I liked it. I designed this outfit myself and several others."

"What if this all goes bad with you or Kael turning?" Hayden posed the more critical question.

"Then we're vampires," Evelyn answered plainly. "No different than the rest."

"Your familiar and Kael's mark just, what, go away?"

"He'd even turn back to normal," Evelyn said, referring to Kael.

"I guess that's something," Hayden said, and then made a backhanded wave to her fingers. "Do your rings have anything special to them?"

"Normally I have to take in energy through my left hand and send it out with my right," Evelyn explained. "But the jewelry carries a few special purposes. A lot of what I'm wearing does."

"But not reproducing the sun's effect, I take it," Hayden thought aloud, his voice clearly expressing his yearning.

"No, not even to fake it, so that vampires would run away," Evelyn herself seemed to rue that fact.

"Hmm, I'll have to work on that," Hayden mused.

* * *

Because of the time they'd left, the four of them didn't bother stopping in the small town along the way back to the city. Evelyn passed the time watching news videos on her cell, as Hayden drove with an expression that hinted his mind was elsewhere.

"They've sent the National Guard to power stations and utility plants," Evelyn informed Hayden, while she pulled one of her earpieces out. "And apparently some asshole on the radio is claiming that bringing the army and navy home is an attempt to take over the country through martial law."

"Oh, that guy," Hayden recalled with an upraised chin. "He says that about everything. One time he said Title Nine was a transgender plot to impose sex changes on male athletes. Whatever side isn't running the country always claims the other is trying to impose dictatorship."

"Tell me something," Nick spoke up as he moved forward to between cab seats. "How'd you know to wake up when that vampire in the wedding dress showed up?"

"I set up thirteen double-A's around the Judds' house," Evelyn replied. "It's sort've like a home security system, but it only warns me of things that will bring harm."

"Ah," Hayden nodded. "Was that the same day you first checked out the grove?"

"Yes," Evelyn answered, looking straight ahead, and then warned, "Hayden, look."

"Yeah, I see it," the chemical engineer told her. "At least we don't have to drive off the road."

The police barricade of almost two weeks ago lay in ruins, with dried blood splattered over asphalt and machine alike, but few bodies.

"How well would you and Kael handle that gorilla if we saw it again?" Hayden asked her.

"I guess that depends on if we see it before it sees us," Evelyn answered. "You don't typically encounter those in medieval Europe or colonial era Ireland."

Around one in the afternoon they turned off the freeway into the city. To Evelyn's surprise there were more people out than she would've thought after the outbreak.

"Hayden," Evelyn said, pointing to a gas station. "Pull over."

"I'm not sure there's going to be gas left, or if there is it'll be locked down," Hayden doubted.

"I've got that covered," Evelyn assured him.

He drove up to a station pump.

Nick and Kael climbed out as Evelyn and Hayden did. Looking the pump over, Evelyn then waved Hayden on. He took the nozzle out, removed the truck's fuel cap, and inserted the nozzle into the filler pipe. Evelyn went over to the magnetic card reader and studied it for a minute.

"Kael," she called. "Get me a knife, will you?"

He and Nick both came over. Along with a knife, Kael offered her a bow and one of the swords that the group had from before fleeing the city. Nick produced one of the guns and a holster from their first scavenging run. Remembering Isaac's reasoning for getting more firearms, Evelyn didn't question it.

"It's a nine millimeter, so the recoil shouldn't be too bad," Nick said, and then thought of something else. "That karma thing you mentioned with the familiar, does it apply to anything that you don't use your, I guess, power on?"

"No," Evelyn answered, and strapped the modern weapon to her right side under the dress.

Evelyn slung the bow, a quiver and a Celtic-style longsword that she suspected Kael had specifically picked out, onto her back. Then she took the large folding knife, inserted the tip into the reader and grabbed one of her batteries.

"If we had time I'd have gotten at the wiring and used that," Evelyn said, as the LCD screen flickered in chaos with no coherent numbers coming up.

"Just electrical power?" Hayden asked.

"I'd need some kind of physical contact to the fuel to use some of that," Evelyn explained, and then spoke to Nick and Kael. "We should grab some gas cans too, and fill those up."

The pair made several trips, bringing back four at a time for Evelyn to fill. Then they boarded the truck and left. Hayden slowed by a windowless building for reasons Evelyn couldn't guess, but moved on after apparently seeing what he needed to.

Nothing stirred around the place.

Next, Hayden drove toward the lab again, and explained himself, "We left in a rush, and there's some things I left, thinking at the time they weren't useful."

"Like what?" Evelyn asked, realizing from movement in Hayden's forehead he'd had an idea.

"Full spectrum solar simulators," the chemist answered. "We were going to using them to figure out how to burn vampires without sunlight. That is until our little mirror test I showed all you guys proved to us it wasn't light."

"What's the point then?" Evelyn wondered if this was chewing up valuable daylight for nothing.

"Running a solar simulator alone didn't damage the turned corpses of course," Hayden recounted, and raised an index finger. "And it also didn't invoke the behavioral repulsive response, the acting of fear."

"You think you can change that," Evelyn realized aloud.

"We put together a lot of what we needed, because our deliveries didn't arrive in time," Hayden explained. "However, we only used certain spectra one at a time, in order to pin down which one would work. I think it's the full spectrum and at the equivalent intensities of the sun that does it."

"What are the spectra you think you'll need?" Evelyn's curiosity was perked up.

"Infrared for sure, and visible likely," Hayden started to list, as he pulled into the lab's receiving bay and shut off the engine. "From what I know of the functional groups in the uni-molecular crap, I'm sure microwaves are in the mix and maybe radio. There might be something in the skin that picks up UVA and UVB, so I'll have to account for that as well."

"I may be a witch, Hayden," Evelyn chided with a smirk, as they got out of the cab. "But if this works you'll have proved yourself to be a wizard."

"'Told you guys that a chemical engineer was better than an undead expert," Hayden beamed.

Nick and Kael entered the bay first with bows drawn. Hayden carried the spear gun that was his hallmark. Evelyn readied her bow, but also pinched a double-A lengthwise between her index finger and the base of her thumb. It would normally affect her aim, but for now she'd use the power.

The four of them cleared their way to Hayden's original offices and labs without encountering any vampires. Then, Hayden led them to the custodial closet to grab a large rolling bin. He and Kael pulled it back to his labs to load up with new equipment. Some of that, Evelyn realized, appeared built in haphazard fashion. It made the rat restraining board look like NASA precision quality.

Next to go was a small fridge filled with many quarts of fluid too thin to be exclusively blood, and not sufficiently red. In explanation, Hayden described that it included lymph and cytoplasm along with anticoagulants to prevent clotting. Hayden packed a supply of dry ice, which happened to be on hand, into the fridge. It would be without power for hours.

"Okay," Hayden announced, sounding upbeat. "Let's get rambling."

"Do we try for that building your mystery employers wanted to check out?" Nick asked as he and Evelyn covered the door.

"Yeah," Hayden affirmed. "We'll be pushing it to get back before dark."

"Hayden?" A distant voice called out from elsewhere in the building. "Is that you?"

211

"Shit," Hayden cursed under his breath and gestured for Nick and Evelyn to stay at the door.

"Who is that?" Kael whispered, as he and Hayden re-joined Evelyn and Nick before the door.

"It's James," Hayden said, with a dread Evelyn picked up on through his voice.

"I thought you said everyone with you died," Evelyn said, clearly hoping for elaboration.

"They did," Hayden replied at a whisper. "Or so I thought. I didn't actually see James die, but he was grappling with that vampire that we un-staked. I was pretty sure James wouldn't make it."

"Hayden?" The man's voice inquired again. "It's me, James."

"Yeah," Hayden muttered. "That's the problem."

"Ah, look, I know it looked bad back in that shooting range, but I pulled through," James called out in assurance. "Really, I managed to stab that rod back into the thing's heart and stop it."

"Maybe we should check, just in case," Nick hissed.

Hayden refused with a vigorous head shake. "I don't know. He could just be trying to get our guard down. He'd have been by himself for nearly two weeks."

"I should warn you," James shouted out, sounding further away. "There're some vampire dogs that sometimes shelter in this building during the day. I don't know if I cleared them all out."

"Sounds like he's okay," Nick ventured at normal volume, and reached for the door.

212

"Whoa, wait," Evelyn stopped him from opening it, and then looked to Hayden.

"I'd rather not leave him behind again, if he's alive," Hayden said. "We need to be sure."

"How about those dogs first?" Kael offered. "We can verify his story without approaching him."

"Okay," Evelyn agreed. "Let's start in the opposite direction from James."

"Yeah," Hayden accepted, and then opened the door to enter the hall.

Kael went out next, and put away his bow in favor of his Athame. He reached up over his shoulder to unsheathe the weapon in its short form and drew it out to half-length. Evelyn and Nick stepped out last, and the four of them advanced down the hall in caution. At each door, Kael was careful to open it without sound and peek inside.

"Have you been keeping up on the news?" James called out. "This plague has gone global. Every major continent's been swamped. Australia too. That video of the dolphins going after American navy ships was unreal. They say the government's not even going to try reinforcing the islands or Alaska. Apparently some Pentagon geniuses decided that the mainland was the big asset to defend."

Evelyn tried to shut the guard out of her thoughts, as the group approached the cafeteria. Hayden went ahead of Kael, and when Evelyn herself entered she realized why Hayden had gone in without concern. The entire room was well lit with banks of windows on three walls. That was the

213

reason why a partly burnt dog stood out so well, that it caught everyone's attention in an instant.

Evelyn rushed over to inspect it close up. A number of tables were knocked over and those still upright were in disarray. The animal had been staked with a wooden peg, the kind that Evelyn recalled seeing on construction sites with string stretched between them. The head and the lower body were each under tables close to the wall, unburned, and another table on its side shielded the corpse from evening incineration.

Nick and Kael set their weapons aside to grab the third table to lift and move it over, so that the dog would eventually burn as the sun came through the west windows. Hayden went over to wrap a hand on the wooden weapon, but stopped himself in afterthought. Unsure of his motive, Evelyn suspected that the sight of a removed stake might inform human vampires that someone was still around. Then Hayden gave her a slow blink and then a nod, having gotten the unspoken hint.

"C'mon Hayden," James' growing sense of desperation only just reached Evelyn's ears.

"That's one," Hayden remarked while looking around. "I thought he said there were more."

"Hayden," Evelyn addressed him, pointing to a second door on the north wall from which they had come. "Where does that go?"

"Best check there too," Hayden said without answering her.

Hayden took the lead again, but Evelyn stood at his side, ready to guide any and every shot anyone made. With a growing jitter, Hayden reached for the door. He pulled it just an inch, not even providing a crack to see through, and paused.

"I should tell you, Hayden," James' voice jolted the chemical engineer.

"Shit," Hayden swore through gritting teeth.

"The daytime's getting bad too," James shouted on. "You got people out there fighting over food and medicine. There were even a few shootings. Why can't we just be like New York? You remember that power outage back in two-thousand three? No looting, no shooting, just people calmly walking outside in the night and helping each other out."

"Everyone's gotta bring that up," Evelyn lamented with a bit of a sneer.

"You did that?" Hayden asked. "Eight states lost power."

"Call it tween angst," Evelyn whispered, her bow aimed down the hall as they advanced. "I worked it out by making trees grow faster. Trees always relax me, and I didn't know any better."

"You think that's bad...," Kael started to say.

"If you ever tell anyone," Evelyn gnashed quietly. "So help me, you'll pay for it in spades!"

Raising a hand in surrender, Kael clammed up and checked another door.

"What?" Nick asked, as they saw Kael stop.

Opening the door wider, Kael revealed a bathroom and a bloodbath. Evelyn saw paw prints everywhere, confirming James' account of dogs. Evelyn often wondered why none of the priestesses of today or those who came before ever developed a way to learn what the blood had been spilt from.

She had sketched out some recipes here and there, but never got around to trying them out. Being a witch was bad enough even in most of today's culture. It then occurred to her that tinkering with what could easily be misinterpreted as a blood ritual was just asking for trouble.

Evelyn stepped in with Kael, leaving Nick and Hayden to keep watch in the hall. Shards from all the broken mirrors cluttered in the sinks, around faucets and on the floor between sinks. From the faint blackened streaks and smears, she imagined a person on their back, scurrying away from something at their feet. Splatters all around hinted at multiple attackers, but not their identities. Evelyn could make out that there had been at least two dogs and maybe more.

However, the handprint Evelyn saw was from the dying act of trying to stand. It told her the victim had been human. That she learned while leaning close, for everywhere blood had fallen had been licked at.

"Honestly," James called out again. "I can't tell you why I keep coming back here. Force of habit, I suppose. Nothin' else to do. No one to talk to at home."

Evelyn trotted out in a hurry, with Kael behind her, both mindful of their steps.

"Someone was killed in there," Kael said to the others.

"'Wife's out doin' her thing," James went on. "My kids are okay, for now anyway."

"Sounds like he's closer," Hayden observed under his breath.

216

"They were smart," James continued, and Evelyn could hear his steps as he told his story. "They saw what was happening and hauled ass out of the house."

"That's too bad," Hayden called back, getting three startled looks. "About your wife, I mean."

"What're you doing?" Evelyn whispered in Hayden's ear after pulling him close.

"This man greeted me coming into work for the last fourteen years," Hayden answered. "Just let me have this. Feels wrong to let him keep going on like that."

"Remember when you first met her at the company barbeque?" James asked.

His footsteps had stopped.

"Bright yellow dress with the flowers?" Hayden asked, and then nodded. "I recall. She kept going on about that movie with the southern women and the armadillo cake."

"She always thought of herself as a tough blossom," James said. "I think about her at times."

"I thought about you too, James," Hayden said, causing Evelyn to glance at him in sympathy.

"You know that thing about not having a reflection in the mirror?" James asked, seeming locked into a character he couldn't shake after the curtains closed. "It's malarkey. You might've noticed what I did to the bathroom. I hate it. Seeing myself like that... Or I should hate it, anyway."

"James wouldn't have wanted to come back, that's true," Hayden agreed in memory of his friend. "And killing his wife? I can't imagine he could live with himself. Good thing he doesn't have to."

217

The corpse of James, the security guard at last rounded the corner. Despite the calm of his voice, there burned a lust in the dead man's face that Evelyn feared would haunt her sleep for years. It was gradual at first, but James' head shaking speeded up and carried increasing hate.

"Why do you have to go there?" the vampire yelled, as he broke into a sprint unhindered by the utility belt and all the weapons of his job. "I thought we were friends!"

Evelyn beamed a hard stare to a spot at the lower right side of the badge on the blood-encrusted shirt. Her two fingers holding the battery tightened. Hayden brought up the spear gun with a mournful calm, and Evelyn approved, "Do it, Hayden. Send him home."

One mechanical clink and a twang of bungee stood in for James' funerary hymn.

Chapter 10: Baby Bats

After calling and explaining to Isaac that the four of them would be staying in the city for the night, Hayden hung up. He also chose to use the rest of the day to scout around for anything of value to take back. The vicious struggle for survival among the living had taken its toll, Hayden noticed, seeing a few bodies in the streets. However, a healthy fear of the dead shooed the city's survivors back into whatever hidden corners they could find a whole hour before dusk.

"It's not a lot," Nick said from in back. "But better than I thought we'd find."

"Makes me wonder why people fight over it," Hayden remarked, as he pulled around to the building in question. "That much ambition for kicking ass, you'd think they'd bring it into the dark."

"Look," Evelyn pointing out at the robed figures starting to converge on the large windowless structure. "You don't think they're vampires, do you?"

"I'd expect them to be chasing people down," Hayden replied. "Though, their reaction to even a hint of daylight should prevent them from attempting it before the sun's down."

"What if they can learn?" Kael asked, coming up front to see.

"Alina's corpse does throw a little English at us," Hayden agreed. "But no, my guess is the

219

heliophobia is hard wired, just like their drive for hunting people."

"Even James back there?" Kael asked, and gave Hayden a face suggesting he meant no offense.

"Yeah, even him," Hayden sighed. "That other stuff I tend to think of as finding a final recording of someone who knew they were dying."

"Should we go in?" Evelyn asked.

"Building looks pretty secure," Hayden observed, as he leaned forward for a better survey.

Hayden pulled around into a back lot, and the four of them climbed out. Hayden had them lock their doors and then went around checking that they were secure. Then he, Evelyn, Kael and Nick ventured toward the front entrance of the building. They fell in line with those wearing robes.

"Ah, newbies," someone said, while turning to see them. "What's with all the hardware?"

"Getting' tired of needing to find food around town," Hayden bluffed. "So I figured, let's try something new. After everything else what's to lose?"

"Right," the robed man said with a rising tone that was the current popular expression.

It came time for them to enter. A lanky tower of a man at the door wearing gloom for clothes, black lipstick, and red contacts stayed them. "Cover fee's five dollars."

"Serious?" an incredulous Kael asked.

"Nah, I'm kidding," the man said, revealing either plastic insert or caps made to look like classic vampire teeth. "Go on in, but you'll have to stay in until dawn. That's the rule."

"Easy enough," Hayden said, as he entered into a stew of colognes, perfumes, cigarette smoke and a few other odors he couldn't make out.

"Hey," the doorman called. "Don't you want to enter the drawing?"

"Ah," Hayden stalled trying to play up a casual uncertainty. "Let me think about it."

"That's cool," the man said, and ushered the others in.

Evelyn edged up to Hayden side and leaned close. "These aren't Goths."

"I'm not up on my new age or hipster subcultures," Hayden's old school societal rebel admitted, as he looked around at the scene of a horror movie bar. "Back in my day they said heavy metal was trying to convince us to sell our souls to the devil. Of course that was real heavy metal."

"They're not new agers either," Evelyn corrected. "And definitely not hipsters. I know clothing design, and this isn't quite the Gothic look."

"God," Nick, turning around in caution, hissed toward Hayden's other ear. "I feel like they're all going to get ugly and rush us any second now."

"Like some blood?" a vampire-costumed girl asked. She gave Hayden a start with her bright yellow eyes and her display of four upper vampire teeth through an unsettling smile.

"No thanks," Hayden refused, and pretended to look for someone while adding. "Tryin' to quit."

"That's funny," she said, and then offered up glasses of red syrupy stuff to the others.

"I think it really is blood," Kael said, stepping around in front of Hayden. He looked at the girl as she continued her rounds. "But something's different about it."

"Like what?" Evelyn asked him.

"Not sure." Kael shook his head, and took a whiff before saying, "Kind've bacon-like, I guess."

"Pig's blood then," Hayden observed and picked out a table. "They probably cleaned out our supplier after the outbreak went into full swing."

"Good evening everybody!" Someone shouted into a microphone from a stage.

Hayden turned to see the doorman now serving as an announcer pacing around the stage and surveying the audience. Cheers rose up, as did a sea of hands tipped with black or blood red fingernails. The tall vampire-wannabe issued a hoarse guttural yell – the kind that Hayden had heard from death metal music that he recalled some of the kids of his older son's age were into.

"And how are we tonight?" he gurgle-screamed out.

"Goddamn nervous," Kael uttered at normal volume, which Hayden barely heard.

"Are you ready for the death of the sun?" the announcer roared.

"I'm not sure these are your typical pseudo-Goths," Evelyn said close to Hayden's ear.

"Here it is darlings!" he shouted in his vocal cord-abusing voice, and swung a finger to a monitor.

"Die, die, die, die!" the crowds shouted at a live feed from one of the cameras outside.

222

The shadow of city outline slowly merged with the darkening sky as the last sliver of the sun sunk below the horizon. That served to introduce a metal band that involved more growling lyrics as far removed from singing as Hayden's own untested efforts at football would be to the Crimson Tide he practically worshipped.

"That's a rad tat, bro," someone from the next table shouted to Kael.

Kael flashed him a metal sign with index finger and pinkie raised before facing the others with worried side-cast eyes. Despite his martial arts dress and that he still had Evelyn's knife sheathed on his shoulder, Hayden would've thought Kael was a kid being brought to their first horror movie.

"Alright," the manager announced at the end of the musical number that left Hayden's ears ringing. "Time for our first drawing! Whose ready to enter eternity?"

Screams and cheers roared up again, making Hayden wince. Kael subtly plugged his ears by pretending to rest his head on his fists. Hayden had to remind himself that just one day ago Kael turned into the effigy of an animal noted for its sharp hearing among other senses. For Evelyn's description he was probably still in possession of keen ears.

"I said, who's ready to enter eternity?" the announcer repeated, drawing out the last word.

The audience shouts came louder than before, and then he continued, "Mistress Manslaughter's coming with the Cauldron of Souls. Who will be our first crossover?"

223

The foreboding tone of his voice belied his gleaming smile and exhilarated crowd. Then a woman appeared who, as best Hayden could figure, deliberately styled her hair to drape over her face, slick with something probably meant to be blood. Her dress seemed as if it once was for children's seminary prior to be ripped and stained red. Where it didn't cover Hayden saw pale skin, but doubted very much she was a vampire under such controlled conditions.

Held out before her, as though bringing a dead cat to a gravesite, was a red smeared goldfish bowl –clearly the lottery in question. Once she stood next to the announcer the girl tilted her head back in a jerky fashion of that Hayden became unnerved by. Doubly so, once he saw the crazy crooked stare in the one eye that appeared from under the parting of hair.

And yet, her eye was perfectly normal. Hayden recognized that through the haze of the stage mist and smoking lingering in the room after the first performance. With theatrical exaggeration the announcer eyed the crowd while reaching into the bowl, as though he were about to draw a rabbit out for five year olds at a birthday party. It was the girl's bloodcurdling scream, as the manager grabbed a slip of paper, which made Hayden jolt in his seat.

Looking around, Hayden noticed that Kael, Evelyn and even Nick appeared ashen at the played out snuffing of life, when the announcer pulled out the paper ticket to read off, "Amanda Hale!"

Another girl, or woman, Hayden couldn't be sure, jumped up with a squeal of delight. Her friends gave her a bosom buddies' hug before urging her to race up to the stage. She proudly stood to the announcer's side bobbing on her toes and clapping.

"Definitely not Gothic," Evelyn said to Hayden without looking away. "She acts like it's the latest in thing to do until the next trendy fad comes up."

"Amanda," the announcer said. "You've been chosen by fate to embrace the night forever."

She screamed in excitement, and many in the crowd also did. Others looked a little despondent that it wasn't them instead. Hayden suspected what was coming, but a part of his brain refused to accept the conditions required for what would be next.

"What's first on your list when you kiss the sun goodbye?" the announcer asked.

"I'm going to be an awesome vampire!" Amanda declared with her hands up and clasped together ready to bow. "First, I'm going straight to my parents' house and give them the biggest fucking surprise of their lives! And I'm never going to be afraid of the night again! Whooh!"

"Alright baby!" the announcer shouted in spirit with the girl's own screamed plans.

Hayden thought Amanda's voice had carried a hint of burning resentment.

"There's no way," Hayden denounced under his breath, shaking his head as Evelyn and Nick looked to him. "I had one strapped down without limbs, and it still caused a problem."

225

"Are you ready?" the manager's question built into a crowd-stoking shout. "I am ready!" Amanda shouted also to the crowd.

"Chaos and Carnage," the announcer called to some point offstage. "Are you boys ready to feed the hunger that can't be stilled? Are you ready to offer up a maiden to the night?"

Two sizeable figures, which Hayden assumed were men, emerged wearing medieval style armor with high black hoods of Dark Age executioners. They escorted Amanda backstage, and the monitor came up again. This time it was a scene of an Egyptian sarcophagus and there were six robed figures standing around it. The two armored men brought Amanda into view, and the six lifted the top off the coffin.

Hayden leaned close, thinking his eyes deceived him. The floor of the casket was a sickly gray that writhed as if dead flesh were the River Styx. It occurred to him, when it zoomed in to get a close-up of the sarcophagus' contents, that the camera wasn't part of any regular security surveillance system. Small hairless forms, many whose eyes hadn't opened before being fed on and dying, Hayden thought might've been rats.

Some were, he noticed after a moment, but the sporadic flap here and there revealed to him that infant bats had also been added. He even saw puppies and kittens, those of which at least had the beginnings of fur, emerging from the smaller vampiric offspring.

The two presumed executioners picked the girl up, and she helped by leaning back into their arms. They then raised her over the Egyptian coffin and lowered her in. Each man was careful to adjust their grip, so as to not invite bites from the wriggling masses of newborn dead. Most unable to see, the tiny forms latched their jaws onto her as if from instinct, and blood swelled up from all over her body. Amanda called out from the many sharp pains, but she didn't scream in terror.

"Jesus fucking Christ," Nick cursed, gawking with his mouth open.

Hayden had started the counter on his wristwatch the moment he saw red, and it gave him the excuse to look at the soon-to-be-late Amanda Hale as little as possible.

She lost healthy color in less than a minute, and passed out in about equal time after that. Her body disappeared under a swell of underdeveloped little horrors that would never mature.

At eleven minutes, twenty seconds, a pockmarked human hand emerged.

Hayden stopped the watch there and stared in fascination, as the corpse of Amanda pulled itself out of the mass of vampire animals. Her eyes displayed the same clouded lifelessness he'd seen in every other vampire. Amanda's prior teen energy and cheer had disappeared forever under the swarm of dead feeders.

"Why isn't she rushing for the guys in there?" Kael wondered.

"They must've split the moment she was placed inside," Hayden guessed.

A sound of an electric garage door opened, which Hayden envisioned was probably for freight.

The vampire who was Amanda turned to look while still sitting up in the sarcophagus. Climbing out, the vampire disappeared from the camera's field of view. The monitor switched to an outdoor security camera that had no color. A stylized metal goblet waited some ten yards away from the door. The corpse paced closer to then scoop it up and chug the contents without hesitation.

The door closed, as indicated by the diminishing area of light out on the asphalt, while the vampire girl was distracted by the bait. Cheers rose up from the audience, and the announcer himself was taken by the euphoria. He yelled into his mike and raised a hand high to show two fingers in a fang gesture. Hayden, Evelyn, Kael and Nick were the only ones disturbed by what they'd witnessed.

"The Boat of Eternity has claimed tonight's first offering!" he shouted to adoring fans.

To follow-up there came the same band as before, performing a new number.

Hayden wondered if it were to disguise the prospect that the dead Amanda might be pounding on a door to get in and feast on those still living and waiting their turn.

"Turned in under twelve minutes," Hayden said to them.

"Do you think it's because of the rate of fluid loss?" Evelyn asked.

"I can't see how that would work," Hayden doubted. "Nothing on the WHO videos shows anything turning that fast. Then again they didn't have nearly so many vampires feeding all at once."

228

"Hey guys," the same girl who had offered blood before came around. "Would you like to order something from our menu? There's regular food there if you're not ready for our house special."

"Uh, yeah," Hayden said, looking at all the mats placed around the table. "Give us a minute."

"Sure thing," she said and poured service-sector charm in her smile. "Remember, it's all free."

"We should definitely hit them up on the food," Kael advised.

"I don't think I can eat anything after seeing that," Evelyn gulped with a sour face.

Hayden figured that even with a seeming metaphysical transformation, Kael's living curse– or whatever his tradition considered it - still required metabolic energy. Hayden checked out the menu before settling on a premade sandwich and a stiff drink. When the waitress-of-the-damned came back, Nick asked for the strongest coffee the establishment could make along with a couple hotdogs and a packaged pastry. Kael saw some fresh cooking happening and ordered three burgers.

"Do you think that sarcophagus is real?" Evelyn asked.

"As in swiped from a museum?" Hayden queried back, and then nodded while swallowing a bite. "It's possible. I'm sure the alarms went off, or whatever the security is, but who's to stop them from just walking out with it? But I'm pretty sure that has nothing to do with how fast they're turning."

"If they change that quick what's that going to do with how much of them is left?" Kael asked.

229

"Even if there's no breakdown of neural synapses," Hayden began. "The hormones aren't being produced. Other parts of the autonomic nervous system stop working for lack of need. Certain proteins and enzymes no longer function, because they're now at room temperature. So it's really just about having a better recording of a once living mind than what normally happens."

"Do you think they know?" Evelyn posed the question that had Hayden looking around.

"Nope," Hayden doubted and shook his head before taking a drink. "And they don't care."

After eating, the wariness of the past couple of days snuck up on them while they were sitting down. Nick, Kael and Evelyn had caught a few hours of sleep during the drive, but Hayden with his bloodshot eyes had been up since yesterday morning.

Adrenalin had kept him up through the last night, but under the perception of this place being secure, he felt overcome with exhaustion. Kael and Nick promised to keep watch through the night. Despite the loud music and rambunctious crowd Hayden was out like a light.

* * *

Every time that chick with the ghost girl hairdo screamed out the drawing of a name, Evelyn woke up. On the sixth drawing she noted it was a rather buff guy talking about how he kept himself perfectly shaved and worked on just the right shape to his nails in case his name was drawn. He was wholly unaware that being turned didn't quite work that way, but it had become the accepted gospel of

230

the modern mythology. He, like the five before him, also believed it would be him in eternity.

Though, as the man was lowered into the sarcophagus, Evelyn realized he was changing his mind at the last minute. Immersed in the underdeveloped horde, he began thrashing and screaming.

"Hayden," Evelyn called out while pushing on his arm. "Look at this."

"All that preparation and he wasn't ready," the host declared and added theatrical laughter reminding Evelyn of Hayden's ringtone. "Too late, dude! You're already immortal!"

While a groggy Hayden studied the screen, Evelyn heard something from the ceiling. It reminded her of gravel or rain on a tin roof. With the night's show wrapping up, the announcer called up one last performance. The host went around welcoming new people.

"Kick-ass show, right?" the host said to Hayden, as Kael woke up.

"What's that?" Evelyn asked, pointing to the ceiling.

"Those're bats," the announcer proudly beamed, and returned to his shtick, "Dawn's coming and they've been satiated by mother night."

Evelyn noticed Nick's hand tightening on a shotgun grip, but Hayden subtly shook his head.

"How is it they don't get in?" Evelyn dreaded the prospect of another aerial frenzy.

"The power of Boat of Eternity," the host boasted with a grandiose spread of his arms, and then waved that off. "I got a couple friends who

231

helped me mount these steel wire grates in the vents.

"Where're your friends now?" Nick's voice tensed as his jaw clenched.

"Oh, one of them won the drawing tonight!" The host declared with pride.

At that Hayden snapped right out of it. "Kael, Nick, Evelyn, we're leaving."

"Nah, it's alright," the host insisted. "We won't be that strong when we enter eternity."

"We?" Nick's voice cracked into a hard edge, and he jumped up to pin the host to the table with a shotgun barrel to the taller man's neck as he shouted, "We, mother fucker? Like those other people you killed tonight? You want eternity? Huh? I'll give you eternity, you little shit!"

"Nick, Nick," Hayden soothed. "C'mon. You're not helping them with this."

"No, Nick's got a point," Evelyn realized herself saying, and gave the immigrant smuggler plenty of room for the mess his twelve gauge would make. "Why should we let this continue?"

By now the two semi-executioners had arrived, and many of the crowd gathered to see what was happening. Most figured it was part of the announcer's act, to have the supposed vampire hunters intrude into the den of darkness. Given the lyrics of the music Evelyn was hearing she could understand their grins. But the two medieval clad men knew better.

"Want me to test that armor for 'ya?" Nick had slipped out his double-barrel colt to aim at them.

232

Evelyn had slipped her own pistol out, but kept it hidden under her long coat.

"Nick, at least let me get some things out of him," Hayden bartered for time.

"So long as the fucker don't twitch and his goons step off," Nick warned.

"How did you accelerate the turning process?" Hayden asked.

"Where did you get the sarcophagus?" Evelyn had her own concerns.

"We harvested those newborn animals using vampire rats," the host answered, switching his fearful glance between Hayden and Nick, and then looked to Evelyn. "It's just something we swiped from the museum after the vampires spread. I thought it looked cool and read the plaque about the Boat of Eternity thing. That's how I came up with this whole thing. It's harmless."

"Harmless?" a raging red-faced Nick repeated as if in question. "How many people did you harmlessly kill in your little fucked up funhouse?"

"It's not like that," the host proclaimed in defense. "They're still there. They don't die."

"Yes, they do, son." Hayden now exercised a hard patriarchal scolding tone. "There may be more of their minds left intact, but that's not all of what makes a person."

"It's them," the host insisted, and jolted at the thought Nick would shoot him for it. "I was going to go through with myself once everyone else had who wanted to."

"Why would you want to?" Evelyn asked, unable to accept the vampire-themed subculture

233

actually making the real step the way she'd seen it tonight. "The whole world's going to shit and you help it along? I don't see any reason for not letting Nick here splatter your brains."

"That's the point," the host agreed, trembling more and more. "They are winning. Everyone's going to die because of this. Why not die in a way that lets you make it, I figure."

A metallic pop sounded from the building's ducts, causing all eyes to search up.

"Damn," Hayden cursed, and then turned to his watch. "Inside or out, we're screwed either way for the next twenty minutes. At least outside we can try for the truck and make a break for it."

"It's alright, they can't get in," the host bawled out, seeing that Nick wasn't relenting.

"That," Hayden pointed to the ceiling as he leaned over the man, "is your pal busting through."

The host did finally get the point of Hayden's growing alarm.

"Everyone," Evelyn shouted over the noise louder than humanly possible using a battery in her palm. "Everyone, please! Vampires are breaking in! We're leaving right now. When we leave here you need to book it to wherever you were taking shelter and fast. Got it?"

"But we want them to turn us," one said, and got agreement among others.

"If it's not done his way," Evelyn spat out in a moment's anger, waving to the host still under Nick's gunpoint. "Then there's going to be a lot of brain damage. You'll be retard vampires."

234

That got the message across, Evelyn thought, as they started moving toward the doors.

"Nick, let him up," Hayden said softly. "He'll get his in time."

With the shotgun no longer commanding his cooperation, the host made a break toward where his supposed drawing winners were taken. Evelyn put her handgun away and led Hayden, Kael and Nick to one of the fire exits. She found that the door had been chained and locked, but that wouldn't pose any problem at all.

"Kael, Athame," Evelyn demanded with her open hand over her shoulder.

"Yeah," Kael said, and complied by setting the handle into her awaiting grasp.

Switching it over to her left, while still holding the battery, Evelyn then ran her ring finger and thumb along the blade edge, ending with a feminine flick. The edge heated up to a glow where she made contact, and Evelyn felt its heat on her face and hands.

Taking the knife back into her right hand, Evelyn grabbed the chain near the lock with her left. She inserted the blade tip into the padlock's loop and pivoted it, so that the knife cut through one side with all the ease of butter. Then she unhooked the lock and threw off the chains.

Passing the knife back, Evelyn kept her D-cell in hand, and drew out her longsword.

"Everyone ready?" Hayden asked, as he pulled up the spear gun and loaded it.

235

"Ready to rock," Kael snarled. He drew the knife to full length, to the amazement of patrons behind him.

"Those fuckers up in the ceiling are ready," Nick observed, as drop ceiling panels fell to the floor.

Evelyn kicked open the door and ran out with Kael positioning himself unerringly to her side. At first, Evelyn looked to the East to see hope-inducing predawn, but a grinding scramble from the roof turned her around on her heel. A few turned bats fluttered down toward the emerging crowd, but a human vampire was perched up there sizing up its opportunity.

Dropping three stories without care or harm, the vampire grabbed the nearest person as others fled screaming. Nick ran up to it and the struggling victim to point twin barrels into the night stalker's neck. One squeeze later and the fiend fell back, its arms and legs in a spasm.

Seeing bats come at her and Kael, Evelyn raised up the sword despite the weapon's appreciable weight. She swept the edge back and forth with less expertise than Kael would have, but not in a reckless manner of someone who never practiced. Evelyn sliced through bats with each stroke, and Kael either batted others away or cut a wing off with each hot-edged attack.

Then Evelyn felt repeatedly bumped, and nearly knocked down once, by the escaping mob. Kael had caught her, and then positioned himself to body check patrons away. However, as Evelyn turned for the truck she was confronted by another ambulatory corpse merged with the masses.

More out of reflex, Evelyn jumped back a step with her sword arm drawn. The thing gave her a shark-tooth grin as it lunged. Evelyn lanced her sword straight into the dead woman's chest, and then her grip on the handle flinched tighter for an instant.

Flames erupted from just inside the left breast, where her sword pierced, as the now limp body fell.

That's when Evelyn recognized Amanda Hale, the first lottery winner.

Drawing the Celtic blade out, Evelyn quickly swung it around to take Amanda's head off, before her never-decaying corpse could regain motility. Evelyn turned to wave the others on toward the security truck. Other human and canine vampires snagged fleeing people and took to sucking on them where they fell. Hayden loosed a spear into one, which Evelyn guided on target, without Hayden knowing it. Nick, meanwhile, fired a barrage of forty-five caliber pairs at another human vampire. True to Nick's statement a couple weeks ago, he blasted a good-sized hole into the advancing vampire's chest, though a few bullets bounced off the exposed sternum.

By the time it was close enough to grab Nick's jacket he was able to shove the pistol barrels through the ribcage to fire off the eighth and final twins that were loaded into two clips. Evelyn saw bits of flesh blast out the vampire's back, and the thing lost its power to move. It nearly took Nick down as it collapsed. No time to reload, Nick put

237

the pistol away, and pulled out lawn pegs into each hand.

However, the motley collection of the night's creatures had their prizes, as most of the patrons escaped into the coming dawn. Evelyn grabbed a door handle on the truck, and realized it was locked. Again, she raised her sword, ready to back it up with power and turned her head back and forth searching for the next assailing vampire.

"Hayden," Evelyn yelled, as he Kael and Nick caught up. "Keys!"

Running around to where Evelyn waited, Hayden opened the door facing away from the club. He shouldered the spear gun and fumbled with the keys. Then he unlocked the truck and ushered everyone in. Once Hayden got into the driver seat, Evelyn took the passenger side, and set the sword down at her feet to get a lawn stake ready.

Evelyn saw human vampires dragging their prey inside. One of the turned dogs had fed as long as it could, before giving up to advancing morning. However, the fire door had closed once the human vampires fled into it. The canine corpse clawed and scratched at the door with no outside handle, as dawn's rays beamed over the horizon. Yelps that tore at Evelyn's heart strings sounded, as the rapidly cooking thing ran around to the other side of the building. She didn't know if it made it, but caught herself hoping it had.

"God damn, that was fuckin' intense," Nick cussed out his exhilaration.

Evelyn wondered why Hayden hadn't turned the engine over to escape, but then reminded herself

238

that it was no longer necessary. Instead, she saw Hayden texting away on his phone. From an inconspicuous lean Evelyn spied Hayden's online social chirping account.

"Why aren't we moving yet?" Kael demanded.

"The sun's out," Evelyn called back. "We're safe now."

"Goddamn stupid son-of-a-bitch," Evelyn heard the chemist condemn under his breath and then mocked the host's confessed plan. "Oh, let's just die now so we don't have to later. Dumb shit, should'a let Nick kill him. People need to know that having all pistons firing doesn't mean it's you."

"Are you going to tell those guys about this?" Evelyn asked, trying to look into Hayden's eyes.

"What guys?" he threw back, still staring at his phone.

"The people who keep calling you about your research," Evelyn elaborated.

"I don't know yet," Hayden said, his hands trembling as he typed with his thumbs. "Maybe you're right about their intentions. I can't wait to hear their 'fight fire with fire' argument. This is a weird time to admit it, but back when I was a little kid I used to always side with Smokey the Bear, 'Only you can prevent forest fires.' God, I loved seeing those commercials come on."

Evelyn was moved by Hayden's confession to being a childhood tree-hugger. "That's sweet."

"Wasn't sure this would actually work on them," Nick remarked, perched between front seats, as he pulled out his handgun again and traded an empty pair of clips for full ones.

"What happened with 'it's too close for shotguns'?" a curious Evelyn asked with a smirk.

Raising his eyebrows in a shrug, Nick answered. "I kept thinking of that head severing thing."

"You figured why not blow out their spinal column," Hayden observed.

"Worked pretty good, didn't it," Nick crowed with a grin.

"A little too good," Evelyn pointed out all the gore on Nick's jacket sleeve.

"Ya'know, what the fuck." Nick dismissed it, waving a hand out after putting the gun away. "The way I see it, it's not like I can't just pick up a new one free of charge."

"What do we do about that asshole in his little shop of horrors?" Evelyn asked Hayden.

"One way or the other he's dead," a spurning Hayden declared. "Fuck him."

Hayden opted to do another quick set of errands around the city for whatever goods the group might need. Raiding an army/navy surplus and sporting goods store, Evelyn stumbled across a large cache of military food rations, which Kael said were called MRE's. They loaded them into the truck, as Nick went searching for more ammo. In the third building they checked out the group stumbled across other survivors out foraging, but no one spoke. Evelyn, Kael, Hayden and Nick just traded back uncertain glances to those given to them by other refugees from the night.

Maybe it was seeing their arsenal that held the strangers back and kept them honest. Or it was Evelyn's own neo-medieval protective clothing, she realized on second thought. She and Kael had to chop back advancing rats in the building's stockroom, but that proved easy. At least no tiny, winged terrors had roosted in the buildings that they scavenged through.

Chapter 11: Magic Man

"It's surprising things have held up as well as they did," Hayden said to Evelyn, as he worked on the mess of electronics. "Power, water, sewage, gas all working after two weeks."

In the background was David's emergency radio tuned to a channel providing news reports day and night. While Hayden had brought back stored blood in a small refrigerator, he provided none of it to the still cryptobiotic vampire. Though Hayden didn't tell anyone, he frequently thought about just pushing Alina Galca's corpse out the front door into the morning sun.

"Ah," Hayden yelped in a jolt to his Vincent Price ringtone. "The only people I get calls from."

"Same old Hayden." Evelyn shook her head at his persistent choice of phone rings.

"Hello," Hayden said into the phone, while still looking over his spectral array.

"We saw your last posting." It was indeed the man Hayden figured called from the *USS John C. Stennis*. "You say this guy figured out how to accelerate the turning process, but no specifics."

"We had to leave in something of a rush," Hayden explained, turning to see Evelyn and Valerie taking interest in his conversation. "It could be the number of entry points."

"What about who orchestrated these drawings?" the voice asked. "We'd like a word with him."

"I'm afraid that's not an option," Hayden replied. "Last we saw of him he bolted into that nest of turned infant corpses. Either he made it or the vampires entering the building got him beforehand. But whichever it was he's surely prowling the night now."

"But his specimens turned in under fifteen minutes, correct?" The voice had a cruel way of stripping away the humanity of Amanda Hale and others who had gone to their deaths willingly.

"Yes, by nearly four minutes," Hayden affirmed. "So there would've been next to no neural synaptic breakdown. But that didn't stop those corpses from coming after the rest. One had installed screens into the ventilation system, and after he turned those were the first thing he went for."

"Why do you suppose that is?" the voice asked.

"Well, look," Hayden began. "None of the body's hormones or neurotransmitters are produced. This unimolecular crap substitutes specialized functional groups for that. The brain gives direction to the body still, but this goo that's centralized in the heart is what gives the turned dead motility and its requirements are their motivation. You get a smarter vampire if this is repeated, but they're just more dangerous that way. I'd work on a different angle to this problem if I were you."

"You work your angle and we'll work ours," the caller advised him. "I'm sure that's why you stopped off at your facility before checking out the gathering."

"Any chance you could spare a few more of those Free Electron Lasers?" Hayden wanted to test how the voice would respond to his ventured guesswork.

"What makes you think we're so well equipped?" The mystery person guarded well his words.

"The *Stennis* made pretty short work of those vampire dolphins," Hayden explained, wondering if the other man was just going to hang up as an omission. "Nothing we have burns that fast, other than the sun. That leaves us the old Peter Cushing approach."

"The remote nature of your current location should help you out," the caller said.

"I see then," Hayden said, looking up through the ceiling. "I'm surprised you haven't sent anyone here. We could use the help, if you need another scouting mission."

"You're doing well enough," the voice refused. "We don't have time for door-to-door."

So they don't know exactly where we are, Hayden thought. Just the general area.

"Are they sending someone?" Evelyn mouthed the question to Hayden.

He shook his head quickly, and then spoke into the phone again. "Well, thanks for considering it."

"You said this man stole the Egyptian sarcophagus for use in his little show," the voice said.

"Yeah, but honestly that was for theatricality," Hayden dismissed. "He said as much."

"How can you be sure?" the voice pressed.

"Look, there's some properties in this crap that defies my understanding, but it's not some hooky ancient curse, I'm pretty sure," Hayden stated. "Dark Matter maybe, but not black magic."

"I appreciate your insight, Dr. Cornell," the voice concluded before hanging up.

"Hmm." Hayden vocalized his musings while pulling back his phone to look at it.

"What?" Valerie asked.

"I think that's the first sign of gratitude and genuine human warmth I got from these people," a bemused Hayden revealed, himself somewhat taken aback by it.

"My god!" Evelyn gasped with a comical face of shock. "It truly is the end of the world."

"Whatever the hell happened to those guys out there," Hayden said returning to his electronic work. "It must've really rattled their cage. 'Rocked their boat' a little, if you'll excuse the pun."

"I still say they're trying to make vampires they can control," Evelyn insisted.

"You're probably right about that," Hayden remarked, crouched down and looking up into the housing for a mirror that directed the Xenon Arc Lamp's light onto the working surface.

Hayden added filters as the machine was originally designed for them, but also installed several other features to augment what he believed missing from the solar simulator.

"Okay, Valerie," Hayden called out, as he rolled the simulator on a cart with near the gurney-strapped vampire. "Let's plug her in and see how well I got this."

She did so, and then Evelyn brought out a bag of blood for Hayden. He attached surgical tubing into it and inserted the other end into the mouth without removing the gag. He then hung the bag onto a medical drip pole and applied a couple downward squeezes to get it started.

"Tell me," Evelyn spoke up. "When was the first time you knew bites didn't turn people?"

"Oh, yeah," Hayden recalled and added while still being vague, "I forgot about him."

"Who?" Valerie asked, looking between the two adults.

"See, I had this other lab aid," Hayden recounted. "He probably would've joined that vampire hangout if he knew about it. Anyway, once I let my lab workers in on what we had been handed, he got excited without saying why. I didn't think anything of it at the time. Though, we later found out he was into one of those supernatural role playing clubs. Only this wasn't like D and D, just vampires and, I guess, some other Halloween creatures. I'm not sure if Halloween was the main theme."

"Oh, I know what you're talking about," Evelyn recalled. "Yeah, it's more about the vampires."

"So there we are," Hayden resumed his tale, waving to Evelyn and Valerie while giving the simulator one last look-over. "Testing aspects of the condition and whatever. But a few mornings we found traces of blood on the Alina corpse's mouth.

Three days apart each time. Then, when that stopped, we would find someone had been feeding the vampires without logging quantities or taking notes of effects. It made us trim down the renewed limb formation. There were syringe marks and really small cuts in places most people wouldn't think to check. Kinky places, a couple times."

"He was letting himself get bit," Evelyn deduced. "And when that didn't work he fed her blood, so he could extract it and drink from her like in the movies, or injected the stuff into himself."

"Pretty much," Hayden acknowledged. He leaned on the simulator cart once finishing.

"What did you do once you found out who it was?" Valerie asked.

"After a quick lockdown and quarantine, you mean?" Hayden asked, but didn't wait for either of them to answer. "I made him disappear— I fired his ass."

That got a grin out of Evelyn. It made Valerie burst out laughing, covering her mouth. By then Hayden noticed a sucking sound coming from the vampire.

"Yeah, that's it," Hayden said, looking down at the slow-working mouth. "Suck that down."

"How much should you let it have?" Valerie asked with some dread as she kept back.

"While they seemed to get extra mass out of thin air," Hayden waved his hand in a magic gesture while saying. "It doesn't materialize in observable matter. So this bag shouldn't be enough for more than a small fraction of an inch on each limb. But when we're done I'll cut that back again."

247

For good measure, Hayden pinched the shorter upper stretch of tubing closed with a clasp, and disconnected the longer portion. The woman's corpse sucked more eagerly in simulated desperation, whining moans included, while trying to suck dry the tube.

"Tough shit, bitch," Hayden cursed at the dead fiend.

He then rolled the hood of the simulator over by the vampire's head and scooted the machine to the edge of the cart. Then he noticed Evelyn's fascination at the body's stumps. Hayden saw tiny bits of necrotic flesh wriggle just enough to be perceptible, and knew that the molecular network was reforming cells. Many times he'd studied microscopic video of the phenomenon, and recalled the seeming Lego block assembly of missing cells.

"You say they're not thinking or feeling people anymore," Evelyn said with a sympathetic face. "But you still love to hate them, don't you."

"After everything they destroyed, you bet," Hayden seethed without realizing it.

"I'm not so sure we were doing that well before they came along," Evelyn muttered to herself.

"Anyway," Valerie interjected with discomfort. "Let's see if it works."

"Right," Hayden agreed, raising a finger to that idea. "Sorry, there."

He checked his settings and the filters once more before preparing to turn on the solar simulator. Finally, he spoke out in comical flare, "In the name of Sir Newton and Max Planck, I bid get thee behind me! The power of optics compels you! The power of optics compels you!"

Evelyn and Valerie both lost it and broke up laughing, as Hayden switched on the Xenon Arc Light and added array. The reaction was instantaneous, though wasn't quite the full terror that Hayden got from the body using reflected sunlight. It was more like seeing someone recoil from a gun put in their face fearing it would go off. Useful, Hayden supposed, but he wanted something that would stop vampires in a straight up charge to turn away fleeing for their non-life existences.

"Kind of a let-down, huh," Valerie surmised from Hayden's expression.

"Very much a let-down," Hayden admitted, stepping back to continue gauging the vampire's attempted wriggling away from the pseudo-sunlight. "I might have the various intensities wrong. Except, they recoil from sunlight regardless of what latitude, time-of-day or clouded conditions exist."

"Maybe there's something else other than light reflected by the mirror," Evelyn suggested.

"Other than the magic particle that cooks them, I can't figure out what it would be," Hayden said, and then turned off the simulator. "I'm going to have to play with this some more."

"I'll leave you to your conjuring then," Evelyn chided with a smirk.

"Oh, I been meaning to ask you," Hayden spoke up as the pagan priestess turned to leave. "The moon phases that powers Kael up. How do you think that works?"

"Until late medieval times, the keepers or our stories used to tell themselves that it was the moon's power to craft magic, given by the sun, that was reaching its zenith," Evelyn explained.

"Not the sun directly, but only reflected off the moon," Hayden muttered to himself.

"I may be a high priestess in my religion, Hayden," she prefaced. "But I still have to embrace the realities of science when they affect us. There's a guy in our faith who thinks that the magnetic part of the sunlight is passing through the Earth's field to merge with reflected light off the moon and the three are interacting somehow. He claimed it was a more complex form of something called the Photoelectric Effect, but of course he's never attempted to reproduce it. Personally, I figured it was somehow tied to gravity like with the tides, but I've got no way to prove that."

"And the mark?" Hayden queried on. "How's that work?"

"We say that the familiar and the mark are both within the light and between the light," Evelyn revealed, though sounded a little wary to tell Hayden, a Christian, this. "I'm, ah, not sure that helps. There's not much else I can say that will make scientific sense. But the pentagram like the one on Kael's hand does contain the mathematical Golden Ratio."

"Really?" a mildly amazed Hayden said, and then thought to grab his note pad and a pen.

It signaled for Evelyn to come over and draw out the pentagram first. To Hayden's surprised she reproduced it with free-hand flawless precision.

Then she ran a line between two tips, and darkened a line down the outside of the second tip. She repeated that through the pentagon at the center of the pentagram, to be followed by a dart shape above what now revealed a kite outline.

"One plus the square-root of five all divided by two," Hayden whispered to himself.

"The angles are thirty six, seventy-two and one hundred eight," Evelyn pointed out with the tips, the angles between them and the inside angles of the pentagon. "We call them single, double and triple angles. And then there's one other thing."

"Kind've like the trinity: Father, Son and Holy Ghost," Hayden pondered aloud, as she drew on.

"Actually, that comes from pagan beliefs," Evelyn corrected. "Only it was Maiden, Mother and Crone. Christians swiped the idea and our holidays to make forced conversions go easier."

She finished two circles centered on two corners of the pentagon that were at far ends from each other. The center of one circle marked the circumference of the other.

"I suppose your trinity could refer to the sun, Earth and the moon," Hayden speculated.

The image complete, Evelyn stared at him a moment, before saying, "What made you say that?"

"Have you ever heard of the double-slit experiment?" Hayden asked gawking at the circles.

"I think it was something I saw in grade school," Evelyn recalled.

"What you've drawn here reminds me of that," Hayden pointed out. "Isaac Newton cast a light onto a surface with two slits and studied what shone through those onto another surface. There were spots where wave overlap reinforced each other and other places where they cancel out."

"Your wheels are turning, I see," Evelyn said, studying Hayden's face.

"I think your fellow pagan was onto something," Hayden said, now fully transfixed by the augmented pentagram drawing. "There could very well be a complex array of angles and wave interactions that trigger Kael's transformation. But where does his wolf form go when he's not showing it? Does he change mass, and how does he recover human form?"

"It's said that the wolf hides under the skin," Evelyn replied. "That's why medieval superstition was that cutting a suspected werewolf's skin open would reveal fur. It doesn't, but they didn't know any better. And no, his weight doesn't change. Maybe it's a multiple dimension thing."

"I was never one to buy into that," Hayden told her. "Too much philosophizing and no evidence to show for it. The only hypothesis that made any sense was micro- dimensions at the quantum level."

"What are micro-dimensions?" Valerie asked.

"It's like seeing a string as a one-dimensional thing, but the ant walking on it sees it differently because of its perspective," Hayden explained using a common layperson translation. "They think that if we were to unravel particles they'd reveal other dimensions out to the world we know."

252

"That's pretty cool," Evelyn praised. "Kind've like pagan ideas of the hidden world."

"Yeah," Hayden agreed, rising up to his full height and shifting his focus at her. "Just like that."

"Does that mean you're more flexible on the idea of a goddess?" Evelyn chided.

"Hmm," Hayden pretended to think and quickly added, "No. But you've given me some ideas here. I'll tinker around and see what comes out."

Hayden had helped cook breakfast, but ate little before resuming this morning. He kept working through lunch, and had to be poked into eating dinner. By then he'd crunched quite a few numbers and dug around on the net for additional resources on his application. Also, he posted more to his online Hay-Corn account about the new approach and read some feedback. It seemed that other scientists were taking interest in his posting among the countless thousands of responses.

Where those scientists hid, or how they kept safe, Hayden didn't know. Yet a few of them seemed to be linked to the contract work his lab was doing, while others were from the National Academy of Science and DARPA. Or so they claimed anyway.

Hayden had no way to verify.

That night came a crash of breaking glass and another attempted intrusion into the shelter around one in the morning. However, from the scratching, Hayden and others suspected it was a turned animal, possibly a medium sized dog. Evelyn woke first, and managed to get others up before the noise started, bringing Hayden to think about her little home security trick.

The unwelcome visitation was enough to keep Hayden up for several more hours, which he spent reading news reports and social media gossip regarding the vampire plague. Hound of Hells, as Hayden recalled the internet terms being kicked around, though joke references to Poodles or Pomeranians of Perdition and Chupacabra Chihuahuas had also quickly emerged.

The vampire lions mostly stayed in or lingered on the outskirts of major cities. They were increasingly referred to as Blood Kings, for the leonine habit of staking out such huge territories. It was becoming the accepted belief that it was one turned lion for one city except for the largest metropolitan areas of the country. Manhattan's five boroughs were each staked out by a single vampiric male big cat, yet other vampire types filled those domains with them. No one seemed to agree on what to tag the turned foals which tended to run the highways and open plains near places of daytime shelter.

What Hayden took away from all this online chatter was that in small clusters people or, rarer still, individuals were hanging on. Rumors spread about resistance groups of slayers rising up to take back the night, but Hayden didn't see anyone showing themselves to be part of that. Despite what he, Evelyn, Kael and Nick had done back in the city, Hayden didn't consider himself in that camp.

The next morning, a numb Hayden joined the rest to enter the kitchen after clearing the house.

Only there they found destruction and disarray. The screen doors, which Isaac and David had fixed from when the Blood King and human vampires had broken in, again saw damage. This time only one glass door had been shattered.

However, on the walls, floor, the dining table and kitchen counters were written in blood: Fuck you Hayden and Fucking Hayden, along with variations of those themes.

"Er... okay," Hayden muttered, as shocked as the rest by the sight.

"Friend of yours?" David asked with a tone so casual, Hayden wondered if he were joking.

"We did put that security guard out where it would get hit with sunlight, right?" Nick asked.

"The cafeteria, yep," Hayden acknowledged. "I even busted out a window to be sure it'd get full effect. Best I can figure is someone else I knew was turned and prowled in here."

"But how would they know you're here?" Evelyn ventured the big question.

"I don't know," he answered, and then cast his attention upwards. "But we should check the house again to be sure. Maybe look around outside for places they might be hiding, too."

"Ah," Nick raised a hand. "I'll take upstairs this time. Isaac, you game?"

"Yeah, be right wit'cha," Isaac accepted, and the two armed themselves for the top floor.

"Kael," Evelyn addressed him directly. "We'll run through the ground floor."

"Sure thing," Kael answered, giving the ceremonial knife a deft flip around his hand.

255

"Hayden, I think you an' me oughta take a look outside," David suggested.

Once he retrieved his spear gun, Hayden followed David Judd outside. They walked around the house as the more obvious place to find signs giving away the literate intruder. With fresh snowfall the previous evening, picking out prints was easy. Those of a dog with extra-long claws stood out most, though David also found a pair of shoeprints. Hayden honestly couldn't remember ever having enough interest in the shoes of people in his life to make out these. At best he and David agreed that they belonged to a man, or last least someone wearing a man's shoes.

"Anyone you bumped heads with lately?" David asked, the pair starting to backtrack the trail.

"A lab aide I fired over a month ago, who was trying to turn himself into a vampire," Hayden admitted, and wondered if David already heard him telling Evelyn.

"Haven't seen 'em since?" David pressed the line of inquiry.

"Nope," Hayden replied without hesitation. "I didn't tell anyone where we are that I can recall."

"What about those gov'ment people out on that ship?" David pried further.

"They know the general area I'm in," Hayden confessed shaking his head. "Probably because their satellites saw which way I left the city. The guy hinted at not knowing exactly where, but I suppose he could've lied. But in any event, I didn't tell them."

"You don't think they got Wanda after she left, do you?"

"If they did, I can't see why she'd name me rather than, say, Evelyn," Hayden observed.

After a couple hundred yards it was apparent the tracks weren't stopping to any place nearby, and the large gap between strides indicated the source wasn't slowing down. With that, Hayden and David headed back to the house to help clean up. Not finding a body nearby made Hayden wonder where the blood had come from.

Anh Judd now allowed Hayden to cook more often, though she reined in how much bacon he prepared. Venturing out every few days, the group found fewer stores with working power. Atop that, Hayden couldn't imagine factory farms still being in operation, and so entertained the idea that bacon could become the new gold.

Eating quickly, Hayden then went right back to work. Sometime after, he wasn't sure how long, Evelyn came into the room to assist. He had the solar simulator open to rework his arrangement around the Xenon Arc Lamp, and then reset the filters before closing it all up.

"Alrighty then," Hayden said to himself, as he rolled the cart with the simulator over the vampire's face once more. "Let's try this again."

"She appears to recognize it," Evelyn observed.

"I hope so. Makes me think I'm on the right track," Hayden said, glancing at Evelyn a brief moment. He added as he set the machine in place, "I have a question for you."

"What about?" she asked in turn.

"I did a little digging and found that there's four items in Wicca ceremonies," Hayden revealed his side-line research. "Symbolically they're the sword, the spear, shield and cauldron."

"In Wicca, yes," Evelyn acknowledged. "But what our real gifts stem from is older than that."

"No, no, I remember," Hayden accepted her correction, and rested his hand on the switch. "But I saw that you only had the knife, which literally is in fact a spear in Kael's hands rather than a more obvious sword, and the cauldron."

"The pentacle is the representation of the shield," Evelyn stated. "Though, as you can guess it's more about the protective power of the sun shielding us from the Shadow Side."

"And the sword?" Hayden asked.

"Do you recall the Arthurian legions?" Evelyn posed, as Hayden switched on the light.

"That's a little better," Hayden exclaimed, and then turned to Evelyn, after turning the solar simulator off. "Oh, yeah, I suppose so."

"And the sword?" she pressed on.

"Right, Arthur pulls it out of a stone," Hayden answered, thinking only of movies he'd seen.

"That's the more recent versions of the tale," Evelyn corrected. "Actually, there's more than one sword in many accounts, and that's not including Norse or Celtic versions. Excalibur came from the Lady in the Lake, and was returned to her on Arthur's orders as he lay dying."

"I don't recall seeing you do any swimming," Hayden joked.

"Ah-hah," Evelyn let out the humorless laugh, and then grinned with real amusement before continuing. "The idea of a physical sword is a metaphor, Hayden."

"A metaphor of what?" he asked.

"A masculine property or power drawn from a feminine source," Evelyn revealed.

"Like Kael's werewolf thing given to him by your sisterhood?" he asked.

"No, like I said, the pentagram represents a shield," Evelyn explained. "Kael and the others who are marked are assigned protective powers, even if that means pre-emptively going out to defeat threats. The wolf is seen as protective and loyal to family in a lot of traditions."

"Then what?" Hayden shrugged, having no idea where this was leading.

"In our tradition we haven't seen it manifest for many centuries." Evelyn's answer sounded as if she were more let-down than Hayden. "But the keepers of our stories suggest it emerges after a long quest or hard fought battle. One on which the fate of all depends."

"But no specifics?" Hayden inquired. "That must be frustrating for you guys."

"As much so as figuring out vampirism is for you, I'm sure," Evelyn suggested.

"Yeah," Hayden agreed, turning to look at Alina's corpse with his jaw unconsciously clenching. "The sooner I pick apart this riddle the sooner I can roll this human disaster outside in the day and be done with it. Tired of looking the

259

damned thing and tired of hearing Corneliu's fuckin' name."

"So now that you got closer to what you wanted, what's next?" Evelyn switched gears.

"Built like this," Hayden waved at the device. "It doesn't really work as a repellant.

Gratifying as it is to watch the thing freak out, that doesn't address the problem of vampires running around out there. I have to figure out a way to make it practical and not such a pain in the ass to set up."

"Is there anything more I can do?" Evelyn offered.

"I've been thinking about your diagram," Hayden said to her, but his mind turned inward. "It's interesting that full moon light powers Kael in proportion to the golden ratio of what his normal abilities are, but that the sun itself doesn't do anything for him directly."

"You mean because the moon only reflects light from the sun," Evelyn observed.

"Yes," Hayden affirmed with a nod with an absent stare at his assembled electronics. "The spectrum reflected off the moon isn't the same as that coming directly from the sun. But I can't shake the feeling there's something else I'm missing. Maybe there's light outside the visible spectrum bouncing around the atmosphere after the sun's below the horizon."

At that point Hayden became distant, and Evelyn dipped low and prompted, "What?"

"That's it," He declared, raising up a hand. Then he looked to her. "Polarized light."

"You mean for Kael's transformation?" Evelyn asked.

"Yeah, possibly for that too," Hayden alluded to what his mind tripped over. "But no, to get the maximum repulsion effect on vampires. I'm not sure if I can produce that with everything I got here, but that might be why they freak out at sunlight more than simulated solar spectra. It's not just the wavelengths, but also the angle they enter the eye relative to each other."

"What wavelengths become polarized?" Evelyn inquired further.

"Well," Hayden started to explain, as he sat down and pulled over another cart with his laptop to do a search. "The most obvious is UV, because I was reading somewhere that bees navigate by it. However, each spectrum polarizes at different angles. If I can calculate the right spectra from that and then bounce them in the correct angle I should get both of these riddles hammered out."

"Let's get started then," an excited Evelyn responded.

"And you will be critical, since this is more your stuff," Hayden admitted. "I wouldn't have thought all that pagan astrology meant anything, but throw in whatever you think's relevant."

Hayden first went online to fish up the equations he needed. Next, he brought out his forty year old solar calculator, given to him by his father as a kid, to help crunch the numbers. Then he and Evelyn measured off angles within the room and tacked up string to key points. There, Hayden would later attach more Xenon Arc Lamps and filters when he got them. A check with the priestess and her sworn protector affirmed that his change started when the sun set and the full moon rose. That allowed Hayden to establish reflected spectra from the moon and finish out the pentagram web he cast up on its side floor-to-ceiling in the small lab room.

The next day he, Evelyn, Isaac and Kael drove out in one of the trucks to scavenge more supplies. The finds were easy, because in the midst of this crisis virtually no one was thinking of raiding laboratory suppliers anymore. Another day after that and Hayden's polarized lighting array was installed. David Judd gazed in amazement at his storm cellar becoming a semi-pagan light therapy chamber. Hayden actually forgot to ask David if it was okay, but the older man never complained.

A couple hours before it was time to lock up for the night, Hayden brought Kael and Evelyn into the lab room. He placed tape on the floor to mark off where to place a chair. With all the prior work done, Hayden forced himself to not go about compulsively rechecking his angles, as though mischievous fairies would've snuck in to tamper with his work and screw with his head.

"Alright Kael, sit here," Hayden waved to the uncertain young man. "Perfect."

"Oh wait," Evelyn shot out having just remembered something. "Kael, you'll want to change out to your other clothes, in case this works."

"Those're only for the full moon," Kael said, confused.

262

"Then," Hayden stammered and waved to the door nodding quickly. "You'll definitely want to."

Kael threw Hayden a look that he couldn't interpret, but left for a couple minutes and returned.

"What was the martial art you were in?" a suddenly curious Hayden asked.

"Hun Gar Kung Fu," Kael said, turning to look up at Hayden. "It's the high school archery team story that was bullshit. I'm not bad with a bow, but... well. Evelyn can explain how she does it."

His curiosity peaked by the suggestion, Hayden brushed that aside, as he turned on the collection of lights. David still stood halfway into the door. Everyone else was busy elsewhere in the house. The moment of history was observed only by the four present, plus one animated corpse.

Kael doubled over in the chair right away clutching at himself gnashing, "Fuckin' shit!"

"It's alright, Kael," Evelyn assured. "You've done this twelve to thirteen times a year."

"Son of a..." Kael's voice deepened and grew hoarser.

His skin began to gray up and human hair seemed to withdraw the same time wolf fur sprouted. Leaning over to see other details, Hayden watched the thumbnail on Kael's clinched fist shrink back to the root and a claw extend upward from underneath to form an arc. When his hands could no longer form fists the other claws became apparent. Very likely, his teeth disappeared into the gums with canine dentation rising in their stead. The cracking of bones and skin stretching with the grind

263

of leather alarmed Hayden, but Evelyn waved him back from turning off the lights. All in all the process ran twelve minutes. In the end stood not the Kael Hayden was used to seeing but a powerful lupine form huffing loudly through its nostrils.

"Wow, uh, I didn't think it took that long," Hayden stuttered, gazing at the transformed Kael.

"That's about right, actually," Evelyn said. "Just that with vampires working to get at us, keeping track of time wasn't the biggest thing on anyone's mind."

"Right," Hayden agreed, leaving his mouth open in awe of the results.

"You did it," David congratulated, getting the attention of all three. "Damn, you are smart."

"Behold, the power of optics," Hayden offered in praise to Newton above, and then looked to Evelyn. "If I shut this down, how long will he stay like this?"

"Ah, I think it's, what?" She seemed to ask Kael. "A little over a couple hours?"

The wolf head nodded once in answer.

"Of course," Hayden breathed out. "Thirty-six degrees means two hours, twenty four minutes."

"Should we keep 'em that way in case another one o' them freaks breaks in here?" David asked whoever would answer. "That's if Kael's alright with it."

"Whaddya say, Kael?" Hayden prompted.

Again, one nod and a parted-jaw pant as if he tried to smile.

"And now for working this other configuration," Hayden said, turning in place

264

toward the vampire Alina. "That's right, you dead piece of shit. Your turn's next."

Chapter 12: Nothing New Under The Sun

Evelyn realized that Hayden had done it! The day after his test on Kael, Hayden succeeded with inducing fear in the Shadow Sider, though he still wouldn't call it real fear. Letting that go, Evelyn acknowledged his achievement that, according to traditional stories, none before had matched.

They also reworked the lighting system for Kael, as Hayden realized the planar orientation shouldn't matter, since Kael couldn't possibly be always standing the same way when his change started. And it was true, Evelyn saw after the next night's test.

However, there was more to do.

David Judd inquired whether the house could be protected by Hayden's lighting system. Hayden said he'd need more equipment and lights, which then prompted Isaac to step up and accept the implied shopping list. They also would need more solar cells and another wind generator if they could find one, as Hayden's work was pushing the limits of David's own array. Evelyn decided she too should go, and fully equipped at that. It naturally meant Kael went as well. Salma and Nick joined them, and the five climbed into the second security truck early the next morning with supplies and weapons.

"Hey, wait up," Hayden called out, while walking up with a couple of rigged parabolic devices.

"What're those?" Nick asked pointing.

"They're his arc lamps," Evelyn answered, and then turned to Hayden. "Right?"

"Yeah," he admitted looking down at them, before handing them over. "I set up a xenon arc lamp and filters in each, and then put these reflectors on. They're coated to simulate the polarized light from the sun. I hooked them up to spare car batteries David had lying around, so you should be able to use jumper cables to recharge them if they run out."

"Thanks, Hayden." Nick brought them into the back compartment.

"Good thinking," Salma congratulated him in turn. "If we need to hide out in here we can aim one at each door. I guess we'd better get going."

"Ah, you guys," Hayden added, turning back around before going to the house. "Be careful."

"Of course we'll be careful," Isaac said, furrowing his brow.

"No, I mean," Hayden paused before continuing, "We still don't know who put that blood up."

"It can't be anyone living," Evelyn said. "Not at that hour."

"Possibly, though it could've happened shortly after dawn," Hayden suggested. "It did look pretty fresh. I'm just saying be careful. Whoever it was knew I'm here somehow."

"Ah, I got'cha," Isaac acknowledged with an upward nod, and then produced the directions Hayden wrote out. "Don't worry none. We ain't lookin' for trouble."

Evelyn sneaked a peek at the paper Isaac held. It was a city in the neighboring state, which apparently was another of the suppliers Hayden's lab had bought things from. Isaac figured that it'd take two to three days to get there and back. With the prior fuel salvaging trips Evelyn had accompanied, they had the gas needed. However, she still worried for those left at the house.

"Will you guys be okay while we're gone?" Evelyn asked.

"We're fine," Hayden dismissed her concern. "I got one covering the inside of each door to the shelter."

"Alright, we'll see you later then," Evelyn said, before Kael closed the rear compartment.

"Who's on shotgun?" Isaac asked, referring to the front passenger seat.

"I'm on it," Nick volunteered.

They pulled out from the dirt road, where it re-joined asphalt, and headed west. From there Isaac turned northwest, more or less, on the winding road system common to the state, and then hit the freeway. Evelyn, Kael and Salma sat in back, with the door open to the cab, and munched on MRE's. Evelyn sighed and relaxed against the side wall while gazing out toward the windshield and morning light.

"Hey, check this out," Isaac called to everyone.

Cramming into the doorway between cab and rear compartment, the three in back looked to where Isaac and Nick were staring. They passed a sizeable power plant that was around a hundred yards away from the freeway. Evelyn saw how it had been turned into a military camp with razor wire, barricades and army vehicles all arrayed as if making a last stand. In all likelihood, the place had an extra layer of mines or other explosives out beyond the wire. Soldiers and armed men in civilian clothing walked perimeters, but their guns didn't look like anything Evelyn thought was a typical army weapon.

"Nick, you're the expert on guns," Evelyn prompted.

"If you say so," Nick sounded less confident. "I mainly know how to use them."

"What're they holding, or can you tell from here?" she asked.

"Looks kinda like a gun," Nick suggested, while squinting a bit with a hand up against the window from the morning sunlight. "'Cept the front half doesn't seem to have a barrel. Looks more like a big stapler or hole-punch or— something."

"Reminds me of a nail gun, actually," Isaac said, periodically glancing away from the road. "Okay, Kael, guess you're right. The government did put together army vampire killers."

"I'm betting they improvised after the fact," Nick remarked, craning his neck to stare back at the expansive facility. "Those cannons probably shoot white phosphorous shells. They sure laid out a

269

shitload of that razor wire. No fiend's gonna jump that."

Not far after they passed a sewage processing plant that, likewise, had been put under guard. As before some men wore camouflage, which Evelyn figured meant they were military, while others remained in civilian clothing, though the manner of dress made her think of security contractors mentioned on the news a few times. They didn't have the fully decked out perimeter defense of the power plant, suggesting sewage was less important than electricity.

Further away from human habitation and still under the protecting sun, Evelyn sat back in the compartment with Kael at one side and Salma on the other. Part of the new ritual for travel was Evelyn going through her phone, but this time it was for text messages from the others in the sisterhood.

"How's it going back home?" Kael asked, leaning over to scan the lists of messages.

"The ninth familiar hasn't shown up yet," Evelyn said, looking to Kael's hand. "How are you feeling?"

"Starting to feel the downslide, now that Hayden's pentagram lighting is wearing off," Kael said.

"You're not kidding about that familiars stuff?" Salma now had both of their attentions.

"Our oldest sister passed away about a month and a half ago," Evelyn said, and tilted her head toward Kael. "So I figured it would be safe to go looking for him while we awaited a baby girl who

270

would have the familiar. There's a few women in our religion who're expecting, so we hope it'll be any time now. At this point if the familiar comes through a baby outside our religion we'll have a hard time trying to get to them safely."

"Do you need all nine to do– you know, your thing?" a curious Salma asked.

"There's a few rites that take all nine," Evelyn admitted. "But most require seven or less."

"How're the others of the Mark handling things?" Kael asked, looking down somewhat ashamed.

"Their first moon run went pretty good," Evelyn assuaged his worries with a hand on his shoulder. "You don't have to feel bad about taking off. After everything I told them about finding Hayden and the work he's done, Michael thinks you were meant to lead me to him."

"Who's Michael?" Salma asked the two of them.

"He's the leader of the Order of the Mark," Evelyn revealed.

"How big's this order?" she wanted to know.

"A couple hundred," Evelyn replied. "Though, they don't venture out in those numbers. Anything more than twenty has always risked exposing us to everyone."

"Still," Salma doubted. "I'd think everyone would be glad you're around."

"Eh-heh," Kael gave the undercover a humorless toothy grin before his expression drooped.

271

"Yeah, not likely," Evelyn agreed. "In the thirteenth century we were accused of spreading vampirism along with the bubonic plague. We lost scores of the Marked to fighting off the Vatican's armies and four of the sisterhood to the bonfire."

"Can't let the sheep know pagans succeeded where God's chosen failed," Kael remarked.

"That wasn't the only reason," Evelyn told Salma while glancing to Kael. "But they seemed to care less that we saved people, including the pope's relatives, than the fact we were heathens."

Somewhat self-consciously, Salma turned toward the crucifix necklace she wore.

Evelyn always knew the Catholic crosses from others, for the basic reason that Jesus was shown on them. However, Evelyn didn't hold it against Salma. On thinking about it, she had no business doing so.

Before nightfall Isaac already had reached the next state, and pulled off well away from the road into a field. Evelyn, needing to stretch her legs, stepped out to admire the surroundings. Not even hills broke up the view to the horizon in any direction.

"This is some beautiful country out here," she observed, as the others came out.

"It's good for spotting trouble way off," Nick added.

"Now how we all going to handle these lights?" Isaac asked. "Leave the doors open and the lights on all night, or lock up and wait to turn them on in case those things try bustin' in?"

"I don't know about anyone else," Salma said, looking to the others. "But we're going to be way out here I'd sleep better with the doors closed."

"Hayden didn't say how long the batteries would last," Evelyn explained. "Just that we could use the truck to recharge them."

"Two things," Isaac prefaced with fingers up. "I wanna be easy on our fuel in case shit gets crazy, or crazier. The other is leaving the engine on all night might draw somethin' to us."

"Locked up and lights off it is then," Nick agreed.

They ate quickly before settling into the security compartment to sleep. Nick didn't cradle any of his guns like they were stuffed animals. He did rest his head on the leather bundle they were wrapped into, except one holstered on his hip. Kael kept the Athame within arm's reach outside the sheath. Evelyn slept in her armor, but she did so sitting up. The swords, bows, crossbows and lawn pegs all lay in a pile in the middle of the truck where everyone could get at them.

A hoarse scream ripped Evelyn from sleep, and she grabbed a battery from off her belt before thinking about it, and saw the others wake up in an instant. When she heard the second, she wasn't sure it was human. Nick and Isaac had the arc lamps on by the time more screams came.

"'The fuck's going on out there?" Isaac cursed with worry.

"Kael, the back door," Evelyn instructed, as she went for a lawn stake.

"Kael, don't get the back door," Salma countermanded the order.

"Kael," Evelyn reiterated, and then glanced to Salma. "It'll be fine. I just want to see."

"I don't," Salma insisted.

Yet Kael opened the door while keeping the Athame firmly in hand. Evelyn positioned herself closer on her well-protected knees to look outside. The light cast a sixty degree swath outside, but even without that Evelyn noticed the starlight offered more visibility than in years past.

Within the coverage of Hayden's lamp, Evelyn saw nothing moving or anything which was motionless that might've seemed out of place from her memory of it before dusk. Another vocalization to her left had Evelyn leaning out of the doorway to investigate. There were several dark lumps running back and forth in a way to suggest creatures running on all fours. Yet they didn't have the outline or movement of dogs and were too big for house cats. When one stood up against the approach of another Evelyn realized what she witnessed.

"Isaac, would you take a look out here with that infrared scope?" Evelyn requested.

"Yeah," he replied and produced it while coming to the door next to her.

"I think they're baboons," Evelyn supposed. "But I can't tell if they're turned."

"There's at least one that doesn't show up well," Isaac observed, and then turned the scope elsewhere quickly. "Ah, wait, found a second one. Yeah, they're suckin' down on one of the live monkeys now. The rest are haulin' ass away from them."

"Should we put them down, you think?" Kael suggested from inside.

"So long as they're not fuckin' with us, I say leave it be," Nick offered his opinion.

"They will sooner or later," Evelyn reminded, still transfixed by the sight.

"Wait," Isaac paused and adjusted something on the scope. "I don't think that second one's a baboon. I'll just check around to be sure there ain't any more on the other side."

Isaac stepped out of the truck completely, but stayed within the light of the lamp. He panned the scope to the other side of the truck and, walking to the side opposite of the vampires, looking forward. He came back quickly, but not so fast as to imply anything else was coming.

"All clear, but for those two," Isaac revealed. "One of them looks like a man."

"What do you think, Kael?" Evelyn asked.

"I say do it," he answered. "They're feeding right? From what Hayden said they tend to keep what they have rather than go for more. We might as well pick them off and go back to sleep."

"I agree," Evelyn said, and then turned to others. "Watch the back door. We'll take the other lamp and go deal with this."

Following her cue, Kael grabbed the front-aimed lamp and stepped out with Evelyn, who wore a sword on her back. She heard Salma mumble something involving the Spanish word, loco, but brushed it off. They strode from the truck some dozen yards, while Evelyn held a lawn peg like a dart to be tossed. Kael had the lamp in his left, with his other poised to flip the switch on with the thumb of his right while holding the ceremonial knife.

The baboon's back was to her, allowing Evelyn to line up the shot with ease. The pop of her metaphysically-assisted catapult of the peg caused both feeding vampires to turn, but not in time for the first to evade the projectile. It let out one primate scream before slumping over the victimized baboon. The second, however, rose up to full human height, and rushed at them fast.

Kael flipped on the lamp, which caused the vampire to slide to just around ten feet away with arms up over a face of stark terror. The thing fell over while trying to turn around and flee. Evelyn withdrew the sword and ran for the scrambling corpse, forcing Kael to catch up. With the aid of the D-cell in her left, she had no trouble at all plunging the heavy sword into the vampire's back using her right hand alone. Kael jumped atop the stilled body and drove his Athame into the base of its skull. Using his upper body, he twisted the knife with both hands until something in the spine popped. From there he quickly cut away the soft parts of the neck until the head was separated.

He rose up and cast the arc lamp at his clothes to see little in the way of grass stains. It was late winter, and the grasses had yet to return to their healthy green.

"That was easy," Kael commented.

Evelyn, however, approached the other animal that they fed from. There had only been two

276

vampires sucking on it, and they only just started. However, to be cautious she swept the sword down to make a clear sever with searing heat imbued into the blade. Kael decapitated the other baboon that Evelyn had brought down, and then waved the lamp around in all directions.

"Do you see anything else?" Evelyn asked tensely, turning around.

"No," Kael shook his head. "What time is it, anyway?"

"A little before three," Evelyn answered after putting the battery away and fishing out her phone to turn the screen on. "At least we know Hayden's light works on them."

"Still," Kael began to say. "It'd be nicer if it burned vampires, instead of just freaking them out."

"Take what you can get and be grateful," Evelyn schooled, trying not to sound like a minister.

"Whoa," Kael stopped up before heading back to the truck.

Evelyn turned to where Kael had aimed the vampire-repelling light. The human corpse appeared to have a crisp set of all black clothes and army-style boots. What's more, it appeared equipped for deployment, though Evelyn didn't know all that much about what kind of equipment that would be. She was, however, pretty sure it didn't include the type of gun that remained strapped to the dead body's side. Kael turned the headless body over and knelt down for a closer look.

"Didn't Isaac say those other weapons looked like nail guns?" Kael asked, turning up to her.

"Yes he did," Evelyn recalled, and turned toward the truck with a hiss. "Isaac! Over here."

Isaac scanned around before hopping out and trotting over with a crossbow in hand and lawn pegs tucked into his belt. "What's up?"

"Doesn't look bloodied up at all," Kael remarked, causing Isaac to look down.

"Damn, just like at the plant," Isaac said, toeing the strange weapon.

"Except they weren't in all black," Evelyn observed.

"You think this guy was at that club?" Kael inquired, while carefully freeing the gun.

"I don't see why he would," Evelyn doubted. "Certainly not with all this on him."

"This is cool," Kael said, pulling free one of several knives off the dead man.

He set the blade onto the muzzle of the weird gun with a solid click, causing Evelyn to realize something. "A bayonet in case they're too close."

"You think he was bein' sent out to hunt vampires?" Isaac asked.

"No reason to think he'd be out here for anything else," Kael suggested. "But by himself?"

"Maybe that's why he got ate up," Isaac postulated.

"There's no signs he was attacked," Evelyn said, and walked over to point her sword at the collar. "That blood is from his feeding here. If he was himself attacked he was cleaned up and redressed after."

"A lot of those other vampires looked pretty clean themselves," Kael reminded her. "They have to know that rolling around like they're in a horror show's gonna scare people off."

"Still," Evelyn iterated. "I think we should take it with us to show Hayden."

"Creepy, but alright," Isaac agreed with reluctance. "Chillin' with another dead man."

Evelyn took one arm and leg as Isaac grabbed the others, and she knew she surprised him at how well she handled the load. Kael covered their retreat into the truck while bringing the head. After covering up the remains they went back to sleep, which proved easier than Evelyn imagined. It seemed they had all gotten used to the idea of hordes of living dead prowling the night.

The next morning Evelyn awoke to the sound of the truck getting back on the road. She pulled out her phone to check for messages first, and then to dial.

"Hayden?" Evelyn asked.

"Yeah, did you find that warehouse yet?" he asked.

"No," Evelyn replied, and then looked out the opened front door to the cab. "Looks like we're just about to the city. It's something else. We came across a vampire in, I guess, it's like tactical gear."

"Such as?" Hayden drew out.

"We found this odd gun and a bunch of bayonets on the guy," Evelyn described. "Like he was expecting to leave them in when used, and replace it with another. I see Nick looking over the gun, and it looks like it has shotgun shells and some kind of darts loaded into it the way you'd load a nail gun. Hayden, the vampire didn't look like it was attacked when turned. All the clothes were new."

"And you just saw the one?" Hayden asked.

"Of people, yeah," Evelyn replied. "There was a turned baboon as well. They were going after living baboons, which I imagine got out of a zoo somewhere."

"What happened with it?" he pressed.

"Well, Kael and I went out of the truck last night to stake and decapitate them."

"You brought it with you, right?" Hayden stated more than asked.

"Yes," Evelyn said looking at the others. "We figured you'd want to see it. Here's the other weird thing. We drove by this electrical plant with soldiers and other people guarding it holding something similar to this nail gun thing. Hayden, I think they're trying to use vampires."

"'Guess that's why the *U.S.S. Stennis* guy was so curious about that club," Hayden suggested, and brought his attention back to something else. "Did those lights work?"

"Yes," Evelyn assured with a vigorous nod. "Yes, they did, and very well. Thanks. You should've seen it, Hayden. This guy came at us full speed and it stopped him dead in his tracks."

A laugh from Hayden made Evelyn realize the pun. "Hah! Nice one."

"I think this'll work," Evelyn praised. "And when it does everyone who's left out there will be able to protect themselves with Hayden Lights. You gotta post this stuff online and teach people how to make them. You're a genius, Hayden!"

She got back stammering more than anything else, showing that in fact Hayden did have a humble side, despite his prior boasting about chemical engineers. Evelyn said goodbye and ended the call with a gleam of a smile for Salma and Kael to see, as she leaned back against the side wall.

"Huh," Isaac voiced from up front.

Evelyn glanced over, still in her warm and fuzzy moment, to see a city devoid of power, but with a helicopter flying around. Kael crept up to the cab, but stayed low while also watching the aircraft circle around overhead. In the following minutes of driving further into the city, Evelyn suspected it was a military helicopter. That was confirmed, when it turned to let her see gunners in each door with their weapons aimed down at an angle.

"Anyone else get the feeling they're not doing rescue flights?" Nick asked with trepidation.

"Yeah," Kael agreed. "Maybe it's just a wolf thing, but it looks like the kind of circling a raven or vulture would do waiting for something to die."

"Or looking for where something was killed," Evelyn proposed.

"Seeing if their vampire slew any other vampires," Salma rephrased, as she leaned forward to look.

"Turn this way," Nick said, though Evelyn didn't see where he pointed. "In case it's us they want."

"Shit," Isaac said, and then elaborated what concerned him as he looked back, "See if there's anything on that dude like a cell phone or something else with GPS."

281

"Yeah," Kael said and hopped over to the corpse and start searching.

"Make sure you don't expose it to sunlight," Evelyn reminded.

"Can I at least leave the head out?" Kael asked. "Fuckin' thing keeps staring at me making hungry faces and working those teeth."

Evelyn doubted he really was asking, and just cracking a joke. However, from her vantage point, Evelyn couldn't see any point in knowing the dead man's face.

"There's nothin' on this guy, Isaac," Kael called up. "Unless it's hidden, I suppose."

Evelyn crawled up to the cab in order to look into the side-view mirrors and out the windows. Yet, from the sound of its rotors the helicopter didn't swing around to follow them. They found the supplier a little before ten a.m. and pulled into the dock. The five of them picked weapons, took both arc lamps and climbed out to gather around at the entrance near the rollup doors.

Nick gave Isaac a rundown on the strange nail gun, having figured out most of its features. Then he passed it over before drawing back a crossbow. Next, he readied his odd double-barrel colt pistol for a shoulder holster and ensured his shotguns were within easy reach on his back. His last step, before entering, was in lighting up another cigarette and then positioning himself to one side of the door.

"You sure smoking's a good idea?" Salma asked, having her crossbow ready at the other side.

"If they're in there they'll come at us anyway," Nick reasoned with a shrug. "It might as well be while we're near an exit. No reason to add suspense, anyway."

Salma threw him an expression conceding the point before she tried the handle. Entering into the receiving area brought on a literal deathly quiet that unsettled Evelyn. In the back of her mind, slow eerie horror movie music played, and she forced herself to focus on something pleasant.

"Okay," Nick read off the list loud enough for anyone inside to hear, his cigarette bobbing up and down. "So! Solar cells we need, and Hayden's suggesting some new kind here. He says we might find a couple wind generators small enough for the parts to fit into the truck. And then there's the shit he needs for his funky lights. Whatever else you think is useful and we can get to fit, grab it."

Salma shook her head and smiled at Nick, who threw back his own charming smirk.

"Should we split up?" Kael suggested meekly, having committed Horror Mistake Number One.

"I'll go wit'chu guys," Isaac nodded and strolled over.

Tearing the list neatly in half, Nick passed over the Hayden Lights portion to Evelyn, who laughed despite herself. Salma swatted Nick's shoulder as he led her off elsewhere. Reading Hayden's writing, Evelyn realized he had even named the department they should look for what he needed. Isaac led the way with Kael close to his side, ready with the Athame and the lamp. Evelyn watched their rear with a bow drawn and a battery between her finger and thumb.

Despite being a warehouse the place was well lit by natural lighting coming from windows near the top of a high ceiling. Isaac pointed out that such windows were a fire safety feature, should a blaze start inside. Either growing pressure would blow windows out, venting flammable smoke into the air, or fire departments could break them as needed to direct air flow.

"Here's what we're looking for." Isaac pointed with his gun.

Evelyn read off inventory numbers for which Isaac and Kael scanned the monster racking. Kael found a pallet jack and an unused pallet to stack everything they found.

Then he and Isaac began loading it up, while Evelyn kept watch for them. Forty minutes later and they had the pallet stacked to over seven feet. Isaac slung the experimental nail gun on a shoulder, before pushing the load to aid Kael pulling the pallet jack handle.

Coming back to the truck, they loaded it up. Kael positioned a lot of the stuff around the vampire corpse and atop it to ensure it remained safe from burning. Once done, they realized that Nick and Salma hadn't called out or come back yet.

"Should it take that long to find shit that big?" Kael asked Isaac and Evelyn.

"Something tells me they found some corner where they could get more acquainted with each other," Evelyn remarked. "Though how this place could be romantic I can't figure."

"There's crazy, white people crazy, and then there's Nick," Isaac listed off.

"Just to be sure——," Evelyn's voice trailed off as she started down where they had headed.

The three of them followed where they figured Nick would go, and then came to an intersection of isles that offered no clue which way he and Salma would have turned. Isaac, Kael and Evelyn all turned around to see anything out of place. Taking a second glance down a long row of shelves, Evelyn noticed the walkway at the far end lit up particularly brightly.

"This way," she said to the others. "Looks like they set up the Hayden Lamp."

Coming down the end of the isle and turning, they saw that in fact the lamp was sitting on the floor. It had been aimed toward another walkway close to the back wall leading to the receiving bay. Isaac drew out the weaponized nail gun and held it up to his shoulder, before he and Kael started down a hall away from the open supplies floor.

"Kael, turn the lamp on," Evelyn instructed, and once he did she called out, "Nick? Salma?"

"Yeah, here," she heard Nick answer back from inside a room.

"Just in case," Evelyn said, slinging her bow before trading up for a D-cell and drawing out lawn pegs.

Walking down, she and Kael peeked into offices as Isaac kept an eye ahead. At the end they reached an office with no window to the outside. They stepped in with the Hayden Light leading the way. There they discovered living black clad men holding nail guns on Nick and Salma, who were on their knees with their hands behind their heads and stripped of weapons.

"Ah, got a speck of trouble here," Nick half turned toward them, understating the issue. "But at least we found everything we needed for power. It's all out on an isle near the lamp."

Evelyn nodded to him with slow unease, before eyeing the four men, "Yeah, ah, we'll look later."

"Wha's up fellas," Isaac chinned to them, just as tense. "As you all can see we're not dead."

"Upscom," one of the four said into his headset. "Operation Glinda has the packages."

"Glinda," Nick chided. "'You kidding me with that shit?"

"I think I know where this is going," Kael hissed toward Evelyn through barely parted lips.

"You." The lead man indicated Evelyn with a gun barrel, and then pointed it at Kael. "You and that man are coming with us. The rest of you can go."

"Fuck if we are," Kael challenged him hotly, and stepped in front of Evelyn.

All four nail guns pointed at Kael, and Evelyn saw each man tense up as if before a wild animal rather than a man. The leader repeated his order, "You're coming with us one way or the other."

From the corner of her eye, Evelyn saw Isaac's hand move to aim his weapon back at them. Realizing what would follow, she threw out her left forearm as if bracing herself from an attack. The discharge from one of their weapons resulted in a ping off thin air, causing Isaac and Kael to jump, but otherwise no harm came to them. It escalated from there.

Nick slipped something out of a pocket, and after a light snap, threw a knife at one of the men. Kael rushed a second operative the next instant with Isaac firing back before Kael could reach the gunmen. Evelyn attempted to split her concentration on the four guns and where she thought they would aim. The quartet of discharges sounded out of rhythm, before one of them stumbled with a knife in his neck and another fell backwards with a nail in his recoiling head.

Evelyn was pretty sure she deflected at least two shots, and thought it was all over. Kael had opened the throat of the man to his left with a cross-body slash of the knife blade from the bottom of his fist-hold. He followed up in a blink by reversing the motion into the temple of the man to his right, keeping his left leg back and locked straight for added force to both hands. However, Kael let go of the knife and stood wavering like a willow.

"Kael!" Evelyn screamed with realization, as she ran forward to catch him in her arms.

Nick scrambled over the man he took down, retrieved his knife, only to put it back in. Many times. His shouts were the angriest Evelyn had ever heard from the easy-going human smuggler. Evelyn's eyes swept Kael up and down to find one nail in his thigh, and the other lodged into his stomach. Salma and Isaac rushed over to help, each applying pressure on a wound, for Kael's leg bled profusely enough to reveal an artery had been hit.

Having recovered his arsenal, Nick walked the line of four downed men and discharged twin forty-five caliber bullets into the heads of three of them with a final cursing, "Mother fuckers!"

Going to work as only she could, Evelyn produced her esoteric first aid. She dumped half the aged bottle's contents onto Kael's leg wound while leaving the vampire slaying projectile undisturbed. The other half went to his stomach, as Salma wrapped the gauze around his thigh.

"Shit," Isaac cursed, turning his head up at the sound of an approaching helicopter.

"We gotta roll, guys," Nick warned, while fishing something out of his bundle.

"Stomach's bandaged," Salma called out with a voice reminding Evelyn of the Latina's police training. "Isaac, help me carry him to the truck."

"I got'cha buddy," Isaac assured Kael with a father's tone, as he wrapped up on Kael's chest and lifted him up. "You hold the fuck on, a'ight."

While four of them beat a hasty retreat, with Evelyn leading the way, they didn't see Nick following just yet. He arrived after stripping the four tactical-clad men of their weapons and web gear. Now spoiling for a fight, Evelyn strode confidently in front with bow drawn. Nick scooped up the second Haydon Light on the way, and placed it and the commandeered weapons onto a cart already laden with their earlier finds. He pushed it along after them, huffing with each step.

On returning to the truck, Isaac and Salma eased Kael into the front seat, where Evelyn stayed with him. They ran back to help Nick toss equipment into the back with haste, before Salma and Nick climbed in after and closed up. Isaac rushed up to jump into the driver seat, but Evelyn didn't get in just yet. The passenger door open, she stood there stewing with a downcast face.

Deciding to go through with it, she went around back and opened the rear door. The rotary aircraft drew closer, as Evelyn detached one of the Hayden Lights from the high powered car battery. She left two wires attached and shoulder strap that Hayden added. Next she dug out a handful of ball bearings she'd borrowed from David, unsure at the time what they might be useful for until now.

The helicopter hovered into view over nearby commercial buildings. Evelyn came around and stood some dozen yards the front of the security truck. Taking the battery's wires into her tightly balled fist, she felt the weight of the ball bearings in her right. She sized up the machine some two-hundred feet in the air. Knowing next to nothing about the machine's armor, she decided its rotor head was a good place on which to concentrate.

Evelyn imagined herself a baseball pitcher for a brief instant, as she drew her arm back. The thunderous explosion, from which she managed to shield herself and the truck using her bracer, shattered the windows of the warehouse. The ball bearings left searing trails in the air, at first in a spread, but arcing together toward the rotor assembly. The next horrendous crack accompanied the rotary blades shooting off to the four winds in a spray of burning metal and crushing the main cabin's roof. The machine fell out of the air in a rotating tumble and disappeared below the roofs of structures in a crash. All that rose after was a smoke cloud from the mayhem she had wrought.

Prepared for the consequences, Evelyn nonetheless collapsed where she stood, racked by pain. She blacked out just after hearing distant shouts of people kneeling over her and hands lifting her up. Amid the sense of burning, ruptured organs and broken bones of six men trice over, she dreamt of beautiful trees backed by bright blue sky and flush with wind through their leaves.

Chapter 13: The Truth Will Out

"Hayden!" Isaac yelled at the top of his lungs as he walked into the front door. "We need some help up here!"

Running out of the lab and up to the ground floor, Hayden saw Kael and Evelyn both being carried into the living room. It was a little before noon two days after they had left for supplies. Isaac laid Evelyn onto one of the couches, and then Nick and Salma followed with Kael. It was obvious Kael was hurt, but Evelyn, without a mark on her, just lay in a state of shock.

"What the hell happened?" Hayden demanded of anyone who would answer.

"Fuckin' assholes from a helo were waitin' for us," Nick spat, and then furiously stabbed a finger at the floor. "I mean the fuckers were sittin' in that warehouse until we showed up."

"They wanted Evelyn and Kael," Salma added, looking frightful at the prospect.

"Wanted them as in dead?" Hayden asked, still not sure what happened.

"I don't think so," Nick sat, as he plopped down in a recliner. "Something called Operation Glinda, what-the-fuck-ever that is. I guess they know she's a witch and wanted her for something."

"They had these," Isaac explained showing Hayden the oddest gun he'd ever seen. "They fire some kind of nail or spike using shotgun shells. We found a dead guy who had one and was dressed up

291

the same as they were. Evelyn didn't think he was attacked when turned."

"They're trying to make vampire soldiers," Nick explained, shaking his head.

"Evelyn told me over the phone," Hayden said, and waved at Kael. "So why'd they shoot him?"

"He fuckin' manned up and refused," Nick replied. "As to Evelyn, well, I guess it's because she iced a helicopter crew. She drained that car battery completely and blasted the shit out of them."

"Evelyn," Hayden kneeled down by her and took one hand in both of his asking softly, "Evelyn. What happened? What's going on?"

"Those people on the aircraft carrier lied to you, Hayden," Isaac laid it out plain. "I'll bet they had you guys check out that night club so they could track you back here."

"No, it's something else," Hayden suggested, himself accepting the possibility that they all had been used for some ulterior motive. "You said one of them was turned?"

"Hayden," Evelyn hissed, as if her entire body ached for speaking. "Get Kael into your lab. Get him in there and leave the moon lighting on. Please, Hayden!"

"Shit," Hayden cursed, and then went for Kael. "Someone give me a hand."

Isaac beat Nick to it, because he was already standing, and assisted Hayden in carrying Kael down into the shelter. Nick, Salma and a weeping Valerie followed. Salma brought one of the mattresses into the lab to lay Kael on. Nick flipped on the lights, unsure at first why transforming Kael would help. However, that was before Kael's eyes shot open with a body-racking twinge.

As before, his bones cracked and skin ground like wrung leather. Kael reached for the nails to pull them out. At first Hayden dropped down to stop him, unsure if he'd bleed, but noticed the opening of the wound was trying to seal itself. Then he and Salma each pulled on a projectile, cautious to the risk of doing damage on the way out. The rather long bullets were tipped with strakes at the ends to prevent them from exiting the body; by the time they came out, Kael's body was already covered with wolf fur. It alarmed the others who hadn't seen it before now.

"Should've known better," Hayden griped to himself, while parting fur around the stomach injury. "Of course he should be able to heal because of this."

"Painful as that all looks when he's turnin', I don't care what the perks are," Isaac said. "A curse is a curse. I'd just as soon stay straight up normal."

Closing of the wound took several nerve-racking minutes, and full healing came slower. Granted, it far outpaced Evelyn's healing additive, Hayden realized as he looked up at the array of lights. Nick, Isaac and Salma all explained everything that had transpired on the way to the city and while there.

"It's working at least," Nick noted, before leaving.

Once more that Vincent Price laugh jolted Isaac, who closed his eyes and turned his head up in condemnation, "Hayden, man, seriously. Lose that shit. I can't take it."

Hayden himself had jolted, before pulling out his phone, answering Isaac, "Me neither. But I'd rather be jumpy and on edge at this point."

"I'll bet it's them assholes," Isaac complained, before Hayden raised a finger in front of his lips.

"Hayden speaking." He didn't even bother with hello, with everyone else here.

"We've been very up front with you, Hayden," the man started off in a bad mood. "And you didn't deem it important to let us know there's goddamn werewolves now?"

"Up front," Hayden shot back, leaning forward. "Bull-fucking-shit, up front! That kid saved our asses more than once! So what if he turns into an animal? And what's the big idea sending a bunch of fucking black ops goons to abduct and shoot up my friends?"

"What're you talking about?" the voice griped.

"Some men came after some of us, when we went out to get stuff." Hayden refused to let up. "So don't give me any shit. While you're at it, why didn't you offer us the kind of shit you're gearing your own guys with when they cruise around?"

"Specifically?" the voice asked, having shut off his anger from a moment ago.

"Some kind of gun using– what, twenty-eight gauge shotgun shells to throw spikes?" Hayden decided he had more right to feel screwed than anyone on the *USS Stennis*. "I'm pretty sure that's useless for anything else. Also, what the hell is Upscom?"

"Son of a bitch," the voice seemed to scold himself. "I don't know if you're going to believe me, but I had no idea they'd send anyone out there to get your people. Hayden, things're messy out here."

Hayden thought he heard the background noise increase, and the sound of the caller walking somewhere, and then Hayden asked, "What's going on with you guys?"

"It's not just military, Hayden," the caller revealed. "We've got people from the State Department, intelligence guys, even the Department of Interior. There's also a lot of private sector personnel aboard. I think three or four different companies. Now don't get all conspiracy theory nuts on me."

"I wouldn't before now, but maybe I should've been," Hayden threw back at him.

"This ship isn't just a carrier anymore. They dismantled three quarters of the fighter air wing, just so they could guarantee the president air launch capability for the long term. We're talking decades, Hayden. They've started indoor farms. The ship itself is quadrupling as an assault vessel, rescue center, a mobile industrial platform and the last bastion of human civilization if it comes to that.

"Europe and Asia are gone. Whoever's left there are on their own. China's multi-million man army didn't mean shit when the epidemic hit them. The only thing the African Union nations have going for them is that half of them're pre-fucked-up, and– well, it's pretty easy to make stakes when you've got that much wilderness. We haven't even bothered checking on South America, because we're not the most popular team down there."

"You still didn't answer any of my fucking questions," Hayden's voice grew ever more heated.

"The ship's machine shops and Three-D printers are working night and day to produce weapons like the one you guys found," the voice finally 'fessed up. "And, not to sound like an asshole, but Upscom's kind've a joke around here. It means Unofficial Parcel Service Command: snatch'n'grabs done by the security contractors we had to take on."

"That's not all they do," Hayden accused. "Is it?"

"One of the big wigs, I couldn't tell you which because I don't honestly know, wanted intel on that club you guys reconned for us," the voice continued. "They sent guys out there to retrieve the turned infant animals. You're right in that the sarcophagus was just razzle-dazzle. But there's something to accelerating the dehydrolysis meta-necrosis."

"The–what?" Hayden asked, taken off guard by the technical term.

"Transforming death after being drained of fluids, Hayden," the caller explained.

"They think if it's sped up the subject's mind will remain intact. Everyone's read your statements on the matter, so don't bother arguing about it."

"Eleven minutes, twenty," Hayden interjected, the memory of studying his watch and the video of

Amanda Hale's murder seared into his brain. "That's faster than neurological degeneration. Eleven minutes, twenty seconds, and they're just as violent and bloodthirsty as ever. It just makes them more of a bitch to deal with. And yes, that's been a repeatable experiment." Hayden thought about James.

Meanwhile, the caller continued, "I'm not saying you're wrong about that point, Hayden. But there're people on here who're pretty sure it can be done."

"People who know where exactly where we are?" Hayden hoped the question would take the caller off guard. "People who've been sending their lab rats here to leave me little love notes?"

"Hayden, I swear to you, I don't even know the town," the voice managed to sound sincere, but Hayden refused to be wooed by the caller's apparent compassion. "I can't say no one does, but if they do they're not telling the CAG, the Master at Arms, Operations Department or even the command staff. We saw the flame job your girl did on that corpse. Sat video found werewolves running around Vermont at platoon strength. But despite what you might think, the surveillance satellites offering our highest resolution can't loiter overhead all day."

"What about the original guy who would call me?" Hayden pressed.

"He's dead, Hayden," the voice insisted. "Trust me on that."

"Like lying down dead?" Hayden asked, starting an agitated pacing around the small room as the others watched. "Or runnin' around suckin' people dry dead?"

"Dead as in cut in half by a snapped Arresting Cable and lost at sea," the voice iterated with a harder tone, and then shifted gears on Hayden. "That's not the only accident we've been pressed to explain. Your girl there brought down an SH-60 Sea Hawk, killing the entire crew."

"I already know about that," Hayden, unphased, replied as he looked at a transformed Kael. "'Serves you assholes right for not coming clean with us."

"Hayden, whatever she did it shredded and burned a milled titanium rotor head," the caller added, himself sounding shocked by the fact. "The recovery team said the thing's completely perforated and would've melted were it not exposed to open air. The last image we got suggests she doled out more kinetic energy than fifteen rounds from a five-inch gun. Whatever your werewolf pal's capabilities are, that woman's bag of tricks kicks the shit out of anything we've ever seen."

"Don't count on a repeat performance," Hayden snapped, thinking of the karmic rule Evelyn described to him. "And for the last time, don't fucking send your goddamn goons after us!"

"Hayden, it's not the Navy doing this," the voice pledged to him. "There's times we can't even control our own flight ops. That your little group nailed their recovery team and one of the test volunteers might give them pause, but it will just be a pause."

"You guys had been so hush-hush up to now," Hayden realized aloud. "What gives with the Wikileaks style change of heart?"

"Because there're a lot of people out here riding their bet on you," the voice said.

"Well good!" Hayden was still worked up, but almost felt the caller might be trustworthy some year, and dared offer him a hint, "Because I'm betting my answer to this is better than yours."

"If you have something the Big Fish will want a first look," the voice warned.

"They'll see it when everyone else does," Hayden assured. "I'm not letting this one stay locked up in some vault with triple super secrecy wrapped around it. Too much is at stake for that bullshit."

"I believe you," the voice softened up quite a bit, enough so for the background noise to suggest he was in some part of the ship difficult to be overheard in. "I know you won't believe me, but I got your back on this. We lost families too, Hayden."

Lowering the phone, Hayden felt a flush of shame as he stared at it. He'd forgotten a lot of those people must've thought they were on just another regular tour at sea. A part of him wanted to apologize. Another thought gnawed at him with the warning that it was just a psychological ploy. Yet if it was, Hayden realized everybody had family, and they would be only human in mourning their losses. Confused and uncertain, Hayden simply turned off his phone. Looking up to Salma, Isaac and the yellow eyes of Kael, he realized his inner turmoil must've shown on his face.

"What now?" Salma asked, as she took slow steps closer to him.

"First thing's first, and that's getting this place covered with arc lamps," Hayden explained in a low and slow penitent manner. "After that, I gotta figure out how to get the plans out before these guys decide to shut the net down to stop me."

"You think they'd do that?" Isaac asked, leaning against the door frame with arms folded.

"Unlikely," Hayden reversed himself after a heaving sigh at the floor. He looked up. "But just in case I'd rather err on the side of caution and be proved wrong."

Pushing off from the door, Isaac stepped over to give Kael a slap on his well-muscled and thickly furred shoulder. "Then we better get started, man."

"I'll be up in a minute to help you out," Hayden said, before turning to study Alina's corpse.

What benefit did he see that could be had by keeping the vampire around, Hayden wondered? He and everyone else got used to its leering and broken-record chatter. Much of the time Hayden didn't notice its attempts to bait him or bite him.

Really, why not roll it out into the sun once and for all?

Instead, Hayden covered it back up and went upstairs. For some reason he felt Evelyn and others should be in on that decision. During the rush installation of arc lamps overlooking the corners of the house, Hayden brought it up and met a predictable reaction. Isaac, Salma, Anh and Kael all

300

agreed that having Alina's body around now was unnecessary. David believed that Hayden would somehow find a way to improve the effect, having not understood that light wasn't the reason vampires burned in sunlight. Valerie wondered if something else might be gleaned from the corpse, but wasn't that vested in the opinion. Nick thought it'd make a great surprise for the next "UPS" team sent out.

Evelyn still lay in a semi-state of shock in the living room, so Hayden waited until the day's work was done. The new design of solar cells Hayden had them get were flexible and captured more of the sun's spectrum than just a narrow band of infrared. He suggested installing some on the south side of the house under the Hayden Lights, so that some of the light otherwise wasted on the roof would be reclaimed.

A few jokes passed around about a certain nationality's design of solar power lights, and Hayden admitted it was ridiculous sounding. However, while physical law made it clear a light could never power itself, at last there could be some reclamation of energy.

The wind generators could wait another day, as dusk approached. The extra batteries for storing energy could be installed down in the Judds' shelter before bed. Hayden helped Evelyn downstairs. Nick and Isaac volunteered to stay on the ground floor to witness the effectiveness of the lights. With another arc lamp aimed up the stairs from the shelter, David felt it safe to leave the door open as fallback for the two men, should they need to get inside quickly.

* * *

Blasting, breaking, and burning pain lasted for hours, but the memory of it haunted Evelyn and stole her will to ever want to move again. Those six in the helicopter couldn't move in their last moments without incurring the lingering wrath she had inflicted on them. Their final moments lasted minutes, but only because broken bones stabbed into vital organs until the heat of the flames brought their suffering to an end. However, Evelyn, who hadn't a mark on her, couldn't look to that escape. Her own screaming, Evelyn didn't recall, but others said that's what she did.

Not until they brought her into the Judds' home could Evelyn think clearly enough to plead for Hayden to save Kael using the pentagram lights. She finally willed herself to sit up after everyone had come down to the shelter for the night. Kael, still wearing his second skin, dutifully sat by her ready to offer food or water if she wished. Instead, with a shaky hand, she opened his shirt to see the most threatening injury pretty much healed.

"I could get to like Hayden's gadgets," Kael struggled to utter through a long muzzle not built for articulated consonants. His voice was deep and used flowing vowels with no roughness.

"When we reach out to the others we'll have to consider how to create the effect over a large area," Evelyn suggested, and then took a sip of water before continuing, "Especially now, if ever people are going to have normal lives again."

"Agh, I'm out," Hayden announced, folding his card hand before moving his chair over to the air mattress on which Evelyn was resting. "How're you holding up?"

"Better, but—," Evelyn hesitated for the fleeting fear that the pain of others would find her again. "I'm still not over it. Half the time I think I can still smell blood and other stuff from my own lungs."

"That thing from your familiar, right," Hayden recalled. "A witch's Scared Straight program?"

"Kael told me that guy on the ship called you again," Evelyn changed the subject.

"Yeah, he did," Hayden nodded, clasping his hands between his knees leaning forward from his chair. "He all but 'fessed up to working in a sensitive department on the *USS Stennis*. Apparently, all the carriers are being used as staging centers for whatever they got planned. That might explain why power plants and other utilities are being turned into armed camps. They're nuclear powered, but they still need to ship in food, weapons, fuel for aircraft and a bunch of other crap."

"Hayden," Evelyn wasn't sure how to phrase this. "They allowed this to happen?"

"And put their own families at risk," Hayden pointed out. "Force themselves to live on ships or in bunkers for years and years? I might not like government, but there's a difference between taking advantage of a bad situation and causing a disaster."

"But they are trying to use turned corpses," Evelyn reminded.

"That sailor said not everyone onboard likes the idea," Hayden revealed to her, and then shifted to something else. "Kael's healing ability. How did that normally work?"

"On a new moon it's like anyone else," Evelyn explained. "But as the moon waxes it improves until even some mortal wounds can go away overnight."

"Some?" Hayden rose up at that. "What about regenerating lost limbs and organs?"

"It doesn't work like that," Evelyn shook her head with eyes closed. "The Marked heal as they normally would, only it's so fast that infections don't get in the way and scarring is less severe."

"Now I got to figure out how to release the Hayden Lights design over the net from as many sources as possible simultaneously," Hayden seemed to say to himself, changing the subject again. "I have to think their ability to shut down websites and servers is diminished."

"There's a couple of the sisterhood who could handle that," Evelyn suggested right away.

"I mean someone with a good background in software and internet protocol," Hayden specified.

"Yeah," Evelyn said, scooting back and sitting up. "Amaranth and Rhona. Amaranth was one of the first to do file sharing back in the late eighties."

"Nineties, don't you mean," Hayden contested.

"No, Hayden, eighties," Evelyn insisted. "She was one of the people who got the whole thing started. We're pagans, Hayden, not medieval."

"Fair enough," Hayden smirked, hanging his head, before asking, "Do you think she could do the whole zombie computer thing that lets a file copy itself into thousands of computers and then release it according to an encoded time?"

"Amaranth was responsible for some denial-of-service attacks to the Vatican's website," Evelyn confessed with a mischievous smile. "She's also part of that hacktivist group in the news."

"Damn, we might just pull this off," Hayden praised, before getting up. "I'll have to see if David's alright with us using his internet for a little do-gooder underhandedness."

Through the night Nick and Isaac looked through the thermal imaging scopes out the front and back doors. Regularly they saw movement far from the house, but nothing dared approach. The closest came from the grove out back. Yet vampires who caught sight of the lamps recoiled behind the cover of trees to escape what they thought to be their destruction. Hayden Lights had greater reach when given larger reflectors around them, which now repelled vampires hundreds of yards.

When morning came David decided a celebration was in order, and Hayden hosted with a breakfast cook-off the likes of which they hadn't seen since the hotel. While others waited around the table to eat, Evelyn sent emails, texts and social media messages to the sisterhood and other members of their tradition. To be sure she got through Evelyn borrowed other cell phones from among the group. Whoever might be monitoring her phone or David's internet access might try blocking the schematics Hayden drafted up. However, they might not yet know who else was sheltering in the house. Evelyn sent the last by the time she heard Hayden announce breakfast was served.

After finishing up her meal, Evelyn sought the solace of trees. The others continued installing solar panels and started erecting wind generators. Straying further from the hammering noise and conversation, Evelyn stepped deeper into the grove.

Hyun's grave and David's buried cow remained, but David had apparently filled in the hole where the vampire rats had been. Fresh top soil had been scattered over it, making it look as though it had never been. Closer to a pagan practice of purification than a Christian exorcising of unclean spirits, Evelyn thought.

Days old lion prints were still present but faded, lending Evelyn to believe at least that danger didn't await nightfall. However, as she went further, to the point the house and its activity ceased to exist, she noticed more footprints of people. This time, with the soil thawed by spring, as yet to arrive, she could even make out the tread. Then realization struck her.

The rats and other animals the club host was using to rapidly turn people were all young. Evelyn's memory of the scorched fiends in the pit had all been that they were all full grown, or just about. Hairless and seemingly meshed together, because of icky silk-like goo within their bodies, but with adult proportions, to be sure. What's more, Evelyn couldn't recall anyone wearing the kinds of boots that would lead to the waffle-tread she saw imprinted into the earth before her.

Without her armored outfit and no batteries on her, Evelyn still opted to follow the tracks for a while. After what felt like three or four miles, she emerged into a clearing. In the middle of that lay two long indentations that could've included wheels at the ends of each. The helicopter Evelyn brought down flashed into mind. With the aid of the familiar, and a tiny portion of bodily energy, Evelyn induced a hallucination of that memory as if it were a hologram only she could see. Evelyn envisioned the machine, flushed out with more detail than her conscious mind could've summoned from memory, landing at this very spot. She noticed the landing gear fit right into the track as a perfect match.

"You fucking assholes," Evelyn whispered, before turning back at a trot.

On reaching the house, Evelyn saw one of the trucks driving off. The protection around the house she placed didn't warn her of any danger. Seeing Hayden coming down off the roof, Evelyn walked around to him.

"'Wondered where you ran off to," Hayden said, sounding again like a concerned father.

"I found more tracks out in the grove," Evelyn warned.

"Nick said he saw vampires running around out back," Hayden reminded.

"With combat boots," she added, and before Hayden could answer that, she continued. "They led out over a few miles to a place where a helicopter landed. One just like that other I hit."

"You saw the helicopter," Hayden asked, misunderstanding her.

"No, but I saw the impression where it landed," Evelyn clarified. "I had to channel the familiar to get a clearer memory of the thing and picture it on the spot. "

"When you say clearer memory...," Hayden restated, before she jumped in.

"Meaning all its little parts and whatever," Evelyn elaborated. "Every bolt, screw, slab of metal, everything. They're probably the same people who picked up those turned rats."

"Wait," Hayden stopped her there with his hand. "That was the weirdo running the club."

"No, Hayden," Evelyn refuted. "He only used baby animals. I guess they were easier to handle, but none of them were adults. And it's not likely he would head straight over here by chance to get the adults he said he used to turn the young. Those prints I saw were pretty new."

"But no one's heard anything flying around all day," Hayden said. "Those things are pretty loud, and it'd be hard to sneak around overhead in them."

"Did Isaac or Nick say anything about hearing helicopters last night?" Evelyn asked.

"No, and I'm sure they would've said so otherwise," Hayden answered. "You could ask Isaac and Nick when they get back. We sent them out to see if they can come up with cement mix."

"I'm not sure we should stay here much longer," Evelyn, looking distant, advised him before she realized the thought had even occurred to her.

"And go where?" Hayden wondered, and then led her further from the house with a hand on her shoulder and spoke quieter. "Look Evelyn, we got lucky to find this place and the Judds. I'm sure if they thought about it they'd be grateful we came. That bridal gown vampire would've destroyed their door to get at them. David might be a good shot with his crossbow, but there's a chance he could've missed and then they'd be dead before he could reload."

"Hayden, I'm telling you whoever those people really are, they know we're here," Evelyn insisted, trying to keep her voice down. "They knew enough to meet us at that warehouse full of solar panels. For all I know they sprayed some kind of rust water vampire-attractant all over the place."

"I've been looking at the one you guys brought back," Hayden brought up. "And I agree with you that its clothing and equipment are new-looking. But obviously they lost control of it. And I doubt they'd need to leave a trail for vampires to find us.

"The pickings in larger population centers are probably looking thin. They'd have to go further out and risk getting caught in daylight before finding accessible refuge. You have to admit that those baboons out in the middle of nowhere are kind of unusual for America. From what I saw and read online those Blood King lions are taking kills away from other vampires."

"We still don't know who splattered those messages aimed at you," Evelyn said.

That quieted Hayden right there. True, it was mystifying for secret agents or paramilitary contractors to tell the chemical engineer off in writing, particularly in blood. However, it's not like a vampire would've used up the resource precious to them and yet have done nothing else to the living.

"I don't suppose that guy on the carrier left you a number to reach him by?" Evelyn asked.

"No," Hayden shook his head in disappointment. "He didn't. But I think I know why."

"And—?" Evelyn made a summoning gesture.

"At one point the guy seemed to walk somewhere with a lot of background noise," Hayden revealed. "But he didn't have to go far. He must've been deep inside the ship already. I think I saw a movie like that, where there was this secure room away from the bridge and some other windowless control center. It's where the navy intelligence officers were working."

"Okay, so how's that help us?" Evelyn asked.

"I'm not sure," Hayden replied and mulled something over. "Once I suspected the calls came from a ship I kept wondering why no one identified themselves or explained who gave the orders. When he said that contractors and other civilian people were on the *Stennis* I figured he was one of them, maybe a company rep or something. But that last call now has me wondering why it is the ship's captain or fleet admiral isn't talking to me instead."

"Aren't those guys really busy?" Evelyn suggested. "Maybe they ordered someone else to call."

"But still, why not say so?" Hayden asked, and Evelyn realized Hayden's point.

"Maybe it's a spy thing, or whatever," Hayden then dismissed. "Maybe it's a ship security procedure, who knows. I was never up on those kinds of things. I figured they just did their thing and I cheer for them when they come home."

Hayden returned to installing the last solar panels, and then those still at the house went inside for lunch. A couple of hours later, Isaac and Nick returned with cement mix and equipment that allowed them to pour support for the windmill generators. Evelyn helped while waving off concerns about her pain that was transferred from the helicopter crew. The cement would need to dry and harden before the rest could be set up.

With sundown again approaching everyone went inside, but not to retreat into the shelter. Only Kael went down to Hayden's lab, where the lights would trick his mark into transforming him. The Hayden Lights seemed to assure safety above ground, and so the Judds too felt no need to hide.

By then Evelyn was able to read message back from Amaranth and Rhona. They offered vague descriptions that their plan to release Hayden's designs for the vampire repelling arc lamps was in place. The other design, that which recreated the pentagram angles to induce the Marked to change would, of course, help no one else, and so weren't going to be disseminated.

Arming themselves with the nail guns, Nick and Isaac traded night watch with Hayden and Salma. Kael would stay in the shelter on standby,

311

since he'd been allowed to sleep most of the evening to rest up. Evelyn stayed up, using another shower and change of clothes as an excuse, but the real reason she couldn't sleep was unease.

Finally about to turn in around midnight, Evelyn stopped on hearing Hayden's wicked laughing ringtone. It was near time for Hayden to wake and relieve Nick and Isaac anyway, so he answered it. Evelyn witnessed his expression change as he came downstairs to the main floor. Noticing her, Hayden didn't attempt to hide his alarmed face, though he took her by the upper arm before going into David's hobby room. He selected the speaker option before setting his phone down by David's computer.

"Now run that by me again," Hayden spoke loud enough for the mike to pick up, and then grabbed a chair. "These are the same assholes you got on your ship?"

"The field deployment team is, yes," the *Stennis* aircraft carrier caller replied, letting Evelyn hear his voice for the first time. "But they had a facility somewhere onshore to run their tests."

"And they've been just roaming around collecting small vampire animals, I take it," Hayden stated rather than ask. "Just like the night club."

"They read your posts on the chemistry of the vampiric material," the voice explained. "And coupled with your observations they tested a few ideas out on someone they claim volunteered."

"Wait," Hayden stopped him right there while leaning forward. "The turned rats went missing

312

before we investigated that club. Did they tell you that?"

"No," the caller answered. "but we figured it out. I'm guessing the robes are a psyops thing to keep survivors from wanting to reach out to them. After you told us about their operatives, Command ordered them removed from the ship. Some of those guys are pretty pissed."

Fuck those people! Evelyn wanted to shout, and was about to when Hayden raised a finger.

"Which leaves them this land-based facility, right?" Hayden prodded for clarification.

"Unless they found their own helos, you don't have to worry about them hovering around," the voice assured. "There's one other reason U.S. Com, under orders from the President, insisted we break ties with their firm and drop them off."

"Which is—?" Hayden teased out, as if the voice could see his hand rolling gesture.

"A specimen of theirs is on the loose," the voice started with a vague answer.

"Uh, we know about that," Hayden said, turning his head sideways with uncertainty. "We got it downstairs. The head's severed from the body."

"That's not a specimen, they consider it a volunteer," the caller corrected. "By specimen we mean like the ones you were issued. The adaptive behavior that the World Health Organization documented is a little more than language mimicry with this one. The dumbasses talked openly around it, and I guess their researchers were informed of your work. You and your posts kept coming up in conversation. I don't know if they were aware of

313

your location, but I'm guessing they have a better idea than we do. We can't say whether the thing escaped or the assholes let it loose. But, it knows your name and that you have the other specimen it was found with. Seriously, watch your ass."

With that the voice hung up, leaving Evelyn and Hayden both in silence.

Chapter 14: Necrophilia

For a week, the group allowed themselves to sleep in the other rooms of the house with the exception of Kael in the lab. There always remained one person on guard in the night, though. A wise precaution, Hayden realized during his turn, when he heard a pop of shattered glass.

"Everybody up!" Hayden's voiced caused a few to stir, as he first ran to the living room to awaken Nick and Isaac on the couches. "Get up, we just lost a bulb!"

Nick was up and fully conscious in an instant, suggesting he was used to rude awakenings. Isaac appeared a bit drowsy but no less motivated to scoop up a nail gun and hustle. The three of them ran upstairs to awaken the others in order to get everyone in the shelter.

"David! Anh! Get up!" Hayden shouted while pounding on their bedroom door.

Another pop from a rear corner caused Hayden to look out the panel windows overlooking the back yard. Isaac had Evelyn and Valerie up, and Nick went to wake Salma. Hayden saw that both lights were on the rear side of the house, and decided it was no accident.

"We're in trouble," Hayden shouted in warning.

Moving back for the stairs with the others, Hayden heard the window he'd just stood before shatter. On reflex, he ducked as did others. All except Anh, who just lay by the bedroom door, and David dropped to his knees in order to shake her while screaming her name. Leaning over, Hayden didn't see the entry wound, but guessed that it must've been a bullet that exited from her forehead.

"Evelyn," Hayden yelled, causing her to bolt back up the stairs. "Help us out here!"

"I can't do anything for her," Evelyn said, once she saw Anh.

"'The fuck you mean you can't do anything for her?" Hayden shot, staying low.

"Hayden," Evelyn whispered, which he realized didn't reach David's ears over his own crying and calling for Anh to wake. "I don't need to feel a pulse to know she's gone. I'm sorry."

"David, I'll help you carry her," Hayden turned to say. "David...! C'mon, we can't stay here."

"Go on," David's voice cracked with a hardened tone, and went back into the bedroom. "Just leave me here. I gotta settle up."

"David, you can't," Hayden challenged. "Not in the night."

"Just get down into the shelter, Hayden!" David grew more pissed by the second.

Something told Hayden at that moment not to interfere with a grieving man bent on summoning hell on Earth. He didn't dare take steps two at a time in the semi-dark, but pounded down quickly regardless. He ran from the base of the stairs to the shelter steps, and heard something snap behind him, taking out a front window.

In the shelter, everyone readied weapons, and Evelyn geared up for all-out battle. Hayden swiped up a package of lawn pegs and scoured the room for his spear gun, before Isaac stopped him.

"Hayden," Isaac called out, and handed over a nail gun. "'Baby's ready to rock."

"I was going to say we can't leave David to do this by himself, but—," Hayden got out.

"Yeah, we know," Isaac replied before he could finish. "Besides, those assholes would bust in here after us anyway. I don't think it'd be good pinned up in this place."

"Hey Isaac," Nick called over, and showed the top of the nail gun. "We can mount those thermal scopes on these puppies."

"Alright Hayden," Evelyn said, as she and Kael stepped closer. "What's our plan?"

"First," Hayden announced, looking around. "Let's get those arc lamps."

"Way ahead of you there," Salma said, having produced both.

"Alright, we don't want whoever, or whatever's out there to shoot these," Hayden advised. "So we don't turn them on until we're being charged by vampires. After that, uh, I dunno. Hide around the house, I guess. We can't just rush out there."

"Would a vampire want to shoot us?" Nick asked.

"I—," Hayden paused to think about that, "Maybe to wound us, but depending on who it was they might not want to risk bad aim costing us too much blood."

317

"Unless they're living." Kael struggled to warn them with his elongated mouth.

"How would they keep vampires from turning on them?" Evelyn cast a face of doubt at Hayden.

"It's probably another one of their volunteers." Hayden sneered the last word.

"No more fuckin' around!" Nick went for the door, and started upstairs.

The rest followed, but Nick at the top of the stairs huddled low and held up a hand to stay them. He then raised a finger and waved up toward himself. Kael went first, and then dropped to all fours to crawl where directed by Nick. Next, Isaac went up, and Hayden after. Evelyn emerged afterward, with bow in hand and, Hayden guessed, a battery tucked in her grip. Salma followed, and edged down the wall to the kitchen, where she could try to locate David.

Shot impacts sounded like chucks into the wall, causing Hayden to duck further back behind the wall separating the front room and dining room, with the staircase at his back. Only, on reflection, he quickly realized that the prior shots made no noise he could hear.

"Don't think hiding in trees makes you safe!" David was heard shouting out.

More firing and Hayden realized that David's weapon sounded odd. It took a moment to realize why, when Hayden thought back to a Clint Eastwood movie about Marines. It must've been a keepsake from Vietnam, though Hayden wondered if there had actually been that many AK-47's smuggled back by veterans. Yet, he wouldn't have the chance to go see if that's what David used.

More pops from the front yard bulbs reminded Hayden of what the naval caller had warned about. With all the outside Hayden Lights down, and another shot hitting the house's power line, he felt a tremor up his spine. Everywhere was dark now. Then he heard that gurgling bark of vampire dogs.

"Can you see David out there?" Hayden called out to Salma.

"No," she called back. "I think he's firing from inside the house."

"Ready with that light," Hayden advised her.

He heard ground-beating paws, until Hayden saw the arc lamp light up. Loud yelping sounded a hasty retreat of the dogs. Next, Hayden heard a chuck sound he couldn't place. More impacts knocked from walls and the floor, before he heard Salma scrambling back from the light she left aimed out the back door. It occurred to Hayden that he'd never heard a bullet without the bang.

The last one put the light out once and for all, Hayden realized, as the battery sparked for a moment. After, turned dogs found it safe to rush in again. Someone fired a nail gun off several times in the dark followed by dogs collapsing or tumbling.

"You pricks ain't the only ones seeing in the dark," Nick's voice scoffed.

A window upstairs broke, and David's feisty yelling accompanied more discharges from his appropriated assault rifle. "You wanna a fight, ya' nasty mutt?"

319

Hayden knew the old man's fighting spirit would ebb quickly, when the screaming and rips of clothing followed. More thumps revealed the dead catapulting themselves into the upper floor, as Nick rushed over to the stairs with Kael's claw taps following him. Several more shots from Nick's gun preceded Kael's lupine growls and the sounds of him clashing with the other canines. Soft tearing noises hinted at stabs, and over a short moment the raucous din drew down.

Nick and Kael returned to the stairs at a mournful pace, telling Hayden what he suspected. However, things ratcheted up a second later, when they all heard banging on metal and shattering of glass outside the front of the house. The impacts came so loudly that Hayden would've thought vehicles were repetitively crashing into a pileup of ever-grinding and twisting metal and breaking glass.

As the front door burst open, firing began immediately. Hayden couldn't tell by who, other than the man blotting out the dull cloudy gray defining the doorway. He heard Isaac shout through gritting teeth, and realized that Isaac had riddled the attacker before taking a hit. Yet more shots from the top of the stairs brought the unknown man at the door to his knees and then onto the floor.

A flashlight came on, which let Hayden see that Evelyn had crawled over to help Isaac with what looked like a leg wound and another to his opposite arm. Nick, Salma, Kael and Valerie all scrambled to help, with Evelyn setting pairs of hands on various injuries to apply pressure. She

320

then rushed downstairs, and came back up with her bag to start rendering aid.

"Isaac," Evelyn addressed him, as Hayden sat dumbstruck by the quick turn of events. "Can you hear me? I'm about to do something that's going to make you feel strange. Okay?"

"Have at it," he said with a slur in his weakened state. "Do your voodoo thang."

"Where's that other light," Salma hissed out with alarm.

"It's over here," Evelyn answered at normal volume, without indicating.

"What? Why?" Hayden stammered out, still not all with it.

"There's more coming!" Salma ran over to look around until she found the Hayden Light.

"I see you, Hayden," called a remarkably Romanian accent.

"Aw damn," Isaac condemned, still half alert. "Real life fuckin' Dracula."

"Evelyn, I gotta let go or we're fucked," Nick warned.

"Not yet," she shot back in a flash of anger. "Just wait!"

Hayden turned toward the back door, realizing he hadn't moved from the staircase wall the entire time. Putting the nail gun stock to his shoulder, Hayden hoped it wasn't too dark to see whoever or whatever was coming. A tremor built up in his hands, as he swung his head between the front and back of the house, unsure if more vampires stalked toward him.

"You need to hold them off while I do this, Hayden," Evelyn ordered, while smearing something he couldn't see around where others held Isaac's wounds.

His attention returned to the dining room and bullet-cracked screen doors, rebuilt by Isaac some days after the Blood King attack. Hayden saw something small slink up. It crept so low to the ground he didn't realize it was a cat until it began hissing while clawing at the edge of the door. Then it reared up to paw at the glass, before jumping up toward where the bullet holes were. Its claws caught at one, and it immediately pulled on it with vitriolic spittle-laced hisses.

With one squeeze of the trigger, Hayden punched a nail through the glass into the cat. It wriggled and writhed, informing Hayden that he'd missed the heart. It redoubled its effort to force its face through the hole, making it bigger a chip at a time. Hayden figured it was time to try a lawn peg.

Not having heard any bullet impacts, Hayden figured there had only been one turned gunman. He nonetheless remained tentative when approaching the screen doors. The cat had its face through and was trying to pull its body in after, but the nail kept it back, and its claws offered no traction against glass. Hayden opened the door halfway, noting that the cat recklessly ripped its head back out to come after him. It scratched at air toward him, as Hayden stepped halfway through.

First, Hayden scanned the vast field of a backyard of dead winter grass. Then he turned his attention to the cat growling and hissing while pulling on the side of the door. He could hear dried skin tearing, as the vampire cat's will overtook any concern for self-destruction.

Hayden made a guess, studying the still beautiful long-haired cat, and then stabbed a lawn stake into the small body. It brought on a feline scream that cut off in another instant. To be on the safe side, he wrapped his other hand around the plastic peg and pushed further in with all his bodyweight. Doing this tore the cat nearly in half and ripped it loose of the nail projectile, which clattered with a metallic ring on the dining room floor. Quick to react, Hayden dropped and caught the cat before its body could slide off the commercial-use impaling weapon.

"Son of a bitch, where is she?" That Romanian rage demanded to know as a powerful hand grabbed him.

Hayden was spun around so fast his feet left the ground. He landed on his side, and then tried to point the nail gun at the source of the attack. However, one cold hand clamped around his wrist and another snatched the weapon out of his grip.

A flash of lightning let Hayden see who had a hold of him. The haircut definitely looked medieval to renaissance, but there was no beard or mustache. The clothes were those given to hospital patients, though a little tattered by outdoor wear. Yet its clouded eyes, matching the storm clouds above, Hayden thought, appeared to carry more menace than most he'd seen before.

In a silent snarl that let Hayden see cutting teeth, the dead man lifted him up with ease, and threw him at the screen doors. Glass shattered everywhere, and Hayden felt something hard crack against the back of his head. With a distant stare he realized that he lay under the dining room table and heard bits of glass crack and scrape with each dazed movement he made.

Then all of a sudden the table was no longer there. Instead, the vampire loomed over him and reached down to latch chilled but firm fingers on his throat. Gagging as he lost contact with the floor, Hayden reached for the strong wrist with both his hands out of reflex.

"She's mine, Hayden," the corpse demanded. "Mine!"

Unable to speak, Hayden slapped at the vampire's wrist as if tapping out from a bout of wrestling.

"Nick, help him!" Hayden heard Evelyn scream.

Vertigo overwhelmed Hayden as he again sailed through the air, this time toward the front room. When he slammed into the floor the vampire had already burst into a full sprint over him toward the others. Hayden heard the scuffling, cursing, growling and impacts of people against walls. For a brief moment a Hayden Light came on, but a popping shatter quelled that after a startled scream from the Romanian corpse. It sounded as though someone had been thrown down the stairs toward the shelter, where yet another arc lamp broke.

Finally getting a sense of himself and the situation, a sore and winded Hayden rolled onto one side, still coughing. He realized that Kael had landed next to him, but recovered faster and ran back after the vampire. Hayden wiped his mouth with his left wrist while drawing another lawn peg with his right.

"That's right, Corneliu," Hayden got out between ragged hacking. "I got your wife!"

Between slamming Kael into the railing, which broke from the crash, and backhanding Salma out the front door, Corneliu's body turned toward Hayden. Even in the unlit interior of the house Hayden could tell the posture of someone – something – contemplating murder.

"Where?" The dead man's whole body shook with his enraged yell.

"Fuck," Hayden said in unintentional delay, as he leaned over with his hands on his knees. "Just – huh! Shit, just go down those stairs there. Figure it out yourself, asshole."

Hayden wasn't sure who was thrown down onto the lamp. Yet after Corneliu entered the stairwell toward the shelter, Hayden ran back outside for the nail gun. After a second's search he recovered the experimental weapon and tromped back into the house. There came a detached thought that more vampires would come, but Hayden forced himself to concentrate on the ones he knew of.

Coming to the stairs, Hayden looked down to see Evelyn staring into the main shelter room, still in the position on which she landed. Corneliu stepped right over her without a thought. Maybe he'd fed before arriving, Hayden guessed, but the dead man was driven toward the sole purpose of being reunited with his deceased wife.

Descending the stairs, Hayden strained to make as little sound as possible. He slung the nail shooting weapon around one shoulder before crouching down to help Evelyn up amid the crunching glass. Something poked under a fingernail, as Hayden reached under Evelyn's shoulder, causing him to withdraw his hand with a vigorous shake.

"Hayden, what the hell's going on?" Evelyn asked, as she got up mostly on her own.

"It's Corneliu Galca's body," Hayden whispered, then took a sharp inhale on pulling a piece of glass out of his finger. "'Sounds like they're sweet-talking each other in Romanian.''

"Where're you going?" Evelyn hissed, as Hayden ventured in.

"We only got the one Hayden Light left," he reminded her, after coming back to whisper. "Besides, I'm getting really fucking tired of that dead bitch saying his name. I'll handle this, while you go back to helping Isaac."

Unsure whether anything lay in his way, Hayden made tentative steps in near-total darkness, as Evelyn crept back toward the stairs. He felt around with his toes before shifting his weight to the forward foot. In the lab he could hear Corneliu shuffle around as if in a waltz, all the while he and Alina both sang a melody that reminded Hayden of some god-awful polka.

Using the vampires' voice as a reference, Hayden gauged his placement near the second shelter exit leading outside. He knelt down and felt around the floor. A loud bump of his hand into the light, accompanied by an exclamation under his breath, brought the undead festivities to an end.

* * *

"Valerie," Evelyn queried, while she approached the terrified teen holding the flashlight toward the front door. "Are you alright?"

"Yeah," she squeaked. "Isaac's unconscious, but I don't think he got hurt any worse."

"Salma?" Evelyn listened for a moment, as Kael picked himself up, before she stepped out the front door to find Nick brooding over her. "Is she all right, Nick?"

"One or two broken ribs," Nick answered over Salma's labored breathing.

Evelyn broke out her herbal remedies and another D-cell. As with Isaac, Evelyn selected the greenish white paste. She pulled up Salma's shirt to feel around for the breaks, and then spread the treatment over it. Then she closed her eyes, as her hand again grew warm. Salma sucked in her breath sharply as Evelyn sensed the D-cell rapidly drained.

"What's that do, exactly?" Nick asked, as he surveyed the outdoors for more trouble.

"Exactly, I don't know," Evelyn confessed. "But we believe the paste recipe was formulated to offer the elements needed by the body to heal. Though, I'm using the familiar to speed that up and let the body absorb the ingredients through the skin."

Panicked screams from a man and a woman caught everyone's attention. Valerie jumped out the front door, fearing attack from within the house. Evelyn removed her hand from Salma, to find almost all of the paste gone from her palm and fingers. She wiped the rest onto the porch, before she handed Nick a roll of gauze and took up the Celtic sword.

Stepping back inside, Evelyn saw that Kael was ahead of her, poised before the shelter stairs with the Athame drawn to full length. Allowing Kael to lead her down, Evelyn descended to the source of screaming that didn't stop. She realized whose voices they were.

"Someone get over here quick!" Hayden didn't sound frightened, just in a hurry.

Once at the bottom of the steps, Evelyn saw the light coming from the lab. She and Kael ran over to find Hayden holding the two vampires at bay with his lamp. Both opaque-eyed creatures of the night were crammed into the corner, the man huddled over his quadruple-amputee wife from centuries ago.

"Kael," Hayden said, and then chinned to the dead pair. "Stake'em and cut their heads off."

"Even your specimen?" Kael double-checked after taking one digitigrade step toward them.

"Yeah, I think I've gotten all I can from them," Hayden reconciled aloud with a sigh. "Whatever it is that burns them up is going to take more equipment and facilities than I'll get for a long while."

Taking a pair of lawn pegs out of the pack in his back pocket, Hayden passed them over to Kael, who declined. "Nah, I got it wit' diss."

Rather unceremoniously, Kael lanced the knife blade deep into the man's back, silencing him and rendering his body slack that instant. Pulling the weapon out, he then was quick to roll the body of Corneliu over and, with martial arts finesse, spin the spear from one shoulder to another for momentum. That he used to sweep the blade through the vampire's neck, ending with the spear held firm behind his right arm, his left hand under the right arm pit.

"Corneliu will save me," Alina's voice started the mantra. "Corneliu will save...."

Kael had rotated his right wrist, to then slice up at an angle with a lupine growl.

The head rolled forward down the chest, as the woman's body relaxed into a curve within the corner. After readjusting his grip, Kael pulled the pommel and hilt back to a recognizable knife before sheathing it over his right shoulder. Hayden sat the arc lamp onto the table toward the corner. It was that moment Evelyn realized the moon lighting was also damaged, and then pulled her phone out to look at the time.

"Hayden, he's going to revert back in a couple hours," Evelyn warned.

"I know," Hayden replied, nodding as he reached down to pick up the woman's torso. "Grab those heads. Kael, get the man's body. We'll leave them out the front door for morning."

"What about in the meantime?" Evelyn asked. "We're down to one Hayden Light."

"We'll just have to hide in the trucks again," Hayden said, picking his way through the main shelter room and kicking a few things by accident. "How's everyone else?"

"Isaac and Salma are stable," Evelyn answered. "Bumps and bruises for everyone else."

Back upstairs, the three of them went out the front door and several yards beyond the porch before dumping the remains. Kael rendered one good scratch with the four claws of his right foot as he turned around with a raised head. The thick overcast of night-time clouds let Evelyn see Hayden's slack-jawed stare at the two security trucks.

Getting out a flashlight, Evelyn shined it on the back of one. The door was smashed and dented, and while still attached it was clear they couldn't close it all the way to lock it. She and Hayden both paced around to see the side doors in much the same condition, and noticed the second truck was also severely damaged. Both hoods were ripped off and parts from the engines scattered across the lawn. Evelyn figured it must've been the turned gunman who did it.

Hayden shrugged and let his hands fall limp into a slap of thighs before he turned back to the house. Evelyn trotted after him, only to discover Hayden tromping upstairs with all the nonchalance of daytime. He searched rooms until he found David's body.

Evelyn tightened the grip on her sword.

"Will you help me move him?" Hayden asked with an air of reverence.

"Where to?" Evelyn asked.

"Ah," Hayden paused, and then seemed to look through the wall toward the west. "That grove

330

of trees seems as good a place as any. I'll have Valerie find us some shovels."

"Shovels," Evelyn doubted aloud. "Hayden, it's five hours to dawn."

"These people opened their homes and their lives to us," Hayden reminded her, turning toward her with his head tilted in exasperation. "Just, please, Evelyn. We got one lamp and the nail guns."

"Alright," Evelyn gave in with her own annoyance. "God knows what's prowling around out there, but Christian burial it is."

Nick, Kael, Valerie and Isaac leaned against the wall by the front door, all stared in disbelief at what Evelyn said Hayden wanted to do. Though, Evelyn thought, it was clear at this point the house wasn't safe anymore. Kael gave Isaac a furry shoulder to lean on, and Nick scooped up Salma in his arms. Evelyn escorted Valerie to the garage with a flashlight to find shovels. Then, as Kael and Nick each took their charges out into the back yard with flashlights, Evelyn went back to help Hayden. They carried David out with Valerie holding the arc lamp as well as another flashlight. She followed Evelyn and Hayden back to the house to retrieve Anh. Nick laid Salma down to take up his nail gun and scan the area with the thermal imaging scope.

Despite Kael's youth and strength advantage, Hayden appeared to dig faster under the light drizzle of late winter rain, and produced a grave plot a few feet from where Hyun rested. He then helped Kael finish the second hole, until Kael succumbed to the waning of synthetic lunar power. Undaunted, Hayden interred David and Anh, while Kael

331

strained to keep his transformation as quiet as possible. Evelyn helped cover the Judds up with dirt until Kael could again stand. Evelyn checked her phone for the time, and then went through her messages to find none.

"It's a little over three hours before dawn," Evelyn warned them, while turning her ringtone off.

The whinnying of a horse sounded through the night, causing everyone to take notice and look around. Even Salma sat up with alarm and a grip on the nail gun.

"Did that sound a little too high pitched to anyone else?" Nick asked, aiming his nail gun between trees and looking through the scope.

"David said something about a newly-born horse turning, I thought," Hayden replied.

Next came a scream that didn't quite sound human. Evelyn was reminded of a monkey or chimpanzee, but it had a pitch somewhat too low.

"Shit," Nick cursed. "That fuckin' gorilla thing."

"Turn the Hayden Light on, Val," Evelyn said, herself turning all around.

"What about those guys?" Valerie asked, growing more frightened by the prospect.

"They would've done something by now," Hayden deduced. A flash of lightning drew Evelyn's gaze skyward with a smirk.

"You guys stay close to the trees," Evelyn instructed. "And face out in every direction."

"Away from the trees, don't you mean?" Kael suggested. "You're supposed to stay away from

332

trees during lightning storms. They're more likely to get hit."

"Not if I can help it," Evelyn countered and held her hand out. "Salma, I'll need the night scope, so I can spot for you guys. Kael, you're staying with everybody else."

"Where're you gonna be?" Isaac asked as he rose uneasily to his feet.

"Up there," Evelyn pointed at a patch of sky visible through branches.

"What? No broom?" Nick, ever the smartass, chided.

"Ah, cell phone batteries sown into this," Evelyn explained, pointing to her leather girdle. She made it for flying or to lighten her bodyweight, depending on how much energy she could transfer into it.

Salma slid the scope off the nail gun and leaning over, handed it to Evelyn.

Evelyn then tucked it into her long coat pocket, before she stepped out into a growing downpour. She unsheathed the sword, but didn't take out any batteries. The leather girdle and the storm would provide for that. Raising her arms out to her sides, Evelyn closed her eyes and concentrated. She lost contact with the moist ground and rose up, to everyone's amazement.

Over the grove canopy, Evelyn continued to ascend, the rain's patter below becoming quieter than before. Thunder rumbled and clouds flickered with the electrical power of water vapor colliding, twirling and gusting. Then she took the scope out to survey the ground before putting it away again.

333

"Nick," Evelyn called down loudly. "That gorilla's coming through the trees and fast! Turn around!"

In a line, trees unaccustomed to huge primates swinging through them bowed and bent. A few pops informed Evelyn that Nick was trying to stop the arboreal charge, though without much luck. Evelyn raised her left hand over her head, and gave the sword a shake to test the weight.

"Come and get me, you smelly bastard," Evelyn yelled as loud as she could, and added a scream for good measure, as she hovered forward.

Sufficiently challenged and tempted alike, the gorilla cast its cataract gaze up at her. Evelyn lowered to within thirty feet above the thicker branches. The gorilla vampire flung itself to higher limbs as it closed the distance. Evelyn left hand, still held high, caught an arc of lightning. Yet she felt none of its incinerating heat, nor did she take the jolt to her muscles. Instead, it all went to the familiar and from there to the sword in her right hand.

The dead ape hurled itself at her with more force than any living gorilla could muster. At a mortar shell trajectory, the once-gentle creature with a bruiser's body sailed toward her. Evelyn flew to her right and spun in the same direction. Taking the Celtic blade in both hands, she swung the blade out at shoulder level. Powered by the extra force of her spin and the electrical crackle along the steel, Evelyn barely felt any resistance as the weapon's edge sliced through a meaty wrist and then across a

334

mouth opened wide and armed with canine teeth made into sabers.

Evelyn continued to spin two more full circles before she could stabilize herself. However, she caught a glimpse of the primate monstrosity falling in three pieces. The hand and the portion of head above the jaw tumbled away from where the body snapped branches in a crash and slam into the ground. It bounced once, with slack limbs flailing about to land again a little more than ten feet from the group, giving them quite the start.

"Evelyn," she heard Hayden shout up to her. "Where's that turned horse?"

As before, she pulled out the scope and scanned the patch of woods. Despite not having internal body heat, vampires still stood out in the imager. The motion and near-uniform distribution of heat roughly matching the chilly air gave Evelyn enough of an outline to pick up the filly's galloping stride. The lightweight but bloodthirsty equine darted between trees as if being trained for an obstacle course. Even amid the rainfall it couldn't disguise the pounding of its hooves.

"Northeast, guys," Evelyn yelled down. "It's hauling ass right to you."

Nick and Hayden squeezed off shots when they appeared to have line-of-sight with it. Yet Nick's hits didn't strike the heart and Hayden's unpracticed aim missed entirely. Evelyn realized that, unlike arrows or crossbow bolt, she couldn't get a good look at the projectiles and so guide them in. She put the sword away in favor of a lawn peg. Borrowing static from the air, she gave the plastic stake a flicking toss that turned into air-popping speed.

The throw stuck into a tree trunk after whizzing right over the small horse's shoulders. Readying another, Evelyn paused on hearing other footfalls and breaking of tree limbs. Two human vampires, one a tall lanky man and the other a waif of a girl, sprinted hard through the woods heedless of stealth.

"Hayden, to your left!" Evelyn shouted, after seeing which way Hayden faced.

"You guys make a break for it," Salma's faint voiced reached up to Evelyn's height.

"Fuck that, we can take'em," Nick refused with a stern tone.

Evelyn spotted some other shadowy figures. She couldn't make them out, other than they gave off no body heat, as they barreled through the grove. It occurred to her that this must've been some mad rush to get their kill before the vampires retreated from the eventual dawn. Then she heard many small rapid wing beats, and swept her gaze from side to side while kicking her legs to speed up rotation.

Drawing from the surrounding air again, Evelyn thought about taking up the sword once more. However, she realized it was too heavy for deft use even with strength assistance from the rings on her index fingers. Nail guns fired below, as Evelyn took out the pocket knife, while the water soaking her coat, her hair and exposed skin crackled with nature's fury.

One by one, Evelyn rebuffed animated bat corpses using her bracers like a long distance boxer.

She turned frequently to see which way the next winged terror would attack from, all the while hearing arguments between Nick and Salma about running away as she provided delay.

"Stop being a macho man for a sec!" Salma shouted between discharges of nail guns.

Bats circled back around after being swatted away, having never been touched by Evelyn. When she could, Evelyn flashed the blade to take off a wing or, less often, a head. Then she heard Salma cry out from pain, and looked down to see that the foal had her by the upper thigh.

Kael lay several feet away in a posture Evelyn realized meant he'd been bowled over and kicked by the immature horse form. The equine vampire trotted backwards, dragging Salma half-dangling from its bite hold. Nick bolted after her shooting at the horse, and getting further from the others.

"Nick, don't!" Evelyn's voice was drowned out by rain patter and increasing distance.

Hayden and Isaac were busy shooting at other fiendish shapes coming at them.

Valerie had to swing the Hayden Light around to drive back those she could see, leaving Hayden Isaac and Kael to shoot at other directions not doused by the repelling simulated sunlight. A better situation than Nick and Salma were in, so Evelyn soared off after them.

By now the filly was spinning around, smacking Salma into trees or the ground. Evelyn lowered through an opening in the woods, just as she saw Nick take a risky shot with the nail gun. On landing, Evelyn stood by Nick's side with her sword out. Yet Nick's aim had planted the shotgun propelled-spike into the small horse's left shoulder and quelled the beast. Without waiting for Evelyn, Nick ran over to Salma and knelt down by her.

"Nick," Salma coughed, with blood coming up her mouth. "Nick!"

"I'm here baby," Nick cooed.

Screams, barks and feline hisses rang out all around them, putting Evelyn on high alert. Yet Nick disregarded the danger to stay by Salma's side as she lay dying.

"Don't let me come back, Nick," Salma pleaded, tears welling up in her eyes, her left hand clutching her cross necklace. "Make sure I don't come back."

"I will, I promise," Nick assured.

Part of Evelyn screamed that they should just run, but she remained to guard his back.

"Just go," Nick said with reconciliatory calm. "Get back to the others and get out of here."

"You sure," Evelyn's shaky voice asked.

A silent nod was his only answer.

"I'm sorry, Nick," Evelyn offered, with a reluctant step away.

"Just make sure you kill as many of these fuckers as you can when you can," Nick replied.

"I will," Evelyn promised, before taking off again. "You have my word on that."

Evelyn returned to provide her esoteric air cover to Hayden, Kael, Isaac and Valerie. The five of them stayed within the grove for as long as they could while fleeing from where they heard the most vampires. When the storm loosed a bolt of lightning

338

to or from the ground, Evelyn ensured the tremendous electrical arcs passed through whatever vampire she saw coming at them. A distant crack not quite like thunder reminded Evelyn of a gunshot.

The other mercy offered was that the storm lasted into early morning.

Chapter 15: What's In A Name

Back on the road again, only this time they traveled on foot and headed north.

While the others had salvaged what goods they could, Hayden went through the house pulling vampire corpses out to burn in the sun. He had wanted to burn the house down in a vain hope of destroying bad memories, but Hayden then imagined the voices of David and Anh Judd telling him it should stay for others who might need shelter.

Despite the risks, Hayden suggested they return to the small town that they'd passed through on the way to the house. It was the only place anyone could think of that they could reach before the next night. This time there were no security vans to commandeer, only a beat up SUV they found with the door wide open and dried blood stains on the steering wheel.

"Luckier than the last guy, anyway," Hayden said, after pulling down the driver side sun shade to search for spare keys. "Now to see if the engine will turn over."

The engine started up, and Hayden then checked the fuel gauge, before having Kael top it off with the gas can he carried. Despite serving as Isaac's crutch, Kael carried the heaviest load composed of food and the gas can in his free arm. Evelyn traded off supporting Isaac, and took the time to inspect his bandages.

"Yeah, that's the last of it," Kael called up.

"Okay," Hayden replied. "Kael, help Isaac into the front passenger seat here, and we'll head out."

"Any idea where?" Evelyn asked, as she climbed in.

"Where's your little club live?" Hayden asked in turn.

"Most of them are in Vermont," Evelyn answered. "I flew out from there to a few other cities looking for Kael when he took off."

"Speaking of which," Hayden said, seeing Kael starting off down the sidewalk, and then Hayden leaned out the still open driver side door to holler, "Kael! Where you off to?"

"I wanna check that gas and mart for maps," he explained, half turned around.

"That's one tough kid," Hayden remarked after closing the door and following in the SUV.

The place had plenty of windows, so Hayden didn't fret seeing Kael rush in. As Hayden pulled into the lot, Kael trotted out again, raising a folded map with a flip. He opened a door behind Isaac and hopped in, putting himself and Evelyn on opposite sides of Valerie in the middle.

Following the map, Hayden and Evelyn drove in shifts for five days, staying on the move at night and sleeping in the day. They stopped in towns and cities along the way, to scavenge what they could. Then they came to a large town in Pennsylvania and entered a bulk retail-grocery outlet. The huge building lacked power and had few windows. Yet, as Hayden, Kael and Evelyn stood in the doorway,

341

they all heard mariachi music blasting out from the home electronics section.

"Hayden," Kael called out with a cautious tone.

"Alright, ah," Hayden paused before going on, "Start with food, and then we'll go looking around for some more arrows and anything else useful."

"I got the Hayden Light," Valerie volunteered.

"I think you should stay out here with Isaac," Hayden said.

"It's alright, Hayden," Isaac dismissed, as Kael helped him ease into the SUV. "I'll be okay."

They left one nail gun with Isaac, even though it was still afternoon, and Hayden found himself back with the spear gun. Valerie stayed by Hayden's side with the arc lamp in her hands and a crossbow slung over her shoulder. Kael and Evelyn led the way in with the nail guns.

"Damn, no forty-five cal hollow point?" Hayden recognized Nick's voice immediately.

Evelyn produced two flashlights, one of which she passed to Hayden. Resting his spear gun on his left forearm in order to hold it, Hayden aimed the light only at the floor. Evelyn did likewise as they advanced. Footsteps went from one aisle to the next, just before Evelyn could get a look around the corner. Hayden noticed when she turned her light off and resorted to the thermal imagining scope mounted on the nail gun. Following her lead, he clicked his off also, and that was when the rummaging sounds stopped.

"Whoever's out there," Nick's voice declared loudly. "You picked the wrong guy to fuck with."

Yet Hayden didn't hear the readying of any weapon. He couldn't picture Nick getting through a gauntlet of vampires on just two nail guns and maybe only twenty or thirty shots altogether. Imagination took over from there, leading Hayden's thoughts to picture Nick surrounded.

But the sound of trotting tore Hayden out of it, and Evelyn switched her light on in order to follow. Turning his back on as well, Hayden kept up behind Kael with Valerie between them. It took them deeper into the store, to where virtually no light from outside reached down major lanes or the aisles they branched off to. It occurred to Hayden that he hadn't smelled cigarette smoke the entire time, and recalled Nick much preferred lighting up before entering a place vampires might hide in.

Nick's steps led into the home electronics section, where Hayden couldn't hear them over the music. Kael traded off point with Evelyn and drew the Athame to full length, slinging the nail gun as a backup weapon. The four of them cast flashlight beams down each aisle they reached, and then Hayden saw light coming from a home entertainment display in the middle of the department.

"I think it's meant to lure us in," Kael suggested at a whisper.

Taking another look, Hayden realized someone sat in the recliner with their feet propped up on a low table. He realized the occupant could see all of them, if they could see in the dark, and appeared to be waiting. The light from there was from a flat screen television that Nick had just turned on.

"Val," Hayden whispered, taking up Evelyn's truncation of her name. "When I tell you, turn the Hayden Light on and point it right into his eyes, okay? Keep it hidden until then."

"Yeah, okay," she replied with a rapid nod of trepidation.

Then Hayden just dropped the need for stealth and strode toward Nick with the spear gun pointed at him, but the flashlight turned off. Valerie stuck with him, and held the arc lamp partially behind Hayden's back. Evelyn and Kael stood at their sides, Evelyn ready to shoot if she had to.

"Where's Salma, Nick?" Hayden asked at normal volume.

"She didn't make it." Nick's face turned toward the dark and dropped a little in the semi-gloom of shadow cast by the television from the side of the chair.

"But you did." Hayden's voice grew a little hard with accusation. "That's rather unlikely, don't you think? No arc lights to hold them off, running short on shells, and by yourself no less."

"I've been by myself a lot before running into Wanda and the others," Nick countered, and then waved at them. "Of course you could just use that heat scope to check, if you doubt."

"How do you know we have it?" Hayden challenged.

"Salma and I only had the one," Nick replied. "Of course it'd be a shame if you lost it getting out

344

of those woods. Man, that would sure creep me out."

"Creepy as looking through an unlit store without a flashlight," Hayden asked, wondering how much of Nick he was talking to. "I'm guessing the bullets are for shooting out tires."

"Oh, right," Nick's voice spoke up, as his hand fingered at the high back of the chair. "That's an interesting idea. Only it doesn't work like that with most pistols. Of course armor piercing rounds might do it. I should try that sometime. Why do you insist on calling me Nick?"

"That's how you introduced yourself, isn't it?" Hayden asked.

"You're looking at a guy who got past ICE time after time," he said, and chuckled while wiping at his mouth. "Do you really believe I'd just throw out my real name to complete strangers?"

"Maybe after we ceased to be strangers," Hayden suggested. "After facing worse things than border patrol agents and state police, I don't know."

"Still trying to get back to that fairy-tale world the Judds clung to," Nick analyzed him as if Hayden were on a couch next to his chair. "I would've thought those contractor guys dispelled the myth you all believe in. Land of the free, home of the brave, capital of exploitation and command center of more dirty wars than the rest of the world combined."

"Nothing like a little apocalypse to clean house, huh," Hayden scoffed.

"What's the phrase," Nick posed, holding out both hands, though not far enough for Hayden to see their color. "'You don't seem them fucking each other over for a goddamn percentage.' I mean, I gotta hand it to these kinds of bloodsuckers. They are upfront about what they want to take from you. There's never any mistake about where you stand with them."

"Val," Hayden issued the order.

Raising the Hayden Light, Valerie switched it on. The light blasted into Nick's face, and he threw up his hands instantly while turning away. "Jesus Christ, Hayden!"

Before he realized it, Hayden had the spear gun up and ready to shoot, but gave Nick one last chance. "Put your hands down— I mean it, Nick."

"There," Nick complied, though he squinted at the intense artificial daylight. "Ya' happy?"

Crouching a bit and bending down, Hayden searched Nick's pupils. Hazel, not opaque, as he had feared. The one-time coyote's skin also appeared flush with blood and life. It was at that time Hayden took note of what the television showed. It was a bland studio set not unlike those of the prior reports Hayden thought were on a ship. Only this time the person sitting behind the deck and talking wore a military uniform. Closed captioning allowed Hayden to read what was being said, as Nick had the sound on mute. The logo that the news crawl rolled into indicated the *U.S.S. Stennis*.

"They claim they're doing humanitarian aid drops and rescue flights," Nick pointed out, and then scoffed. "Yeah! Like they can afford to do that much maintenance for helicopters."

346

"How is it you ended up in the same direction as us?" Hayden asked, having lowered the spear gun.

"Those contractors surprised us to west of David's house," Nick began. "East of us wasn't an option. Hell, that guy running the night club's probably still out there. And then there's fucking Florida to the south. So, eh, I figured north. I was planning on New Hampshire, actually."

"Evelyn and Kael's people are in Vermont, if you want to stick with us," Hayden offered.

A thoughtful face and a shrug later, Nick replied, "I could think of worse places to be."

"What is your name, anyway?" Valerie asked.

"Uh," the human smuggler hesitated as he pushed off from the chair and went to a shopping cart filled with his salvage hoard, and then looked over one shoulder. "Let it be Nick."

"Nick it is," Hayden granted. They resumed scavenging. "Nick Farnsworth, human resources manager, job placement specialist and gun slinging vampire slayer."

After loading up a second cart with goods, Hayden and the rest headed for the front entrance, while Nick had turned for the back of the store.

"Where're you going now?" Evelyn asked.

"'Got a motorcycle out back," Nick thumbed as he turned around. "You rode a bike all this way," Hayden said in disbelief.

"Last thing those mercenary pricks would expect," Nick explained.

"Wait," Hayden waved his hand in confusion. "Why aren't you smoking? I thought you would've

347

lit one up before coming in here with the prospect of them hiding out from the day."

"'Quit,'" came back Nick's one word answer, before he pulled his cart to the stockroom.

By the time they brought the cart to the SUV, Nick had loaded up and driven around to the parking lot. He straddled a black motorcycle with side compartments over the rear wheel. An ecstatic Isaac jumped out of the front seat, visibly hurting for the effort, and threw his arms around Nick when the bike stopped.

"Goddamn man," Isaac declared with a broad toothy grin. "'Thought you was gone for good!'"

"Lawn pegs," Nick revealed his secret at last, and pointed to Isaac, who still had an arm around Nick's shoulders. "Good call there. By the way, I'm out if you have any left."

"Shee-it!" Isaac beamed, and then hobbled to the back of the car. "I got'cha covered bro!"

Valerie and Kael loaded up supplies into the back seat, when Hayden stepped up next to them.

"Look, ah," Hayden paused and became nervous. "Val, I know you didn't have a lot of luck with your last foster parents, but– well, I wanted to ask you something."

"Like what?" Valerie turned for the next armful to pass to Kael inside.

"Would you be willing to give an old guy a second chance at being a father?" Hayden asked, looking down at his shoes and rubbing his fingertips at one side of his forehead.

Out of nowhere Valerie hugged him, forcing Hayden to step back to keep his balance. It was that

348

moment Hayden realized everyone was staring at them.

"I'll even call you dad," she cried, her face buried in his shirt, as he hugged back.

Hayden noticed Isaac wiping away tears, and thought of his little girl. On reflection over some of the people following his online postings about vampires, Hayden didn't recall seeing many from Florida. Inwardly, he pledged to find a way back in order to figure out where Isaac's daughter was. But in the meantime, Hayden realized it'd be a lot easier with as many as nine witches and two hundred pentagram-powered werewolves at his back.

With everything loaded and everyone ready to go, Hayden sat in the middle row seat with Valerie and Kael as Evelyn drove out of the parking lot. Nick preferred the bike and cruised ahead of them, a new pack of lawn pegs sticking out his back pocket. He still had his bundle of weapons and one of the nail guns slung across his back. Two more days put them inside Vermont's state borders. By dusk they drove a heavily wooded road up to a fortified wall.

"This wasn't here when I left," Evelyn said, as she and Hayden stepped out from the SUV.

To the sides of the gate large bright lights burned down, and a voice challenged them from a silhouette poised with a weapon aimed at them, "Stop and stay in the light."

"Just do what he says," Evelyn uttered, and looked straight up into the lights with her hands out.

"Evelyn?" The guard seemed to doubt who he recognized. "Everyone was worried after you stopped calling and texting us. Who're these people you brought with you?"

"He seems more trusting that I would've guessed," Hayden observed, noticing the sun was down.

"These're the people I was with all that time," Evelyn shouted up to the guard, and then spoke to Hayden at normal volume. "I think it's because he knows we're not vampires."

"I want them all to step into the Heathen Lights," a second voice demanded.

"Did he just say Heathen Lights?" Hayden checked, wondering if the Vermont accent were that bad.

"Oh god," Evelyn gasped and doubled over with a face holding back laughter. "I forgot to tell you why I stuck around after that whole witch hunt thing!"

"Wait. What?" Hayden felt he missed something, but it would have to wait. Isaac, Val and Nick all followed Kael into the cast of the intense lighting.

"You can put your hands down, guys," the second guard called out.

Then the gate clinked in the middle and parted to the sound of motors, reminding Hayden of garage openers. The two guards stepped out with compound bows down at their sides, one of them putting an arrow away. After approaching the group, they tilted each person's head back, one at a time, to make a close inspection of their eyes.

"Yeah, they're good," the salt and pepper haired man announced.

Kael raised his left hand out, and the others did likewise, revealing their own pentagram marks. Then Kael traded forearm embraces in greeting each man, and a pat on the other's shoulders. The older man waved them back to their vehicles to then enter the community they garrisoned. Once inside the SUV, Hayden turned in the driver seat on noticing Evelyn leaning forward.

"It's your name," Evelyn hinted.

"You mean Cornell being eerily similar to that Corneliu asshole," Hayden asked.

"I mean your first name," Evelyn chinned up at him, leaning back. "It means Heathen."

"Ain't that some shit," Isaac to his right, laughed out and brought a hand over his mouth.

"This goddess of yours have a name?" Hayden asked back to her.

"There's a few, depending on what aspect is being described," Evelyn detailed. "But the highest form is called Morrigan. The parts of her trinity are Fae, Badb and Macha. Why?"

"If I'm going to learn a new prayer book I at least gotta get the names right," Hayden announced.

Following Nick on his bike, Hayden drove past the gate, which closed behind them. In the rear and side view mirrors he studied the structure of the wall. A mix of old and new, which he figured would be like the rest of the town he would find himself calling home.

* * *

Some leapt between roof tops and others across windows, opened or closed, and still more charged toward them on a street that, like the rest of

351

the city, suffered five years of ruin and neglect. Mostly they were human, dog and cat vampires but a number of former zoo monkeys counted among their horde. Evelyn, in full battle dress and with the images of ravens on the sleeves of her long coat, stood with two others of the sisterhood along with some twenty of the Marked.

To quell the advancing they switched on Heathen Lights, and then others came out from behind them to also use the vampire-repelling illumination. Boxed in by their own hardwired fear of harmless simulated sunlight, there was nothing they could do when the Marked, all turned with the full moon above, circled in with swords, axes, spears and knives.

Retrofitted naval strike groups had dedicated themselves to manufacturing and airdropping nail guns and stake-loaded shotgun shells to whoever might find the crates. However, the Marked did just as well without them and so only the garrison back home and newest of initiates carried the stake-firing weapons. They staked hearts and dismembered the Shadow Siders without too much trouble. The animated corpses screamed and curled up from the light, and a few even attempted to lash out.

They only ventured into the outskirts of the city, Bennington, which still had countless more Shadow Siders, of course. But going deeper risked encountering its Blood King, a turned male lion larger than the one Nick had been attacked by five years ago. The world harbored billions of turned, and so this one victory was small indeed.

However, Evelyn, with Kael by her side, and the others of their tradition took action regardless. There was no alternative other than dying to be put into the ground or dying and joining their ranks.

The night's work done, the supernatural empowered force returned to two tractor trailer trucks, both rebuilt and up-armored. Other Marked men had escorted foraging groups led by Isaac and Nick. They returned about the same time as Evelyn's team.

Heathen Lights beamed out from all corners of the trailer and more off the cab, including its original headlights. Hayden had gotten good with miniaturizing the technology, to where regular aluminum flashlights kept the dead at bay.

Isaac entered the first trailer as did Evelyn. After he helped load up the group's gatherings, he turned to take Evelyn in his arms and kiss her. "Hey baby, how'd it go?"

"No surprises tonight," she answered, removing her armor. "Your haul seems pretty good."

"Mostly construction stuff," Isaac waved with a humble turn of his head to the supplies.

The drive back to the community took under an hour, and brought with it the wondrous sight of the morning sun casting light down upon the fortified town. After Hayden's arrival, every house had solar panels and wind generators as well as Hayden Lights. Most food came from within, and other utilities had in recent months also been handled internally. Even Wi-Fi remained a normal part of everyday living. Among survivor groups across the country none of that was unusual at all.

In some ways, Evelyn thought, the outbreak was the best thing to happen to humanity. As Hayden once said on seeing the Judds' house, renewable energy was a revolution that since became the only means of electrical power. Hayden had also started up a training class for manufacturing biofuel which powered both semi-trucks and every other vehicle left that didn't run directly on electricity. Average temperatures rose higher than ever, as weather grew weirder and wilder, of course. At least now humanity wasn't making it worse, while some pretended it didn't happen.

The trucks pulled up to the gate, and waited for it to open. They drove to a large parking lot well covered by Hayden Lights, turned off for morning, and the expedition exited to the welcoming of people from the community. An ecstatic nine year old girl with a skin tone lighter than Isaac's ran up to him, and jumped up in time for her father to catch and hug her.

"My baby girl bein' good while daddy's out?" Isaac asked rhetorically.

"Yeah," Lisa replied, and then peered over his shoulder. "Whaddya get?"

"Buildin' stuff," Isaac answered. "You wanna help daddy move it out?"

"Just a little bit," Lisa said with an adorable gesture, holding a gap between her thumb and finger.

Isaac passed over a box of nails– the regular kind for construction nail guns – and sent Lisa on her way. He took a moment watching her run over to a pickup truck to hand it to a man standing in the bed. Hayden had requested, and then demanded, that the Marked organize a trip to Florida to find Lisa and her mother's parents. When that didn't work, Hayden threatened to go do it himself, and that's when Evelyn, Nick and Kael stepped up to join him. Then the city council of pagan elders relented.

"'Her grandparents talking to you yet," Evelyn asked Isaac.

"The granddad is, yeah," Isaac revealed. "We hang out on weekends. His wife, not so much, but she doesn't glare at me anymore. 'Guess that's progress, right?"

With the goods transferred, the two armored vehicles were driven to a storehouse for safe keeping, and other cars drove to other parts of town. Isaac, Evelyn and Lisa drove to Main Street where their house was. Climbing out, Evelyn looked across to a park to find Hayden surrounded by children of all ages, right up through their teens. His hair had grayed more, but otherwise he was the same old Hayden she first met in that vacant office building. Valerie, his adopted daughter, sat with him and watched the faces of other kids, and Hayden was recounting his stories about first discovering vampires.

Evelyn also reflected on something she and the Sisterhood had learned since Hayden's arrival. Hayden was the sword. He just seemed to know when the Ninth Sister was born with the familiar bonded to her. He picked her out from among other newborns at the rebuilt community hospital. More than that, he possessed an intuition, which Evelyn and the Sisterhood saw as a feminine power, to make discoveries and achievements. His work to reclaiming the night, at least in part, via the Hayden Lights and the Lunar Lighting for inducing the Mark, was just the start of his legacy.

"Hey, Isaac, I'll be in in just a bit," Evelyn called.

"Okay, babe," he called back before going inside.

As Evelyn paced across the quiet street, wetted with early fall rains, and into the park, Hayden ushered the children off to their morning studies. He leaned back on the bench, with his arms draped out to both side, and took in the sounds of birds chirping and the cozy closeness of many trees. Most of the community was enveloped by trees for reasons practical as much as aesthetics.

"Turned quite the tree hugger yourself, I see," Evelyn chided him with a now old joke, as she neared.

"I never get over how beautiful this place is," Hayden praised. "But, onto work. How was it?"

"No trouble, really," Evelyn answered. "Bennington is a bust so far."

"Hmm," Hayden voiced, and then sat up with a finger raised. "I gotta think there's a few people left in there, else the vampires wouldn't be in such numbers."

356

"We show up as witches and werewolves," Evelyn reminded. "So it's no wonder they stay scarce."

"That reminds me," Hayden said, "We need to head over to my place to work some details out."

Hayden and Evelyn walked to his house a couple of blocks away, and Evelyn called Isaac on her cell to let him know she'd be later than she'd said. Once in his home, they went to the den, where Hayden had maps pinned to wall boards and another lain out over his desk and computer keyboard. On many were circles in red felt tip marker. Hayden could've just as easily had it all on his computer, but he seemed to prefer the obsessive mad scientist shtick.

Without warning Vince Price's maniacal laughter broke out.

"Jesus, you still won't give up that ringtone," Evelyn jibed with knowing smirk.

"'Told'ya, I'd rather be on edge and be wrong," he remarked, before answering. "Hello."

Evelyn heard a voice go right into addressing Hayden, but couldn't make out what they said. Hayden stayed the caller at that moment, and directed the call through his computer. "Okay, go ahead."

"Does your little crew feel like taking another trip?" the caller asked.

"Let me guess," Hayden said, and leaned sideways onto his desk. "Your satellites picked up suspected abnormal behavior among the vampires, and it's too far inland for a helo flight."

"Your guessing creeps me out, Hayden," the voice, which Hayden said wasn't the same as the two from five years ago, replied. "But yeah, that's it exactly."

"So, by some stroke of luck, we hack our way through a hell-infested pit of bloodsuckers," Hayden began the gory embellishment, "and find one odd acting vampire among thousands to millions. We take its limbs off, stake it and send to your guys safely covered from the sun. Sound about right?"

"That's about the size of it," the voice admitted. "Oh! And I got a bit of good news here."

"Uh-huh," a skeptical Hayden replied.

"They've decided to rename it the Large Hayden Collider," the caller said.

"They got that thing up and running again?" Hayden asked, furrowing his brows as his head jerked back in mild astonishment. "I would've guessed no one had the juice, and turned it into a museum."

"You'd be amazed at was a handful of Thorium reactors will do when people are pressed against the wall," the voice explained. "They're going to start looking into a Supersymmetry causal agent for why the sun burns vampires, as per your suggestion."

"And they got enough PhD's who didn't get bled out to run the LHC," Hayden asked. "I thought Europe and Asia were pretty much wiped out."

"There're pockets of survivors, but yeah, you can forget pre-outbreak nationalities."

"Now do I just call these guys every now and then and make suggestions?" Hayden inquired on.

"Or post them on your streaming account," the voice suggested. "Whichever you prefer. We all know you won't go over there yourself or take refuge with any of the naval strike groups."

In five years, as far as Evelyn knew, Hayden never once told any of the callers where he was or who he sheltered with. They knew only of Evelyn, though not by name, and her ability to propel objects using whatever power source she could get her left hand onto. They'd seen the Marked from orbit, but had no names for any of them and, hopefully, didn't have their human faces on file.

"Hey, what I'm doing has worked all this time," Hayden refused once more what he hadn't heard offered outright. "You guys'll just have to trust me on this."

"No, that's fine," the voice accepted. "My bosses are tired of trying to convince you. They've even abandoned the idea of issuing you the Medal of Freedom."

"None of us are free, so long as those things own half the day," Hayden remarked.

"Yeah, yeah, yeah," the voice grew a bit exasperated. "You told us often enough."

"You know," Hayden switched subjects. "At some point we'll have to map out how this all started, so we can figure out the source. And we need to know what changed to allow the spread to be so much faster. Your bosses agree on that, right?"

"Hayden, we're years to decades away from that," the caller explained. "Top priority is figuring out the solar particle emission. After we got that, and re-established something like a space launch program, we'll be able to purge any point on Earth we want. Until then it's fantasyland stuff, and we gotta work the problems we know. Hell, no one has estimates on the U.S. census, much less about human populations around the planet. Most of our aid and arms packages don't ever get touched."

"And that other thing?" Hayden queried in vague language.

"They still drop off volunteers and still don't get them back," the voice explained. "The official word is we're not dealing with them, but the Commander-in-Chief won't have us take 'em out either. It's the understanding that all options should be left open."

"I think you see why I don't come in, then," Hayden hinted. "Those assholes did a real number on us, and I'm not forgiving them that. If it's dead but still up and about we're putting it down, period."

"Can't argue that," the caller agreed. "Which is why they're on their own. However, we know that those two specimens had a strong behavioral affinity for each other."

"Yet the male wasn't the least bit bothered by the fact her arms and legs were lopped off?" Hayden turned his head sideways in lingering doubt. "They gotta know that rapid draining from multiple entry points alone isn't doing it."

"The thinking is that it's strong emotional states and reinforced synaptic pathways," the caller reported, himself sounding unconvinced. "But

360

you're right, that doesn't stop them from being a horror show to everyone with a heartbeat."

"Anything else from your end?" Hayden asked, rolling a finger to wrap it up.

"I'll call back once the Big Fish upstairs pinpoint a location for you, but otherwise, no."

"Okay, thank you," Hayden concluded and cut the call with a gleam in his eye.

"You enjoyed hanging up on him first, didn't you," Evelyn smirked.

"Goddamned right," Hayden acknowledged with pride.

"So, I guess the next full moon trip will be for their little quest instead," Evelyn suggested.

"Yeah," Hayden replied, grabbing a seat at last. "Ooh! Knee's killin' me. I just wish they'd stop thinking like regular bureaucrats and take a crapshoot at finding whatever creates vampires in the first place. Otherwise we'll be hiding out like this literally forever."

"What do you think?" Evelyn offered the always loaded question.

"I got a few ideas," Hayden teased, as he raised a map and focused on Eastern Europe. "But most of those land me right around here. I did some checking, and a large mountain range with extremely cavernous guts is about the best place to shelter ancient material that otherwise burns up in sunlight."

Evelyn studied the area within a repetitive circle of red: the Carpathians.

"You're in there somewhere," she listened to Hayden mutter and aim his conjecture, suspicion, as well as an accusatory index finger. "I just know it."

Epilogue: The Blind Weaver

More than a year before an outbreak that changed the world, a collapse on the side of a mountain opened up ancient caverns. Since then a number of animals ventured in to roost or just for temporary shelter against the elements. A few ventured out, though not always in a living state. Into this twenty foot high A-shaped breach, a group of rats scurried to escape the rain outside.

They split off independent of each other, and some sought out whatever morsels might be had. Some snatched up cave-dwelling invertebrates, and reared up to gnaw at them between tiny, cupped hands. One ventured deeper on smelling something just as curious. Bats fluttered about overhead, causing the rodent to freeze and gaze up with large timid eyes.

When the winged creatures settled back down, and some bombarded the cavern floor with guano, the black rat felt it safe to move again. Daylight still leaked into the voluminous cave, and so the rat went on in assumed safety. For even the rats knew that nightfall brought dangers unlike any predator they had known in their long journey to pervade every major continent and countless islands.

Rising up on its hind feet, the rat took in rapid sniffs to investigate the air.

Something else awaited deep in the cave the likes of which the rat had no familiarity with. It crept on, allowing its whiskers to rub and poke at every surface like ten thousand canes of the blind. Small hairless ears listened to a faint breeze that carried an old scent.

Like the other hard-bodied critters, this thing the rat sensed also was an arthropod. In its odor was evidence of a creature capable of breathing air and water alike, and still needing to do so. Light taps of double-clawed legs told the rat it had eight limbs. Living in the absolute dark, which its kind evolved in, rendered useless eyes that its ancestors long ago sacrificed to the inky black.

Another blow of stale air through the cave caused a shimmer to manifest in the middle of the tunnel. Fine threads incapable of existing in direct sunlight glistened with the threat of day. The creator of the web doubtless knew enough to huddle further into everlasting darkness.

It was an abyssal shadowy world which the rat ventured into, until it recognized another smell. A warning, drifting off the body of a dead rat entombed on the silken mesh suspended in air. Its killer, once part of a species, now was the last of its kind and had been so for countless millennia. Changed by an encounter it could never understand, it had become something new and acquired a taste it had yet to satisfy in full. Though, it was obvious lesser fur-bearing creatures would do.

When the rat reared up again, the dead member of its kind twitched in its cocoon. The Weaver itself remained motionless, but for a primitive heart that still beat and book lungs which continued to open and close as a bellows. Having eaten already, the Weaver felt no blind anticipation that might tug on the delicate threads of death it laid out for the unwary and the too-curious.

Yet its prize lacked such satiation. The rodent corpse struggled and writhed to escape its funeral shroud. The living rat backed away in caution, but twitched its nose in concern for its fellow appearing to break loose for freedom. However, when the deceased rat's head emerged, something about its eyes appeared wrong. Even in this gloom the breathing rat smelled, heard and saw something was amiss. The side of his neck was macerated into a jagged open wound that didn't bleed.

Turning to flee and squeal warnings up the cavern passage, it never got the chance. The vampire rat dropped onto it, and sank its newly forged razor sharp incisors into its victim. Too weak to escape the fiend's grasp, the living rat squirmed in futility, until its life seeped down into the corpse's eager throat. The blood drinking rodent's tail whipped and curled like a worm to express basal satisfaction.

After some minutes there now scurried two fiends devoid of life and breath.

THE END

THE END

www.ingramcontent.com/pod-product-compliance
Lightning Source LLC
Chambersburg PA
CBHW011738010726
47496CB00010B/2985